Tom Holt was born in London in 1961. At Oxford he studied bar billiards, ancient Greek agriculture and the care and feeding of small, temperamental Japanese motorcycle engines; interests which led him, perhaps inevitably, to qualify as a solicitor and emigrate to Somerset, where he specialised in death and taxes for seven years before going straight in 1995. Now a full-time writer, he lives in Chard, Somerset, with his wife, one daughter and the unmistakable scent of blood, wafting in on the breeze from the local meat-packing plant.

Find out more about Tom Holt and other Orbit authors by registering for the free monthly newsletter at www.orbitbooks.co.uk

By Tom Holt

EXPECTING SOMEONE TALLER
WHO'S AFRAID OF BEOWULF?
FLYING DUTCH
YE GODS!
OVERTIME
HERE COMES THE SUN
GRAILBLAZERS
FAUST AMONG EQUALS
ODDS AND GODS
DJINN RUMMY
MY HERO
PAINT YOUR DRAGON
OPEN SESAME
WISH YOU WERE HERE
ONLY HUMAN
SNOW WHITE AND THE SEVEN SAMURAI
VALHALLA
NOTHING BUT BLUE SKIES
FALLING SIDEWAYS
LITTLE PEOPLE
THE PORTABLE DOOR
IN YOUR DREAMS

DEAD FUNNY: OMNIBUS 1
MIGHTIER THAN THE SWORD: OMNIBUS 2
DIVINE COMEDIES: OMNIBUS 3
FOR TWO NIGHTS ONLY: OMNIBUS 4
TALL STORIES: OMNIBUS 5
SAINTS AND SINNERS: OMNIBUS 6
FISHY WISHES: OMNIBUS 7

THE WALLED ORCHARD
ALEXANDER AT THE WORLD'S END
OLYMPIAD
A SONG FOR NERO

I, MARGARET

LUCIA TRIUMPHANT
LUCIA IN WARTIME

TOM HOLT

Mightier than the Sword

Contains
WHO'S AFRAID of BEOWULF?
and MY HERO

www.orbitbooks.co.uk

An *Orbit* Book

First published in Great Britain by Orbit 2002
Reprinted 2003, 2004

This omnibus edition © Tom Holt 2002

Who's Afraid of Beowulf?
First published in Great Britain in 1988 by Macmillan (London) Limited
Copyright © Tom Holt 1988

My Hero
First published in Great Britain in 1996 by Orbit
Copyright © Tom Holt 1996

The moral right of the author has been asserted.

A CIP catalogue record for this book is available
from the British Library.

Typeset by Palimpsest Book Production Limited
Polmont, Stirlingshire
Printed in Great Britain by
Clays Ltd, St Ives plc

ISBN 1 84149 133 0

Orbit
An imprint of
Time Warner Book Group UK
Brettenham House
Lancaster Place
London, WC2E 7EN

CONTENTS

Who's Afraid of Beowulf?   1

My Hero   239

ACKNOWLEDGEMENTS

The author would like to thank
Jim Henderson and Iain Carmichael
for their kind assistance.

DEDICATION

For K. N. F.

WHO'S AFRAID OF BEOWULF?

CHAPTER ONE

Someone had written 'godforsaken' between 'Welcome to' and 'Caithness' on the road sign. When he saw the emendation, the surveyor almost smiled.

'Tourists, I expect,' said the archaeologist disapprovingly. She had decided that the Highlands were authentic and good; therefore, any malice towards them must have proceeded from uncomprehending outsiders.

'I hope not,' yawned the surveyor, lighting a cigarette and changing gear. 'I was taking it as evidence that there's one native of these parts who can read and write.' He paused, waiting for a laugh or an 'I know what you mean'. Neither was forthcoming. 'Though there's no reason why any of them should. After all, you don't need to be able to read if you make your living robbing and killing passing travellers, which has always been the staple industry around here.'

The archaeologist looked away. He was off again. An irritating man, she felt.

'Which explains the ingrained poverty of the region,' the surveyor went on remorselessly, 'because only a few bloody fools ever used to come travelling up here. Until recently, of course. Recently, you've had your coachloads of tourists. Theme holidays for heavy sleepers. Anyway, these days the locals don't even bother killing the travellers; they just sell them tartan key-fobs. And they all take the *FT*, to keep track of currency fluctuations.'

The archaeologist had had enough of her companion's diatribe, which had started before the car had got clear of Lairg. Rather ostentatiously she fanned away the cigarette smoke and expressed the opinion that it was all lovely. 'I think it's got a sort of—'

The surveyor made a peculiar noise. 'Listen,' he said, 'I was born and bred in bonnie bloody Caithness, and the only thing it's produced in a thousand years is starving people.' He'd read that in a Scottish Nationalist manifesto, but it sounded clever. 'Five years ago, the inhabitants of Rolfsness pleaded with the Water Authority to turn the wretched place into a reservoir so that they could be compensated and move to Glasgow. But it's too remote even for that. The Army won't have it for a firing range, and the CEGB got lost trying to find it.'

He was getting nicely into his stride now, despite the lukewarm response. The archaeologist managed to interrupt him just in time.

'That reminds me,' she said, tearing her eyes away from a breathtakingly lovely prospect of cloud-topped mountains, 'I wanted to ask you, since you were born here. Are there any old traditions or folk-tales about Rolfsness?'

'Folk-tales.' The surveyor frowned, as if deep in thought. 'Well, there's an old superstition among the shepherds and crofters – but you know what they're like.'

'Go on.' The archaeologist felt a tremor of excitement.

'Well, they *say* that every year on the anniversary of the battle of Culloden – you know about the battle of Culloden?'

'Yes, yes, of course.'

'They *say* that every year, at about noon, the bus from Wick to Melvich stops here for three minutes where the old gibbet used to be. But nobody's ever claimed to have seen it for themselves.'

Dead silence. The surveyor shook his head sadly. Americans, he reflected, have no sense of humour.

'Otherwise, apart from Bonnie Prince Charlie hiding from Butcher Cumberland's men in what is now the bus shelter, where Montrose had been betrayed to the Covenanters, no. Totally unremarkable place. Now, if there was a story that Montrose *wasn't* betrayed to the Covenanters here, that would be a bit out of the ordinary.'

'I see.' The archaeologist sniffed. She should have known better than to ask. 'So nothing about giants or fairies or the Wee Folk?'

'Round here,' said the surveyor grimly, 'the Wee Folk means Japanese businessmen looking for sites for computer factories. Not that they ever build any, of course. Have you ever tasted Japanese whisky? All the hotels up here sell it now. Personally, I prefer it to the local stuff.'

The archaeologist gave up in despair, and they drove on in silence for a while. Then, as they turned a sharp corner on the side of a towering hill, the archaeologist suddenly asked the surveyor to stop the car.

'What is it?' said the surveyor, glancing anxiously in his rear-view mirror, but the archaeologist said nothing. She had no words to spare for such an insensitive person at the moment when she caught her first glimpse of the sea that washes the flat top of the British mainland, and, grey and soft-edged as any dream-kingdom should be, the faint outline of Orkney. On an impulse, she opened the car door and scrambled up to the top of a rocky outcrop.

Here, then, was the earldom of her mind, her true habitation. She felt as Orestes must have done when, coming secretly out of exile, he looked for the first time upon Argos, the land he had been born to rule. That was the sea of her Cambridge dreams, those were the islands she had first pictured for herself sitting on the front porch in Setauket, Long Island, with her treasured copy of the *Orkney-men's Saga* open on her knee. As a promised land it had been to her as she trod the weary road of professional scholarship, laying down her harp beside the waters of Cam, marching more than seven times round the bookshops of St Andrews. As she gazed out over the sea, called 'whale-road' and 'world-serpent', she could almost see the blue sails of the Orkney Vikings, the dragon-prows of Ragnar Lothbrok and Erik Bloodaxe, sweeping across their great grey highway to give battle to Bothvar Bjarki or Arvarodd in the *vik* at Tongue.

'On a clear day,' said the surveyor behind her, 'you can just make out the Old Man of Hoy from here. Why you should want to is beyond me entirely.'

'I think it's wonderful,' said the archaeologist softly.

'I think it's perishing cold. Can we get on now?'

They got back into the van.

'Tell me again what it is you've found,' said the archaeologist briskly.

'Well,' said the surveyor, leaning back with one hand on the bottom of the steering-wheel, 'we were taking readings, and I'd just sent the Land-Rover up ahead when it fell clean through this small mound. Right up to its axles, useless bloody thing, we had to use the Transit to pull it out again. Anyway, we got it out and when we looked down the hole it had made we saw this chamber underground, all shored up with pit props. I thought it was an Anderson shelter or something left over from the war, but the lads all said no, ten to one it was a Viking ship-burial.'

'*They* said that?'

'They all work for the Tourist Board over the summer. So we put a tarpaulin over it and sent for your mob.'

'Didn't you want to look for yourselves?'

The surveyor laughed. 'You must be kidding. Roof might collapse or something. Besides, you aren't supposed to touch anything, are you, until the experts arrive. Or is that murders?'

The archaeologist smiled. 'You did right,' she said.

'The lads get paid by the hour,' said the surveyor, 'and I'm on bonus for being in this wilderness. Besides, if it does turn out to be an ancient monument, the project will be cancelled, and we can all go home with money in lieu. Look, there it is.'

He pulled over on to the verge, and they picked their way over the uneven ground to the site. The archaeologist found that she was faced with a long leaf-shaped mound about fifty to sixty yards long, pointing due north. Under her woolly hat her hairs were beginning to rise, and she broke into a trot, her moon-boots squelching in the saturated peat. The sheer size of it made her heart beat faster. If there really was a ship down there, and if anything at all was left of it, this was going to make the *Mary Rose* look like a pedalo.

The survey team were staring at her over their cans of lager, but she took no notice. As she struggled with the obdurate ropes that held the tarpaulin in place, an old man in a raincoat apparently moulded on to his body got up hurriedly and started to wave his arms at her. To her joy, the archaeologist realised that he was a Highlander, and that the gist of his broken English was that she was on no account to open up the mound. She beamed at him (for surely this was some survival of the ancestral terror of waking up the sleepers under the howe) and said, 'Pardon me?' Her pleasure was somewhat diminished when the surveyor explained to her that what the old fool meant was that he'd spent half the morning nailing the tarpaulin down in the teeth of a gale, and that if she insisted on taking it off she could bloody well put it back herself.

The tarpaulin was thrown back, and the archaeologist nerved herself to look inside and seek her destiny. She had always felt that one day she would make a great discovery, something which would join her with Carnavon, Carter, Evans and Schliemann in the gallery of immortals. On the rare occasions when archaeology had lost its grip on her imagination – seemingly endless afternoons spent up to her knees in mud in some miserable Dartmoor hut-circle – she had consoled herself by trying to compose a deathless line, something which would be remembered beside 'I have looked upon the face of Agamemnon'. Although so far in her career she had found, apart from enough potsherds to line the bottom of every flowerpot in the world, nothing more prestigious than a Tudor belt-buckle, she knew that one day she, Hildy Frederiksen, would join that select band of immortals who have been fortunate enough to be the first men and women of the modern age to set eyes upon the heirlooms of the human race. She knelt down and with trembling fingers checked the contents of her organiser bag: camera (with film in it), notebook, pencil, small brush, flashlight (free with ten Esso tokens) and small plastic bags for samples.

In the event, what she actually said when the beam of her flashlight licked over the contents of the mound was 'Jesus!' but in the circumstances nobody could have blamed her for that. What she saw was the prow of a ship

– a long clinker-built ship of a unique and unmistakable kind. The timbers were coal-black and glistening with moisture, but the thing actually seemed to be intact. As the blood pounded in her ears she thanked God for the preservative powers of peat-bog tannin, took a deep breath, and plunged into the hole like a small, learned terrier.

The chamber *was* intact; so much so, in fact, that the possibility of its collapsing never entered into her mind. The sides were propped with massive beams – oak, at a guess – which vaulted high overhead, while the chamber had been dug a considerable depth into the ground. Under her feet the earth was hard, as if it had been stamped flat into a floor. The ship itself reclined at ease on a stout trestle, as if it was already taking its rightful place in a purpose-built gallery at the maritime museum at Greenwich. It was an indescribably beautiful thing, with the perfection of line and form that only something designed to be functional can have, lean and graceful and infinitely menacing, like a man-eating swan. Every feature she could have hoped to find in an archetypal Viking long-ship was present – this in itself was remarkable, since none of the ships so far discovered looked anything like the authoritative reconstructions in the *Journal of Scandinavian Studies* – from the painted shields beside each of the thirty oar-holes on either side of the ship to the great dragon figurehead, carved with a deep confident design of gripping beasts and interwoven snakes. Although it was strictly against the rules, she could not help reaching out, almost but not quite like Adam in the painting, and tracing with the tip of her left forefinger the line of the surrealistic pattern.

Like a child who has woken to find itself inexplicably inside a confectioner's warehouse, she walked slowly round the great ship, noting the various features of it as if with an inventory. Suddenly the light of her flashlight was thrown back by a sparkle of gold: inlaid runes running back from the prow, glowing bright as neon. She spelt them out, like a child learning its alphabet; Naglfar, the ship of nails, the ferry of the dead. It was so utterly perfect that for a moment she could not bear to look, in case her light fell on an outboard motor bolted to the stern, or a slogan draped across the mast advertising Carlsberg lager.

She touched it again, and the damp sticky feel of the tannin reassured her. Turn the Circus Maximus into a carpark, she said to herself, and wrap fish in the First Folio; preserve only this. As if in a dream, she put her foot on the first rung of a richly carved ladder that rested against the side of the ship.

At the top of the ladder was a small platform, with steps leading down into the hold. She stood for a moment unable to move, for the belly of the ship was piled high with the most extraordinary things, jumbled up together as if History was holding a garage sale. Gold and silver, fabrics, armour and weapons, like the aftermath of an earthquake at a museum. She rubbed her eyes and stared. Under the truncated mast, she could see twelve full sets of armour lying wrapped in fur cloaks, perfectly preserved. No, she was wrong. They were human bodies.

Then the flashlight went out.

The human heart is a volatile thing. A second or so before, Hildy I-Have-Looked-Upon-The-Face-Of Frederiksen had been thanking Providence that she alone had been granted the privilege of being the first living person in twelve hundred years to set foot on the planks of the longship Naglfar. Now, however, it occurred to her as she stood motionless in the complete silence and utter darkness that it would have been quite nice to have had someone there to share the moment with her, preferably someone with a reliable flashlight. She reminded herself sternly that archaeology is a science, that scientists are creatures of logic and reason, that she was a scientist, therefore she was not in the least afraid of the dark. However, being afraid seemed at that particular moment the most logical thing in the world, the reason why fear circuits had been planted in the human brain in the first place. So deathly was the silence that for a moment she took the sound of her own breathing for the snoring of the twelve dead Vikings lying just a few yards away from her under the mast. She tried to move, but could not; her muscles received the command from her brain and replied that they had never heard anything so absurd in their lives. She reflected that burglars must feel like this all the time, but the thought was little consolation.

As suddenly as it had gone out, the flashlight came back on again – the ways of petrol-station flashlights pass all understanding – and Hildy decided that, although it was really nice inside the chamber, it was probably even nicer outside it. As she turned away towards the ladder, she felt something under her foot and without thinking stooped and picked it up. It felt very cold in her hand, and was heavy, like a pistol. She stopped for a moment and looked at it. In her hand was a golden brooch inlaid with enamel and garnets, in the shape of a flying dragon. She half-expected it to move suddenly, like an injured bird picked up in the garden. The beam of the flashlight danced on interlocking patterns and spirals, and she felt dizzy. She knew perfectly well that she ought not to touch this thing, let alone thrust it deep into her pocket, and equally well that no power on earth could stop her doing it. Then she imagined another noise in the chamber and, with the brooch in her pocket, she scurried down the ladder and out of the mound like a rabbit with a ferret the size of a Tube train after it.

As the top of her hat emerged into the light, the

surveyor put his copy of *Custom Car* back in his pocket and asked: 'Are you all right, then?'

'Of course I am,' Hildy stammered. She was shaking, and sweat had turned her fringe into little black spikes, like the horns of a stag-beetle. 'Why shouldn't I be?'

'You were down there an awful long time,' said the surveyor. It had just occurred to him that more portable things than ships are sometimes found in ancient mounds.

'Very interesting,' Hildy said. 'I wish I could be sure it was authentic.'

The surveyor was staring at something sticking out of the pocket of her paddock jacket. She put her hand over it and hitched her lips into a smile.

'So there's nothing like – well, artefacts or anything down there?' asked the surveyor, rather too casually. Hildy tightened her grip round the neck of the brooch.

'Could be,' she mumbled. 'If I'd been brave enough to look. But the roof looks like it might collapse at any minute, so I came out again.'

'The roof?'

'Perilous, if you ask me. I think I heard it moving.'

The surveyor's face seemed to fall. 'Perhaps we should try to shore it up,' he suggested. 'I could go in and have a look. Of course, you needn't go in.'

Hildy nodded vigorously. 'Go ahead,' she said. 'Where's the nearest phone, by the way, in case we have to call for help?'

As she expected, the surveyor didn't like the sound of that. 'On the other hand,' he said, 'it's a job for the experts.'

'True.'

'Best leave well alone.'

Hildy nodded.

It had started to rain, and the survey team were making chorus noises. 'What I'd better do,' the surveyor said, 'since we can't do anything more for the present, is send the lads home and take you back to Lairg. You lot,' he shouted to the survey team, 'get that hole covered up.'

The old man in the raincoat said something authentic, but they ignored him and set about replacing the tarpaulin. 'We'd better wait till they're on their way,' whispered the surveyor. 'Otherwise – well, they might be tempted to see if there was anything of value down there.'

'Surely not?'

Neither Hildy nor the surveyor had much to say on the way back to Lairg. Hildy was thinking of a passage from *Beowulf* which she had had to do as a prepared translation during her first year at New York State, all about a man who stole a rich treasure from a hoard he found in a burial-mound, and woke a sleeping fire-drake in the process. She could remember it vividly, almost word for word, and it had had a decidedly unhappy ending.

The surveyor bundled her out of the car at Lairg and drove away rather quickly, which made Hildy feel somewhat suspicious. So she telephoned the police at Melvich and explained the situation to them slowly and lucidly. Once they had been made to understand that she was not mad or drunk they sounded very enthusiastic about the prospect of guarding buried treasure and promised to send the patrol car out as soon as it came back from finding Annie Erskine's cat. Feeling easier in her mind, Hildy went into the hotel bar and ordered a double orange juice with ice. As she drank it, she drew out the brooch and looked round to see if anyone was watching. But the barman had gone back to the Australian soaps in the television room, and she was alone.

The brooch was an exquisite example of its kind, the finest that Hildy had ever seen. The form was as simple as the decoration was complex, and it reminded her of something she had seen recently in quite another context. Slowly, the magnitude of her discovery and its attendant excitement began to return to her, and as soon as she had finished her drink she left the bar, reversed the charges to the Department of Archaeology, and demanded to speak to the Director *personally*.

'George?' she said calmly (he had always been Professor Wood to anyone under the rank of senior lecturer, but *he* had never found so much as a row-boat). 'It's Hildy Frederiksen here – yes, that's right – and I'm calling from Lairg. L-A-I-R-G.' He was being vague again, she noticed, an affectation he was much given to, especially after lunch. 'I'm just back from a first inspection of that mound site at Rolfsness. George, you're not going to believe this, but . . .'

As she spoke, her hand crept of its own accord into her pocket and closed around the flying dragon. Something seemed to tell her that on no account ought she to keep this extraordinarily beautiful and dangerous thing for herself, but that nevertheless that was what she was going to do, fire-drake or no fire-drake.

In the mound, it was dark and silent once again. For the past twelve hundred years, ever since the last turf had been laid over the trellis of oak-trunks and the horsemen had ridden away to the waiting ships, nothing had moved in the chamber, not so much as a mole or a worm. But now there was something missing that should have been there, and just as one tiny stone removed from an arch makes the whole structure unsound, so the peace of the chamber had been disturbed. Something moved in the darkness, and moved again, with the restlessness that attends on the last few moments before waking.

'For crying out loud,' said a voice, faint and drowsy in the darkness, 'there's some of us trying to sleep.'

The silence had been broken, irrecoverably, like a pane of glass. 'You what?' said another voice.

'I said there's people trying to sleep,' said the first voice. 'Shut it, will you?'

'You shut up,' replied the second voice. 'You're the one making all the noise.'

'Do you two mind?' A third voice, deep and powerful, and the structure of beams seemed to vibrate to its resonance. '"Quiet as the grave," they say. Some hope.'

'Sorry,' said the first two voices. The silence tried to return, as the retreating tide tries to claw its way back up the beach.

'I told you, didn't I?' continued the third voice after a while. 'I warned you not to eat that cheese, but would you listen? If you can't sleep, then be quiet.'

There was a sound of movement, metal scraping on metal, as if men in armour were turning in their sleep and groaning. 'It's no good,' said the third voice, 'you've done it now.'

Somewhere in the gloom there was a high-pitched squeaking sound, like a bat high up in the rafters of a barn. It might conceivably have been a human voice, if a man could ever grow so incredibly old. After the sound had died away, like water draining into sand, there was absolute quiet; but an uneasy, tense quiet. The mound was awake.

'The wizard says try counting sheep,' said the second voice.

'I heard him myself,' said the third voice. 'Bugger counting sheep. I've counted enough sheep since I've been down here to clothe the Frankish Empire. Oh, the Hel with it. Somebody open a window.'

There was a grating sound, and a creaking of long-relaxed

timber. 'Sod it,' said the first voice, 'some clown's moved the ladder.'

The old man grinned, displaying both his yellow teeth, and cut the final cord of the tarpaulin. Two of his fellows pulled the cover free, while the other members of the survey team, who had come back in the expectation of wealth, stood by with dustbin liners. In about fifteen minutes, they were all going to be rich.

'Can you see anything, Dougal?' someone asked. The old man grunted and wormed his way into the hole. A moment later, he slid out backwards and started to run like a hare. The survey team watched him in amazement, then turned round and stared at the mouth of the hole. A helmeted head had appeared out of the darkness, with a gauntleted hand in front of its eyes to protect them from the light.

'All right,' it said irritably, 'which one of you jokers moved our ladder?'

Hildy waited and waited, but no one came. She tried to pass the time by rereading her favourite sagas, but even their familiar glories failed to hold her attention. For in her mind's eye, as she read, the old images and mental pictures, which had been developed in the distant and unheroic town of Setauket, were all displaced and usurped by new, rather more accurate visions. For example, she had always pictured the lonely hall on the fells where Gunnar of Hlidarend, the archetypal hero of saga literature, had made his last stand as being the disused shed on the vacant lot down by the tracks, so that by implication Mord Valgardsson had led the murderers out of the drugstore on the corner of Constitution Street, where presumably they had stiffened their resolve for their bloody deed with a last ice-cream soda. Sigmund and

Sinfjotli had been chained to the log that was the felled apple tree in her own back yard, and there the wolf who was really the shape-changer king had come in the blue night and bitten off Sigmund's hand. Thus was maintained the link between the Elder Days and her own childhood; but the sight of the ship and the heaped gold had broken the link. She had seen with her own eyes a real live dead Viking, who had never been anywhere near Setauket and was therefore rather more exciting and rather less safe. Long Island Vikings were different; they had stopped at the front door, and never dared go into the house. But the Caithness variety seemed rather more pervasive. They were all around her, even under the bed – in the shape of the brooch in her suitcase.

Hildy tried her best not to unpack it from under the shirts and sweatshirts and hold it up to the light, but she was only flesh and blood. It seemed to glow in her hands, to move not with the beatings of her pounding heart but with a movement of its own, as if it were some thing of power. She made an attempt to study it professionally, to see if that would dispel its glamour; undoubted Swedish influences, garnets probably from India but cut in Denmark, yet the main work was in the classical Norwegian style and the runes were those of the futharc of Orkney. She stopped, and frowned. She had not noticed the runes before; but the keen light of the reading-lamp seemed to flow into them, like water into a channel when a dam is opened, so that they stood out tiny but unmistakable on the main curve of the central spiral of the decoration.

Runes. For some reason her heart had stopped beating. Perhaps it was some magic in those extraordinary letters, first created at a time when any writing was by definition magical, a secret mark on silent metal that could communicate without speech to the eyes of a wise lore-master. Runes cannot help being magical, even if what they spell out is commonplace; a rune cut on the lintel will keep the sleepless ghosts from riding on the roof, or put a curse on the house that curdles milk and makes all the fires suddenly go out. Runes were also spells of attraction; to learn the runes, the god Odin had made himself a human sacrifice at his own altar, and ever since they had had a power to command. For all she knew, it was their command that had drawn her, by way of New York State and Cambridge, across the grey sea all the way from Setauket to be the improbable heroine of some last quest.

The strange wonder of the thing did not altogether fade or wither as it lay in her hands: the runes were still runes, and the brooch was still incredible. A Viking brooch in a museum or under the fluorescent tubes of the laboratory of the Department of Archaeology was resentfully tame, like a caged lion, and its voice was silent. Outside on the cold hill the wild lion roared, fascinating and dangerous, while in the incongruous setting of a hotel bedroom it was like – well, like a wild lion in a hotel bedroom, where no pets or animals of any description are in any circumstances permitted.

Rationalised, what that meant was that she was feeling guilty about having stolen it, which was effectively what she had done, something which no archaeologist, however debased, would ever conceive of doing. So why, she asked her suitcase, had she done it?

'I must put it back,' she said aloud.

The only vehicle for hire in Lairg was a large minibus, by all appearances coeval with the longship Naglfar and about as practical for winding Scottish roads. But Hildy was in no position to be choosy, and she set off with an Ordnance Survey map open on the seat beside her, to drive to Rolfsness and put the brooch back in the mound before the team from St Andrews got there. As the deliberately obstructive road meandered its way through the grey hills, she could feel her resolve crumbling like an ancient parchment; the wild animal commanded her to return it to its natural habitat, not to put it back where middle-aged men with careers would come to find it and make it turn the treadmill of some thesis or scholarly paper.

She stopped the van and took it out once more. The dragon's expression had not changed; his garnet eyes were still red and hot as iron on the anvil; his lips still curved, in accordance with the demands of symmetry and form, in the same half-smile of intolerant mockery. She was suddenly aware that blood had been spilt over the possession of this extraordinary thing, and convinced that blood might well be shed for it again.

A loud hooting behind her, and plainly audible oaths, not in Old High Norse but modern Scots, woke her from her self-induced hypnosis. She rammed the van into first gear and drove on to the verge, letting the council lorry pass. Now she felt extremely foolish, and the voice in the runes fell silent, leaving her to her embarrassment. Listening to dragon brooches, said another, rather more familiar voice in her head, is only one step away from talking to dragons, for which they take you to a place where people are very kind and understanding, and where eventually the dragons start talking back. She bundled the brooch back into her pocket and took off the handbrake.

It was nearly dark when she reached Rolfsness, but the new, sensible Hildy Frederiksen defied nightfall as she defied all the other works of sorcery. She parked the bus under a lonely rowan tree and trotted swiftly over to the mound. There was no tarpaulin over the hole and no sign of the police, and her archaeologist's instinct returned, all the stronger for having been challenged. A terrible fear that the mound had been plundered while her attention was distracted struck her, and she started to blame herself. Why, for a start, had she left the mound in the first place, like a lamb among wolves, unguarded against the return of those unsavoury contractors' men? She fumbled for her flashlight and dropped it; the back came off and all the batteries were spilt into the short wiry grass. Her fingers were unruly as she tried to reassemble it, for clearly everything she tried to do today was fated to come to no good. When the wretched thing was mended, she advanced like an apprentice lion-tamer on the hole in the side of the mound, afraid now not of what she might see but of what she might not. With a deep breath that seemed to fill not only her lungs but also her pockets and the very lining of her jacket she poked one toe into the mouth of the hole, as if it were a hot bath she was testing. Something seemed to move inside.

'Now what is it?' demanded a voice from under the earth.

So she had disturbed the plunderers at their work! Suddenly her small familiar body was filled with cold and unreasonable courage, for here was a chance to redeem herself in the eyes of Archaeology by falling in battle with tomb-robbers and unlicensed dealers in antiquities.

'OK,' she said between clenched teeth, 'you'd better come out now. We have this whole area surrounded.'

There was a clanking noise, as of something very heavy moving, and somebody said: 'Why don't you look where you're putting your great feet?' Then a ray of the setting sun fell suddenly on red gold and blue steel, and a man stood silhouetted against the sky on the edge of the mound.

He was a little over six feet tall, clad in gilded chain-mail armour. His face was half-covered by the grotesque mask that formed the visor of his shining helmet, while around his bear-like shoulders was a thick grey fur cloak, fastened at the neck by a brooch in the shape of two gripping beasts. In his right hand was a hand-and-a-half sword whose pommel blazed with garnets, like the lights of distant watch-fires.

'Who the hell are you?' said the man from the mound.

Hildy did not answer, for she could not remember. The man clapped his gauntleted hands, whereupon a procession of twelve men emerged from the mound. Nine of them were similarly armed and masked, and on their arms they carried kite-shaped shields that seemed to burn in the setting sun. Of the other three, one was small and stooping, dressed in a long white robe that blurred the outlines of his body like low cloud over a hillside, but his face was covered by a hood of cat skins and he leant on a staff cut from a single walrus tusk, carved into the shape of a serpent. The second of the three was a huge man, bigger than any human being Hildy had ever seen before, and he was dressed in the pelt of a long-haired bear. On his shoulder he carried a great halberd, whose blade was as long as its tree-like shaft. The third was shorter than the rest of the armed men but still tall, slim and quick-moving like a dancer. He wore no armour, but only a doublet of purple and dark blue hose. Tucked under his arm was a gilded harp, while over his right shoulder was a longbow of ash-wood and a quiver of green-flighted arrows.

They looked around them, shading their eyes even against the red warmth of the setting sun, as if any light was unbearable to them. One of the armed men, who was carrying a spear with a banner of cloth bound to its shaft, turned to the others and pushed his helmet back, revealing a face at once young and old, with soft brown eyes under stern brows.

'Well,' he said. 'Here we are again. So how long do you reckon we've been down there?'

'No idea,' said the man next to him, who carried a silver horn on a woven baldrick. 'Ask the wizard. He'll know.'

The standard-bearer repeated his question, slowly and loudly, to the small stooping man, who made a noise through the cat skins like a rusty hinge.

'He says twelve hundred years, give or take,' said the standard-bearer. No one seemed in the least surprised (except Hildy, of course, and she was not as surprised as she would have expected to be). The horn-bearer cast his eyes slowly round the encircling hills, inexpressibly majestic in the light glow of the sunset.

'Twelve hundred years,' he said thoughtfully. 'Well, if that's true, it hasn't changed a bit, not in the slightest.' He looked round again. 'Pity, really,' he added. 'Miserable place, Caithness.'

Hildy suddenly remembered that she had to breathe sooner or later or else she would die, and it would be a shame to die before she had found out whether the unbelievable explanation for this spectacle, which was nevertheless the only possible explanation, was correct.

'Excuse me,' she said in a tiny voice, 'but are you people for real?' The words seemed to flop out of her mouth, like exhausted salmon who have finally given up on a waterfall.

'Good question,' replied the leader of the men. 'What about you?'

Hildy wanted to say 'I'm not sure', but she realised that the man was being sarcastic, which was the last thing she expected. 'I'm Hildy Frederiksen,' she mumbled, aware that in all this vastness and mystery that one small fact could have little significance. Still, she wanted it put on record before it was wiped out of her mind.

'Well, now,' said the leader, still sarcastic but with a hint of sympathy in his voice, 'you shouldn't have told me that, should you? After all, when strangers meet by night on the fells, they should not disclose their names, nor the names of their fathers, until they have tested each other's heart with shrewd enquiry.' Then his face seemed to relax a little behind the fixed scowl of his visor. 'Don't ask me why, mind. It's just the rule.'

But Hildy said nothing. The other men from the mound were staring at her, and for the first time she felt afraid.

'Damned silly rule if you ask me,' said the leader, as if he sensed her fear. 'The hours I've wasted asking gnomic questions when I could have been doing something else. Is this place still called Rolfsness?'

Hildy nodded.

'Then, allow me to introduce myself. I am Rolf. My name is King Hrolf Ketilsson, called the Earthstar, the son of Ketil Trout, the son of Eyjolf Kjartan's Bane, the son of Killer-Hrapp of Hedeby, the son of the god Odin. I have been asleep in the howe for – how long have I been asleep in the howe, somebody?'

'Twelve hundred years,' said the horn-bearer.

'Thank you. Twelve hundred years, waiting for the day when I must return to save my kingdom of Caithness from danger, from the greatest danger that has ever or will ever threaten it or its people, according to the vow that I made before the great battle of Melvich, when I slew the host of Geirrodsgarth and cast down the power of Nithspél. These are my thanes and housecarls.'

With a sweeping movement of his hand, he lifted his helmet over his head, revealing a magnificent mane of jet-black hair and two startlingly blue eyes. Hildy felt her knees give way, as if someone had kicked them from behind, and she knelt before him, bowing her head to the ground. When she dared to look up, she saw the last ray of the setting sun sparkling triumphantly on the hilt of the King's great sword as, apparently from nowhere, a fully grown golden eagle swooped down out of the sky and perched on his gloved fist, flapping its enormous wings.

CHAPTER TWO

'Will someone,' said the King, 'get this bird off me?'
The last ray of the sun faded as the standard-
bearer made nervous shooing gestures with his hands.
The bird shifted from one claw to the other, but made
no sign of being prepared to leave. The man in the bear-
skin tried prodding it gently with a huge forefinger, but
it bit him and he backed away. In a sudden access of
daring, Hildy rose to her feet and clapped her hands. At
once the eagle flapped its wings, making a sound like a
whole theatre full of people applauding at once, and
soared off into the sky. It circled slowly three times and
disappeared.

'They do that,' said the King, rubbing his wrist vigorously to restore the circulation. 'Comes of me being a
king, I suppose.'

'I'm starving,' said the horn-bearer. Several voices told
him to be quiet. 'But I am. I haven't had anything to eat
for twelve hundred years.'

A babble of voices broke out, and rose quickly in a
sustained crescendo. 'Ignore them,' said the King softly
to Hildy. 'Sometimes they're like a lot of old women.'

Laying aside his helmet on the grass, he took Hildy's arm, and much to her own surprise she neither winced nor shrank back. He led her aside for a few paces and settled himself comfortably on a small boulder.

'Well, now,' he said, fixing her with his bright eyes. 'So what's been happening in the world while we've been asleep?'

Hildy looked back at the champions. They seemed to be discussing something of extreme importance, and from what she could make out it was mainly to do with whose job it should have been to pack the food. She sat down beside the King.

'It's a long story,' she said.

'It would be, wouldn't it?' he replied, smiling. There was something about his smile that made her feel safe, as if she was under the protection of some great but homely power. She sat in silence for a while, gathering her thoughts. Then she told him.

When she had finished, she looked up. The men were still arguing; they seemed to have narrowed the responsibility down to either the standard-bearer or the horn-bearer, both of whom were protesting their innocence loudly and simultaneously.

'That's it, basically,' Hildy said.

'That's it, is it? Twelve hundred years of history? The achievements of men? Men die, cattle die, only glorious deeds live for ever?'

'That's it, yes.'

The King shrugged his shoulders, and twelve hundred years of history seemed to slide down his arms and melt into the peat. 'But you're sure you haven't left anything out?'

Hildy shuddered slightly. 'Lots,' she said.

The King nodded. 'Yes, of course,' he said, 'but I mean something really important.'

'Like what?'

'I don't know, do I?' He frowned. 'No, the hell with that. If it was there, you couldn't have left it out.' He stopped frowning, and looked over his shoulder at the bickering champions. 'Among the Viking nations,' he said wistfully, 'the model hero is regarded as being brave, loyal, cheerful and laconic. Three out of four isn't bad, I suppose. So who are you, Hildy Frederik's-daughter?'

'Frederik*sen*,' said Hildy automatically. 'Oh, I forgot. We did away with -*son* and -*daughter* centuries ago.'

'Quite right, too,' said the King. 'Go on.'

'I'm an archaeologist,' said Hildy. 'I dig up the past.'

The King raised an eyebrow. 'You mean you refresh old quarrels and keep alive old grievances? Surely not.'

'No, no,' said Hildy, 'I dig up ancient things buried in the earth. Things that belonged to people who lived hundreds of years ago.' As she said this, she began to feel uncomfortable. She had forgotten about the brooch.

'Do you really?' said the King. 'We used to call that grave-robbing.'

Hildy wriggled nervously, and as she did so the brooch slipped out of her pocket and fell on to the ground. 'Oh, I see,' said the King softly. 'Archaeologist. I must remember that one.'

Hildy picked the brooch up, trying unsuccessfully to avoid the King's eye. 'I was going to give it back, honestly,' she said. 'That's why I came back again. I'm sorry.'

The King sighed and took the brooch. It seemed to kick out of her hand, as if it was pleased to be leaving her.

'I was wondering where that had got to,' said the King coldly. 'I went to a lot of trouble. . . . Never mind.'

'What is it?' Hildy asked, but the King only smiled rather scornfully and pinned the brooch on to his cloak. Hildy looked away, feeling utterly miserable, like a child who has done something very wrong and been forgiven.

'You were saying,' said the King.

'I came here to explore the mound,' said Hildy. 'The people laying the pipeline—'

'You, of course, know what a pipeline is,' said the King.

'It's a sort of tube, really. It goes under the sea, and—'

The King frowned again. 'Sorry,' he said, 'I shouldn't have interrupted you. Some men were building a tube, and they broke open the mound. Was it an accident, or done on purpose?'

'Oh, purely accident,' said Hildy. 'Then they sent for the archaeologists, in case it was an ancient burial. And I came and—'

'Yes.' The King smiled again, this time quite kindly. 'You're *sure* it was an accident? It's rather important.'

'Absolutely sure.'

Then the King started to laugh, loudly and almost nervously, as if a great fear had been rolled away from his mind. 'That's good,' he said. 'Now, then, a pipeline is a sort of tube, is it? A tube for what?'

So Hildy told him all about oil, and natural gas, and electricity, and even nuclear power and Three-Mile Island, and by the time she had finished the champions had finished quarrelling and come across to listen. But Hildy didn't notice; the King's eye was on her, and she felt absurdly proud that she was the one chosen to tell him, like a child showing off an expensive new toy to a patient uncle. When she had finished with power, she went on with technology; motor-cars and computers and telephones and television. As she did so, she felt that the King's reaction was all wrong; he didn't seem in the least surprised. In fact he appeared to understand everything she was telling him, even about fax machines and the way word-processors swallow whole chapters and refuse to give them back. She tailed off and stared at him.

'I knew you'd left something out,' said the King.

'But how could you have known?' Hildy said. 'I mean, it must all be so strange to you.'

The King raised his eyebrow again. 'What's so strange about magic?' he said. 'Or don't you know anything about the world I lived in?'

'Yes, I do,' said Hildy proudly. 'I've read all the sagas, and the Eddas, and everything.'

The King nodded. 'A wise-woman, evidently,' he said with mock approval. 'A lore-mistress, even. So you should know all about magic, then, shouldn't you?'

'But that's not magic,' Hildy said. 'That's science.'

'And you're not a grave-robber, you're an archaeologist.' The King laughed again, and Hildy blushed, something she had not done for twenty years. 'That is plain ordinary magic, Hildy Frederik's-daughter, only it sounds rather more mundane and there seems to be more of it about than there used to be.' As he said the words, something seemed to trouble him and he fell silent.

'When you've quite finished,' said a voice behind him, 'there's some of us starving and freezing to death over here.'

The King closed his eyes and asked some nameless power to give him strength. In the distance Hildy heard the sound of an approaching car. She looked quickly over her shoulder towards the road, and saw headlights. The champions looked round as well; the lights were getting closer but slowing down, and Hildy realised that the car was going to stop. One of the champions had drawn his sword, and the others were muttering something about whose turn it was to fight the dragon, and who had done it the last time, and it wasn't fair that the same person always had to do the lousy jobs. But Hildy suddenly felt that on no account should the King and his men be seen by anybody else; whether it was just a desire to keep them all to herself, for a little longer at least, or whether she had a genuine premonition of danger, she could not tell.

'Please,' she said urgently to the King, 'you mustn't be seen. Come with me.'

The King looked at her, then nodded. The men fell silent and sheathed their swords. 'This way,' Hildy said, and she made for the minibus, with the King and his champions following her.

'I'm not getting in that,' said the standard-bearer. 'For one thing, it's got no oars.'

'Shut up and get inside,' snapped the King. The standard-bearer climbed in and sat heavily down. His companions followed swiftly, treading on each other's feet in the process.

'Get in here beside me,' Hildy whispered to the King. 'We must be quick.'

She released the handbrake, and without starting the engine or putting on the lights she coasted the van over the bumpy ground down the slope to the road. The police car had pulled up, and she could see the light of the policemen's torches as they climbed up towards the mound. She coasted on down the road until she reckoned that she was out of earshot, then started the engine and drove away.

In the deserted mound, nothing stirred and the darkness was absolute. A golden cup, which had been disturbed by a passing foot as the Vikings had climbed out of the ship, finally toppled and slid down into the hold with a bump. But someone with quite exceptional hearing might possibly have made out a slight sound, and then dismissed it as his imagination playing tricks on him; a sound like two voices whispering.

'That's thirty-two above the line, doubled, and six left makes thirty-eight, and two for his nob makes forty, which means another free go, and I'm going to go north this time, so if I make more than sixteen I can pass and make another block.'

'Nuts to you,' said the other voice disagreeably.

There was a tiny tinkling noise. 'Six,' said the first voice, with ill-concealed pleasure. 'Up six, clickety-click, and buckets of blood, down the ruddy snake.'

'Serves you right.'

Then there was silence – real silence, unless you could hear the sound of grass forcing its roots deeper into the earth. But by now, of course, your eyes would have picked out four tiny points of soft white light, deep in the gloom under the keel of the ship.

'This is a rotten game,' said the first voice. 'Why don't we play something else?'

'Just because you're losing.'

'We've been playing this game for twelve hundred years,' said the first voice peevishly. 'I'm bored with it.'

The tinkling sound again. 'Four,' said the second voice. 'Double Rune Score. I think I'll have another longhouse on Uppsala.'

'I've got Uppsala, haven't I?'

'You sold it to me in exchange for a dragon and three hundred below the line.'

'Oh, for pity's sake.' Deep silence again. 'What was all that moving about earlier?'

'What moving about?' said the second voice. 'I didn't notice any moving about.'

'There was a lot of coming and going, and voices,' said the first voice. 'Clanking metal, and people swearing, and even a bit of light.'

'Light,' repeated the second voice thoughtfully. 'That's that stuff that comes out of the sky, isn't it?'

'That or rain. Is that your move, then?'

'Just about.'

'Right, then, I'm taking your castle, and I think that's check . . . Oh, damn.'

'No, you don't. You took your hand off.'

'Didn't.'

'Did.'

Complete and utter silence. Even the worms seemed to have stopped snuffling in the turf overhead.

'Shall we go and have a look, then?'

'What at?'

'The noise. I'm sure there was something moving about.'

'You're imagining things.'

'No, I'm not. I think it was somebody going out. Or coming in. Anyway, there was something.'

'Look, are we playing this game or aren't we?'

'I'm going to have a look.' Two of the pale lights seemed to move, round the keel of the ship and up the ladder, then down again, and round the inside of the mound. 'Here, come and look at this,' said the first voice excitedly. 'There's a hole here.'

'What sort of hole?'

'Any old hole. I don't know. A hole going out.'

The second pair of lights scrambled up and joined the first pair.

'You're right,' said the second voice. 'It's a hole.'

'So what are we going to do about it?'

'Push.'

A moment or so later, two small forms were lying on the grass outside the mound, dazzled and stupefied by the dim starlight.

'If this is light,' said one to the other, 'you can keep it.'

But the other was cautiously lifting his head and sniffing. 'It smells like light,' he said tentatively. 'Tastes like light. Do you know what this means, Zxerp?'

'It means that by and large I prefer the other one. Rain, wasn't it?'

'It means we're free, Zxerp. After one thousand two hundred and forty-six years, three months and eleven days in that stinking hole we're actually free.'

They were both silent for a moment. 'Bit of an anticlimax, really,' said Zxerp sadly.

'Oh, the hell with you,' said Prexz. Unusually for a chthonic spirit, he was cheerful and optimistic by nature, and ever since he and his brother had got themselves trapped in King Hrolf's mound he had never entirely given up hope of getting out.

'Now what?' said Zxerp. 'You realise, of course, that things will have changed rather since we got stuck in there.'

'And whose fault was that?' asked Prexz automatically – the issue had not been resolved in over twelve hundred years of eager discussion, and minor disagreements over the precise rules of the game of Goblin's Teeth had not helped them to find a solution to it. But Zxerp refused to be drawn.

'I mean,' Zxerp continued, 'things are bound to have changed. Twelve hundred years is a long time.'

'No, it's not,' replied Prexz accurately. Chthonic spirits, like the sources of energy from which they were formed at the beginning of the world, are practically immortal. Like light and electricity, they go on for ever unless they meet some insuperable resistance or negative force; but, having by some freak of nature the same level of consciousness as mortal creatures, they can fall prey to boredom, and Zxerp and Prexz, imprisoned by the staying spell that had frozen the King's company in time, were no exception. It is in the nature of a chthonic spirit to flow imperceptibly through the veins of the earth in search of magnetic fields or feed parasitically on the currents of an electric storm; confinement gnaws at them.

'It is when you're stuck in a mound with nothing to do but play Goblin's Teeth,' said Zxerp. 'I rather think you'll find . . .'

But Prexz wasn't listening. 'Well,' he said, 'only one way to find out.'

The two spirits sat in silence for a while, as if preparing themselves for a great adventure.

'Right,' sighed Zxerp. 'If we're going, we're going. Where *are* we going, by the way?'

'Dunno. The world is our oyster, really.'

'Terrific. Oh, hang on.'

'What?'

'Shall I bring the game, then?'

Prexz scratched his head. On the one hand, the world was full of new, exciting things for a chthonic spirit to do: elements to explore, currents of power coursing through the magma layer to revel in, static to drink and ultrasound to eat. On the other hand, he was winning.

'Go on, then,' he said. 'Might as well.'

'If anybody asks,' Hildy whispered, 'you're the chorus of the Scottish National Opera off to a rehearsal of *Tannhäuser* in Inverness. I'm going to get some food.'

She had parked the van in a backstreet in Thurso, just round the corner from a fish and chip shop. She hated leaving them like this, but the clamour of the King's champions for food was becoming intolerable, and nothing else was open at this time of night, except the off-licence. 'Cod and chips for fourteen and fourteen cans of lager,' she muttered to herself as she trudged up the darkling street. She only hoped she had enough money to pay for all that. And how long was all this going to last, at three meals a day, not to mention finding them all somewhere to sleep?

Back in the van, the standard-bearer was being difficult, as usual.

'But how do we know we can trust her?' he said. 'I
mean, you don't know her from Freyja. She's obviously
some sort of a witch, or how come this thing moves about
without oars?'

The King shook his head. 'We can trust her,' he said.
'But she doesn't seem to know very much. Whether that's
good or bad, I don't know.'

'So you think there's still danger?' said the huge man,
who was bent nearly double at the back of the van.

'There's danger all right, Starkad Storvirksson,' replied
the King thoughtfully. 'That much we can be sure of. I
can feel it all around me. And I think the woman Hildy
Frederik's-daughter is right that we should not reveal
ourselves until we have found out exactly what is going
on. I do not doubt that the power of the enemy has grown
while we have slept.'

When Hildy returned, exhausted and laden down with
two carrier-bags, the King ordered his men to be quiet.
'We had better not stay in this town,' he said. 'Can you
take us back into open country?'

Hildy nodded, too tired to speak, and they drove out
of Thurso for about half an hour to a bleak and deserted
fell under a grey mountain. There the company got out
and lit a fire in a small hollow hidden from the road.
Hildy handed out paper packages of cod and chips and
cans of lager, which the champions eyed with the greatest suspicion.

'I'm afraid it may have got cold,' Hildy said, 'but it's
better than nothing.'

'What is it?' asked the horn-bearer. 'I mean, what do
you do with it?'

'Try taking the paper off,' said Hildy. The huge man

looked up in surprise; he had already eaten the wrapping of his.

'The brown stuff on the outside is called batter,' Hildy said. 'It's made from eggs and flour and things. Inside there's fish.'

'I don't like fish,' said a champion with a silver helmet.

'The small brown things are chips,' Hildy continued. 'They weren't invented in your time. There's beer in the metal tubes.'

The champion in the silver helmet started to ask if there was any mead instead, but the King frowned at him. 'Excellent,' he said. 'We owe you a great debt already, Hildy Frederik's-daughter.'

Hildy nodded; they owed her twenty-two pounds and seventy-five pence, and she could see little chance of her ever getting it back. The authors of all the sagas she had read had been notably reticent about the cost of mass catering.

'You're welcome,' she said wearily. 'My pleasure.'

'In return,' said the King through a mouthful of cod, 'I must explain to you who we are and why we were sleeping in the mound in the first place. But I must ask you to remember that this is a serious business. Wise is he who knows when to speak; wiser still, he who knows when to stay silent.'

'Point taken,' said Hildy, who recognised that as a quotation from the Elder Edda. 'Go on, please.'

The King bent his can of lager into the shape of a drinking-horn and pulled off the ring-pull. 'My father was Ketil Trout,' he said, 'and he ruled over the Orkneys and Caithness. He was a wise and strong king, not loved overmuch by his people but feared by his enemies, and when he fell in battle he was buried in his ship.'

'Where?' Hildy asked, for she still had the instincts of an archaeologist. But the King ignored her.

'I succeeded him as king,' he said. 'I was only fourteen at the time, and my uncle Hakon Claw ruled as regent until I reached the age of sixteen. When I came to the throne, I led my people out to war. I was strong then, tall for my age and burning with the desire to win glory. The people worshipped me, and I foresaw a succession of marvellous victories; my sword never sheathed, my banner never furled, my kingdom growing day by day in size and power.'

The King stopped speaking, and Hildy could see by the light of the fire that there were tears in his bright quick eyes. She waited patiently, and he continued.

'As you can see, Hildy Frederick's-daughter, I was a wicked fool in my youth, blinded with tales and the long names of heroes. That's what comes of paying attention to the stories of long ago; you wish to emulate them, to bring the Elder Days back into the present. But there never was an age of heroes; when Sigurd Fafnir's Bane was digging dragon-traps in the Teutoberger Wald, they were already singing songs about the great heroes and days that would never come again. But I wasted many lives of farmers' sons who could not wait for the barley to ripen, leading armies into unnecessary battles, killing enemies who did not merit killing. What are these songs that they promised me they would make, and sing when I was cold in the howe? You say you have read all the sagas of our people, and studied the glorious deeds of heroes. Is there still a song about the battle of Melvich, or the fight at Tongue, when I struck down Jarl Bjorn in front of his own mainmast?'

Hildy turned away and said nothing.

'They promised me a song,' said the King. 'Perhaps they made one; if they did not, it does not matter very much. I found all those songs very dreary; warflame whistled and wolves feasted when Hrolf the Ring-Giver reddened the whale-road. The arrows always blotted out the sun, I remember, and the poet didn't get paid unless blade battered hard on helmet at least once in the first stanza.'

The King smiled bitterly, and threw more wood on the fire. It crackled and grew brighter, and he continued.

'Then one day I was wounded, quite seriously. Strangely enough, it wasn't a great hero or an earl who did it; it was just a miserable little infantryman whose ship we had boarded. I expected him to hold still and be killed, because I was a hero and he was only a peasant, but I suppose he didn't know the rules, or was too scared to obey them. Anyway, he hit me across the forehead with an axe – not a battle-axe with runes all over the blade, something run up by the local blacksmith. I think it knocked some sense into my thick head, because that was the end of my career as a sea-raider, even though I made a complete recovery. I went back home and tried to take a serious interest in more mundane matters, such as whether the people had enough to eat and were the roads passable in winter. I'm afraid I was a great disappointment to my loyal subjects; they liked their kings bloodthirsty.

'Just when the world was beginning to make a little sense, and nobody bothered to invade us any more because we refused to fight, something started to happen away up north in Finnmark, in the kingdom of Geirrodsgarth, where the sorcerers lived. I think they stopped fighting among themselves and made an alliance. Whatever it was, there was suddenly an army of invulnerable berserks loose in the northern seas; all the fighting men who were too vicious even to be heroes had apparently been making their way there for years, and the sorcerer-king organised them into an army. And that wasn't all. He had trolls, and creatures made out of the bodies of dead men, which he brought back to life, and the spirits of wolves and bears put into human shape. Suddenly the game became rather serious, and the kings and earls settled their differences very quickly, and started to offer high wages to any competent wizard who specialised in military magic. But most of those had joined up with the enemy, and quite soon there were battles about which nobody made up any songs, as the ships from Geirrodsgarth appeared off the coasts of every kingdom in the north.

'There seemed little point in fighting, because the ordinary hacking and slashing techniques didn't seem to work on the sorcerer's army. But I was lucky, I suppose, or my ancestor Odin came to my aid. In a stone hut in Orkney lived a wizard called Kotkel, and he knew a few tricks that the enemy did not. He came to me and told me that I could withstand the enemy, perhaps even overthrow him, if I found a brooch, called the Luck of Caithness; with that in my possession, I could at least fight on equal terms. At that time, all the fugitives from the great kings' armies were pouring into my kingdom, and so I had the pick of the fighters of the age. I chose the very best: Ohtar and Hring, Brynjolf the Shape-Changer and Starkad Storvirksson, Angantyr and Bothvar Bjarki, Helgi and Hroar and Hjort, Arvarodd, who had been to Permia and killed giants, and Egil Kjartansson, called the Dancer. I sent them to find the brooch, and within a month they had found it. Then we went to fight the sorcerer. And we won, at Rolfsness, after a battle that lasted two days and two nights.

'But something went wrong at the last moment. One of us – I can't remember who, and it doesn't matter – had the sorcerer-king on the point of his spear but let him get away, and he escaped, although all his army, berserks and trolls and ghost-warriors, were utterly destroyed. We had failed, in spite of all our efforts, and we knew it. Of course, we did our best to make up. We raised forces in every kingdom in the north and went to Geirrodsgarth, where we razed the sorcerer-king's stronghold to the ground and killed all his creatures in their nests. We searched for him under every rock and in every barn and hay-loft; but he had escaped. Some said he had ridden away on the wind, leaving his body behind, and others assured me that he had sunk into the sea.

'Then the wizard Kotkel came to me and gave me more advice, and I realised that I would have to take it. I ordered my longship Naglfar to be brought up on to the battle-field at Rolfsness and sunk into a mound. While the wizard cast his spells and cut runes into the joists and beams of the chamber, I gathered together my champions and led them into the ship. Then the wizard sang a sleeping spell, and we all fell asleep, and they closed up the mound. That last spell was a strong one; we should not wake until the day had come when the sorcerer-king was once again at the summit of his power and threatening the world. Then we should do battle with him once more, for the last time. And there we have been ever since, Hildy Frederik's-daughter. Quite a story, isn't it? Or aren't there any songs about it? No? I'm not surprised. I think people rather lost interest in stories about heroes after the sorcerer-king appeared; most of them seemed to be in rather bad taste.'

For a while, Hildy sat and stared into the heart of the fire, wondering whether or not she could believe this story, even out on the fells, by night beside a fire. It was not that she suspected the King of lying; and she believed in his existence, and that he had just woken up after twelve hundred years of sleep. But something struggling to stay alive inside her told her that some token show of disbelief was necessary if she was to retain her identity, or at least her sanity. Then it occurred to her, like the obvious solution to some tiresome puzzle, that her belief was not needed, just as the meat need not necessarily consent to being cooked. She had entered the service of a great lord; part of the bargain between lord and subject is that the subject does not have to understand the lord's design; so long as the subject obeys the lord's orders, her part is discharged, and no blame can attach to her.

'So what are you going to do?' she asked.

The King smiled. 'I shall find the sorcerer-king and I shall destroy him, if I can,' he said. 'That sounds simple enough, don't you think? If you keep things simple, and look to the end, not the problems in the way, most things turn out to be possible. That is not in any Edda, but I think it will pass for wisdom.'

The King rose slowly to his feet and beckoned to the wizard, who had been sitting outside the circle of the fire-light, apparently trying to find a spell that would make a beer-can magically refill itself. They walked a little way into the night, and spoke together softly for a while.

Hildy began to feel cold, and one of the champions noticed her shivering slightly and took off his cloak and offered it to her.

'My name is Angantyr,' he said, 'son of Asmund son of Geir. My father was earl of—'

'Not you as well,' moaned the horn-bearer. 'Can't we have a song or something instead?'

Hildy wrapped the cloak round her shoulders. It was heavy and seemed to envelop her, like a fall of warm snow.

'Do you mind?' said Angantyr Asmundarson. 'The lady and I—'

'Don't you take any notice of him,' said the standard-bearer. 'He's not called Angantyr the Creep for nothing.'

'Look who's talking,' replied Angantyr.

'Excuse me,' Hildy said. The heroes looked at her. 'Which one of you is Arvarodd?'

'I am,' said a gaunt-looking hero in a black cloak.

Hildy was blushing. 'Are you the Arvarodd who went to Permia?' she asked shyly. For some reason the heroes burst out laughing, and Arvarodd scowled.

'I read your saga,' she said, 'all about the giants and the magic shirt of invulnerability. Was it like that?'

'Yes,' said Arvarodd.

'Oh.' Hildy bit her lip nervously. 'Could I have your autograph, please? It's not for me, it's for the Department of Scandinavian Studies at St Andrews University,' she added quickly. Then she hid her face in the cloak.

'What's an autograph?' asked Arvarodd.

'Could you write your name on – well, on that beer-can?'

Arvarodd raised a shaggy eyebrow, then scratched a rune on the empty Skol can with the point of his dagger and handed it to her.

'Everyone's always kidding him about his trip to Permia,' Angantyr whispered in her ear. 'All his great deeds, and the battles and the dragons and so forth – well, you heard the saga, didn't you? – and all anyone ever asks him is "Are you the Arvarodd who went to Permia?" And it was only a trading-voyage, and all he brought back was a few mouldy old furs.'

The King and the wizard came back to the fire and sat down.

'The drinks are on the wizard,' announced the King, and at once the heroes crowded round the wizened old man, who started to pour beer out of his can into theirs.

'Don't worry,' said the King to Hildy, 'the wizard and I have thought of something. But we're going to need a little help.'

*   *   *

There are many tall office-blocks in the City of London, but the tallest of them all is Gerrards Garth House, the home of the Gerrards Garth group of companies. Someone – perhaps it was the architect – thought it would be a good idea to have a black office-block instead of the usual white, and so the City people in their wine bars refer to it as the Dark Tower.

The very top floor is one enormous office, and few people have ever been there. It is full of screens and desktop terminals, and the telephones are arrayed in battalions, like the tanks at a march-past. On the wall is a large electronic map of the world, with flashing lights marking the Gerrards Garth operations in every country. On a busy day it almost seems as if the entire world is burning.

The building was entirely dark, except for one light in this top office, and in that office there was only one man: a big burly man with red cheeks and large forearms. He was staring into a bank of screens on which there were many columns of figures, and from time to time he would tap in a few symbols. Then the screens would clear and new figures would come up before him. He did not seem to be tired or impatient, or particularly concerned with what he saw; it looked very much as if everything was nicely under control. Thanks, no doubt, to the new technology.

And then the screens all over the office went out, and came on again. All over them, little green figures raced up and down, like snowflakes in a blizzard, while every light that could possibly flash began to flash at once. Unfamiliar symbols which were to be found in no manual moved back and forth with great rapidity, forming themselves into intricate spirals and interweaving curves of flickering light, and all the telephones began to ring at once. The man gripped the arms of his chair and stared.

Suddenly all the screens stopped flickering, and one picture appeared on all of them, glowing very brightly, while the overhead lights went out, and the terminals began to spit out miles of printout paper covered in words from a hundred forgotten languages.

The man leant forward and looked at the screen closest to him. The picture was of a golden brooch, in the shape of a flying dragon.

CHAPTER THREE

'Admit it, Zxerp,' said a voice, 'you've never had it so good.' The postman, who had just been about to get on his bicycle for the long ride back to Bettyhill, stopped dead in his tracks and stared at the telegraph wires over his head. He could have sworn that one of them had just spoken. He looked around suspiciously, but nothing stirred in the grey dawn.

'I mean,' said the voice, 'I haven't the faintest idea what this stuff is, but it beats geothermal energy into a cocked hat.'

The postman jumped on his bicycle and pedalled away, very fast.

'It's all right, I suppose,' replied Zxerp. 'A bit on the sweet side for my taste, but it has a certain something.' He wiped his mouth with the back of his hand.

'You're never satisfied, are you?' said Prexz, emerging from the wire and hopping lightly down to the ground. 'You want magnetism on it, you do.'

'Hang on,' said Zxerp. He climbed out of the copper core and dropped rather heavily. 'Ouch,' he said unconvincingly. 'I think I've hurt my ankle.'

They strolled for a while down the empty lane, and paused to gaze out over the misty hills. The cloud was low, so that the peaks were blurred and vague; it was possible to imagine that they rose up for ever to the roof of the sky.

'So whose go was it?' asked Zxerp after a while.

'Mine,' replied Prexz. 'Have you got the dice?'

'I thought you had them.'

They searched their pockets and found the dice: two tiny cubes of diamond that glowed with an inner light.

'So what are we going to do, then?' asked Zxerp after each had had a couple of turns. He was in grave danger of being Rubiconned (again) and wanted to distract his companion's attention.

'Do?' Prexz frowned. 'What we like, I suppose.'

'No, but really. We've had a break; we ought to be getting back to work.'

Prexz shook his head vigorously, causing great interference with Breakfast Television reception all over Bettyhill. 'I've had it up to here with work. At the beck and call of every wizard and sorcerer in Caithness, never a moment to call your own – what sort of a life do you call that? I reckon that if we keep our heads down and play our runes right . . .'

He stopped, and put his hands to his head. Zxerp stared at him, then suddenly he felt it, too: words of command, coming from not far away.

'Oh, for pity's sake,' muttered Prexz. 'It's that bloody wizard again.'

'I was just thinking,' said Zxerp through gritted teeth, 'how nice it would be not to have to see that Kotkel again.'

'He was the worst,' agreed Prexz. 'Definitely the worst.'

The words of command stopped, and the two spirits relaxed.

'Perhaps if we just hid somewhere,' Prexz whispered. 'Pretended to be a bit of static or something . . .'

'Forget it.' Zxerp was already packing up the game, putting the Community Hoard cards back into their marcasite box. 'I knew it was too good to last.'

They started to trudge back the way they had come.

'Do you suppose he did it on purpose?' asked Prexz. 'Trapped us in the mound deliberately, or something?'

'I wouldn't be surprised,' said Zxerp gloomily. 'He's clever, that wizard.'

Hildy was not used to sleeping out in the open, but at least it hadn't rained, and she had been so tired that sleep came remarkably easily. She had had a strange dream, in which everything had gone back to normal and which ended with her sitting at a table in the University library leafing through the latest edition of the *Journal of Scandinavian Studies*.

When she opened her eyes, she found that the Vikings were all up and sitting round a fire. They were roasting four rabbits on sticks, which reminded Hildy irresistibly of ice-lollies, and passing round a helmet filled with water.

'Why's it always *my* helmet?' grumbled the horn-bearer.

For a moment, the pure simplicity of the scene filled Hildy with a sort of inner peace: food caught by skill in the early morning, and clean water from a mountain stream. Then she discovered that a spider had crawled inside her boot, and that she had a crick in her neck from sleeping with her head on a tree-root. She evicted the spider nervously and tottered over to the fire.

'Have some rabbit,' said Angantyr. 'It's a bit burnt, but a little charcoal never killed anyone.'

Hildy explained that she never ate breakfast. 'Where's the King?' she asked.

'He wandered off with that blasted wizard,' said the horn-bearer, drying out the inside of his helmet with the hem of his cloak. 'I think it's going to rain any minute now,' he added cheerfully.

She found the King sitting beside the bank of a little river that rolled down off the side of the fell just inside the wood. He turned and smiled at her, and put a finger to his lips. On the other side of the stream the wizard was standing on one leg, pointing with his staff to a shallow pool. The King was lighting a small fire with a tinderbox.

'What's he doing?' whispered Hildy.

'Watch,' replied the King.

The wizard had started mumbling something under his breath, and almost immediately two large salmon jumped up out of the water and landed in the King's lap.

'Saves all that mucking about with hooks and bits of string,' explained the King. 'Had any breakfast?'

'No,' said Hildy. 'But I never—'

'Don't blame you,' said the King. 'Rabbit again, I expect. And burnt, too, if I know them. No imagination.'

The wizard had crossed the stream, and the King set about preparing the salmon, while Hildy looked away.

'Kotkel and I have been thinking,' said the King. 'Obviously, it's no good our hanging about out here having a good time and waiting for the enemy to come to us. On the other hand, we aren't exactly suited for going out and looking for him, although I don't suppose he'll be all that hard to find.'

He threw something into the water, and Hildy winced. As a child, she had had to be taken outside when her mother served up fish with their heads still on.

'So I think we should find somewhere where we can get ourselves organised, don't you? And there are things we're going to need. For example, I was never a great follower of fashion, and far be it from me to make personal comments, but does everyone these days wear extraordinary clothes like those you've got on?'

Hildy glanced at the King, in his steel hauberk and wolfskin leggings. 'Yes,' she said.

'Well,' said the King, 'we don't want to appear conspicuous, do we? So we'll need clothes, and somewhere to stay, and probably other things as well. I'm afraid you'll have to see to that for us.'

Hildy didn't like the sound of that. To the best of her knowledge she had just over two hundred pounds in the bank, and her next grant cheque wasn't due for three weeks.

'The problem is,' continued the King, 'what do we have to trade?'

Hildy had a brilliant idea. On the King's tunic was a small brooch of enamelled gold in the shape of a running horse. She pointed to it.

'Could you spare me that?' she asked.

'A present from my aunt, Gudrun Thord's-daughter,' replied the King, looking down at it. 'I never liked it much. Rich is gold, the gift of earls, but richer still the help of friends. So to speak.'

He unpinned the brooch and handed it to her. Hildy looked around at the vast empty hills and the dense wood before her.

'I know a couple of dealers in antiquities down in London . . . You remember London?'

'Still going, is it?' asked the King, raising an eyebrow. 'You surprise me. I never thought it would last. Go on.'

'They'd pay a lot for this, with no questions asked. Enough to be going on with, anyway.'

'But London is several weeks' journey away,' said the King.

'Not any more,' said Hildy. 'I'd be away two, at the most three days.'

The King nodded. 'I imagine we'll be able to take care of ourselves for three days. It'll give us time to think out what we're going to do. But be careful. For all I know, the enemy is aware of us already.'

For some reason, Hildy felt rather cold, although the King's little fire was burning brightly. She had no notion what this strange enemy was, but when the King spoke his name she was conscious of an inexplicable discomfort, just as, although she did not believe in ghosts, she could never properly get to sleep after reading a ghost story. The King seemed to understand what she was thinking, for he put his hand on her shoulder and said: 'I think you will be able to recognise the enemy when you come across him or his works. I suspect that you know most of them already. It will be like a house or a bend in the road which you have passed many times, until one day someone tells you a story about that place – there was a murder there once, or an old mad woman lived there for many years – and the place is never the same again. Here, in these unchanged mountains, I cannot feel properly afraid of my enemy, even though I fought him here once, and smelt his danger in every fold of the land. But now I think his ships are beached somewhere else, and his army watches other roads. I remember that he used to have birds for spies and messengers, ravens and crows and eagles, so that as we marched we knew that he could see us and assess our strength at every turn. I think he has other spies now; and now it is most important that he does *not* see us. He will look here first, of course, and we are not an army able to do battle; we cannot fight his armies, we can only fight him, hand-to-hand in his own stronghold – if we can find it and get there before he finds us and squashes us under his thumb.'

The King stopped speaking and closed his eyes, but Hildy could not feel afraid, even though fear was all around her, for the King was here with his champions, and he would find a way.

'The salmon's ready,' he said suddenly. 'Help yourself.'

'No, thanks,' said Hildy, 'I never eat breakfast. I'd better get going.'

'Good luck, then,' said the King, not looking up from his salmon. 'Be careful.'

Hildy walked back to the camp, where she had parked the van.

'Going somewhere?' asked Arvarodd, who was sitting by the fire sharpening arrowheads on a stone.

'Yes,' said Hildy. 'I'll be gone for a day or so. The King needs some things before we start out.'

'Going alone?'

'Yes.'

'Risky.' Arvarodd got up and stretched his arms wide. 'Never mind, I expect you'll cope. You know all about everything these days, of course, so I don't suppose you're worried.'

'Yes,' replied Hildy doubtfully, 'I suppose I do.'

'Better safe than sorry, though,' said Arvarodd. He was looking for something in a goat-skin satchel by his side. 'Come over here,' he said softly.

'Well?'

He took out a small bundle of linen cloth and laid it on the grass beside him. 'When I was in Permia,' he whispered, 'I did pick up one or two useful things, although I made sure no one ever found out about them, so you won't have heard of them in any of those perishing sagas. Never saw a penny in royalties out of any of them, by the way. These bits and pieces might come in useful. I'll want them back, mind.'

He unrolled the cloth and picked out three small

pebbles and a splinter of bone, with a rune crudely carved on it.

'Not things of beauty, I'll grant you,' he said, 'but still. This pebble here is in fact the gallstone of the dragon Fafnir, whom Sigurd Sigmundarsson slew, as you know better than I. Improbable though it may sound, it enables you to understand any language of men. This remarkably similar pebble comes from the shores of Asgard. If you throw it at something, it turns into a boulder and flattens pretty well anything. Then it turns back into a pebble and returns to your hand. This bone is a splinter of the jaw of Ymir the Sky-Father. Ymir could talk the hind legs off a donkey, and this makes whoever bears it irresistibly persuasive. And this,' he said, prodding the third pebble with his forefinger, 'was picked off the roughcast on the walls of Valhalla. I never found out what it does, but I imagine it brings you good luck or something.'

He rolled them back up in the cloth and gave it to her. She tried to find words to thank him, but none came.

'You'd better be going,' he said, and she turned to go. 'Be careful.'

'I will. It's not dangerous, really.'

'Did you really read my saga?'

Hildy nodded.

'Like it?'

'Yes.'

'Wrote it myself,' said Arvarodd gruffly, and he walked away.

Danny Bennett's definition of an optimist was someone who has nothing left except hope, and he felt that the description fitted him well. Ever since he had joined the BBC, straight from university, his career had seemed to drift downhill, albeit in a vaguely upwards direction. True, he had made a reputation for himself with the less intense sort of documentary, the sort that people like to watch rather than the sort that is good for them, but although his work interested the public it was not, he felt sure, in the Public Interest. While all around him his colleagues were exposing scandals in the Health Service and uncovering cover-ups with the enthusiasm of small children unwrapping their Christmas presents, he was traipsing round historic English towns doing series on architecture, or lovingly satirical portraits of charming eccentrics. Better, he thought, to suffer the final indignity of producing 'One Man and His Dog' than to be caught in this limbo of unwanted success.

As he sat in the editing suite with visions of the Cotswolds flickering before him, he had in his briefcase the synopsis of his life's work, a startling piece of investigation that would, if carried through with the proper resources, conclusively prove that the Milk Marketing Board had been somehow connected with the assassination of President Kennedy. He had seen its pages become dog-eared with unresponsive reading, and always it had returned, admired but not accepted, along with a command to go forth and film yet another half-baked half-timbered village green. All around him teemed the modern world, sordid and cynical and infinitely corrupt, but he was seemingly trapped in the Forest of Arden.

He wound his way painfully through the material in front of him, and for only the fifteenth time that hour wished a horrible death on his chief cameraman, who seemed to believe that people looked better with trees apparently growing out of the tops of their heads. He picked up the telephone beside him.

'Angie?' he said. 'Is Bill still in the building?'

'Yes, Mr Bennett.'

'Find him, and personally confiscate that polarising

filter. He's used it five times in the last six shots, and it makes everything look like my daughter's holiday snaps. And tell him he's an incompetent idiot.'

'There's been a call for you, Mr Bennett,' said Angie. 'I think somebody wants you to do something.'

Danny Bennett could guess what. There had been a news report that morning about some fantastic archaeological find up in the north of Scotland, and he had felt the threat of it hanging over him all day, like a bag of flour perched on top of a door he must walk through. Five days on some windswept moor, and all the delights of a hotel bar full of sound-recordists in the evenings. He plodded through the rest of the editing, and went to investigate.

'You want to talk to Professor Wood, Department of Archaeology, St Andrews,' he was told. 'He's on site at the moment with an archaeological team. Apparently, there's gold and a perfectly preserved Viking ship. Sort of like Sutton Hoo only much better.'

'And Professor Wood actually found the ship, did he?'

'No, it was one of his students or something. But Professor Wood is the one who's in charge now.'

'But I'll have to talk to this student,' Danny said wearily. 'What was it like to be the first person in two thousand years, and all that. Can you find out who this person is?'

He went to the bar for a drink before going home to pack. One of his colleagues, a rat-faced woman called Moira, grinned at him as he sat down.

'You drew the short straw, then? That Caithness nonsense with the Viking ship?'

'Yes.'

'I'm just off to do an in-depth investigation into a corrupt planning inquiry in Sunderland. Nuclear dumping. Wicked alderman. Rattle the Mayor's chain.'

'Good for you.'

'It will be, with any luck. Plenty of nice gooey evil in these local-government stories.' She grinned again, but Danny didn't seem to be in the mood.

'There's a rumour that there's a story in this Scottish thing, actually,' she said.

'Don't tell me,' said Danny to his drink. 'The Vikings didn't get planning permission for their mound.'

'The girl who found the thing,' said Moira, 'has apparently vanished. Not at her hotel. Hired a van and made herself into air. Can it be that she has looted the mound and absconded with a vanful of Heritage? Or are more sinister forces at work up there among the kilts and heather? You could have fun with that.'

Danny shrugged his shoulders. 'May be something in it,' he said.

'Perhaps' – Moira looked furtively round and whispered – 'perhaps it's the Milk Marketing Board. Again.'

'Oh, very funny,' said Danny.

It took Hildy some time to get used to the idea that she was still in Britain in the twentieth century and that, so far as she could tell, no one was hunting for her or trying to kill her. As she waited for the bus to Inverness, having dumped the hired van outside Lairg, she had the feeling that she ought, at the very least, to be using false papers and a forged driving licence, and in all probability be speaking broken French as well. But she put this down to having seen too many movies about the Resistance, and settled back to endure the long and unpleasant journey.

She made her way uneventfully to the railway station, bought a copy of *Newsweek*, and read it as the train shuffled through northern Britain. It was unlikely, of course, that even in that great rendezvous of conspiracy theories the rising of the sorcerer-king would be reported in so many words, but at the back of her mind she had an inchoate idea of where the enemy might be found. Something the King had said about magic had started her thinking and, although her idea was scarcely distinguishable from healthy American paranoia, that was not in itself a reason for discarding it. God, guts and paranoia made America great.

As she picked her way with difficulty through the various items – for she had been in England a long time now, and found the language of her native land rather tiring in long bursts – she began to feel aware of some unifying theme. There happened to be a long article about a group of companies, a household name throughout the world. Then there was another article about advances in satellite communications, and a discussion of the techniques of electoral advertising. There were several letters about commercial funding of universities, and a great deal about nuclear power, apparently cut from the great bolts of similar material that hang in all editorial offices. The whole thing seemed to make some sort of left-handed sense, and she started again from the beginning. The more she read, the more sense it seemed to make, although what the sense was she could not quite grasp. She told herself that she was probably imagining it, and went to the buffet-car for a coffee.

She had a headache now, and tried to get some sleep, but when she dozed a dream came to her, and she thought she stood on the roof of a very high office-block somewhere in Manhattan or Chicago, from which she could see all the kingdoms of the earth below her. That was curious enough but what was odder still was that large areas of the world were apparently dyed or cross-hatched in a colour she had never been aware of before. Then something rolled out of her pocket, and she stopped to retrieve it. It was the third pebble that Arvarodd had lent her, the one whose use was unknown, and it was the same colour as the cross-hatching.

Then the train went over some points, and she woke up. Once she had recovered her wits sufficiently, she took out the roll of cloth and extracted from it the third pebble. It felt warm in her hand, and something prompted her to put it in her mouth and suck it. It tasted rather bitter, but not unpleasantly so, and she picked up the magazine and started to read it a third time.

By the time the train pulled in to Euston, she was sweating and feeling very frightened. She took the pebble out of her mouth and put it away, then walked briskly to a small and not too horrible hotel she had stayed in before. She did not sleep well that night.

The next morning, promptly at nine-thirty, she walked down to Holborn, where the dealers in antiquities have their lairs. There she converted the golden brooch into seven thousand pounds cash money. It seemed strange to be walking about with so much money in her pocket, but she was in no mood to entrust it to a bank.

Next she went to the London University bookshop, where she bought a number of Old Norse and Anglo-Saxon texts, of such great popularity that the prices on the backs were still in shillings, and then to the British Museum, where she spent several hours in the Reading Room. After a cup of coffee and a hamburger, she caught a train for Inverness. It took even longer than the train down, but the journey passed quickly, for she was used to working on trains.

She stayed the night in a hotel in Inverness, and spent the next morning among the secondhand-car dealers, trying to find a fourteen-seater van. Most of those that were within her price range had no engine or less than the conventional number of wheels, but eventually she found something suitable, which she christened Sleipnir, after the eight-legged warhorse of the god Odin. Then she went to Marks & Spencer and bought fourteen suits; she had to guess at the sizes, but she knew that you can always change things from Marks & Spencer if they don't fit. The woman at the cash-desk gave her a suspicious look, and Hildy could not really blame her; but the worst she could be suspected of doing was organising a cell of Jehovah's Witnesses, which was not a crime, even in Scotland. Shoes were more of a problem, but she decided on something large and simple in black; timeless, she thought to herself. They would need to be, after all.

There were other things, notably food and blankets and camping-stoves, and by the time she had got everything there was not much money left and she was exhausted. She filled the van up with petrol – how do you explain petrol to Viking heroes? This wagon has no horses, it moves by burning dead leaves – and started off on the long drive to Caithness.

'Don't talk daft,' said the horn-bearer, 'that's the Haystack.'

'You're the one who's talking daft, Bothvar Bjarki,' replied Arvarodd. 'That's Vinndalf's Crown. You find Vinndalf's Crown by going left from the Pole Star until you reach the Thistle, then straight down past the Great Goat.'

'If that's all you know about the stars,' replied Bothvar Bjarki, 'it's no wonder you ended up in bloody Permia. Where were you trying to get to – Oslo?'

Arvarodd gathered up his cloak and moved pointedly to the other side of the fire. There the huge man and another champion were sitting playing chess on a portable chess-set made out of walrus ivory.

'Is that checkmate?' asked the huge man.

'Afraid so,' replied his opponent.

'I always lose,' said the huge man.

'You can't help it if you're stupid, Starkad,' replied his opponent kindly. 'A berserk isn't meant to be clever. If he was clever, he wouldn't be a berserk. And you're a very good berserk, isn't he, Arvarodd?'

'Yes,' said Arvarodd. The huge man beamed with pleasure, and his smile seemed to light up the camp.

'Thank you, Brynjolf,' said Starkad Storvirksson. 'And you're a very good shape-changer.'

'Thank you, Starkad,' said Brynjolf, trying to conceal the fact that he had had this conversation before. 'How about another game, then?'

'Don't you want to play, Arvarodd?' Starkad asked, looking at the hero of Permia. Starkad loved chess, even though he invariably lost, although how he managed to do so when everybody cheated to make sure he won was a complete mystery.

'No, not now,' Arvarodd said. 'I'm going to get some sleep in a minute.'

'Can I be black, then?'

'But white always moves first, Starkad,' said Brynjolf gently. 'Don't you want to move first?'

'No, thank you,' said the berserk. 'I've noticed that I always seem to lose when I play first.'

If Brynjolf closed his eyes, it was only for a moment. They played a couple of moves, and Brynjolf advanced his king straight down the board into a nest of black pieces.

'Tell me something, Brynjolf,' said Starkad softly, marching his rook straight past the place Brynjolf had meant it to go, 'why do Bothvar and the others call me Honey-Starkad?'

Brynjolf stared at the board and scratched his head. Yet again, it was impossible for him to move without check-mating his opponent. 'Because you're sweet and thick, Starkad,' he said.

'Oh,' said the berserk, as if some great mystery had been revealed to him. 'Oh, I *see*. It's your move.'

'Checkmate,' said Brynjolf.

CHAPTER FOUR

The job description had never said anything about this, thought the young man as he scooped up the armfuls of paper that had spilled out of the printers during the night. The Big Bang, yes. The New Technology, certainly. The waste paper, no.

He paused, exhausted by the unaccustomed effort, and cast his eyes over a sheet at random. It said:

ƙØ£♦¥⁒{ॱ‐nⁱⁱ⁚꞉}

And probably meant it, too. It might be BASIC, or it might be FORTRAN, or any other of those computer languages, except that he knew all of them and it wasn't. If he was expected to do a reasoned efficiency breakdown on it and report intelligently in the morning, they were going to be disappointed.

'What are you doing with those?'

The young man jumped, and several yards of continuous stationery fell to the floor and wound themselves round his feet, almost affectionately, like a cat.

'It's last night's printout, Mr . . .' He never could remember the boss's name. In fact he wasn't sure anyone had ever told him what it was.

'Leave that alone.' The old sod was in a worse mood than usual. 'Have you looked at it?'

'Well, no, not in any great detail *yet*. I was hoping . . .'

'Put it down and clear off.'

'Yes, Mr . . .'

No point in even trying to place it tidily on the desk. The young man let it slither from his arms, and fled.

'And find me Mr Olafsen, now.'

The young man stopped. One more stride and he would have been out of the door and clear.

'I'm not positive he's in the building, actually, Mr . . .'

'I didn't ask you if he was in the building. I asked you to find him.'

This time the young man made it out of the door. There was something about his employer that he didn't like, a sort of air of menace. It was not just the fear of the sack; more like an atmosphere of physical danger. He asked Mr Olafsen's secretary if she knew where he was.

Apparently he was in Tokyo. Where exactly in Tokyo, however, she refused to speculate. He had been sent there on some terribly urgent business with instructions not to fail. In the event of failure, he should carry the firm's principle of conforming to local business methods to its logical conclusion and commit hara-kiri.

'*He* was in a foul mood that day – worse than usual,' went on the secretary. 'You might try phoning the Tokyo office. I don't know what time it is over there, and they might all be out running round the roof or kicking sacks or whatever it is they do, but you might be lucky.'

A series of calls located Mr Olafsen at a golf-course on the slopes of Mount Fuji, and he was put through to his employer.

'Thorgeir, there's trouble,' said the boss. 'Get back here as quick as you like.'

'Won't it wait? If I can get round in less than fifty-two, we'll have more semiconductors than we know what to do with.'

'No, it won't. It's dragon trouble.'

'This is a terrible line. I thought you said—'

'I said dragon trouble, Thorgeir.'

'I'm on my way.'

The boss put down the telephone. The knowledge that he would soon have Thorgeir Storm-Shepherd at his side did something to relieve the panic that had afflicted him all day. Thorgeir might not have courage, but he had brains, and his loyalty was beyond question. That at least was certain; any disloyalty, and he knew he would be turned back into the timber-wolf he had originally been, when the sorcerer-king had first found him in the forests of Permia. Timber-wolves cannot wear expensive suits or drive Lagondas with any real enjoyment, and Thorgeir had become rather attached to the good life.

'Why now?' the sorcerer-king asked himself, for the hundredth time that morning. With repetition, the question appeared to be resolving itself. There was the little matter of the Thirteenth Generation, the final coincidence of hardware and software that the sorcerer-king had vaguely dreamt of back at the start of his career under the shade of ancestral fir-trees, when artificial intelligence had been confined to stones with human voices and other party tricks. It had been a long road since then, and he had come a long way along it. No earthly power could prevent him, since no earthly power would for one instant take seriously any accurate description of the threat he posed to the world and its population. But the dragon and the King had never been far from his mind ever since he had abandoned his mortal body on the battlefield at Rolfsness and escaped, rather ignominiously disguised as a Bad Idea.

The sorcerer-king leant his elbows on his desk and tried to picture the Luck of Caithness, that irritatingly elusive piece of Dark Age circuitry. As a work of art, it had never held much attraction for him. As a circuit diagram it had haunted his dreams, and he had racked his memory for the details of its involved twists and curves. For of course the garnets and stones that the unknown craftsman had set in the yellow gold were microchips of unparalleled ingenuity, and in the endless continuum of the interlocking design was vested a system of such strength that no successor could hope to rival or dominate it.

The sorcerer-king shook his head, and struck one broad fist into the other. He had tried everything he knew to avoid this day, and made every possible preparation for it, but now that it had come he felt desperate and hopeless. Yet, if it were to come to the worst, he was still what he had always been, and old ways were probably the best. He rose from his desk and took from his pocket the keys to the heavy oak trunk that seemed so much out of place among the tubular steel of his office. The lock was stiff, but it turned with a little effort, and he pushed up the lid. From inside he lifted a bundle wrapped in purple velvet. He took a deep breath and gently undid the silk threads that held the bundle together, revealing a decorated golden scabbard containing a long beautiful sword. He drew it out and felt the blade with his thumb. Still sharp, after all these years. He made a few slow-motion passes with the blade, and the pull of its weight on the muscles of his forearm reminded him of dangers overcome. With a grunt, he swung the sword round his head and brought it down accurately and with tremendous force on a dark green filing-cabinet, cleaving it from A to J. At that moment, the door opened.

The young man had not wanted to go back into the

boss's office. As he turned the handle of the door, he could hear a terrific crash, and he nearly abandoned the mission there and then. But the letters had to be signed.

The sorcerer-king had just lifted his sword clear of the filing-cabinet, feeling rather foolish. He stared at the young man, who stared back. At last the young man, with all the fatuity of youth, found speech.

'Jammed again, did it?'

'Did it?' The sorcerer-king was sweating, despite the air-conditioning.

'The filing-cabinet. I think it's dust getting in the locks.'

The sorcerer-king glanced down at the filing-cabinet, and at the sword in his hands. 'Come in and shut the door,' he said pleasantly.

The young man did as he was told. 'If it's about the luncheon vouchers,' he said nervously, 'I can explain.'

'So can I,' said the sorcerer-king. Of course, there was no need for him to do so, but suddenly he felt that he wanted to. He had kept this secret for more than a thousand years, and he felt like talking to someone. 'Sit down,' he said. 'What can I get you to drink?'

He laid the sword nonchalantly on his desk and produced a bottle from a drawer. 'Try this,' he suggested. 'Mead. Of course, it's nothing like the real thing . . .' He poured out two glasses and drank one himself, to show his guest that the drink was not poisoned.

The young man struggled to find something to say. 'Nice sword,' he ventured. Then he recollected what Mr Olafsen's secretary had been saying about Japanese business methods.

'"Nice" is rather an understatement,' said the sorcerer-king, and added something about the cut and thrust of modern commerce. The young man smiled awkwardly. 'Tell me, Mr Fortescue,' he continued, 'do you enjoy working for the company?'

'Er,' said Mr Fortescue.

The boss seemed not to have heard him. 'It's an old-established company, of course. Very old-established.' He leant forward suddenly. 'Have you the faintest idea how old-established it is?'

The young man said no, he hadn't. The boss told him. He also told him about the fortress of Geirrodsgarth, the battle of Melvich, and the intervening thousand years. He told him about the dragon-brooch, the King of Caithness, and the wizard Kotkel. He told him about the New Magic and its relationship with the New Technology, and how the Thirteenth Generation would be the culmination of all that had gone before.

'I realised quite early,' said the sorcerer-king, 'that magic in the sense that I understood it all those centuries ago had a relatively short future. It wasn't the problem of credibility – that was never a major drawback. But it's basically a question of the fundamental problem at the root of all industrial processes.' The sorcerer-king poured himself another glass of mead and lit a cigar.

'Look at it this way. In all other industries, the quantum leap from small-scale to large-scale, from workshop to factory, craftsman to mass-production, hand-loom to spining jenny, is the dividing-line between the ancient and the modern world. Do you follow me?'

'Not really.'

'Magic, I felt, fell into the same category. In my day, you had a small, highly skilled workforce – your sorcerers and their apprentices – turning out high-quality low-volume products for a small, largely high-income-group market. Result: the ordinary bloke, the man on the Uppsala carrier's cart, was excluded from participation in the field. Magic was not reaching the bulk of the population. Given my long-term objective – total world dominance – this was plainly unacceptable. What was the use of a lot of kings and heroes being able to zap each other to Kingdom Come when Bjorn Public could take it or leave it alone? Especially since, as my own experience will testify, a little well-applied brute force and ignorance can put an end to the whole enterprise? You appreciate the problem.'

'Thank you for the drink. I really ought to be getting back . . .'

'There had to be a breakthrough,' continued the sorcerer-king, 'a moment in the history of the world when magic finally had the potential to get its fingers well and truly round the neck of the human race. There were several key steps along the way, of course. The Industrial Revolution, electricity, the motor-car, and of course television – all these were building-blocks. All my own work, incidentally. They may tell you different down at the Patents Office, but who needs all that? He who keeps a low profile keeps his nose clean, as the sagas say.

'And then I came across an old idea of mine I'd jotted down on the back of a goat-skin hood in the old days – the computer. Originally it was just meant to be an alternative to notches in a stick to tell you how much cheese you needed to see you through the winter, and for all I cared it could stay that way. Except, I got to thinking, how'd it be if everyone had one? I mean everyone. A Home Computer. A little friend with a face like a telly, and its little wires leading into the telephone network. All things to all men, and everything put together. You do everything through it – bank through it, vote through it, work through it, be born, copulate and die through it. Good idea, eight out of ten. But the extra two out of ten is the incredible tolerance the profane masses have towards the evil little monsters. "Computer error," they say, and shake their heads indulgently. Three hours programming the perishing thing, and then it goes *bleep* and swallows the lot.' The sorcerer-king chuckled loudly over his drink and blew out a great cloud of cigar-smoke, for all the world like a story-book dragon. 'Swallows is right. I saw that possibility a mile off. You don't think, do you, that all those malfunctions are genuine? Ever since I got the first rudimentary network established, I've had everything most carefully monitored. Anything I fancy, anything that looks like it might be even remotely useful – *gulp!* and it hums along the fibre-optics to my own personal library.'

Up till then, the young man had been profoundly unconvinced by all this. He had never believed in God or any other sort of conspiracy theory, and he could never summon up enough credulity to be entertained by spy thrillers. But even he had sometimes wondered about the telelogy of his own particular field of interest. All computer programmers have at some stage come face to face with the one and only metaphysical question of what happens to all the stuff that gets swallowed by the computer. Here at last was the only possible explanation. He sat open-mouthed and stared.

'Now do you see?' said the sorcerer-king.

'Yes,' said the young man. 'That's clever. That's really clever.'

The sorcerer-king smirked. 'Thank you. Of course,' he continued, 'another fundamental cornerstone of modern commerce is diversification of interests. We may not be the world's biggest multinational, but we hold the most key positions. With an unrivalled position in the Media – don't you like that word, by the way? It gives exactly the right impression. I suppose it's because it sounds so like the Mafia. Anyway, with that and a manufacturing base like ours, we have the establishment to support a truly global concern. So it would be pretty nearly perfect. If it wasn't for the setback.'

'What setback?'

'The dragon. But never mind about all that.' The sorcerer-king was feeling relaxed again. His own narration of his past achievements gave him confidence, for how could such an enterprise, so brilliant in its conception and so long in the preparation, possibly fail? He smiled and offered the young man a cigar. 'Fortescue,' he said, 'I think your face fits around here. I've had my eye on you for some time now, and I think that you could have a future with us after the expansion programme goes through. How would you like to be the Governor of China?'

'What is the point,' said Angantyr Asmundarson, 'of having the coat and the trousers the same colour?'

There was no answer to that, Hildy reflected. 'I'm sorry,' she said, 'but I thought . . .'

'I think they're fine,' said Arvarodd firmly, as if to say that Hildy was not to be blamed for the follies of her generation. 'What are these holes in the side?'

'They're called pockets,' Hildy replied. 'You can keep things in them.'

'That's brilliant,' said the hero Ohtar, who had been familiar to generations of saga audiences as an inveterate loser of penknives and bits of string. 'Why did we never think of that?'

'Gimmicky, I call it,' grumbled Angantyr, but no one paid him any attention. By and large, the heroes seemed pleased with their new clothes – except of course for Brynjolf the Shape-Changer. He had taken one look at his suit and changed himself into an exact facsimile of himself wearing a similar suit, only with slightly narrower lapels and an extra button at the cuffs. The King's suit, of course, fitted perfectly. Even so, like all the others he looked exactly like a Scandinavian hero in a St Michael suit, or a convict who has just been released.

'While you were away,' said the King, taking her aside, 'Kotkel found two old friends.'

'*Old* friends?' Hildy said with a frown. 'Don't you mean . . . ?'

'Kotkel!'

The wizard came out from behind a tree. He had apparently found no difficulty in coming to terms with the concept of pockets; his were already bulging with small bones and bits of rag. He signalled to the King and Hildy to follow him, and led them out of sight behind a small rise in the ground.

'Meet Zxerp and Prexz,' said the King.

At first, Hildy could see nothing. Then she made out two faint pools of light hovering above the grass, like the reflection of one's watch-glass, only rather bigger. 'His familiar spirits,' explained the King. 'It seems they got shut in the mound with us. Probably just as well. They are the servants of the Luck of Caithness.'

'Do you mind?' said one of the pools of light.

'Kotkel has been telling me how the thing actually works,' the King went on, ignoring the interruption, 'and these two have a lot to do with it. The brooch itself is a . . . a what was it?' The wizard made a noise like poultry-shears cutting through a carcass. 'A jamming device, that's right. It interferes with the other side's magic. But in order to do this it requires a tremendous supply of positive energy, which is what these two represent.'

'Glad to know someone appreciates us,' said the pool of light.

'Quarrelsome and unco-operative energy,' continued the King sternly, 'but energy nevertheless. When Kotkel has put together all the right bits and pieces, he can link these two up to the brooch, and all the enemy's magic will be useless. Once that has been achieved, we can get on with the job. He won't be able to use any of his powers to stop us, or even know we're coming, just like the first time. Then it'll just be the straightforward business of knocking him on the head – always supposing that that will be straightforward, of course. But we'll cross that bridge when we come to it.'

'That sounds perfectly marvellous,' said Hildy a little nervously. There was, she suspected, something to follow.

'The problem, apparently,' continued the King, 'lies in getting the right bits and pieces. Kotkel isn't absolutely sure what he'll need. He says he won't know what he wants until he sees it.' The King shook his head.

'What sort of things does he need?'

'That,' said the King, 'is a very good question.'

Hildy had been to enough academic seminars to know that a very good question is one to which no one knows the answer – counter-intuitive, to her way of thinking; surely that was the definition of a truly awful question – and her face fell. 'So what now?'

'I think the best plan would be for us to go somewhere where the wizard would be likely to see the sort of thing he might want, don't you? And that would probably have to be some sort of town or city.'

'But wouldn't that be rather dangerous?'

The King smiled. 'I hope so,' he said mischievously. 'I wouldn't like to think that the greatest heroes in the world had been kept hanging around all this time just to do something perfectly safe.'

'What I like least about this country,' Danny Bennett started to say; and then he realised that he had said the same about virtually everything worthy of mention that he had encountered since the aircraft which had brought him there had landed. 'One of the things about this country which really gets up my nose is the way you can rely on all their schedules, timetables and promises.'

'Talk a lot, don't you?' said his senior cameraman. It was raining at Lairg, and the van which was supposed to be meeting them to take them up to Rolfsness had entirely failed to appear. All the shops and the hotel were mysteriously but firmly shut; and the only public building still open, the public lavatory, was filled up with camera and sound equipment, placed there to keep it dry. As a result, the entire crew had been compelled to take what shelter it could, which was not much. There was, of course, a fine view of the loch to keep them entertained; but the presence of ground-level as well as air-to-surface water was no real consolation.

'It's a process of elimination, really,' Danny continued. He believed in making the most of whatever entertainment was available, and since the only entertainment in all this wretchedness was his own coruscating wit he was determined to enjoy it to the full. 'If they say there's rooms booked at such and such or that the van will be there at whenever, you can rely on that. You can be sure that that hotel is definitely closed for renovation, and that that particular time is when all the vans in Scotland are in for their MoT test. Yes,' Danny continued remorselessly, 'I like certainty. It gives a sort of shape to the world.'

The cameraman felt obliged to make some sort of reply. 'I was in Uganda, you know, when they had that coup.'

'Oh, yes?'

'We were stuck waiting for a bus then, an' all.'

'Really.'

'Bloody hot it was. Came eventually, of course.'

That, it seemed, was that. Danny opened his briefcase and, shielding its contents against the weather with his sleeve, began to read through his notes one last time. Not that there was much point. Without any material from the archaeologists, who were up at Rolfsness in nice dry tents, he couldn't hope to start planning anything. The one thing that might make this into television was an interview with this missing female who had been the first into the mound. There was probably a perfectly good reason why she had gone missing, of course, and he felt that if he was now to be reduced to a curse-of-the-pharaohs angle it was probably not going to work in any event; still, there is such a thing as the Nose for a Story. He reminded himself, for about the hundredth time that afternoon, that a routine break-in at a Washington hotel had led to the full glory of Watergate. As usual when he was totally desperate, he tried to think in children's-story terms, and as he isolated each element he made a note of it in his soggy notebook. Buried treasure. Mysterious disappearance. Remote Scottish hillside. Vikings. A curse on the buried treasure. The fast-breeder reactor twenty miles or so down the coast. Did anyone happen to have a note of the half-life of radioactive gold?

Through the swirling rain, a small man in a cap was approaching. He asked one of the cameramen if Mr Bennett was anywhere.

'I'm Danny Bennett.'

'It's about your van, Mr Bennett. The one you were wanting to go up to Rolfsness,' the small man said. 'I'm afraid there's been a wee mistake.'

'Really?'

'Afraid so, yes.'

That seemed to be all the man was prepared to say. So far as he was concerned, it seemed, that would do.

'What sort of a mistake?'

'Well,' said the man, 'I hired my van out on Tuesday, just for the day, and it hasn't been brought back yet. So it isn't here for you.'

'Oh, that's bloody marvellous, that is. Look, can't you get another one? It'll take forever to get one sent up from the nearest town.'

'There is only the one van.'

Danny wiped the rain out of his eyes. 'Is there any chance of its being returned within the next couple of hours? Who hired it? Is it anyone you know?'

'Not at all,' said the man. 'It was a young woman who hired it. The one who came to look at the diggings up at Rolfsness, the same as yourself.'

Danny looked at him sharply. 'You mean Miss Frederiksen? The American girl?'

'That's right,' said the man. 'And now I'll be getting back indoors. It's raining out here,' he explained. 'Sorry not to be able to help.'

'Hold it,' Danny shouted, but the man had disappeared.

'What was that about our van?' asked the chief sound-recordist.

'It's not coming,' Danny answered shortly.

'Thought so,' said the sound-recordist. The news seemed almost to please him. 'Just like Zaire.'

'What happened in Zaire, then?'

'Bleeding van didn't come, that's what.' The sound-recordist wandered away and joined his assistant under the questionable cover of a sodden copy of the *Observer*. Danny walked swiftly across to the telephone-box, with which he had dealt before. When you admitted that the thing did actually take English money and not groats or cowrie shells, you had said pretty much everything there was to say in its favour. However, after a while he managed to get through to a van-hire firm in Wick and arranged for substitute transport. Then he reversed the charges to London.

So cheerful was he when he came out of the phone-box that he almost failed to notice that the rain had got heavier and perceptibly colder. He had – at last – the bones of a story. Of course, none of the researchers had come up with anything new about the Frederiksen woman. But they had called up her supervisor, a certain Professor Wood. Apparently, when she telephoned him from Lairg (God help her, Danny thought, if she was using this phone-box), her manner had been rather strange. Incoherent? No, not quite. Excited, of course, about the discovery. But not as excited as you would expect a career archaeologist to sound after having just made the most remarkable discovery ever on the British mainland. How, then? Preoccupied, Professor Wood had thought. As if something was up. Something nice or something nasty? Both. Something strange. Strange as in mysterious? Yes. And she had started to say something about a dragon, but then apparently thought better of it.

Danny Bennett sat down and wrote in 'Dragon?' in his list of potential ingredients. Then he stared at it for a while, put down 'Query Loch N. Monster double-query?' and crossed it out again. He then started to draw out the complicated wheel-diagrams and flow-diagrams from which his best work had originated. He felt suddenly relaxed and happy, and soon he was using the red biro that meant 'theme' and the green felt-tip that signified 'potential concept'. A television programme was about to be born.

'That's settled, then,' said the King. 'And if we can't find the bits we want in Wick we'll try somewhere else. And so on, until we do find it.'

The heroes had taken their briefing in virtual silence, since no one could think of any viable alternative, Angantyr's suggestion of declaring war on England having been dismissed unanimously at the outset. After a formal toast and prayer to Odin, the heroes sat down to polish their weapons and pack for the journey.

Hjort and Arvarodd, who had already packed, and

Brynjolf the Shape-Changer (who didn't need to pack) lingered beside the fire, playing fivestones.

'I don't know about all this,' grumbled Hjort. 'Complicated. All this stealth and subtlety. I mean, we aren't any good at that sort of thing, are we? What we're good at is belting people about.'

'True,' said Brynjolf wistfully. 'But it doesn't look as if there's much to be gained from belting people about these days.'

'Isn't there, though?' replied Hjort emphatically. 'I reckon there'll be some belting-about to be done before we're finished here. Don't you agree, Hildy Frederik's-daughter?'

Hildy, who was carrying an armful of blankets over to the van, nodded without thinking.

'You see?' said Hjort. 'She's clever, she is.'

'That's right enough,' said Arvarodd briskly. 'There's more to that woman than meets the eye.'

'Just as well,' said Hjort. 'I like them a little thinner myself.'

Arvarodd scowled at him. 'Well, I do,' protested Hjort. 'I remember one time in Trondheim – before they pulled down the old market to make way for that new potters' quarter—'

'That girl has brains,' said Brynjolf hurriedly. 'Brains are what count these days, it seems.'

'Dunno what we'll do, then,' said Hjort. 'Never had much use for brains, personally. Messy. Hard to clean off the axe-blade.'

'I reckon she's an asset to the team,' went on Brynjolf. 'As it is, we're strong on muscle and valour, but a bit short on intellect. There's Himself, of course, and that miserable wizard, but another counsellor on the staff is no bad thing. I reckon we should adopt her.'

'What, give her a name and everything?' Hjort looked doubtful.

'Why not?' said Arvarodd enthusiastically. 'Except that I can't think of one offhand.'

'I can.'

'Shut up, Hjort. Yes, we must think about that.'

Just then, there was a shout from the lookout.

'Hello,' said Hjort, suddenly hopeful. 'Do you think that might be trouble?'

'Who knows?' said Arvarodd, buckling on his sword-belt over his jacket and reaching for his bow. 'Anything's possible, I suppose. Who's moved my helmet?'

The heroes had enthusiastically formed a shield-ring, looking rather curious perhaps in shields, helmets and two-piece grey polyester suits. The King stalked hurriedly past them. 'Not now,' he said shortly.

'But, Chief . . .'

'I said not now. Get out of sight, all of you.' He crouched down behind a boulder and looked out over the road. Two vans had stopped there. A moment later Hildy and Starkad (who was the lookout) joined him.

'Just drew up, Chief,' whispered Starkad. 'You said to call you if—'

'Quite right,' replied the King. 'Who are they, Hildy Frederik's-daughter?'

Hildy peered hard but could make nothing out. 'I don't know,' she said. 'Probably nobody.'

Out of the first van climbed a man in a blue anorak with a map in his hand. He walked up to the top of a bank, looked around him, and made a despairing gesture.

'What's he looking for, do you think?' muttered the King. 'You stay here. I'm going to have a look.'

Before Hildy could say anything, the King slipped over the boulder and crept down towards the road to where he could hear what the people in the vans were saying. The man in the blue anorak had gone back and was shouting at the driver.

'How was I to know?' replied the driver. 'One godforsaken hillside looks pretty much like another to me.'

'We'll have to go back to that last crossroads, that's all,' said the man in the blue anorak. 'Rolfsness is definitely due north of here.'

'Why don't we just go back to Lairg and see if the pub's open?' growled the driver. 'It's too dark to film anyhow. We're not going to do any good tonight.'

'Because I want to get there as soon as possible and talk to those archaeologists. We've wasted enough time as it is. We've got a schedule to meet, remember.'

'Please yourself, Danny boy. Since we've stopped, though, I'm just going to take a leak.'

'Hurry up, then, will you?'

To the King's horror, the driver jumped out and walked briskly over the rise. The heroes were just over there, hiding. He closed his eyes and waited. A few moments later, he heard a horrified shout, followed by the war-cries of his guard. The driver came scampering back over the rise, pursued by Hjort, Angantyr and Bothvar Bjarki, with the other heroes at their heels and Hildy trotting behind shouting like a small pony following the hunt.

The senior cameraman, who had been about to open a can of lager, dived for his Aaten and started to film through the side-window. The assistant cameraman also kept his head and groped for a light meter, but Danny Bennett was flinging open the van door. 'Not now, for Christ's sake; they're gaining on him,' shouted the senior cameraman, but Danny jumped out and ran to meet the driver. As he did so, one of the maniacs in the grey suits stopped and fitted an arrow to his bowstring.

'ƒ8,' hissed the assistant cameraman to his colleague. 'If only there was time to fit the polariser . . .'

The King jumped up and shouted, and the archer stayed his hand. The heroes stood their ground while the driver leapt into the van, which pulled away with a screech of tyres, closely followed by the second van. A moment later, they were both out of sight. The heroes sheathed their swords and started to trudge back up the rise.

'Who were they?' the King asked Hildy. 'Any idea?'

Hildy had seen the cameras. 'Yes,' she said nervously. 'And I think we're in trouble.'

When they had made sure they were not being followed, the camera crew pulled in to the side of the road and all started to talk at once. Only Danny Bennett was silent, and on his face was the look of a man who has just seen a vision of the risen Christ. At last, he was saying to himself, I have been attacked while making a documentary. There must be a story in it; and not just *a* story but *the* story. Who the men in grey suits had been – CIA, MI5, Special Branch, maybe even the Milk Marketing Board – he could not say, but of one thing he was sure. He was standing on the brink of the greatest documentary ever made. Sweat was running down his face, and in front of his eyes danced the tantalising image of a BAFTA award.

CHAPTER FIVE

Kevin Fortescue, Governor of China elect, met Thorgeir Storm-Shepherd at the Docklands stolport and drove him back to Gerrards Garth House. On the way, he made it known that he had been let into the secret of the company's history. Thorgeir seemed surprised at this.

'Why?' he said.

'Mr . . . the boss said he thought I had a lot of potential. In fact, he's offered me China.'

'China?'

'I told him I'd give him my decision in the morning, but I'm pretty sure I'm going to take it. I think it would be a good move for me, career-wise. I've got the impression I'm stagnating rather in Accounts.'

Thorgeir made a mental note to water down the sorcerer-king's mead with cold tea before leaving the country next time. He had the feeling that the sorcerer-king was due for a change of direction, career-wise. But it would not be prudent to let the feeling develop into an idea.

The sorcerer-king had come down to the lobby to meet him. 'How was Japan?' he asked.

'Susceptible,' replied Thorgeir, 'highly susceptible. And I did get the semiconductors after all. Just time before the helicopter arrived for a birdie on the last hole.'

'Good,' grunted the sorcerer-king. 'No point in letting things slide just because there's a crisis. You've met our new colleague?'

'Yes,' said Thorgeir. 'What possessed you to do that?'

'Seemed like a good idea at the time.'

'You said that about Copernicus, and look where that got us.'

'Anyway,' the sorcerer-king said, 'he'll come in handy. I've had an idea.'

Thorgeir knew that tone of voice. Sometimes it led to good things, sometimes not. 'Tell me about it.'

'It's like this.' The sorcerer-king reached for the mead-bottle, and poured out two large glasses. 'Our problem is quite simple, when you look at it calmly. Our enemy has reappeared.'

'How do you know that, by the way?'

The sorcerer-king explained about the late-night messages. Thorgeir nodded gravely. 'So King Hrolf is back, and that dratted brooch. We could do one of two things. We could go and look for him, or we could wait for him to come to us.'

'This is meant to be a choice?'

'We could wait for him to come to us.' The sorcerer-king leant back in his chair and put the tips of his fingers together. 'If he tries that, he will be at a certain disadvantage.'

'Namely?'

The sorcerer-king grinned. 'One, he's been asleep for over a thousand years, and things have changed. Two, there's no way he can hope to understand the modern world well enough to endanger us without at the very least a three-year course in business studies and a post-graduate diploma in computers. We are talking about a man who had difficulty adding up on his fingers. Three, he has just crawled out of a mound, in clothes that were the height of fashion a thousand years ago but which would now be a trifle conspicuous. He is likely to be arrested, especially if he strolls into the market-square at Inverness and tries to reclaim his ancient throne. Four, just supposing he makes it and turns up in Reception brandishing a sword, his chances of making it as far as the lift are slim. Very slim. I don't know if you've dropped into Vouchers lately, but I didn't hire them for their math-ematical ability.'

'Fair enough,' said Thorgeir patiently. 'So?'

'So, since he's not a complete moron, he's not likely to come to us. So we have to go to him. But on whose terms?'

The sorcerer-king leant forward suddenly and fixed Thorgeir with his bright eyes. This had been a discon-certing conversational gambit a thousand years ago, but Thorgeir was used to it by now. After over a millennium of working with the sorcerer-king, he was getting rather tired of some of his more obvious mannerisms.

'Ours, preferably,' Thorgeir said calmly. 'Explain.'

'His best chance,' said the sorcerer-king, 'is to use the brooch again. He jams up our systems, blacks out our networks, and fuses all the lights across the entire world. Then he sends us a message – probably, knowing him, by carrier-pigeon – to meet him, alone, on the beach at Melvich for a rematch. Personally, I am out of condition for a trial by combat.'

Thorgeir nodded. He, too, had grown soft since his timber-wolf days. Apart from retaining a taste for uncooked mutton and having to shave at least three times a day, he had become entirely anthropomorphous. 'We can rule that out, then,' he said. 'I never did like all that running about and shouting.'

'Me neither. So we have one course of action left to us. We find him before he's ready, and we kill him. That ought not to be difficult.'

'Agreed.'

The sorcerer-king poured out more mead. 'In that case, where is he likely to be? He's just risen from the grave, right? And he's on foot. All we need to know is where he was buried, and we've got him. Simple.'

Thorgeir smiled, and drank some of his mead. Now it was his turn.

'Over the last thousand years,' he said, in a slow measured voice, 'I, too, have been turning this problem over in my mind, and the big question is this. Given that King Hrolf was the greatest of the Vikings, and his companions the most glorious heroes of the northern world, how come there is no King Hrolf Earthstar's Saga?'

He paused, for greater dramatic effect, and took a cigar from the box on the desk. Having lit it, he resumed.

'And, for that matter, why are the sagas of all the other heroes of northern Europe so reticent about the greatest event of the heroic age, namely our defeat and overthrow? You'd have thought one of them might have seen fit to mention it.'

The sorcerer-king frowned. With the exception of the latest Dick Francis or Jeffrey Archer, he rarely opened a book these days, and he had never been a great reader at the best of times.

'There is no record of the final resting-place of King Hrolf Earthstar,' said Thorgeir. 'If there had been, I'd have bought the place up and built something heavy and substantial over it five hundred years ago. There is no

trace or scrap of folk tradition in Caithness about King
Hrolf or the Great Battle or anything else; just a lot of
drivel about Bonnie Prince Charlie. The only clue is a
single place-name, Rolfsness, which happens to be the
site of a certain battle.'

'There you are, then,' said the sorcerer-king.

'There you aren't. I've been back hundreds of times.
If there had been anything there, I'd have felt it. And
there is no record whatsoever of what became of Hrolf
Earthstar while we were floating around as disembodied
spirits. He just vanished off the face of the earth. For all
I know, he could have sailed west and discovered
America.'

'You think he's in America?'

Thorgeir closed his eyes and counted up to ten. 'No,
I think he's probably somewhere in Europe. But where
in Europe I couldn't begin to say.'

The sorcerer-king smiled. 'You'd better start looking,
then, hadn't you?' he said, and poured himself another
drink.

'Those people,' said Hildy, 'were from television.'

'What's that?' asked one of the heroes.

Hildy racked her brains for a concise reply. 'Like a
saga, only with lights and pictures. By this time tomorrow, everyone in the country will know we're here.'

The King frowned. 'That could be serious,' he said.
'We can't have that.'

'But how can we stop it?'

'That's easy.' The King stood up suddenly. 'Where do
you think they've gone?'

'Back the way they came, probably to Lairg. They'll
want to get the film off to London as quickly as possible.
But—'

'We can't make any mistake about this. Kotkel!'

From a small pouch in his pocket, the wizard took a couple of small bones and threw them in the air. As they landed, he stooped down and peered at them intently. Then he pointed towards the south and made a noise like a buzz-saw.

'They went that way,' the King translated.

Hildy had never been fond of driving, and at speeds over thirty miles an hour her skill matched her enthusiasm. But somehow the van stayed on or at least close to the road as they pursued the camera crew along the narrow road to Lairg, and caught up with them in a deserted valley beside a river.

'What do we do now?' Hildy asked as the van bumped alarmingly over a cattle-grid.

'Board them,' suggested Angantyr. 'Or ram them. Who cares?'

'Certainly not,' Hildy shouted.

'Stop here,' the King said. 'Brynjolf!'

'Not again,' pleaded the shape-changer. 'Last time I sprained my ankle.'

No sooner had Danny Bennett realised that the second van had suddenly stopped for no reason than he became aware of a huge eagle, apparently trying to smash the windscreen. The driver swore, and braked fiercely, but the bird merely attacked again, this time cracking the glass. The senior sound-recordist, who had done countless nature programmes in his time, was thoroughly frightened and tried to hide under his seat. The eagle attacked a third time, and the windscreen shattered. The driver put up both his hands to protect his eyes, and the van veered off the road into a ditch.

When Danny had recovered from the shock of impact, he tried to open his door, but a man in a grey suit with a helmet covering his face opened it for him and showed him the blade of a large axe. If this was the Milk Marketing

Board, they were probably exceeding their statutory authority.

'Who are you?' Danny said.

'Bothvar Bjarki,' said the man with the axe. 'Are you going to surrender, or shall we fight for a bit?'

'I'd rather surrender, if it's all the same to you.'

'Be like that,' said Bothvar Bjarki.

The camera crew were rounded up, while Starkad, apparently without effort, pushed the two vans into a small clump of trees and covered them with branches. The King had found a hollow in the hillside which was out of sight of the road, and the prisoners were led there and tied up securely. Meanwhile, at Hildy's direction, Starkad and Hjort found the cans of film and smashed them to pieces. When Hildy was satisfied that all the film was destroyed, the heroes got back into their vans and drove away.

As the sound of the engine receded in the distance, the assistant cameraman broke the silence in the hollow.

'Reminds me of the time I was in Afghanistan,' he said.

Danny Bennett asked what had happened that time in Afghanistan.

'We got tied up,' said the assistant cameraman.

'And what happened?'

'Someone came and untied us,' replied the assistant cameraman. 'Mind you, that time we were doing a report for "Newsnight".'

Danny had never worked for 'Newsnight', and people had been known to die of exposure on Scottish hillsides. He pulled on the rope around his wrists, but there was no slack in it. A posthumous BAFTA award, he reflected, was probably better than no BAFTA award at all, but awards are not everything.

'If I can raise my wrists,' he said to the assistant cameraman, 'you could chew through the ropes and I could untie you.'

'I've got a better idea,' said the cameraman. 'You could shut your bloody row and we could get some sleep while we're waiting to be untied.'

'But perhaps,' Danny hissed, 'nobody's going to come and untie us.'

'Listen,' said the assistant cameraman fiercely, 'I dunno what union you belong to, but my union is going to get me a great deal of money from the Beeb for being tied up like this, and the longer I'm tied up, the more I'll get. So just shut your noise and let's get on with it, all right?'

Danny's head was beginning to hurt. He closed his eyes, leant back against the assistant cameraman (who was starting to snore) and tried to make some sense of what was happening to him.

The men had been partially disguised as Vikings, with helmets and shields and swords; but they had been wearing grey suits, which tended to spoil the illusion. They had, as he had expected, destroyed the film; but that was all. Not even an attempt to warn him off. Only the barest minimum of physical violence. And then there was that girl – Hildy Frederiksen, beyond doubt. Who was she working for, and what lay behind it all? And where in God's name had they got that incredible bird from?

The obvious clues pointed at the CIA. Whatever they do in whichever part of the world, they always wear grey suits. They buy them by the hundred from J. C. Penney or Man at CIA. That would tie in with the Kennedy connection – at last, after all these years, they were trying to silence him – but the Viking motif was beyond him, unless it was something to do with that tiresome ship. Or perhaps they were in fact wearing protective clothing (the nuclear power station angle) *made to look like* Viking helmets. In which case, why? Unless they were all going on to a fancy-dress party afterwards. The more he thought about it, the more inexplicable it seemed; and the more baffled he became, the more convinced he was that something major was going on. All the great conspiracies of history have been bizarre, usually because of the incompetence of the leading conspirators. As the long hours passed, he traced each convoluted possibility to its illogical conclusion, but for once no pattern emerged in his mind. At last he fell asleep and began to dream. He seemed to hear voices coming from a small pool of light hovering overhead.

'Seventy-five to me, then,' said one voice, 'plus the repique on your declaration, doubled. Your throw.'

Danny sat up. He wasn't dreaming.

'Six and a four. I take your dragon, and that's forty-five to me. Four, five, six, – oh, sod it, go to gaol.'

The rest of the crew were asleep. Danny sat absolutely still. The hair on the back of his neck was beginning to curl, and he found it hard to breathe.

'Trade you Hlidarend for Oslo Fjord and seventy points,' said the first voice. 'That way you'll have the set.'

'No chance,' said the second voice. 'Up three, down the serpent four five six, and that's check.'

'No, it isn't.'

'Yes, it is.'

The voices were silent for a while, and Danny swallowed hard. Perhaps it was just the bump he had suffered when the van crashed.

'Good idea, that,' said the first voice.

'Brilliant,' replied the second voice sarcastically. 'You don't imagine we're going to get away with it, do you?'

'Why not?'

'Because he'll notice we're not there, that's why. And he's not going to be pleased.'

The first voice sniggered. 'He'll be miles away by now. And the rest of them. They're going to Inverness. He won't be able to reach us from there.'

'Where's Inverness?'

'I haven't the faintest idea. But it sounds a very long way away to me.'

The second voice sighed audibly. 'You and your ideas,' it said.

'Well, what choice did we have?' replied the first voice irritably. 'I don't know about you, but I didn't fancy having copper wire twisted round my neck and being linked up to that perishing brooch. Last time, my ears buzzed for a week.'

'He'll be back. Just you wait and see.'

Another silence, during which Danny thought he could hear a rattling sound, like dice being thrown.

'Well,' said the second voice, 'we'd better make ourselves scarce anyhow. No good sitting about here.'

'Just because I'm winning . . .'

'Who says you're winning?'

The voices subsided into a muted squabbling, so that Danny could not make out the words. He longed for the voices to stop, and suddenly they did.

The reason for this was that Prexz had just caught the vibrations from an underground cable a mile or so away to the south. He had no idea what it might be, but he was hungry, and it seemed irresistible.

'Put the game away, Zxerp,' he said suddenly. 'I can feel food.'

But Zxerp didn't answer. 'I said I can feel food,' Prexz repeated, but Zxerp glowed warningly at him.

'There's a man over there listening to us,' he whispered.

'Why didn't you say?'

'I've only just noticed him, haven't I?'

Prexz cleared his throat and turned his glow up a little. 'Excuse me,' he said.

'Yes?' replied Danny.

'Would you happen to know anything about a cable running under the ground about a mile from here and going due north?'

'I would imagine,' Danny replied, his heart pounding, 'that it has something to do with the nuclear power station on the coast.'

'*Nuclear* Power?' Prexz said. 'Stone me. Did you hear that, Zxerp? Nouvelle cuisine.'

The two pools of light rose up into the air and seemed to dance there for a moment.

'By the way,' said Prexz, 'if the wizard comes looking for us . . .'

'The wizard?'

'That's right, the wizard. If he comes looking for us, you haven't seen us.'

'Before you go,' whispered Danny faintly, 'do you think you might possibly untie these ropes?'

'Certainly,' said Prexz. As he did so, Danny was aware of a terrible burning sensation in his hands and arms. 'Is that all right?'

'That's fine, thank you,' Danny gasped. Then he fainted.

'What a strange man,' Prexz said. 'Right, off we go.'

The Dow up three – that won't last – early coffee down, tin's still a shambles, and soon they'll be giving copper away with breakfast cereal. Who needs to buy a newspaper to learn that?

Thorgeir had adapted splendidly to most things in the course of his extremely long life, but the knack of reading the *Financial Times* on a train still eluded him. How one was supposed to control the huge unruly pages was a complete mystery. He was sorely tempted to get the boss to buy up the damned paper, just to make them print it in a smaller format. With a grunt, he retrieved the news headlines. Earthquake in Senegal, elections in New Zealand, massive archaeological find in Scotland . . .

Massive archaeological find in Scotland. Like a raindrop trickling down a window, his gaze slid down the pink surface and locked on to the small paragraph. At Rolfsness, in Caithness; archaeologists claim to have unearthed a ninth-century Viking royal ship-burial. Unprecedented quantities of artefacts including treasure, armour and weapons. Gold prices, however, are unlikely to be affected.

His fellow-passengers saw the small thin-faced man go suddenly white as he read his *FT*, and assumed that he had failed to get out of cocoa before the automatic doors closed. Thorgeir tossed the paper down on the seat beside him, and fumbled in his briefcase for his radiophone.

'Have you seen it?' he said. 'In the paper?'

'What are you going on about, Thorgeir?' said the sorcerer-king, his voice faint and crackly at the other end.

'Front page of the *FT*.'

'Hang on, I've got that here.' Thorgeir could picture the sorcerer-king retrieving the paper from the early-morning mess on his desk.

'The news section, about a third of the way down.'

'You've called me up to tell me about the Chancellor?'

'Stick the Chancellor; it's the bit below that.'

When the sorcerer-king panicked, he tended to do so in Old Norse, which is a language admirably suited to the purpose, if you are not in any hurry. Thorgeir listened impatiently for a while, then interrupted.

'Who have we got in archaeology?'

There was silence at the other end of the line. Twelve hundred years he's managed without a Filofax, reflected Thorgeir. The moment he gets one, nobody knows where they are any more. Marvellous.

'In Scotland?'

'Preferably.'

'There's a Professor Wood at St Andrews. What do you want an archaeologist for, anyway? I'm going over to Vouchers.'

Thorgeir frowned. 'No, don't do that,' he said quietly. 'Get Professor Wood. It says in the paper he's in charge of this dig at Rolfsness. Tell him I'll meet him there.'

'I'm still going over to Vouchers.'

'You do whatever you like. By the way, where's this train I'm on going to? I've forgotten.'

'Manchester.'

'Thanks.' Thorgeir switched off the phone and consulted his train timetable. He was feeling excited now that the enemy had been contacted, although he still could not imagine how he had overlooked something as obvious as a ship-burial on his many visits to that dreary place. Then it occurred to him that any wizard with Grade III or above would have been able to conceal the traces of life in such a mountainous and isolated spot from any but the most perceptive observer, and King Hrolf's wizard had been a top man. Pity they hadn't headhunted him back in the 870s. What was that wizard's name? Something about the pot and the kettle.

In the age of the supersonic airliner, a man can have breakfast in London and lunch in New York (if his digestion can stand it); but to get from Manchester to the north coast of Scotland between the waxing and the waning of the moon still requires not only dedication and cunning but also a modicum of good luck, just as it did in the Dark Ages. By the time Thorgeir had worked out an itinerary, the view from the train window had that tell-tale hint of First World War battlefield about it that informs the experienced traveller that he's passing through Stockport. Thorgeir closed his briefcase and leant his head back against the cushions. Kotkel. Hrolf's wizard was called Kotkel, and he had had quite a reputation around Orkney in the seventies. Winner for three years in succession of the Osca (Orkney Sorcerers' Craft Association) for Best Hallucination. No slouch with a rune, either.

'That's all I needed,' groaned Thorgeir.

Telephone wires were humming all over Britain, for they had just had to shut down the nuclear reactor on the north coast of Scotland. There was, it had been decided, no need to evacuate the area; there was no danger. It was just that someone had contrived to mislay the entire output of electricity from the plant for just over half an hour. Even the lights had gone out all over the building.

'Has anyone,' the controller kept asking, 'got a fifty pence for the meter?' The senior engineers led him away and got him an aspirin, while his deputy made another attempt to get through to Downing Street.

No one had yet got around to checking the underground cable that ran due south from the plant, which was where the fault actually lay. It lay on its back, its eyes closed, and it was singing softly to itself.

'For ye defeated,' it sang,
'King Hrothgar's army,
And sent them home,
To think again.'

The fault's companion was scarcely in a better state He had never even claimed to be able to hold his electricity, and he had very nearly been sick. It was just as well that he had not, or the entire National Grid would have been thrown into confusion. He gurgled, and went to sleep.

'Prexz,' said the fault, 'I just thought of something.'

Prexz moaned, and rolled on to his face, vowing never

to touch another volt so long as he lived.

'How would it be,' Zxerp said, 'how would it be if . . .'

'Don't want any more,' mumbled Prexz. 'Had too much already. Drunk. Totally drunk. Going to join Electronics Anonymous soon as I feel a little better.'

'Don't be like that,' whined Zxerp.

'Think they put something in it at the generator,' continued Prexz. 'Going to sleep it off. Shut up. Go away.'

'Wimp,' snarled Zxerp. 'You're no fun, Prexz. Don't like you any more.'

Prexz had started to snore, sending clouds of undecipherable radio signals to jam up the airwaves of Europe.

'I don't like it here,' said Zxerp. 'I want to go home.'

No reply. Zxerp shook his head, which made him feel worse, and he fell heavily against the cable. There was nothing in it, and he was feeling terribly thirsty. He was also feeling guilty.

'Poor old wizard,' he said. 'Always been good to us. Never a cross word in twelve hundred years. Prexz, shouldn't we go and find the wizard? Shouldn't have run away from the wizard like that. Not right.'

Zxerp started to cry, and negative ions trickled down the side of his nose, electrolysing it. At the government listening post in Cheltenham, a codes expert picked up his tears on the short-wave band and rushed off to tell his chief that the Russians had developed a new cipher.

Thorgeir heard about the closedown of the power station over the radio as he drove his hired car past Loch Loyal. The shock made him swerve, and he nearly ended up in the water.

He pulled over and examined an Ordnance Survey map, but that told him nothing he did not already know, and his own personal map, which was traced in blood on soft goat skin and was somewhat out of date. But a call to London on his radiophone told him all he needed to know, and he asked that a helicopter should be laid on to meet him at Tongue. He also enquired whether there was an equivalent to the Vouchers department at the company's Glasgow office.

'Yes? Then, send a couple of them up. Tell them to bring plenty of vouchers.'

He pushed down the aerial so violently that he nearly snapped it off, and drove on towards the coast. As he turned a bend in the road beside a small clump of trees, he noticed and just managed to avoid a patch of broken glass in the middle of the carriageway. In doing so he stalled the engine, and while he was persuading it to start again his eye fell on the windscreen of a van among the trees. Someone had apparently been to the trouble of covering this van up with tree-branches. For some reason this seemed terribly significant, and Thorgeir went to investigate.

What he found was two vans with broken windscreens and a good deal of smashed camera gear. As he stood scratching his hed, the wind carried back to him what sounded like an argument from the hill on the other side of the road. Something about due north having been over those hills there ten minutes ago, and it reminded someone of that time in Iraq.

Thorgeir looked at his watch. He had plenty of time before he was due to meet the helicopter, and he was starting to get a tingling sensation all down the side of his nose, where his whiskers had once been.

'Told you someone would come and find us,' croaked the assistant cameraman. 'Just like that time in Cambodia.'

'That wasn't Cambodia,' said the assistant sound-recordist, 'that was Kurdestan.'

'We *started* in Iraq,' replied the senior cameraman. 'That's the bloody point.'

'Thank you,' gasped Danny Bennett to the stranger. He was hoarse from arguing. For a long time, he had thought that he had imagined the sound of a car engine. 'We've been wandering round in circles all day. That fool of a cameraman's got one of those compasses you buy at filling stations, and we'd been walking for hours before we realised that it was being attracted by his solar calculator.'

'Are those your vans up there?' said the stranger.

'Yes.' Suddenly, Danny seemed to notice something about his rescuer and recoiled violently.

'What's up?' said the stranger.

'Sorry,' Danny said. 'It's just that suit you're wearing.'

'My suit?' The stranger looked affronted.

'It's a very nice suit,' Danny said. 'It's just that it's grey. But it's not from Marks and Spencer.'

'I should think not,' said the stranger irritably. 'Brooks Brothers, this is. OK, the lapels are a bit on the narrow side, but—'

'It's a long story,' Danny said. 'And you'd probably think I was mad.'

'I already think you're mad,' said the stranger, smoothing out the creases on his sleeve, 'so what have you got to lose?'

So Danny told him. He explained about the ship-burial, the first attack, the second attack, the eagle and the men in the grey suits. The stranger seemed entirely unsurprised and utterly convinced by it all; in fact he seemed so interested that Danny was on the point of telling him about his President Kennedy theory when the stranger interrupted him.

'Was there an old man with them, by any chance? Very old indeed, with a horrible squeaky voice?'

'Yes,' Danny said, 'I think so.'

'And what about the others?' The stranger described the men in grey suits. Danny nodded feebly.

'Do you know them, then?' he asked.

'Oh, yes. They and I go way back.'

Danny dug his fingernails into the palms of his hands. 'Who are they, then?'

The stranger grinned in a way that reminded Danny of an Alsatian he had been particularly afraid of as a boy. 'I don't really think you want to know,' he said. 'Not in your present state of mind.'

'Yes, I do,' Danny said urgently. 'And what has Hildy Frederiksen got to do with it?'

The stranger raised an eyebrow. 'Who's Hildy Frederiksen?'

'The archaeologist. The one who found the burial. She's with them.'

'You don't say.' The stranger had stopped grinning. 'Listen,' he said, taking hold of Danny's sleeve.

'Yes?'

'Who do *you* think those men are?'

Danny blinked twice. 'Are they from the CIA?'

'In a sense. You're a TV producer, Mr . . .'

'Bennett, Danny Bennett.'

'I envy you, Mr Bennett. You've stumbled on to something big here. Really big.'

'Have I?'

The stranger nodded. 'This is once-in-a-career stuff. If I were you, I'd forget all about that ship-burial and get after the men in the grey suits.'

'Really?' The roof of Danny's mouth felt like sandpaper.

'Just don't quote me, that's all. The road's over there. It was good meeting you.' The stranger started to walk away.

'So you don't think I've gone crazy, then?' Danny called after him.

'No,' replied the stranger.

'I didn't tell you about the little blue lights, did I?'

The stranger stopped and turned round. Strange-shaped ears that man has, Danny thought. Almost pointed.

'Tell me about the little blue lights,' said the stranger.

'If you must hum,' said Prexz, 'hum quietly.'

'I'm not humming,' Zxerp replied, 'you are.'

'No, I'm not. And do you mind not shouting? I feel like I've got a short just above my left eye.'

'It must be that cable, then,' replied his companion. 'Humming.'

'Will you shut up about that cable?'

Prexz closed his eyes and resolved to keep perfectly still for at least half an hour. If that didn't work, he could try a brief electric storm.

'Prexz.'

'Now what?'

'It's not the cable. It's coming from up there.'

Prexz opened his eyes. 'You're right,' he said. 'And it isn't a humming. More like a buzzing, really.'

'I don't like it, Prexz. Shouldn't we take a look?'

'Please yourself,' grunted Prexz. He lay back against the cable and dozed off. Zxerp tried to follow his example, but the buzzing grew louder. Then it stopped. After a moment, another sound took its place. Prexz sat upright with a jerk.

'It's that perishing wizard,' he groaned.

'It's not, you know,' whispered Zxerp. 'Do you know who I think that is?'

The two chthonic spirits stared at each other in horror as the summons grew louder and louder, until they could resist it no longer. Something seemed to be dragging them up to the surface. As they emerged into the violent light of the sun, they were seized by strong hands and copper wire was twisted around their necks. They were trapped.

CHAPTER SIX

After breakfasting on barbecued rabbit and lager (from the wizard's now perpetually refilling can) in the ruined broch just south of the Loch of Killimster, King Hrolf Earthstar and his heroes – and heroine – drove into Wick in search of thin copper wire, resistors, crocodile clips and other assorted bits and pieces needed by the wizard for connecting the two chthonic spirits up to the Luck of Caithness. Of course, it had not occurred to any of them to check that the two spirits were still in the small sandalwood box into which the wizard had sealed them with a powerful but imperfectly remembered spell; but even a wizard cannot be expected to think of everything.

The fog and low cloud, which had been hovering over the tops of the mountains for the last few days, had come down thickly during the night, and Hildy, who was not used to driving under such conditions, made slow progress along the road to Wick. The town itself seemed, as usual, deserted, and Hildy felt little trepidation about leading her unlikely-looking party through the streets. As it happened, such of the local people as were out and about did stop for a moment and speculate who these curious men in grey suits might be; but after a little subdued discussion they decided that they were a party of Norwegians off one of the rigs, which would account for their uniform dress and long shaggy beards.

There is an electrical-goods shop in Wick, and if you have the determination of a hero used to long and apparently impossible quests you can eventually find it, although it will of course be closed for lunch when you do.

'I remember there used to be a mead-hall just along from here,' said Angantyr Asmundarson. His shoes were hurting, and he liked the town even less than he had the last time he had visited it, about twelve hundred years previously. 'They used to do those little round shellfish that look like large pink woodlice.'

'I thought you hated them,' said the King. 'You always used to make a fuss when we had them back at the castle.'

'I never said I did like them,' Angantyr replied. 'And, anyway, I don't expect the mead-hall's there any more.'

Oddly enough it was, or at least there was a building set aside for roughly the same purpose standing on the site of it. Hildy was most unwilling that the company should go in, but the King overruled her; if Angantyr didn't get something to eat other than rabbit pretty soon, he suggested, he would start to whine, and that he could do without.

'All right, then,' Hildy said, 'but be careful.'

'In what way?' asked the King.

Hildy could not for the moment think of anything that the heroes should or should not do. She tried to imagine a roughly similar situation, but all she could think of was Allied airmen evading the Germans in occupied France, and she had never been keen on war films. 'Don't draw attention to yourselves,' she said, 'and keep your voices down.' As she said this, something that had been nagging away at the back of her mind resolved itself into a query.

'By the way,' she asked the King, as she brought back a tray laden with twelve pints of Tennants lager and twelve packets of scampi fries, 'how is it that I can understand everything you say? It's almost as if you were speaking modern English. You should be talking in Old Norse or something, shouldn't you?'

'We are,' said the King, wiping froth from the edges of his moustache. 'I thought you were, too. And what's English?'

At this point, the wizard made a sound like a slate-saw. The King raised an eyebrow, then translated for Hildy's benefit.

'He says it's a language-spell he put on us all. He says it would save a great deal of trouble. Unfortunately,' the King went on, 'he couldn't put one on himself. He tried, using a mirror, but it didn't work. He's now got a mirror that can speak all living and dead languages, but even we can't understand most of what he says because he's got this speech impediment and he mumbles.'

Not for the first time, Hildy wondered whether the King was having a joke at her expense, or whether her new friends were just extremely different from anyone she had ever met before. However, the King's explanation seemed to be as good as any, and so she let it go. The thirteen helpings of grilled salmon and chips she had ordered (and paid for; the money wasn't going to last much longer at this rate) arrived and were soon disposed of, despite the heroes' lack of familiarity with the concept of the fork. However, even though they did not know what to use them for, they displayed considerable unwillingness to give them back, and Hildy had to insist. All in all, she was glad to get them all out of the hotel before they made a scene.

'And who do you suppose they were?' asked the waitress as she cleared away the plates.

'English, probably,' said the barman.

'Ah,' replied the waitress, 'that would account for it.'

By now the keeper of the electrical shop had returned from lunch, and Hildy, the wizard and the King went in while the heroes waited outside. After a great deal of confusion, they got what they wanted, and Hildy led them back to where the van was parked. She considered stopping and buying some postcards to send to her family back in America, but decided not to; 'Having a wonderful time saving the world from a twelve-hundred-year-old sorcerer' would be both baffling and, just for the moment, untrue. She did, however, nip into a camping shop and buy herself a new anorak. Her paddock-jacket was getting decidedly grubby and it smelt rather too much of boiled rabbit for her liking.

'Where to now?' she asked, as they all climbed into the van.

'Home,' said the King.

Hildy frowned. 'You mean Rolfsness?' she asked. 'The ship? I don't think—'

'No, no,' said the King, 'I said Home.'

'Where's that?'

The King, who had already grasped the principle of Ordnance Survey maps, pointed to a spot just to the north-east of Bettyhill. 'There,' he said.

'Why?' Hildy asked.

'I live there,' replied the King simply. 'I haven't been home for a long time.'

Hildy looked again at the map. It was a long way away, and she was tired of driving. But the King insisted. They filled up with petrol (Hildy now had enough Esso tokens for a new flashlight, but she couldn't be bothered) and set off. Their road lay first through Thurso and then past the now functioning nuclear power station, and the turning for Rolfsness; but the area seemed deserted. Hildy wondered why.

Eventually they crossed the Swordly Burn and took the turning the King had indicated. There were quite a few houses along the narrow road, but Hildy found a small knot of trees where the van could be hidden, and they packed all their goods into the rucksacks she had bought and the heroes wrapped blankets over their shields and weapons. The company looked, Hildy thought, like a cross between an attempt on Everest and a party of racegoers with a picnic lunch.

They had walked about a mile from the road when they came to a small narrow-necked promontory overlooking the Bay of Swordly. Below them the cliffs fell away to the grey and unfriendly sea, and Hildy began to feel distinctly unwell since she suffered from attacks of vertigo. There was only a rudimentary track heading north, over a broad arch of rock, apparently leading nowhere. Hildy hoped that the King knew where he was going.

Suddenly the King scrambled off the path and seemed to disappear into the rock. The heroes and the wizard followed, leaving Hildy all alone on the top of the cliff. She was feeling thoroughly ill and not at all heroic. This was rather like going for walks with her father when she was a child.

'Are you coming, then?' she heard the King's voice shouting, but could not tell where it came from.

'Where are you?' she shouted.

'Down here.' The sound seemed to be coming from directly below. She tried to look down, but her legs started to give way under her and she stopped. After what seemed a very long time, the King reappeared and beckoned to her.

'There's a passage just here leading down to the castle,' he said. 'Mind where you put your feet. I never did get around to having those steps cut.'

This time Hildy summoned all her courage and followed him. A door in the rock, like a small porthole, stood open before her, and she dived through it.

'That's the back door,' said the King, pulling it shut. It closed with a soft click, and the tunnel was suddenly pitch-dark. The passage was not long, and it came out in a sort of rocky amphitheatre perched on the edge of the cliff. Just below them were the ruins of ancient masonry; but all of a much later period, medieval or perhaps sixteenth-century. The amphitheatre itself, with a deep natural cave behind, was little more than a slight modification of the original rock.

'I see they've mucked up the front door,' said the King with a sigh. 'Still, that's no great loss.' He looked out over the sea, and then turned back to Hildy. 'Unless you know what to look for,' he said, 'this place is invisible except from the sea, and now the front gate's been taken out the only way down here is that door we came through, which is also impossible to find unless you know about it. Someone's been building down there, but this part is exactly as it was. Let's see if the hall's been got at.'

He led the way into the cave. The heroes had evidently had the same idea, for another small door had been thrown open, and the sound of voices came out of it. Hildy followed the King into a wide natural chamber.

In the middle of the chamber was a long stone table, on which Starkad and Arvarodd were standing, poking at the ceiling with their spears. 'Just getting the windows open,' Arvarodd grunted, 'only the wretched thing seems to have got stuck,' and he pushed open a stone trapdoor, flooding the chamber with light. Hildy looked about her in amazement. The walls were covered in rich figured tapestries, looking as if they had just been made but recognisable as typical products of the ninth century. The table was laid with gold and silver plates and drinking-horns, with places for about a hundred. Beside the table was a hearth running the length of the chamber, and the rest of the floor was covered in dry heather that crackled under Hildy's feet. Against the wall stood a dozen huge chests with massive iron locks, and in the corners of the room were stacks of spears and weapons. Everything appeared to be perfectly preserved, but the air in the chamber was decidedly musty.

'The doors and shutters on the windows are airtight,' explained the King. 'We knew a thing or two about building in my day.'

'What is this place?' Hildy asked.

'This,' said the King with a hint of pride in his voice, 'is the Castle of Borve, one of my two strongholds. The other is at Tongue, but I never did like it much. The Castle of Borve is totally impregnable, and the view is rather better, if you like seascapes. On a clear day you can see Orkney.'

The heroes had got the chests open, and were busily rummaging about in them for long-lost treasures; favourite cloaks and comfortable shoes. Someone came up with a cask of mead on which a preserving spell had been laid, while Arvarodd, who had lit a small fire at one end of the hearth, was roasting the last of the sausages Hildy had bought in Marks & Spencer at Inverness. The heroes had discovered that they liked sausages.

'The Castle of Borve,' said the King, 'was built for my father, Ketil Trout, by Thorkel the Builder. My father was a bit of a miser, I'm afraid, and, since he was forever going to war with all and sundry, usually very hard up.

So when he commissioned the castle from Thorkel, the finest builder of his day, he stipulated that if there was anything wrong with the castle on delivery Thorkel's life should be forfeit and all his property should pass to the King. Actually, that was standard practice in the building industry then.'

Hildy, who had had bad experiences with builders in her time, nodded approvingly.

'The trouble was that there was nothing at all wrong with the castle,' the King continued, 'and Ketil was faced with the horrible prospect of having to pay for the place, which he could not afford to do. So he persuaded the builder to go out into the bay with him by ship, on the pretext of inspecting the front gate. Meanwhile my mother hung a rope over the front ramparts, which, seen from the sea, looked like a crack in the masonry. Ketil pointed this out to Thorkel as a fault in the work, and poor old Thorkel was left with no alternative but to tie the anchor to his leg and jump in the sea. This was really rather fortuitous, since apart from my father he was the only other person to know the secret of the back door, which we came in by. Oddly enough, ever after my father had terrible trouble getting anyone to do any work on the place, which was a profound nuisance in winter when the guttering tended to get blocked.'

The heroes had drunk half of the enchanted mead and were beginning to sing. The King frowned. 'Anyway,' he said briskly, 'that's the Castle of Borve for you. Back to business.'

He clapped his hands, and the heroes cleared a space on the table. The wizard laid out the various items he had obtained in Wick, and the King laid the dragon-brooch beside them. The wizard set to work with some tools he had retrieved from one of the chests, and soon the brooch was festooned with short lengths of wire, knitted into an intricate pattern. Then he made a sign with his hand, and Ohtar brought over the sandalwood box. The wizard picked it up, shook it and held it to his ear.

'Now what?' demanded the King impatiently. The wizard made a subdued noise, like a very small lathe.

'You haven't!' shouted the King.

The wizard nodded, made a sound like a distant dentist's drill, and hid his face in his hands.

'I don't believe it,' said the King in fury. 'You stupid . . . Oh, get out of my sight.' The wizard promptly vanished, turning himself into a tiny spider hanging from the ceiling.

'What's the matter?' Hildy asked.

'He's only gone and lost them, that's all,' growled the King. 'Here, give me that box.'

He threw open the lid, but there was nothing inside except the chewed-up remains of a couple of torch-batteries Hildy had put in for the two spirits to eat. For a moment there was total silence in the chamber; then the King threw the box on the ground and jumped on it.

'Now look what you've made me do,' he roared at the spider swinging unhappily from the roof.

'But what's happened?' Hildy wailed. She felt that she was in grave danger of being forgotten about.

'I'll tell you what's ruddy well happened,' said the King. 'This idiotic wizard has let those two spirits escape, that's what. He was supposed to have sealed them in his magic elf-box . . .' The King stepped out of the smashed fragments of the magic elf-box, which would henceforth be incapable of holding so much as a bad dream. 'Now we've got nothing to work the brooch with. Without them it's useless.'

The heroes all started to complain at once, and even the spider began cheeping sadly. The King banged his fist on the table and shouted for quiet.

'Let's all stay calm, shall we?' he muttered. 'Let's all sit down, like reasonable human beings, and discuss this sensibly.' He followed his own suggestion, and the rest of the heroes, still murmuring restlessly like the sea below them, did likewise. The spider scuttled down his gossamer thread and perched on the lip of the King's great drinking-horn.

'All right, Kotkel,' snapped the King to the spider, 'you've made your point. You can come back now.'

The wizard reappeared, hanging his grizzled head in shame, and took his place at the King's left hand. The company that had, a few moments ago, resembled nothing so much as a football team stranded in the middle of nowhere with no beer had become, as if by some subtler magic, the King's Household, his council in peace and war. A shaft of sunlight broke through the stone-framed skylight into the chamber, highlighting the King's face like a spotlight – Thorkel the Builder had planned the effect deliberately, calculating where the sun would be in relation to the surrounding mountains at the time when the Master of Borve would be likely to be seated in his high place. Hildy found herself sitting, by accident or design, in the Counsellor's place at his right hand, so that such of the sunlight as the King could spare fell on her commonplace features. A feeling of profound awe and responsibility came over her, and she resolved, come what may, to acquit herself as well as she could in the King's service.

Arvarodd of Permia, who carried the King's harp, and Angantyr Asmundarson, who was his standard-bearer, rose to their feet and pronounced in unison that Hrolf Ketilsson Earthstar, absolute in Caithness and Sutherland, Lord of the Isles, held court for policy in the fastness of his House; let those who could speak wisely do so. There was total silence, as befitted such an august moment. Then there was more silence, and Hildy realised that this was because nobody could think of anything to say.

'Well, come on, then,' said the King. 'You were all so damned chatty a moment ago. Let's be having you.'

To his feet rose Bothvar Bjarki, and Hildy suddenly remembered that he had been the adviser of the great king Kraki, devising for him stratagems without number, which generations of skalds had kept evergreen in memory.

'We could go back and look for them,' suggested Bothvar Bjarki.

'Oh, sit down and shut up,' said the King impatiently. 'Has anyone got any *sensible* suggestions?'

Bothvar sat down and started to mutter to himself. Angantyr was sniggering, and Bothvar gave him a look. Hildy, thoroughly bewildered, realised that she was on her feet and speaking.

'Perhaps,' she stammered, 'the wizard can find them. Wasn't there that bit in *Arvarodd's Saga* where someone put a seer-stone to his eye . . . ?'

'Have you got a seer-stone, Kotkel?' demanded the King, turning to the wizard. Arvarodd, sitting opposite Hildy, seemed to be blushing slightly. He leant across the table and whispered: 'Actually, I made that bit up. I wanted a sort of mystical scene to counterpoint all the starkly realistic bits. You see, the structure seemed to demand . . .' Hildy found herself nodding, as she so often had at Cambridge parties.

The wizard was turning out his pockets. From the resulting pile of unsightly junk, he picked out a small blue pebble, heart-shaped, with a hole through the middle. He breathed on it, grunted some obscure spell, and set it in his eye like a watchmaker's lens.

'Well?' said the King impatiently.

There was a sound like a carborundum wheel from the wizard. 'Interference,' whispered Arvarodd. 'Ever since they privatised it—'

But the wizard shook his head and took out the stone. Then he leant across the King and offered it to Hildy.

'Go on,' the King said. 'It doesn't hurt.'

Hildy closed her mouth, which had fallen open, and took the stone from the wizard's hand. It felt strangely warm, like a seat on a train that someone has just left, and Hildy felt very reluctant to touch it. But she held it up to her eye, squinting through the hole. To her amazement, and horror, she found that she could see a picture through it, as if it were a keyhole in a closed door.

She saw a tower of grey stone and glass, completely unfamiliar at first; then she recognised it as an office-block. Pressing the stone hard against her eye, she found that she could see in through one of the windows, and beyond that through the open door of an office. Inside the office was a glass case, like a fish-tank, and inside that were two pools of light. There were wires leading from the tank into the back of a large square box-like trunk, which she could not identify for a moment. Then, with a flash of insight, she realised that the box was a computer, and that whoever it was that had control of the two spirits was using them to cut down on his electricity bills.

She thought she could hear voices; but the voices were very far away – they were coming from the picture behind the stone.

'And two for his nob makes seven, redoubled,' said the voice. 'Proceed to Valhalla, do not pass Go, do not collect two hundred crowns.' The other voice sniggered.

It's them, Hildy thought. She felt utterly exhausted, as if she had been lifting heavy weights with the muscles of her eyes, and her head was splitting.

'I give up,' said the first voice. 'I never did like this game.'

'Let's play something else, then,' said the other voice equably.

'I don't want to play anything,' retorted the first voice. 'I want to get out of here, before they plug us in to something else. I don't mind being kidnapped, but I do resent being used to heat water.'

'Impossible,' said the second voice. 'We're stuck. I suggest we make the most of it.' The first light flickered irritably, but the second light ignored it. 'My throw. Oh, good, that's an X and a Y. I can make "oxycephalous", and it's on a triple rune score—'

'There's no such word as "oxycephalous",' said the first voice, 'not in Old Norse.'

'There is now,' replied the second voice cheerfully. 'Up the tree, six, and I think I'll see you.'

Hildy's eyes were hurting, but she struggled to keep them open, as she had so often struggled at lectures and seminars. With a tremendous effort of will, she forced herself to zoom backwards, widening her angle of view. She saw the office-block again, standing in a familiar landscape, but one which she could not put a name to. Then she made out what could only be a Tube station, stunningly prosaic in the midst of all the magic. With a final spurt of effort she read the name, 'St Paul's'. Then the stone fell from her eye, and she slumped forward on to the table.

When she came round, she found the heroes gathered about her. She told them what she had seen, and what she deduced from it. The King sat down again, and put his face in his hands.

'We must take a great risk,' he said at last. 'I shall have to go to this place and recover the two spirits. Otherwise, there is no hope.'

'You mustn't,' Hildy protested. 'They'll catch you, and then there really won't be any hope.' She dug her fingers into the material of her organiser bag until they started to ache. 'Let me go instead.'

The King suddenly lifted his head and smiled at her. 'We'll both go,' he said cheerfully, almost lightheartedly. 'And you, Kotkel. Only this time you'll do it properly, understand? And you, Brynjolf,' he said to the shape-changer, who was trying unsuccessfully to hide behind the massive shoulders of Starkad Storvirksson, 'we'll need you as well. And two others. Any volunteers?'

Everyone froze, not daring to move. But after a moment Arvarodd stood up, looked around the table, and nodded. 'I'll come,' he said quietly. 'After all, it can't be worse than Permia.' He laughed weakly at his own joke, but all the others were silent. The King looked scornfully about him, and sighed. 'Chicken,' he said, 'the whole lot of you.'

Starkad Storvirksson rose to his feet. 'Can I come?' he asked mildly. If no one else was prepared to go, he might at last get his chance to do something other than fighting. Fighting was all right in its way, but he was sure there was more to being a hero than just hitting people.

'No, Starkad,' said the King kindly. 'I know *you're* not afraid. But not this time. I'll explain later.'

Starkad sat down, looking dejected, and Brynjolf patted him comfortingly on the shoulder. 'It's because you're so stupid, Starkad,' he said gently. 'You'd only be in the way.'

'Oh,' said Starkad happily. 'If that's the reason, I don't mind.'

'I'll go,' said Bothvar Bjarki suddenly, and all the heroes turned and stared at him. 'What this job needs is brains, not muscle.' The King muttered something inaudible under his breath, and said that, on second thoughts, five would be plenty. Bothvar scowled, but the heroes cheered loudly, and raised the toast; first to Odin, giver of victory;

then to the six adventurers; then to their Lord, King Hrolf Earthstar. Then Ohtar remembered that there had been another cask of enchanted mead in the back storeroom, and they all went to look for it.

'The others had better not stay here,' said the King to Hildy, while they were gone. 'They'll have to hunt for food and find water, and I saw too many houses on the road back there. I'll send them up into the mountains.' From the back storeroom came sounds of cursing; someone, back in the ninth century, had left the top off the barrel. The King grinned. 'It'll give them something else to complain about until we get back.'

'Will they be all right?' Hildy asked doubtfully. 'They don't seem terribly practical to me.'

The King nodded. 'I should think so,' he said. 'Take Angantyr Asmundarson, for instance. To join the muster at Melvich, he marched all night from Brough Head to Burwick – that's right across the two main islands of Orkney – and since there was no boat available he swam over from Burwick to the mainland, in the middle of a storm. Then he ran all the way from Duncansby Head to Melvich, on the morning before the battle, and still fought in the front rank against the stone-trolls of Finnmark. Complaining bitterly about his wet clothes and how he was going to catch his death of pneumonia, of course, but that's just his way.' He paused, and contemplated his fingernails for a moment. 'Put like that, I suppose, it rather proves your point. Only a complete idiot would have gone to so much trouble to get involved in a battle. Come on,' he said briskly, 'it's time we were going.'

Thorgeir Storm-Shepherd was feeling his age, and since he was nearing his thirteen-hundredth birthday this was no small problem. He could not, he reflected, take the long journeys like he used to, when a flight from Oslo to

Thingvellir, perched uncomfortably between the shoulder-blades of the huge mutant seagull that his employer had bred specially for him, had just been part of a normal day's work.

He had not been idle. What with dashing about by train, car and helicopter, interviewing Danny Bennett and capturing the two chthonic spirits, then hurrying back to Rolfsness to clear the area of Professor Wood and his archaeologists, he felt he had earned a rest. But now he was back in London, and the sorcerer-king was in the bad mood that usually attended the tricky part of any enterprise.

The two spirits were safely locked up in a spellproof perspex tank, and the Professor had been shunted off to the British Museum to ferret about among the Old Norse manuscripts one more time, just in case anything had been overlooked. Still, the Professor was a useful man. Another practical benefit of commercial sponsorship of archaeology. It had, of course, been fortuitous that a freak and entirely localised storm had threatened to flood the site at Rolfsness, forcing the excavation team to close up the mound and go away, but Thorgeir was not called Storm-Shepherd for nothing. He was glad that he had kept his hand in at that particular field of Old Magic, useful over the past thousand years only for betting on draws in cricket matches and then washing them out. He leant back in his chair and ruffled the papers on his desk. As well as being a Dark Age sorcerer, he was also one of the key executives in the world's largest multinational, and work had been piling up while he was away. As he flicked through a sheaf of 'while-you-were-out' notes, he reflected that it was a pity that he had never mastered the art of delegation.

The intercom buzzed, and his secretary told him that his boss was on the scrambler. Thorgeir disliked the machine, but it was better than telepathy, which had until recently been the main method of in-office communication between himself and the sorcerer-king, and which invariably gave him a headache.

'Now what?' said the sorcerer-king.

'That's that,' replied Thorgeir, 'at least for the moment. Without those two whatsits, the brooch is useless.'

'Why can't they just plug it into the mains?'

'Even if they could, they couldn't get enough power from the ordinary mains,' Thorgeir explained patiently. 'But they can't. They need direct current, and you'd need a transformer the size of Liverpool to convert it. The only power source in the world big enough to power that brooch is sitting in a perspex tank in Vouchers. You have my word on it.'

'So now what?'

'With the brooch out of action, they're up the fjord without a paddle.' Thorgeir grinned into the receiver. 'Lucky, wasn't I?'

'Yes,' said the sorcerer-king, 'very.'

Thorgeir stopped grinning. 'So we have all the time in the world to find them and dispose of them. They can't do us any harm.'

'You said that the last time, before Melvich.'

'That was different.'

'So is this different. How do you know they can't modify it?'

'Trust me. Let me rephrase that,' Thorgeir added hurriedly, for that was a sore point at all times. 'Rely on it. They can't. All they can do is try breaking in here and springing the two gnomes.'

'Just let them try.'

'Exactly. So relax, won't you? Enjoy yourself. Set up a new newspaper or something. The situation is under control.'

'I hope so.' The sorcerer-king rang off.

Thorgeir shook his head and returned to his work. The papers from the Japanese deal were starting to come through, and he didn't like the look of them at all. Come the glorious day, he said to himself, I'll turn that whole poxy country into a golf-course, and we'll see how they like that. But before he could settle to it the telephone went again. This time it was Professor Wood, ringing from the call-box outside the British Museum. Thorgeir sat up and reached for a pen and some paper.

After a few minutes, he put the phone down carefully and read back his notes. Things were starting to take shape. In a nineteenth-century collection of Gaelic folk-tales, the Professor had found a most interesting story, all about a chieftain called Rolf McKettle and his battle with the Fairies. Allowing for the distortions inevitably occurring over a millennium of the oral tradition and home-made whisky, it was a fair and accurate report of the battle of Melvich, and it went on to tell the rest of the story, including where the King had been buried and who was buried with him.

The Professor would be round in about half an hour. Thorgeir dumped a half-hundredweight of unread contracts in his out-tray and went to tell his boss. 'Not,' he reflected as he got into the lift, 'that he'll take kindly to being called a fairy. But there we go.'

How long he had been there, or where exactly there was, Danny had no idea, but he was beginning to wonder whether the senior cameraman might not have been right after all. It had been the senior cameraman, armed with the map, who had insisted that the big cloudy thing over to their right was Ben Stumanadh, and that the road was just the other side of it. Danny had been a Boy Scout (although he had taken endless pains to make sure that no one in the Corporation knew about it) and he knew that the assertion was patently ridiculous, and that the cameraman was determined to lead the crew into the bleak and inhospitable interior, where death from exposure was a very real possibility. He had reasoned with him, ordered him, and finally shouted at him; but the fool had taken no notice, and neither had the rest of the crew. Finally, Danny had washed his hands of the lot of them and set out to walk the few miles to the road, which he knew was just over to the left.

Of course the mist hadn't helped, but the further he had gone, the more Danny had become convinced that either the map had been wrong or that someone had moved the road. As exhaustion and hunger, and the loss of both his shoes in a bog had taken their toll, he had inclined more and more to the latter explanation, especially after his short but illuminating chat with the two brown sheep which had been the only living things he had seen since meeting the strange man who had pointed them all in the wrong direction. Shortly after he had arrived at that conclusion, his eyes started playing tricks on him, and he had spent the night in what appeared at the time to be a fully equipped editing suite, complete with facilities for transposing film on to video-tape. In the cold (very cold) light of morning it had turned out to be a ruined shieling, and he had somehow acquired a rather disconcertingly high fever. But at least it kept him warm, which was something.

Rather optimistically, he tried out his arms and his legs, but of course they wouldn't work, just as his car never used to start when he had a particularly urgent meeting. He felt surprisingly calm, and reflected that that was probably one of the fringe benefits of going completely mad. If he wasn't deeply into the final stage of hallucination that came just before death by exposure, he wouldn't be imagining that the men in the grey suits were coming over the hill towards him.

'Just like old times,' one of them was saying. 'Out on the fells with no shelter and nothing to eat but rabbit and perishing salmon. If I have to eat any more salmon, I'll start looking like one.'

Since over his suit he was wearing a coat of silvery scale armour he already did; but of course, Danny reflected, since the man was not really there he was not to know that. He groaned softly, and slumped a little further behind the stones. If he had to see visions in his madness, he would have preferred something a little less eccentric.

'If you hadn't been so damned fussy,' said another of the men, 'we could have had one of those sheep.'

'He said not to get into any trouble,' said the salmon-man. 'Stealing sheep counts as trouble. Always did.'

'There might be deer in that forest we passed,' said a third man.

'Then, again, there might not,' replied the salmon-man, who seemed a miserable sort of person. Danny decided he didn't like him much and tried to replace him with a beautiful girl, but apparently the system didn't work like that. 'And if you think I'm going to go rushing about some wood in the hope that it's full of deer you can think again,' the salmon-man said. The others didn't bother to reply. Danny approved.

'That'll do,' said one of them. He was pointing at the shieling, and Danny realised that they intended to make their camp there. That was a pity, since he had wanted to spend his last hours on earth in quiet meditation, not making conversation with a bunch of phantasms from the Milk Marketing Board. In fact, Danny said to himself, I won't have it. An Englishman's fallen-down old shed is his castle, even in Scotland. 'Go away,' he shouted, and turned his face to the stone wall. The words just managed to clear his lips, but they fell away into the wind and were dispersed.

'There's someone in there,' said Starkad Storvirksson.

'So there is,' said Ohtar. 'I wonder if he wants a fight.'

'Better ask him first,' said Angantyr. 'It's very bad manners to fight people without asking.'

'I thought we weren't supposed to fight anyone,' Starkad said.

'We can if we have to defend ourselves,' said Ohtar, but his heart wasn't in it. The man hardly looked worth fighting anyway. In fact he looked decidedly unwell. Ohtar turned him over gently with his foot.

'Ask him if he's got anything to eat,' Angantyr whispered. 'Tell him we'll trade him two rabbits and a salmon for anything in the way of cheese.'

'Hold it, will you?' said Ohtar. 'It's that sorcerer from the van, the one who wouldn't fight with Bothvar.' He turned to his companions and smiled. 'Things are looking up,' he said. 'We've got ourselves a prisoner.'

CHAPTER SEVEN

'Have some more rabbit,' said Ohtar kindly. Although Danny had done nothing but eat all night, he felt it would be rude to refuse. Obviously the strange men prided themselves on their hospitality.

'Are you sure you'll have enough for yourselves?' he asked desperately, as Ohtar produced two more burnt drumsticks, still mottled with little flecks of singed fur. The man they called Angantyr made a curious snorting noise.

'Don't you mind him,' said Ohtar. 'Plenty more where that came from.'

'Well, in that case . . .' Danny sank his teeth into the carbonised flesh and tried not to remember that he had been very fond of his pet rabbit, Dimbleby, when he was a boy. 'This is very good,' he said, forcing his weary jaws to chew.

'Really?' Ohtar beamed. He had been field-cook to King Hrolf for most of his service, and this was the first time anyone had paid him a compliment. 'You wait there,' he said and, gathering up his sling and a handful of pebbles, walked away.

'You've made his day,' said Angantyr, sitting down beside Danny and absentmindedly picking up the second drumstick. 'Personally,' he said with his mouth full, 'I hate rabbit, but it's a sight better than seagull. You ever had seagull?'

'No,' Danny said.

'Very wise,' said Angantyr, and he spat out a number of small bones. 'Not that you can't make something of it with a white sauce and some fennel. Don't get me wrong,' he added, 'I'm not obsessive about food, like some I could mention. Five square meals a day is all I ask, and a jug or so of something wet to see it on its way. But I draw the line at seaweed,' he asserted firmly. 'Except in a mousse, of course.'

'Of course,' Danny agreed.

Having looked to make sure that there was no more rabbit lying about, Angantyr lay back against the wall of the ruined bothy and pulled his helmet down over his eyes. 'Ah, well,' he said, 'this is better than work. What do you do with yourself, by the way? I know you're a sorcerer of sorts, but that could mean anything, couldn't it?'

'I'm a producer,' Danny said.

'Good for you,' Angantyr said. 'Me, I'm strictly a consumer.' The early-morning sun was shining weakly through a window in the cloud, and the hero was in a good mood. 'That was always the trouble with this country,' he went on. 'Too few producers and too many consumers. I admire you people, honestly I do. Out behind the plough in all weathers, or driving the sheep home through the snow. Rotten job, always said so.'

'No, no,' Danny said, 'I'm not a farmer, I'm a producer. A television producer.'

Angantyr sat up, a caterpillar-like eyebrow raised. 'What's that, then?'

'You know . . .' Danny said weakly. 'I work out the schedules, supervise the crews, that sort of thing.'

'You mean a forecastle-man?' Angantyr suspected that his leg was being pulled. 'Get out, you're not, are you?'

'Not that sort of crew,' Danny said, wishing he had never mentioned it. 'Camera crews. Keys, grips, gaffers, that sort of thing. I make television programmes.'

'Don't mind me,' said Angantyr after a long pause. 'I've been asleep for a thousand-odd years.'

'No, but really.' Danny nerved himself to ask the question that was eating away at the lining of his mind. 'Who are you people?'

Angantyr looked at him sternly, remembering that he was a sorcerer. But he looked harmless enough, and they had smashed up all his magical instruments in the Battle of the Vans.

'If I tell you,' he said, lowering his voice, 'you won't turn into a bird or something and fly away? Give me your word of honour.'

'On my word of honour,' said Danny. Obviously, he reflected, the man really didn't know what a television producer was, or he would have demanded a different oath.

'We're King Hrolf's men,' whispered Angantyr. 'We went to sleep in the ship, and now we've been woken up for the final battle.'

'You mean the ship at Rolfsness?' Danny asked. Something at the back of his mind was making sense of this, although he wished it wouldn't. By and large, he preferred it when he thought he was going mad.

'That's right,' said Angantyr patiently. 'We were asleep in the ship for twelve hundred years, and now we've woken up.'

Danny closed his eyes. 'Then, what about the grey suits?'

'You mean the clothes? That Hildy got them for us. She said we'd be less conspicuous dressed like this.'

'Hildy Frederiksen?'

'Hildy Frederik's-*daughter*. Can't be Frederik*sen*, she's a woman. Stands to reason.' Angantyr shook his head. 'Funny creature. But bright, I'll say that for her. It was lucky we met her, really, what with her knowing the sagas and all. Between you and me,' he whispered into Danny's ear, 'I think old Arvarodd's gone a bit soft on her. No accounting for taste, I suppose, and there was that time at Hlidarend—'

'Could we go through this one more time?' Danny said. 'You were actually *in* the ship when Frederiksen went into the mound?'

'Course we were.' It suddenly occurred to Angantyr that the prisoner might find this hard to believe, if he didn't know the story. So he told him the story. Even when he had done this, the prisoner seemed unconvinced.

'I'm sorry,' Danny said, when Angantyr put this to him. 'I'm not calling you a liar, really. But it's all the magic stuff. You see . . .'

Angantyr remembered something he had overheard the King saying to Hildy, or it might have been the other way around. 'Just a moment,' he said. 'You call it something else now, don't you? Technology or something.'

'No, that's quite different,' Danny interrupted. He had a terrible feeling that there was something wrong with his line of argument. 'Technology is healing the sick, and doing things automatically. Magic is—'

'Watch this,' Angantyr said, and from his pocket he pulled a small doe-skin pouch. 'Here's a bit of technology I picked up in Lapland when I went raiding there.' He emptied the contents of the pouch on to the ground, and picked up two small bones and a pebble. Then he drew his knife, and with a single blow cut off his left hand just above the wrist. Danny tried to scream, but before the muscles of his larynx had relaxed from the first shock of what he had seen Angantyr picked up his severed left hand with his right hand and put it on Danny's knee.

'Hold that for me, will you?' he said cheerfully. Then he popped the pebble into his mouth, took back the severed hand and drew it back on to his wrist like a glove. Then, with his *left* hand, he took the pebble out of his mouth, wiped it on his trouser-leg and put it back in the pouch. 'How's that for technology?' he said. 'Or do you want to try it for yourself?'

Danny assured him that he did not.

'It's a bit like grafting apples,' said Angantyr, 'only quicker. What was the other thing you said? Doing things automatically. Right.'

He threw the two small bones up in the air and blew on them as they fell. One started to glow with a bright orange light, and the other burst into a tall roaring flame. Angantyr blew on it again, and it grew smaller, like a gas jet being turned down. Then he whistled, and the flame stopped.

'That's just a portable one,' he said, putting the bones and the pouch away. 'You can get them bigger for lighting a house and cooking large meals. And they're more controllable than an open fire for gentle simmering and light frying. Cookability, you might say.'

Just then, Ohtar came back, throwing down a large sack. Angantyr turned and looked at him cautiously.

'Couldn't find any rabbits,' said Ohtar, sitting down beside them and opening the sack. 'Will seagull be all right?'

According to the road signs at Melvich, they had finished digging up the A9 at Berriedale, and the main road along the coast was fully open again. Hildy was relieved; she had not been looking forward to going back down the Lairg road, for she felt sure that if their enemy had heard about them he would be watching it, and probably the Helmsdale road as well. The main road would be much safer, as well as quicker.

She still had her doubts about leaving the rest of the heroes to their own devices, even in the wilds of Strathnaver; but she consoled herself with the thought that it would have been even more dangerous to take them to London, not to mention the expense of food, accommodation and Tube tickets for them all. As she turned these questions over in her mind, she realised, with no little pride, that she had become the effective leader of the company, and as she drove she found herself composing the first lines of her own saga. 'There was a woman called Hildy Frederiksen . . .'

'Mind out,' said the King suddenly, 'you're going out into the middle of the road.'

'Sorry,' Hildy mumbled. It was like having driving lessons with her father. Even now, seven years after she had passed her test, he still tended to give her helpful advice, such as 'Why aren't you in third?' and 'For Christ's sake, slow down,' when she was doing about thirty-five along the freeway. She hurriedly put *Hildar Saga Frederiksdottur* back on the bookshelf of her mind, and concentrated on keeping closer in to the side of the road.

The King, she felt, was adapting remarkably quickly to the twentieth century, asking perceptive questions and making highly intelligent guesses about the various things he saw as they drove along. Even when they had passed through Inverness, the King's first sight of a major town had not seemed to throw him in any way. When she asked him about this, he simply said that he had seen many stranger things than that in his life, especially in Finnmark, and he expected to see many things stranger still. That,

Hildy reckoned, she could personally guarantee. Large container-lorries seemed to intrigue him, but aircraft he regarded as inefficient and somehow rather old-fashioned. The one thing he did find fault with was what he called the 'decline of civilisation'. Coming from a Viking, Hildy thought, that was a bit much, but the King refused to be drawn on the subject, and Hildy guessed that he meant all that noble-savage stuff that you got in Victorian academic writing.

Rather than risk staying the night in a hotel, they left the motorway at Penrith and found a deserted corner of Martindale Common, near where, disconcertingly enough, the King had fought a battle with the Saxons.

'A race of men I never did take to,' the King added, as they roasted the inevitable rabbit. 'What became of them, by the way?'

Hildy told him, and he said that he wasn't in the least surprised. 'A nation of shopkeepers,' he muttered, 'bound to do well in the end.'

Hildy had written a paper on early Saxon trade, and would have discussed the matter further, but the King seemed not to be in the right mood. In fact, she thought to herself, he's been strange all day. Preoccupied.

The next day, after filling up with petrol at a service station (enough tokens now for a cut-glass decanter, only she didn't want one), they pressed on towards London. In the back, Arvarodd and the wizard were playing the same complicated game of chess that had kept them occupied all the way from Caithness, and the journey seemed not to trouble them at all. It was only when they stopped outside Birmingham for more petrol and a sandwich that Hildy noticed that the shape-changer was nowhere to be seen. 'Not again,' she muttered to herself, and asked where he'd got to.

'Down here,' said one of the chess-pieces.

'We left the black rook behind,' Arvarodd explained.

'But don't you mind?' Hildy asked the black rook. The rook shrugged its rigid shoulders.

'It passes the time,' he said. 'And chess-pieces don't get travel-sick.'

'It's just that black always seems to win,' Arvarodd said. They had drawn for colours before setting off, and he was playing white. 'Not that I mind that much, of course. I generally lose to Kotkel anyway.'

'Do chess-pieces get hungry?' Hildy asked. She had only bought enough sandwiches for four.

'This one does,' said the rook firmly. Then the wizard grabbed him by the head and used him to take Arvarodd's queen.

They arrived in London late in the evening, and Hildy realised that she had made no plans for their stay there.

'That's all right,' said the King absently. 'We can sleep in this thing.'

Hildy started to explain about yellow lines, traffic wardens and loitering with intent, but the King wasn't listening. He was looking about him and frowning deeply.

'Of course,' Hildy said, 'this must be all totally strange to you.'

'Not at all,' said the King. 'It's most depressingly familiar.'

'It can't be,' said Hildy.

'I assure you it is. Isn't it, lads?'

Arvarodd looked up from the chessboard. 'Hello,' he said, 'I've been here before. It's just like—'

'It's just like Geirrodsgarth,' explained the King, 'where the sorcerer-king had his first stronghold, and which we erased from the face of the earth, so that not even its foundations remained.'

Hildy shook her head. 'Surely not,' she said.

'I started to worry when we went to Wick, but it might

just have been coincidence. At Inverness I felt sure. All the other cities we have passed confirmed my suspicions. The enemy has built his new city as a replica of the old one, except that it's much bigger and rather more primitive.'

'Primitive?'

'Oh, decidedly so. For a start, the whole of Geirrodsgarth was covered over with a transparent roof. But I suppose it's because he could only influence its design, not order it entirely according to his wishes. All the buildings in Geirrodsgarth were square towers like those over there.' He waved his hands at a grove of tower-blocks in the distance. 'I suppose he found the Saxons rather more stubborn than the Finns. That's shopkeepers for you.'

In the end, Hildy parked in a side-street in Hoxton, beside the Regent's Canal; it would somehow not be safe to go any further. She was aware of some vague but localised menace, and something of the sort was clearly affecting the King and the wizard, who huddled together in the back of the van and talked in low voices. Hildy realised that the wizard had put aside the language-spell, so that she could not understand what was being said. She felt betrayed and rejected. In a strained voice she said something about going and getting some food, and opened the door. The King looked up and said something, but of course she could not understand it. Arvarodd, however, translated for her.

'He says you shouldn't go,' he said.

'But I'm hungry,' Hildy replied. 'And I'm sure it'll be all right.'

The King said something else. 'He says go if you must, but take the shape-changer with you.'

'Don't I get any say in the matter?' asked the black rook. 'Two more moves and it'll be check.'

Arvarodd picked up the rook and offered it to Hildy. 'Just slip him in your pocket,' he said.

'No, thanks,' said Hildy stiffly. 'I don't want to spoil your game.'

'Just to please me,' said Arvarodd. Startled, Hildy took it and put it in her pocket. Then she opened the door and slipped out.

It took a long time for her to find a chip-shop, and she had a good mind not to buy anything for the King or the wizard. In the end, however, she bought five cod and chips, five chicken and ham pies, and a saveloy for herself, as a treat. She failed to notice that the two youths in leather jackets who had been playing the fruit machine had followed her out.

Halfway back to the van they made their move. One stepped out in front of her, waving a short knife, while the other made a grab for her bag. Hildy froze, clutching the parcels of food to her breast, and made a squeaking noise.

'Come on, lady, give us the bag,' said the youth with the knife, "cos if you don't you'll get cut, right?'

He took a step forward. At that moment, something fell from Hildy's pocket and rolled into the gutter. The knifeman looked round, and suddenly dropped his knife. Apparently from nowhere, a terrifying figure had appeared. At first it looked like a gigantic bear; then it was a wolf, with red eyes and a lolling tongue. Finally, it was a huge grim man brandishing a broad-bladed axe. The two youths stared for a moment, then started to run. For a few moments, they thought that they were being pursued by a vast black eagle. They quickened their pace and disappeared round the corner.

'I knew that stuff you sold me was no good,' said one to the other.

'Are you all right?' said Brynjolf, returning and perching

on a wing-mirror. He ruffled his feathers with his beak, and then turned back into a chess-piece. 'Sorry to be so long,' he said. 'I couldn't make up my mind what to be. The bear usually does the trick, but the wolf is more comfy.'

'That was fine,' Hildy mumbled. She was breathing heavily, and there was vinegar all over her new anorak. 'Thank you.'

'Not at all,' said a voice from her pocket. 'Who were they, by the way?'

'Just muggers, I think,' Hildy replied. 'That's sort of thieves.'

'I don't know,' said her pocket. 'Young people nowadays.'

'Don't say anything to the King,' said Hildy. 'He'd only worry.'

'Please yourself.'

Hildy didn't tell the King when she got back, but she gave Brynjolf the saveloy. It was, she felt, the least she could do.

The next morning, they left the van and set off on foot. They went by Tube from Old Street to Bank, and changed on to the Central Line for St Paul's. The concept of the Underground seemed not to worry the King or the wizard, but Brynjolf and Arvarodd didn't like the look of it at all.

'You know what I reckon this is?' Arvarodd whispered to the shape-changer.

'What?'

'Burial-chambers,' replied the hero of Permia, 'like those shaft-graves on Orkney only bigger. They must go on for miles.'

'And what are we in, then – a coffin?' Brynjolf looked around the compartment. 'Can't see any bodies.'

'Must be the tombs of kings,' replied Arvarodd. 'Look, there's a diagram or something up on the side.'

Brynjolf leant forward and studied the plan.

'I reckon you may be right,' he said, returning to his seat. 'I think there are several dynasties down here. Those coloured lines joining up the names must be the family-trees. Funny names they've got, though. Look, there's the House of Kensington all buried together: South Kensington, West Kensington, High Street Kensington—'

'Kensington Olympia,' interrupted Arvarodd. 'They must have been a powerful dynasty.'

'Them and the Parks,' agreed Brynjolf. 'And the Actons away in the west. Hopelessly interbred, of course,' he added, looking at the numerous intersections of the coloured lines at Euston. 'No wonder they got delusions of grandeur.'

Hildy overheard the end of this conversation but decided not to interrupt. It would be too complicated to explain; and, besides, as a trained archaeologist she felt that their explanation was rather better than the conventional one.

They got off at St Paul's and were faced by the escalator. This Hildy felt she would have to explain, but the heroes seemed to recognise it at once – they must have had them in Geirrodsgarth. At the foot of it, Arvarodd stopped and studied the notice.

'Dogs must be carried on the escalator,' he read aloud. 'I knew we should have brought a dog. I suppose we'll have to flog up all those stairs now.'

'All right,' said Brynjolf wearily, 'leave it to me.' He sighed heavily and turned himself into a small terrier, which Arvarodd picked up and tucked under his arm. 'Only, if you've lost your ticket,' said the dog, 'you're on your own.'

Once they reached street-level, the object of their quest was obvious. Before Hildy could point to it and identify it as the building she had seen through the stone, her companions were staring at the soaring black tower that dominated the rest of Cheapside.

'That's him all over,' said the King. 'No originality.'

'Well,' said Arvarodd, 'do we go in, or what?' His hand was tightening around the grip of the sports-bag in which he was carrying his mail shirt and short sword.

'No,' said the King.

'Why not, for crying out loud?' Hildy could see that Arvarodd was sweating heavily; but he was not afraid. There was something uncanny about him, and Hildy edged away.

'Because we wouldn't get past the front gate,' replied the King quietly. For his part, he was as cold as ice. He stood motionless, but his eyes were flicking backwards and forwards as he considered every scrap of evidence that the view of the building had to offer. 'Or, rather, we would, which would be all the worse for us. I don't think physical force is the answer.'

'I don't see that we have that many options,' muttered Brynjolf. 'Unless you'd like me—'

'Certainly not,' snapped the King. 'Your magic wouldn't work in there.' He turned sharply on his heel and walked away.

'Now what?' Hildy whispered to Arvarodd. 'He's not going to give up now, is he?' Arvarodd shook his head.

'He is the King,' was all he would say.

The King was talking with the wizard, and they seemed to have agreed on something, for the King turned back and approached Hildy.

'Tell me,' he said, 'how would the power to work all the machines get into that building?'

Hildy told him about the mains and the underground cables. He nodded, and suddenly smiled.

'And all the houses and buildings in the city are connected to the same source of power?' he asked.

'I think so,' Hildy said. 'I can't be certain, of course.'
'What we need, then,' said the King, 'is a building.'

'Down the tree, four spaces over, and that's check*mate*.'

The power-level in the computer wavered suddenly. The grim-faced man got up from his desk and banged on the side of the tank.

'Any more of that,' he said savagely, 'and I'll take that game off you.'

'Sorry,' chorused the pale glow inside the tank.

'Well, all right, then,' said the grim-faced man, 'only let's have less of it.' He scowled and returned to his desk.

'For two pins,' said Prexz, 'I'd run straight up his arm and electrocute him.'

'You wouldn't dare,' replied Zxerp scornfully. 'And, besides, he might have rubber soles on his shoes, and then where would you be?'

'As I was saying,' said Prexz through clenched teeth, 'checkmate.'

'Who cares?' Zxerp stretched out his hand and knocked over his goblin to signify surrender. 'What does that make the score?'

Prexz consulted the card. 'That's ninety-nine thousand, nine hundred and ninety-nine sets and eight games to me, and four games to you.'

'Inclusive?'

'Exclusive,' replied Prexz, making a mark on the card. 'So I now need only one more game for one match point. You still have some work to do.'

'I might as well concede, then,' said Zxerp. He pressed his feet against the side of the tank and put his arms behind his head. 'Then we can start again from scratch.'

'Don't be so damned pessimistic,' replied Prexz. 'A good match to win, I'll grant you, but it's still wide open.'

'We should have brought draughts instead,' yawned Zxerp. 'I'm hungry.'

'You're always hungry. Is there any of that static left, or have you guzzled it all?'

'Help yourself.' There was a faint crackling noise and a few blue sparks. 'That box of tricks over there fair takes it out of you,' Zxerp went on. 'I'll need more than static to keep electron and neutron together if I've got to keep that thing going much longer.'

Prezz turned and glowered at the computer. It winked a green light at him, and started to print something out. Just then, Prezz felt a vibration in the wire running into his left ear. Zxerp could feel the same thing. He started to protest, but Prezz hissed at him to be quiet.

'It's coming in over the mains,' he whispered.

'Tastes all right,' said Zxerp. 'A bit salty perhaps . . .'

'Don't eat it, you fool, it's a message.'

'The old file-in-a-cake trick, huh?'

'Something like.' Prezz closed his eyes and tried to concentrate. 'I think it's the wizard.'

'Kotkel?' Zxerp leant forward.

'He's talking through the mains running into that machine we're linked up to. Honestly, the things he thinks of.'

The two spirits lay absolutely still. 'We're going to try to get you out,' they heard, 'so be ready. But it won't be easy. Don't try to reply or you'll blow the circuit. Bon appétit.'

'Very tastefully put,' said Zxerp, and he burped loudly.

The proprietor of the hotel gave Hildy a very strange look as she went past, and she could not blame him. After all, she had come in just under an hour ago with four strange-looking men and hired a room; and now they were all going away again. Still, it had been worth the embarrassment, for the wizard had managed to talk to the two captives via the shaver socket – how he had managed it she could not imagine – and they seemed to have received the message. The thing to do now was get away fast, just in case their message had been intercepted and traced.

The van was still where she had left it (why was she surprised by that? It was just an ordinary van parked in an ordinary street) and they all climbed in and drove off, entirely uncertain as to where they were going and why. The King was sitting in the back with the wizard and the shape-changer, and they were all deep in mystical discussion. But Arvarodd sat in the front, and he seemed to be in unusually good spirits.

'Don't you fret,' he said, as they drove through Highgate. 'We've been in worse fixes than this, believe you me.'

'Such as?' Hildy cast her mind back through the heroic legends of Scandinavia in search of some parallel, but the search was in vain. Usually, the old heroes had overcome their improbable trials with brute force or puerile trickery.

'Offhand,' said Arvarodd, remorselessly cheerful, 'I can't think. But it looks to me like a straightforward impregnable-fortress problem. Let's not worry about it now.'

'What's gotten into you?' Hildy asked gloomily. She found the words 'straightforward' and 'impregnable fortress' hard to reconcile.

'You worry too much,' Arvarodd replied, to Hildy's profound irritation. 'That's what comes of not having faith in the King. That's what kings are for, so people like you and me don't have to worry.'

Hildy, who had been brought up to vote Democrat, objected to this.

'The King doesn't seem to realise—' she started to say.

'The King realises everything,' said Arvarodd. 'And, even if he doesn't, who wants to know?' The hero of Permia yawned and folded his arms. 'If the King says, "Charge that army over there," and you say, "Which one?" and he says, "The one that outnumbers us twentyfold in that superb natural defensive position just under that hill with the sheep," then you do it. And if it works you say, "What a brilliant general the King is," and if it doesn't you go to Valhalla. Everyone's a winner, really.'

'That's what you mean by a straightforward impregnable-fortress problem?'

'Exactly. You have two options. You can work out a subtle stratagem to trick your way in, with an equally subtle stratagem to get you out again afterwards, or you can grab an axe and smash the door down. We call that the certain-death option. On the whole, it's easier and safer than all the fooling about, but you have to go through the motions.'

'So you think it'll come to that?' Hildy asked.

'No idea,' Arvarodd said. 'Not my problem.'

After more petrol – if she collected enough tokens, Hildy wondered, could she get a Challenger tank, which really would be useful in the circumstances? – they parked in a side-road on the edge of Hampstead Heath and held a council of war.

'The situation as I see it is this,' said the King. 'The tower, which would be unassailable even if we were in a position to attack it, which we aren't, is guarded night and day. Our enemy has control of the two spirits, who are essential to us if we are to have any hope of survival, let alone success. Because of the risk of detection, and because detection would mean certain defeat at this stage, we cannot make a more detailed survey of the ground, so to all intents and purposes we know absolutely nothing about the tower, how to get into it or out of it. Again, because of the risk of detection, if we are going to do anything we must do it now. I am in the market for any sensible suggestions.'

'Why not attack?' Brynjolf said. 'Then we could all go to Valhalla and have a good time.'

The wizard made a noise like worn-out disc brakes, and the King nodded. 'The wizard says,' translated the King, 'that the cause is not yet hopeless, that courage and wisdom together can break stone and turn steel, and that we have a duty that is not yet discharged. Also, Valhalla is looking pretty run-down these days what with nobody going there any more, the towels in the bathrooms are positively threadbare, and he's in no hurry. He says he has this on the authority of Odin's ravens, Hugin and Munin, who bring him tidings every morning, and they should know. Anyone else?'

Before anyone could speak, the van was filled with a shrill whistling, and Hildy realised that it was coming from her bag. At first she thought it was her personal security alarm, but that went *beep-beep* and, besides, she had left it in St Andrews.

'It's the seer-stone,' said Brynjolf, shouting to make himself heard.

'You mean like a sort of bleeper?' Hildy rummaged about and found the small blue pebble. It was warm again, and the noise was definitely coming from it. With great trepidation, she put it to her eye, and saw . . .

'Really,' Danny said, 'we'll come quietly.'

The police sergeant raised himself painfully on one elbow. 'Oh, no, you don't,' he groaned. 'You said that the last time.'

'You shouldn't have tried to handcuff him,' Danny said. 'He didn't like it.'

'I gathered that,' said the police sergeant, spitting out

a tooth. 'If it's all the same to you, I'm going to go and call for reinforcements.'

'Are you refusing to accept our surrender?' said Ohtar angrily.

'Yes,' said the police sergeant. 'I wouldn't take it as a gift.'

'Please yourself,' Ohtar said, fingering a large stone. 'The last person who refused to accept my surrender made a full recovery. Eventually.'

The police sergeant looked round at his battered and bleeding constables, and at the eight grim-faced salmon-poachers standing over them. It seemed that he had very little choice.

'If you're sure,' he said.

'We're sure,' said Ohtar impatiently. 'We've got orders not to get into any trouble.'

'It's the others,' Hildy said. 'They've gotten into trouble.'

CHAPTER EIGHT

It is 520 miles from London to Bettyhill as the crow flies, but if the crow in question is a fully trained shape-changer in a hurry the journey takes just over two and a half hours.

Brynjolf perched on the window-sill of the police station and preened his ruffled feathers. Apart from turbulence over Derby and a nasty moment with a buzzard passing over Dornoch it had been an uneventful flight, and he knew that the tricky part of his mission still lay ahead of him. Cautiously he peered in through the window, and listened.

'No, I don't know who they are,' the man in blue was saying, 'but they beat the hell out of us. Maybe you should send up some water-cannon or something.'

The reply to this request was clearly not the one the man in blue was expecting, for he said, 'Oh, very funny,' and slammed the phone down. Brynjolf hopped away from the window-sill, spread his wings and floated away to consider what to do next.

Very tricky, he said to himself, and to assist thought

he started to sharpen his beak on a flat stone. Shape-transformation is, however, only skin-deep, and he gave it up quickly. Getting the heroes out would be no problem in itself; it was one that they could handle easily by themselves. But getting them out inconspicuously, so as not to cause any further disturbance, would be difficult. He went through his mental library of relevant heroic precedent – heroes rescued by sudden storms, conveniently passing dragons, or divine intervention – but something told him that such effects might be counter-productive. The obvious alternative was the false-messenger routine, but that required a fair amount of local knowledge to be successful. He had no idea who the men in blue took their orders from, what they looked like or what identification would be needed. He had almost decided to turn himself into the key of the cell door and have done with it when he thought of what should have been the obvious solution: the duplex confusion routine or Three-Troll Trick.

First he turned himself into a fly and crawled into the building through a keyhole in the back door. Once inside, he buzzed tentatively round until he had located the cell where the prisoners were being held. It was a small cell and they all looked profoundly uncomfortable. Then he made a second trip and counted up the number of men in blue. There were only three of them; just the right number.

The Three-Troll Trick, so called because trolls fall for it every time, is essentially very simple. The shape-changer simply waits until only one of the gaolers is supervising the prisoners; then he turns himself into an exact facsimile of one of the other gaolers and, claiming to have received instructions from a higher authority, releases the prisoners, who get away as best they can.

He then disappears, and leaves the other gaolers to discover the error and beat the pulp out of the one they believe has betrayed their trust. In a more robust age, the presumed traitor would not survive to clarify the misunderstanding; even if things had changed drastically over the years, Brynjolf reckoned, the mistake would still be put down to administrative confusion and quietly covered up. He set to work, and as usual the system worked flawlessly. The real gaoler lent him his key to the cell, the door swung open, and the heroes, looking rather sullen, trooped out.

What Brynjolf had overlooked was the fact that nearly three hours' confinement in a cramped cell, with Angantyr keeping up a constant stream of funny remarks, had not improved Bothvar Bjarki's temper, which was at the best of times chronically in need of all the improvement it could get. Also, Brynjolf had inadvertently chosen to impersonate the policeman who had been foolish enough to aim a blow at Bothvar's head just before the fight started. So when Brynjolf, acting out his part to the full, shoved Bothvar Bjarki in the back and said, 'Move it, you,' in his best gaoler's snarl it was inevitable that Bothvar should wheel round and thump him very hard on the chin. It was also inevitable that Brynjolf, who had never really liked Bothvar because of his habit of paring his toenails with an axe-blade when everyone else was eating, should forget that he was playing a part, revert to his own shape, and return the blow with interest. The fact that he rematerialised with three extra arms was pure reflex.

Brynjolf realised in a moment what he had done, but by then it was too late. The other two men in blue had come rushing up when they heard the commotion, and they were standing open-mouthed and staring.

'That,' Bothvar said as he picked himself up from the ground, 'is what comes of trying to be clever.'

'I'll deal with you later,' Brynjolf replied. The three policemen, guessing who he meant to deal with first, made a run for the door, but the massive bulk of Starkad Storvirksson was in the way. After a one-sided scuffle, the policemen landed in a heap on the ground, and Starkad, remembering his manners, shut the door.

'Here,' said a voice from the back of the room, 'let me deal with this.'

Brynjolf turned and looked for the source. 'Is he one of them?' he asked, pointing to Danny Bennett.

'No,' said Ohtar, 'he's that sorcerer from the van, when you turned into an eagle.'

'Him,' Brynjolf exclaimed. 'What's he doing here?'

'We found him on the fells,' said Angantyr, putting a tree-like arm round his new friend's shoulders. 'Strange bloke. Eats a lot, very fond of seagull. But he's on our side now. You'll sort it all out for us, won't you?' And he slapped Danny warmly on the back, nearly breaking his spine.

Danny stepped forward and bent over the policemen.

'I'm afraid,' he said, 'there's been a slight misunderstanding.'

'You don't say,' said the sergeant.

'You see,' Danny continued, 'my – my friends here weren't poaching salmon. Like me, I'm sure they're firmly opposed to bloodsports of every sort.' The sergeant laughed faintly, but Danny ignored him. 'In fact they're part of a team investigating a massive conspiracy to undermine democracy. Really, we need your help.'

The sergeant was curiously unmoved by this appeal. He groaned and rolled over on to his face. Danny sighed; he was used to this obstructive attitude from policemen.

'If it's all right by you,' he said, 'I'll just go through and use your phone.' He stepped over them and left the room.

'Is that all sorted out, then?' said Angantyr. 'No hard feelings?' One of the policemen raised his head and nodded. 'Good,' said Angantyr. 'We'll just tie you up and then we'll get out from under your feet.'

Meanwhile, Danny had got through to his boss in London.

'What the hell are you doing up there?' said his boss. 'I've just had a very strange call from a film crew who claim to have been beaten up by lunatics and stranded on a deserted hillside. They also said you'd wandered off and died of exposure. I think they're claiming compensation for bereavement because of it.'

'Listen,' Danny said, 'I haven't much time.'

'Oh, no,' said his boss. 'You're not being followed by the Wet Fish Board again, are you? I thought we'd been through all that.'

'It's not the Wet Fish Board, it's—' Danny checked himself. The important thing was to stay calm. 'I'm on to something really big this time.'

'Whatever you're on,' said his boss, 'it can't be legal.'

'This story's got everything,' Danny continued. 'Multinationals, nuclear power, spiritualism, ley lines, the lot.'

'Animals?'

Danny thought of the eagle that had wrecked his van. 'Yes,' he said, 'there's a definite wildlife angle. Also ecology and police brutality.'

The boss was silent for a moment. 'This has nothing at all to do with milk?'

'This is bigger than milk,' Danny said. 'This is global.'

Something told Danny that his lord and master wasn't convinced. Desperately, he played his ace.

'You don't want to miss out on this one,' he said. 'Like when you didn't run the thing about that little girl's pet hamster getting lost inside Porton Down, and the opposition got it. Got her own series in the end, didn't she?'

'All right,' said Danny's boss. 'Tell me about it.'

'What took you so long?'

The crow flopped wearily off the roof of the van, and perched on the King's wrist.

'Lost my way, didn't I?' it muttered, folding its rain-drenched wings. 'My own silly fault. Next time I go as a pigeon.' The crow disappeared and was replaced by an exhausted shape-changer.

'Well?' said the King, offering him the enchanted lager-can. Brynjolf swallowed a couple of mouthfuls and wiped his mouth with the end of his beard.

'Not so good, I'm afraid,' he said. 'Everyone safely rescued, but there were complications.' He told the King what had happened.

'And,' he continued, 'there's more. You remember those sorcerers in the vans that Hildy told us we should stop?'

'What about them?'

'One of them, the chief sorcerer, has turned up again. Apparently, the lads captured him wandering about in the hills. Angantyr thinks he's on our side now.' He paused to allow the King to draw his own conclusions.

'And is he?'

'Who can tell? After the scuffle, he went off to use one of those telephone things. Could be he really is on our side, but I wouldn't bet on it.'

'We'll soon know,' Hildy said, and looked at her watch. 'We must find somewhere with a TV set.'

There was a set in the third pub they tried, but it was showing 'Dynasty'. There were several protests when Hildy switched the channels, including one from Brynjolf, but when the King stood up and looked around the bar nobody seemed inclined to make too much of it. The nine o'clock news came on. Hildy gripped the stem of her glass and waited.

First there was a Middle East story, then something about the Health Service and an interview with the minister ('I know him from somewhere,' Arvarodd said, leaning forward. 'Didn't he use to farm outside Brattahlid?'), followed by a long piece on rate-capping and a minor spy scandal. Then there was a beached whale near Plymouth – the Vikings licked their lips instinctively – and the sports news. Hildy started to relax.

'And reports are just coming in,' said the presenter, marble-faced, 'of a major manhunt in the north of Scotland, which is somehow connected with the recent discovery of a Viking ship-burial and the disappearance of an American archaeologist, Hildegard Frederiksen.'

Panoramic shot of an unidentifiable mountain.

'Ten men, believed to be violent, escaped from police custody today at Bettyhill. They have with them a BBC producer, who they are believed to be holding hostage. Police with tracker dogs are searching for the men, who are thought to be armed with swords, axes and spears. Reports that the men are members of an extremist anti-nuclear group opposed to the Caithness fast-breeder reactor project are as yet unconfirmed. The connection with the burial-mound containing a rich hoard of Viking treasure discovered at nearby Rolfsness is also uncertain. A spokesman for the War Graves Commission refused to comment. The man held hostage, Danny Bennett, is best known for his evocative depictions of Cotswold life, including "The Countryside on Thursday" and "One Man and His Tractor", which was nominated for the Golden Iris award for best documentary.'

'I didn't know you could disappear, Hildy,' said Brynjolf admiringly. 'Do you use a talisman, or just runes?'

Back at the van, the King and his company debated what to do for the best.

'I still say we should make an attack and get it over with,' said Arvarodd. 'Stick to what we know, and don't go getting involved with all these strange people. If we stick around now, and the enemy does come looking for us, we're done for.'

'I'm not so sure.' The King's eyes were shining, as they had not done since they left the Castle of Borve. 'I think our enemy may have got quite the wrong idea from that little exhibition.'

'How do you mean?'

'Think,' said the King, smiling. 'Doesn't it give the impression that we're all still up there, being chased across the hills by those soldiers, or whatever they are? He won't be able to resist the temptation to go up there and see if he can't find us and finish us off. After all, he has nothing to fear from us, so long as he has the spirits safe here.'

'He might take them with him,' Hildy suggested.

'He wouldn't do that. He wouldn't risk them falling into our hands. But if he thinks we're on the run up there – more important, if he thinks we're so weak that we can be chased around by those idiots Brynjolf was telling us about' – the King grinned disconcertingly – 'then he's not going to be too worried about what we can do to him. He'll be concentrating more on what he can do to us. And that'll give us a chance, especially at this end.'

If that was the King's definition of a chance, Hildy said to herself, she didn't like the sound of it. 'But what about the others?' she said. 'What if he catches them?'

'They'll have to look after themselves,' said the King shortly, and Hildy could see he was worried. 'If the worst comes to the worst, Valhalla. That doesn't really matter at this stage.'

'But surely,' Hildy started to say; but Arvarodd trod

on her toe meaningfully. The pain, even through her moon-boot, was agonising. 'Maybe you're right,' she mumbled.

'And meanwhile,' said the King suddenly, 'we have work to do.'

Half-past three in the morning. There were still lights in the windows of Gerrards Garth House; like a crocodile, it slept with its eyes open. Two of the lights, having failed to draw the telex machine into conversation, were playing Goblin's Teeth.

'Are you sure about that?' said Prexz.

Zxerp smiled. 'Yes,' he said. 'Checkmate.'

'But what if . . . ?' Prexz lifted the piece warily, then put it back. He was worried.

'Ninety-nine thousand, nine hundred and ninety-nine sets and nine games to you,' said Zxerp, 'and *five* games to me.' Could it be that his luck was about to change?

Prexz knocked over his goblin petulantly. 'All right, then,' he said, as casually as he could, 'I'll accept your resignation.'

'Who's resigning?' Zxerp was setting out the pieces.

'You offered to resign after the last game. I'm accepting.'

'I've withdrawn,' said Zxerp, shuffling the Spell cards.

'Can't do that,' replied Prexz. 'Rule fifty-seven.'

'Yes, I can,' said Zxerp. 'Rule seventy-two. Mugs away.'

Sullenly, Prexz threw the dice and made his opening gambit. ChuChullainn's Leap; defensive, but absolutely safe. There was no known way to break service on ChuChullainn's Leap.

'Checkmate,' said Zxerp.

In the street below, a van had drawn up outside the heavy steel doors. The King loosened his short sword in its scabbard and pulled his jacket on over it.

'Remember,' he said. 'You two wait down here, keep quiet, and do nothing. Just be ready for us when we come out.'

Hildy nodded, but Arvarodd made one last effort. 'Remember Thruthvangir,' he said.

The King stiffened. 'That was different,' he said. 'The lifts weren't working.'

'They might not be working now,' Arvarodd wheedled, 'and then where would you be?'

'For the last time,' said the King, 'you stay in the van and keep quiet. If we need help, we'll signal.'

He opened the back doors and jumped lightly out, followed by the wizard and the shape-changer. They ran silently across to the doors – Hildy was amazed to see how nimbly the wizard moved – and crouched down beside them. The wizard had taken something out of his pocket and was inserting it into the lock.

'Is that an opening spell?' Hildy whispered.

'No,' replied Arvarodd, 'it's a hairpin.'

The great door suddenly opened, and Hildy braced herself for the shrill noise of the alarm. But there was silence, and the door closed behind them.

'Well,' said Arvarodd, 'they're on their own now.' He shrugged his shoulders and ate the last digestive.

'I still don't understand,' Hildy said. 'Why tonight?'

'Obvious,' said Arvarodd with his mouth full. 'The Enemy, we hope, has gone off to Scotland. Tomorrow he'll probably be back, having guessed that we aren't there. So now's our only chance.'

'But that's not what the King said earlier.'

'Him,' Arvarodd grunted. 'Changes his mind every five minutes, he does.'

'The King said,' Hildy insisted, 'that it was too danger-ous to try it now. That's why he was so glad that the others had won us some time.'

Arvarodd sighed. 'If you must know,' he said, 'he's worried about the others. He doesn't think they'll be able to cope on their own. Probably right. He knows he ought to leave them to it but, then, he's the King. His first duty is to them. It's going to be Thruthvangir all over again.'

'What happened at Thruthvangir?'

'The lifts didn't work.' Arvarodd scowled at the steel doors. 'That's why he left me out. My orders are, if he doesn't make it, to go back to Scotland and try to save the others. I should be flattered, really.'

So that was what they had all been whispering about while she was getting petrol. 'Arvarodd,' she said quietly, 'just how dangerous do you think it is?'

'Very,' said Arvarodd, grimly. 'Like my mother used to say:

> "Fear a bear's paw, a prince's children,
> A grassy heath, embers still glowing,
> A man's sword, the smile of a maiden."

There's a lot more of that,' he continued. 'Scared me half to death when I was a kid.'

Hildy, who had, from force of habit, taken out her notebook, put it away again. The verses suggested several fascinating insights into various textual problems in the Elder Edda, but this was neither the time nor the place. 'If it's that dangerous,' she said firmly, 'we must go and help him.'

'But . . .' Arvarodd waved his hand impatiently.

'He is the King,' said Hildy cleverly. 'Our duty is to protect him.'

'Don't you start,' Arvarodd grumbled. He rolled the biscuit-wrapper up into a ball and threw it at the windscreen.

Hildy sat still for a moment, then took the seer-stone

from her bag and put it in her eye. She saw the King and his companions crossing a carpeted office. They had not seen the door open behind them, and two men in blue boiler-suits with rifles. Hildy wanted to shout and warn them. The door at the other end of the office opened, and the King shouted and drew his sword. There was a shot and Hildy cried out, but the King was still standing; the man had shot the sword out of his hand. The wizard was shrieking something, some spell or other, but it wasn't working; and Brynjolf was staring in horror at his feet, which hadn't turned into a bear's paws or the wings of an eagle. The guards were laughing. Slowly, the King and his companions raised their hands and put them on their heads.

'Can you see them?' Arvarodd was muttering. There was sweat pouring down his face.

'Yes,' Hildy said. 'It's no good; they've been captured. Their magic isn't working.' She looked round, but Arvarodd wasn't there. He had snatched up his bow and quiver, and was running towards the steel doors. Wailing, 'Wait for me,' Hildy ran after him.

The door was still open. Hildy tried to keep pace with Arvarodd as he bounded up the stairs but she could not. She stopped, panting, at the first landing, and then looked across and saw the lift. Against all her hopes, it was working. She pressed 4 – how she knew it would be the fourth floor she had no idea – and leant back to catch her breath. The doors slid open, and she hopped out.

What on earth did she think she was doing?

She turned back, but the lift doors had shut. Down the corridor she could hear the sound of running feet. She opened the door of the nearest office and slipped inside.

It was a small room, and the walls were covered with steel boxes, like gas-meters or fuseboxes. She had a sudden idea. If she could switch off the lights, perhaps the King could escape in the darkness. She pulled out her flashlight and started to read the labels. Down in a corner she saw a little glass box.

'MAGIC SUPPLY', read the label. 'DO NOT TOUCH'. And underneath, in smaller letters: 'In the event of power supply failure, break glass and press button. This will deactivate the mains-fed spell. The emergency spell will automatically take effect within seven minutes.'

With the butt of her torch Hildy smashed the glass and leant hard on the button. A moment later, the guards' rifles inexplicably turned into bunches of daffodils.

'Daffodils?' asked the King, as he banged two heads together. The wizard shrugged and made a noise like hotel plumbing.

'Fair enough,' said the King. 'Let's get out of here.'

They sprinted back the way they had come, nearly colliding with Arvarodd, who was coming up the stairs towards them.

'What happened?' he said.

'Our magic failed,' replied the King. 'Then theirs did. No idea why.'

'Have you seen Hildy?' At that moment, Hildy appeared, running towards them. 'Quick,' she gasped, 'we've only got three minutes.'

A shot from an ex-daffodil bounced off the tarmac as they drove off.

'Far be it from me to criticise,' said Thorgeir, gripping his seat-belt with both hands, 'but aren't you driving rather fast?'

The sorcerer-king grinned. 'Yes,' he said. He drove even faster. Childish, Thorgeir said to himself, but, then, he's like that. Mental age of seventeen. Only a permanent adolescent would devote hours of his valuable time to laying a spell on a Morris Minor so as to enable it to burn off Porsches at traffic lights. 'I want to get back to London as quickly as possible,' he explained.

'Then, why didn't we fly?' asked Thorgeir.

'We can do that if you like,' said the sorcerer-king mischievously. 'No problem.'

'Stop showing off,' Thorgeir said. A land-locked Morris Minor was bad enough. 'You don't seem to appreciate the situation we're in.'

'On the contrary,' said the sorcerer-king, putting his foot down hard. 'That's why I'm in such a good mood.'

'You seem to have overlooked the fact that they got away,' Thorgeir shouted above the scream of the tortured engine. He shut his eyes and muttered an ancient Finnish suspension-improving spell.

'Only by a fluke,' replied the King. 'Next time they won't be so lucky. Next time we'll be there.'

'You think there'll be a next time?'

'Has to be.' The sorcerer-king removed the suspension-improving spell and deliberately drove over the cat's eyes. 'What else can he do?'

Thorgeir, whose head had just made sharp contact with the roof, did not reply. The sorcerer-king chuckled and changed up into fourth.

'The trouble with you,' he said, 'is that you can't feel comfortable unless you're worried about something.' Thorgeir, who was both worried and profoundly uncomfortable, shook his head, but for once the sorcerer-king had his eyes on the road. 'You don't believe in happy endings. Look at it this way,' he said, overtaking a blaspheming Ferrari. 'If they had anything left in reserve, why did they try to pull that stunt last night? They're finished and they know it. That was pure Gunnar-in-the-snake-pit stuff, a one-way ticket to Valhalla. Not that I begrudge them that, of course,' said the sorcerer-king magnanimously. 'If they want to go to Valhalla, let them. Nice enough place, I suppose, except that the food all comes out of a microwave these days and the wish-maidens are definitely past their prime. A bit like one of those run-down gentlemen's clubs in Pall Mall, if you ask me.'

Thorgeir gave up and diverted his energies to worrying about the traffic police. Last time, he remembered, the sorcerer-king had let them chase him all the way from Coalville to Watford Gap, and then turned them all into horseflies. Turning them back had not been easy, especially the one who'd been eaten by a swallow.

'Now you're sulking,' said the sorcerer-king cheerfully.

'I'm not sulking,' said Thorgeir, 'I'm taking it seriously. Who did you leave in charge, by the way?'

'That young Fortescue,' said the sorcerer-king. 'Since he's in on the whole thing, we might as well make him useful. Or a frog. Whichever.'

Thorgeir shuddered. Much as he deplored unnecessary sorcery, he felt that the frog option would have been safer.

In fact, the Governor of China elect was doing a perfectly adequate job back at Gerrards Garth House. He had seen to the removal and replacement of the anti-magic circuit, debriefed the guards and written a report, all in one morning. At this rate, he felt, he might soon count as indispensable.

After putting his head round the door at Vouchers to make sure that the prisoners were still there, he sent for the chief clerk of the department and asked him about the arrangements for tracking the getaway van the burglars had used. All that was needed was a simple tap into the police computer at Hendon, he was told, to get the registered owner's name and address. Then it would be perfectly simple to slip the registration number on to the computer's list of stolen vehicles and monitor the police band until some eagle-eyed copper noticed it.

'But what if they get arrested?' Kevin asked.

'Then we'll know where they are,' replied the Chief Clerk. 'Easy.'

'No, it's not,' Kevin objected. 'They won't get bail without having plausible identities or anything, and they'll probably resist arrest and be kept in for that. And we can't go bursting into a police station to get them; it'd be too risky.'

The Chief Clerk's smile was a horrible sight. 'No sweat,' he said. 'Lots of things can happen to them. In the police cells, on remand, being transferred, on their way to the magistrates' court, anywhere you like. Easiest thing would be to wait till they're convicted and put away. We can get to them inside with no trouble at all. But I don't suppose the Third Floor will want to wait that long. Best thing is if they do resist arrest. Dead meat,' he said graphically. 'I think our police are wonderful.'

Kevin Fortescue was relieved to get back to his office, for the Chief Clerk gave him the creeps. Still, he reflected, you have to be hard to get on in Business. He dismissed the thought from his mind and took his well-thumbed *Oxford School Atlas* from his desk drawer.

'Winter Palace in Chungking,' he said to himself. 'Not too cold and a good view of the mountains.'

Danny Bennett was being shown round the Castle of Borve.

'Mind you,' said Angantyr Asmundarson, as Danny expressed polite admiration, 'it's perishing cold in winter and one hell of a way to go to get a pint of milk. Or was,' he reflected. 'We used to have our own house-cows, of course. Enchanted cows, naturally. But they were enchanted to yield mead, honey and ale, which is all very well but indigestible on porridge. Couple of Jerseys.'

Danny ducked his head under a rock lintel. The one thing he wanted was access to a television set, for his story, if it was going to break at all, would be doing so at this very minute, and it was too much to hope that anyone would tape it for him.

'That's the mead-hall through there,' said Angantyr, 'and the King's table. The main arsenals and the still-room are round the back.'

This man would make a good estate agent, Danny reflected. He nodded appreciatively and smiled. Why hadn't he bought one of those portable wrist-watch televisions, like he'd seen them wearing at the Stock Exchange?

'So how long do you think we can stay here for?' he asked.

'Indefinitely,' said Angantyr. 'You see, this place is totally hidden. Unless you know how to find it . . .'

'Yes,' said Danny, 'but you'll have to go out occasionally, to get water and food and things.'

'No need,' said Angantyr proudly. 'There's a natural spring – still there, we checked – and as for food, there's any amount of seagulls. You like seagull,' Angantyr reminded him. 'You're lucky.'

Danny repressed a shudder. 'Actually—' he started to say.

'Last time we were besieged in here,' Angantyr went on, 'we stuck it out for nine months, until the enemy got bored out of their minds and went away. We were all right, though,' said Angantyr smugly. 'We remembered to bring a couple of chess sets.'

'I can't play chess.'

'I'll teach you. It's pretty easy once you've got it into your head that the knight can go over the top of the other pieces. And there's other things to do, of course. I used to make collages with the seagull feathers. Anyway,'

Angantyr said, 'we probably won't be here too long this time. It'll all be over soon, one way or another. That reminds me.' He dashed off, and Danny sat down on a stone seat and took off his shoes. His feet were killing him after the forced march from Bettyhill. The Vikings walked very quickly.

Angantyr came back. He was holding a helmet and a suit of chain armour, and under his arm was tucked a sword and a spear.

'Try these,' he said. 'They should be small enough. Made for the King when he was twelve.'

Danny tried them on. They were much too big, and so heavy he could hardly move in them. 'Thanks,' he said, as he struggled out of the mail shirt, 'but I won't be needing them anyway, will I?'

'Don't be so pessimistic,' Angantyr said. 'There's always a bit of fighting at a siege. I remember when we were stuck in Tongue for six months—'

'You don't understand,' said Danny, 'I'm a non-combatant. Press,' he explained. 'And anyway, if there is any violence, these wouldn't help.'

'What do you mean?' said Angantyr, puzzled. Danny explained; he told him about CS gas and stun-grenades, machine-pistols and birdshot.

'You mean Special Effects,' said Angantyr. 'Don't you worry about that. All our armour is spellproof.'

'Spellproof?'

'Guaranteed. All that stuff,' he said, dismissing all human endeavour from Barthold Schwartz to napalm with a wave of his hand, 'is obsolete now.'

'No, it's not.'

'Well, it *was*. Don't say you people still believe in the white-hot heat of magic and so on. Very old-fashioned. No, all our gear's totally magic-resistant. Unless, of course, the other side's got counter-spells.'

'Counter-spells?' All this reminded Danny of something.

'Counter-spells. Of course, most of those were done away with after the MALT talks. It was only when the Enemy started cheating and using them again after we'd all dumped ours that things got unpleasant and we had to use the Brooch. That was the biggest counter-spell of them all, you see.'

'I see.' Danny rubbed his head. There was another story here, but one he had no wish to get involved in.

'Of course,' went on Angantyr, 'the Enemy's probably still got all his, and they don't make you invulnerable against conventional weapons. Still, it does even things up a bit.'

'Even so,' Danny said, 'I'm still a non-combatant. I don't know how to use swords and things.'

Angantyr shrugged his shoulders. 'Have it your own way,' he said. 'You'd better have the armour, all the same.'

Danny decided it would be easier to agree. 'I'll put it on later,' he said.

At that moment, Starkad, who had been left on watch, came running down the narrow spiral stairway. He was shouting something about a huge metal seagull with wings that went round and round. A moment later, Danny could hear the sound of rotor-blades passing close overhead and dying away in the distance.

'Dragons?' Angantyr asked. Danny told him about helicopters. 'It means they're looking for us,' he said. 'They might have those infra-red things that can trace you by your body-heat. Unless those count as magic.'

But Angantyr hadn't heard of anything like that. Danny felt vaguely proud that the twentieth century had at least one totally original invention to its credit.

'Don't like the sound of that,' Angantyr muttered.

'That's what I've been trying to tell you,' Danny said. 'This castle may have been impregnable once, but—'

Angantyr shook his head. 'Still is,' he replied. 'I don't mean that. It's just the noise that thing makes. It'll frighten off all the seagulls.'

'So now what do we do?' said Arvarodd.

'Speaking purely for myself,' said the King, 'I'll have the pancake with maple syrup. What is maple syrup?' he asked Hildy.

They were sitting in a deserted Little Chef in the middle of Buckinghamshire. How they had got there, Hildy had no idea; she had just kept on driving until the petrol-tank was nearly empty, then pulled in at the first service station for fuel and food. Her heroism of the previous night had thoroughly unnerved her, and she wanted to go home to Long Island.

'It's a sort of sweet sticky stuff you get from a tree,' she said absently. 'What *are* we going to do?'

'I haven't the faintest idea,' said the King. He was taking it all very calmly, Hildy thought. Why, if it hadn't been for her . . .

'If it hadn't been for you,' said the King suddenly, 'Odin knows what would have happened back there. That was quick thinking.'

'Pure luck,' Hildy said.

'Yes,' agreed the King, 'but quick thinking all the same. Five pancakes, please,' he ordered. 'All with maple syrup.'

'Do you think they'll follow us?' Hildy asked.

'They'll try,' said the King, 'but not too hard. We must get rid of that van first. Isn't that number written on the back and front some sort of identification mark? They're bound to have seen that. We'll sell the van in the next town we come to and get something else.'

Hildy realised that she should have thought of that. She made an effort and pulled herself together. 'And after that?' she said.

'After that, we'll do what we should have done in the first place.'

'What's that?'

'We'll get hold of that bloody wizard,' said the King grimly, 'and hold his head underwater until he thinks of something.' The wizard made a soft grinding noise, but they ignored him. 'After all, he got us into this mess.'

They stared aggressively at the wizard, who took a profound interest in his pancake. He seemed to have lost his appetite, however, and put his spoon down.

'Get on with it,' said the King. The wizard snarled and draped his paper napkin over his head. There was an anxious silence; then from under the napkin came a noise like a coffee-mill which went on for a very long time.

'Are you sure?' said the King. The coffee-mill noise started up again.

'Positive?'

The napkin nodded.

'What did he say?' Hildy demanded.

'Well,' said the King, leaning forward, 'he reckons that there's a brooch with a spell-circuit – you know, like the dragon-brooch – that might be able to cut off the magic inside the tower, and it should be possible to run it off a much weaker source of power, like a car battery.'

'How does he know about car batteries?' Hildy asked.

'Worked it out from first principles,' said the King. 'Anyway, if we get hold of this brooch, we might have a chance. According to Kotkel, it was made by Sitrygg Sow, who had the design from Odin himself. But he's only seen it once, and he's never tried it out for himself. It's a very long shot.'

'But God knows where it's got to,' said Hildy. 'Even if it still exists, it's still probably buried somewhere.'

'In that case,' said the King, 'all we'll need is a shovel and a map. You see, it belonged to a king of the Saxons down in East Anglia, and it was buried with him. One of the Wuffing kings, can't remember which one. But he was the only one buried in a ship, that I can tell you. In a minute, I'll remember the name of the place.'

'Sutton Hoo,' Hildy murmured.

'That's it,' said the King. 'How did you know that?'

'Is this brooch,' Hildy asked, 'also in the shape of a dragon?' There was a bright light in her eyes, and her hands were shaking.

'That's right,' the King said. 'More of a fire-drake, actually. Never had any taste, Sitrygg.'

'Gold inlaid with garnets?'

'Yes.'

'Then,' said Hildy, 'I know where it is. It's in London. In fact, it's in the British Museum.' She rummaged about in her organiser bag for her copy of the latest *Journal of Scandinavian Studies*. 'Is this it?' she said, thrusting the open book under the wizard's nose. The wizard pointed to plate 7*a* and nodded.

'Is that good or bad?' asked the King.

CHAPTER NINE

'Originally,' said the lecturer, 'this was believed to have been the king's standard, to which his troops rallied in time of war. It has now been reidentified as a hat-stand.'

He looked round his audience. For once, he noticed, there were a couple of intelligent faces among them. One of them, a big man with a beard, was nodding approvingly. He decided to tell them about the quotation from *Beowulf* after all.

'He's wrong, of course,' whispered Brynjolf to Hildy, 'but he wasn't to know that. Only idiots like the East Saxons would use a hat-stand for a battle-standard.'

Hildy sighed. The neatly argued little paper intended for the October edition of *Heimdall* in which she proved conclusively that the Chelmsford Standard was in fact a toast-rack would have to be shelved.

'These,' said the lecturer, pointing at a glass case, 'are among the earliest finds from the period of Scandinavian settlement in Sutherland and Caithness. The Melvich Arm-Ring . . .'

Arvarodd was staring. Hildy prodded him in the ribs,

but he didn't seem to notice. 'That's mine,' he whispered.

'Are you sure?' asked Hildy.

'Course I'm sure. Given to me when I killed my first wolf. Sure, it's only bronze, but it has great sentimental value.'

'Keep your voice down,' Hildy hissed.

'Bergthora said if I didn't chuck it out and get a new one she'd give it to a museum,' went on the hero of Permia. 'I never thought she'd do it.'

'Who was Bergthora?' Hildy asked. Arvarodd blushed.

'Although the workmanship is crude and poorly executed,' continued the lecturer, 'and not at all representative of the high Urnes style that was shortly to . . .'

'He's getting on my nerves,' Arvarodd said. Hildy glowered at him.

The lecturer moved on and started to tell his audience about a set of drinking-horns. The King and his party hung back.

'Remember,' he said, 'we're just here to have a look, so don't get carried away. We'll come back later when it's not so crowded.'

'And here we have the crowning glory of our Early Medieval collection,' the lecturer said proudly, 'the Sutton Hoo treasure. Until recently, this was the richest find ever made on the British mainland. Now, however, the recently discovered Rolfsness treasure . . .'

Arvarodd muttered something under his breath, but the wizard was pointing. So was the lecturer.

'The dragon-brooch,' he was saying, 'is one of the most interesting pieces in the entire hoard.'

When the lecture was over, and Hildy had managed to distract Arvarodd's attention when the lecturer asked if there were any questions, the King and his company went for a drink. They felt that they had earned one.

'Simple theft is what I call it,' Arvarodd complained.

'How would he like it if I took his watch and put it in a glass case and made funny remarks about it?'

'Shut up about your arm-ring,' said the King. 'They've got all my treasure down in their basement, and I'm not complaining. Well, almost all. That reminds me.'

From his finger he drew a heavy gold ring. Hildy had often admired it out of the corner of her eye.

'While we're here,' he said, 'we'd better sell this. I don't suppose there's much money left by now.'

Hildy, as treasurer, nodded sadly. She hated the thought of such a masterpiece going to some unscrupulous collector, but buying the new car had more or less cleaned them out, and even then they'd only been able to afford a horrible old wreck, held together by body putty and, after the wizard had been at it, witchcraft. She took the ring and put it in her purse.

'Back to business,' said the King. 'After we've got this brooch, we'll have to move quickly. I'm still worried about the others . . .'

At that moment the television above the bar announced the one o'clock news.

'There have been dramatic new developments,' said the newsreader, 'in the manhunt in the north of Scotland, in which the police are seeking the eight armed men who are believed to have abducted a female archaeologist and a BBC producer. Helicopters equipped with infra-red sensors . . .'

Picture of the Castle of Borve.

'Don't worry,' said Angantyr Asmundarson.

But Danny was very worried. He'd seen the police marksmen getting into position all morning, and the way Angantyr was testing his bowstring had made him shiver.

'How many do you reckon there are?' asked Hjort over his shoulder, as he plied a whetstone across his axe-blade.

'About ten each,' Angantyr replied. 'Still, if we wait a

bit longer some more may turn up.'

'Cheapskate, that's what I call it,' Hjort grumbled. 'Hardly worth sharpening up for.'

'Anyway,' said Bothvar Bjarki, 'I'm having the one with the trumpet.'

'No, you're not.'

'We drew lots,' Bothvar whined.

'You cheated,' said Hjort. 'You always cheat.'

'I did not,' replied Bothvar angrily, surreptitiously slipping his double-headed coin into Danny's jacket pocket. 'Anyway, look who's talking.'

Danny wasn't listening. He was calculating whether it would be possible to slip out unobserved while the heroes were squabbling. But, if he did, the police might shoot him. And if he were to put on one of the mail shirts the police would take him for one of the heroes and would undoubtedly shoot him.

'This is Superintendent Mackay,' came a voice from outside. 'We have you completely surrounded by armed police officers. Throw out your weapons and come out.'

That, Danny realised, could have been better phrased, given that the heroes were armed with javelins and throwing-hammers. He ducked under the parapet and put his hands over his head.

'You missed!' jeered Bothvar, as Hjort picked up another javelin.

'Of course I missed,' said Hjort, standing up to throw again. A bullet sang harmlessly off his helmet and landed at Danny's feet. 'There's few enough of them as it is without frittering them away with javelins.'

'I don't think they meant it like that,' Danny shouted. 'I think they want you to surrender.' A CS-gas canister whizzed over the parapet, spluttered and went out.

'Surrender?' Hjort's face fell under his jewel-encrusted visor. 'Are you sure?'

'Doesn't look like it to me,' said Angantyr cheerfully, as he caught a stun-grenade in his left hand. He looked at it, threw himself a catch from left to right, and hurled it back. It exploded. 'If they want us to surrender, they shouldn't be shooting at us.'

'They've stopped,' said Hjort wistfully. 'Call this a siege?'

'Here, Danny,' Angantyr said, 'what's the form these days?'

But Danny wasn't there. As soon as the shooting had stopped, he had slipped away and crawled back into the hall. Frantically he unbuttoned his shirt, which was white enough if you didn't mind the stewed seagull down the front of it, and tied the sleeves to the shaft of a javelin. He looked around, but all the heroes were at the parapet. Very cautiously, he started to climb the spiral stair.

'Reports are just coming in,' said the newsreader, 'that the police have made an attempt to storm the ruined castle where the ten men have barricaded themselves in. According to the reports, the attempt was unsuccessful. It is not yet known whether there were any casualties. A spokesman for the Historic Buildings Commission . . .'

The King clenched his right fist and pressed it into the palm of his left hand. His face was expressionless. 'I hate this job,' he said.

Hildy had taken out the seer-stone, but the King told her to put it away. 'I don't want to know,' he said. 'They'll have to look after themselves.'

'If I know them,' said Brynjolf, 'they'll be having the time of their lives.'

'Remember,' said the superintendent, 'the last thing we want is a bloodbath.'

The man in the black pullover grinned at him, his white teeth flashing out from the black greasepaint that covered his face. 'Sure,' he said, and stuck another grenade in his belt for luck. He hadn't been jolted about in a helicopter all the way from Hereford just to ask a lot of terrorists if they fancied coming quietly. 'How many of them are there?'

'Ten, according to our intelligence,' said the super-intendent.

'One each,' said the man in the black pullover. He sounded disappointed.

Just then, there was a rattling of rifle-bolts. A solitary figure with a white flag had appeared on the side of the cliff. 'Hell,' said the man in the black pullover.

'Put your hands on your head,' boomed the mega-phone, 'and walk slowly over here.' The man dropped the white flag and did as he was told.

'Be careful,' said the man in the black pullover, 'it could be a trap.' But his heart wasn't in it. He started to take the grenades out of his belt.

'It's that perishing sorcerer of yours,' muttered Hjort, staring out over the parapet. 'He's gone over to the enemy.'

'Has he indeed?' said Angantyr grimly. 'We'll soon see about that.' He bent his great ibex-horn bow and sighted along the arrow.

'Don't do that,' said Hjort. 'You'll frighten them away. And there's some more just arrived. In black,' he added, with approval.

'What's going on?' said Bothvar, dropping down beside them. He had been searching everywhere for the magic halberd of Gunnar, which he'd put away safely before going into the mound at Rolfsness. Eventually he'd found it down behind the back of the treasure-chests. 'I do wish people wouldn't move my things.'

'We've just been betrayed by a traitor,' said Angantyr.

'That's more like it,' said Bothvar.

*　　*　　*

'And we're now going over live to the armed siege in Scotland,' said the newsreader. 'Our reporter there is Moira Urquhart.'

The sorcerer-king leant forward and turned up the volume. 'Are you taping this?' he asked.

Thorgeir nodded. 'I'm having to use the "Yes, Minister" tape, but it's worth it.'

'They'll repeat it again soon, I expect,' said the sorcerer-king. 'Look, isn't that Bothvar Bjarki?' The camera had zoomed in on a helmeted head poking out above the parapet. 'I'd know that helmet anywhere.'

'I've just thought of something,' said Thorgeir. 'That armour of theirs . . .'

'One of the terrorists seems to be shouting something,' said the reporter's voice over the close-up of the helmeted head. 'We're trying to catch what he's saying . . . Something about a seagull . . . It could be that they're demanding that food is sent in.'

'I never could be doing with seagull,' said the sorcerer-king, spearing an olive. 'Except maybe in a casserole with plenty of coriander.'

'Fried in breadcrumbs, it's not too bad,' said Thorgeir. 'Isn't that Angantyr Asmundarson beside him?'

'It seems that the terrorists are in fact assuring us that they have plenty of food,' said the reporter. 'In fact they're telling us that they're capable of withstanding a long siege and inviting us to storm the castle. In fact,' said the reporter, 'they've started slow hand-clapping.'

'Childish,' said the sorcerer-king.

'And since not much seems to be happening at the moment,' said the reporter, 'I'm now going to have a few words with the BBC producer, Danny Bennett, who was held hostage by the terrorists and managed to escape a few minutes ago. Tell me, Danny . . .'

'Who's he?' asked Thorgeir.

'Search me,' said the sorcerer-king.

'They aren't terrorists at all,' Danny Bennett was saying. 'More like . . . well, it's a long story. Big, but long.' He mopped his brow with the corner of the blanket they had insisted on putting round his shoulders. 'And they didn't kidnap me.'

'You mean you went with them voluntarily?'

'Sort of,' Danny said. 'That is, they rescued me when I was wandering about lost in the mountains. I'd got separated from the rest of the crew, you see. And then they told me all about it, and it was such a big story that I decided I'd stay with them. Until the shooting started, of course.'

'I see.' The reporter was trying to get a good look at the back of Danny's head, to see if there were any signs of a recent sharp blow. Still, she reflected, it was good television.

'I can't say much about the story just now,' Danny went on, 'because it's all pretty incredible stuff and, anyway, I told Derek all about it over the phone from the police station at Bettyhill . . .'

'You mean you were in contact with the BBC at the time of the breakout?' The reporter was clearly interested. 'Are you trying to say there's been a cover-up?'

'How the hell do I know?' Danny said. 'There isn't a telly in that bloody cave.'

'What were you saying about their armour?' said the sorcerer-king.

'Oh, yes,' said Thorgeir Storm-Shepherd. 'It'll be enchanted, won't it?'

'Sod it,' said the sorcerer-king. 'Hang on, something's happening.'

'The hell with this,' said Bothvar. He was hoarse from shouting. 'If they're just going to sit there, when they know about the secret passage and everything . . .'

'Maybe they don't,' said Angantyr. 'Maybe he hasn't told them.'

Bothvar laughed, but Angantyr wasn't so sure. Danny hadn't seemed the treacherous type to him. 'Maybe he went to negotiate,' he suggested.

'Without telling us?'

'We wouldn't have let him go if he'd told us,' said Angantyr. Bothvar considered this.

'True,' said Ohtar, testing the edge of his sword with his thumb. 'And he did say he liked my cooking. Can't be all bad.'

'And what does that prove?' said Bothvar. 'The man's either a liar or an idiot. How are we for javelins, by the way?'

'Running a bit low,' said the hero Hring, who was quartermaster. 'They don't throw them back, you see.'

'That's cheating,' said Bothvar. 'If they go on like that, we'll have to stop throwing them. Still, there's rocks.'

'I think he went out there to try to negotiate,' repeated Angantyr Asmundarson. 'Otherwise they'd have made an assault on the hidden passage by now.'

'Could be,' said Hjort. He could see no other possible explanation for the enemy's lack of activity. 'After all, they outnumber us at least eight to one.' He said this very loudly, in the hope that the enemy might overhear him. They obviously needed to be encouraged.

'And he did try to warn us about the big metal seagulls they used to find us. And about the Special Effects,' Angantyr continued. 'I think he got frightened and went out to try to negotiate.'

'Frightened?' said Bothvar incredulously. 'What by?' He picked a spent bullet out of his beard and threw it away.

'In which case,' said Hring, 'they've detained a herald.'

'That's true,' said Bothvar. 'We must do something about that.'

'The King did say we were only to defend ourselves,' said the hero Egil Kjartansson, called the Dancer, or more usually the Wet Blanket. 'No attacking, those were his orders.'

'But this is different,' said Angantyr. 'Detaining a herald is just like attacking, really. You've got to rescue your heralds, or where would you be?'

There was, of course, no answer to that. 'All right then,' said Egil Kjartansson, 'but don't blame me if we get into trouble.'

'Hoo-bloody-ray, we're going to do something at last.' Hjort rubbed his hands together and put his left arm through the straps of his shield. 'Starkad! Hroar! Come over here, we're going to attack.'

The remaining heroes rushed to the parapet, while Hring distributed the javelins. Starkad Storvirksson, who was the King's berserk, lifted his great double-handed sword and began the chant to Odin.

'Can it,' Bothvar interrupted him. 'We've wasted enough time as it is.'

With one movement, like a wolf leaping, Starkad Storvirksson sprang up on to the parapet and brandished his sword. Then he hopped down again.

'Bothvar,' he said plaintively, 'I've forgotten my battle-cry.'

'It's "Starkad!", Starkad,' said Bothvar. 'Can we get on, please?'

With a deafening roar of 'Starkad!' the berserk vaulted over the parapet and led the charge. After him came Bothvar, wielding the halberd of Gunnar, with Angantyr Asmundarson close behind and Hroar almost treading on his heels. Then came Egil Kjartansson, his shield crashing against his mail shirt as he ran; Hring and Hjort,

running like hounds on a tantalising scent, and finally
Ohtar, who had finished up the seagull flan because
nobody else wanted any more, and had raging indiges-
tion as a result. In their hands their swords flashed, like
the foam on the crests of the great waves that pounded
the rocks below them, and as they ran the earth shook.
A man with a megaphone stood up as they charged,
thought better of it, and ducked down; a moment later,
Bothvar's javelin transfixed the spot where he had been
standing, its blade driven down almost to the shaft in the
dense springy peat.

'That'll do me,' said the man in the black pullover, as
the spear-shaft quivered beside him. 'Let 'em have it.'
His men shouldered their automatic rifles and started to
fire.

'Don't bother with shooting over their heads,' said the
man in the black pullover.

'We're not,' said one of his men. He looked worried.

'Told you,' said Thorgeir, pointing at the screen. The
picture was wobbling fearfully, as if the cameraman was
running: a close-up of one of the heroes, dribbling an
unexploded grenade in front of him as he charged.

'Can't think of everything, can I?' grumbled the
sorcerer-king. 'Anyway, we can fix that later.'

'It's unbelievable,' panted the reporter. 'All the bullets
and bombs and things seem to be having no effect on
them at all. They're just charging . . . And the police are
running away . . . For Christ's sake, will you get me out
of here? This is Moira Urquhart, BBC News, Borve
Castle.'

The picture shook violently and the screen went blank.
Someone had dropped the camera.

'Pity,' said the sorcerer-king. 'I was enjoying that.'

*   *   *

Bothvar Bjarki leant on his halberd and tried to get his breath back. 'Swizzle,' he gasped.

'You're out of condition, you are,' said Hjort, mopping his forehead with the hem of his cloak.

Overhead, the helicopters were receding into the distance, their fuselages riddled with javelins and arrows, flying as fast as they could in the general direction of Hereford. 'Chicken!' Hjort roared after them. He tied a knot in the barrel of an abandoned rifle and sat down in disgust.

'I nearly got the leader of those men in black,' said Starkad Storvirksson. 'I thought for a moment he was going to stand, but in the end he jumped on to the metal seagull along with all the others.' He dropped the piece of helicopter undercarriage he had been carrying and went off to help Hring pick up the arrows.

'Never mind,' said Angantyr. 'It was a victory, wasn't it?'

'I suppose so.' Bothvar yawned. 'Anyway, they might come back.' He chopped up a television camera to relieve his feelings. 'Oh, look,' he said, 'there's glass in these things.'

Angantyr sheathed his sword. 'You know what we haven't done?'

'What?'

'We haven't rescued the herald,' Angantyr said. 'That's no good, is it?'

'Maybe he wasn't a herald after all, only a traitor,' said Ohtar. He had found a lunch-box dropped in the rout and was investigating the contents. 'Anyway, we did our best.' But Angantyr jumped up and started to search. He did not have to look far. Danny, with a disappointing lack of imagination, had climbed a tree, only discovering when he reached the top that it was a thorn-tree and uninhabitable.

'Hello,' Angantyr said, 'what are you doing up there?'

'Help!' Danny explained. 'I'm stuck.'

With a few blows of his sword, Angantyr chopped through the tree and pushed it over. Danny crawled out and collapsed on the ground. 'What happened?' he said.

'We came to rescue you,' said Angantyr. 'You did go to try to negotiate, didn't you?' he asked as an afterthought. Danny assured him that he had. 'And you didn't tell them about the secret passage?'

'Of course not,' Danny replied. He had tried to, but no one would listen.

'That's all right, then,' Angantyr said cheerfully. 'You've got thorns sticking in you.' Danny followed Angantyr back to where the other heroes were sitting and thanked them for rescuing him. He didn't feel in the least grateful, but having seen the heroes in action he reckoned that tact was probably called for.

'No trouble,' said Ohtar. He bit into a chocolate roll he'd found in the lunch-box and spat it out again. 'Don't like that,' he said.

'You're supposed to take the foil off first,' Danny said.

'Gold-plated food,' said Ohtar admiringly. 'Stylish.'

The spokesman from Highlands and Islands Development Board was refusing to comment, and Thorgeir switched the set off. The sorcerer-king was counting on his fingers.

'So that leaves four unaccounted for,' he said. 'The King, the wizard, Arvarodd of Permia and Brynjolf the Shape-Shifter.'

'Plus that lady archaeologist makes five,' said Thorgeir. 'Trouble is we haven't the faintest idea where they are.'

'You're worrying again,' said the sorcerer-king. He turned to his desk and tapped a code into his desktop terminal.

'Trying the Hendon computer again?' Thorgeir asked.

The sorcerer-king shook his head, and pointed to the screen. On a green background, little Viking figures were rushing backwards and forwards, vainly trying to avoid the two ravening wolves that were chasing them through a stylised maze.

'I had young Fortescue run it up for me this morning,' said the sorcerer-king. 'He's good with computers, that boy.'

Thorgeir shook his head sadly, but said nothing. There had been a word in one of the Old Norse dialects that exactly described the sorcerer-king. 'Yuppje,' he murmured under his breath, and went away to get on with some work.

The new car, despite being a useless old wreck, had a radio in it, and the King's company were listening to the news.

'The search is continuing,' said the newsreader, 'for the ten men who routed police and SAS units in a pitched battle in the north of Scotland yesterday. They are believed still to be in the Strathnaver district. Two companies of Royal Marines have reinforced the police, and Harriers from RAF Lossiemouth are on standby. In the House of Commons, the Defence Minister has refused to reply to Opposition questions until the conclusion of the operation.'

The King shrugged his shoulders. 'Might as well leave them to it,' he said. 'They seem to be coping.'

'You should have told me about the armour,' Hildy said.

'You should have told me about the Special Effects,' replied the King. 'Now you see what I mean about the decline of civilisation. But we can't leave things too long. It depends on what he's doing. If he's gone up there or sent someone to put a counter-spell on the lads, it'll all be over in a matter of minutes. Of course, he'll have to find them first. But with luck . . .'

Hildy parked the car, praying that it wouldn't be clamped while they were inside the Museum, for that would interfere quite horribly with their well-planned escape. Still, she reflected, so many things could go wrong with this lunatic enterprise that it was pointless to worry about any one of them.

The King, the wizard, Arvarodd and Brynjolf had put their mail shirts on under large raincoats bought that afternoon with part of the proceeds of the King's ring and hung short swords by their sides. For her part, Hildy had been given a small flat pebble with a rune scratched on it which was supposed to have roughly the same effect as an enchanted mail shirt, and she had put it in her pocket wrapped up in two handkerchieves and a scarf, to protect her against the side-effect (incessant sneezing). She had also found the magic charms that Arvarodd had lent her on her first trip to London; she offered to return them, but Arvarodd had smiled and told her to hang on to them for the time being.

Past the guards at the big revolving door without any trouble. Up the main staircase and through the Egyptian galleries, then out along a room full of Greek vases and they were there.

The lecturer was giving the afternoon lecture. This time his audience consisted of five Germans, three schoolboys, a middle-aged woman and her small and disruptive nephew. No point in even considering the *Beowulf* quotation.

'Well,' said Brynjolf, as they stood in front of the big glass case that contained the shield, harp and helmet, 'what's the plan?'

'Who needs a plan?' replied the King. 'But we'll just wait till these people go away again.'

'That's all wrong, of course,' said Arvarodd, contemplating the helmet, which teams of scholars had pieced together from a handful of twisted and rusty fragments. 'You imagine wearing that.'

Unfortunately the lecturer, who was just approaching the Sutton Hoo exhibit, took that as a question. After all, it was a comment he had often been faced with, and by now he had worked out a short and well-phrased answer. He gave it. Arvarodd listened impatiently.

'Here,' he said when the lecturer had finished, 'give me a pencil and a bit of paper.' Resting the paper on the side of the glass case, he drew a quick sketch of what the helmet should have looked like. 'Try that,' he said.

'But that . . . that's brilliant,' said the lecturer, his audience quite forgotten. 'So that's what that little bobble thing was for.'

'Stands to reason,' said Arvarodd.

The lecturer beamed. 'Tell me, Mr . . .'

'Arvarodd,' said Arvarodd.

The lecturer stared. Perhaps it was something in the man's eyes, but there was something about him that made the hair on the back of the lecturer's head start to rise. The palms of his clenched hands were wet now, and he found it difficult to breathe. He narrowed his eyebrows.

'Arvarodd?'

'That's right,' said Arvarodd.

The lecturer took a deep breath. 'Aren't you the Arvarodd who went to Permia?' he asked.

Arvarodd hit him.

'That,' he said, 'is for stealing my arm-ring.' He strode across to the glass case, drew his short sword, and smashed the glass. Alarms went off all over the building.

'Quick,' said the King. With his own short sword, he smashed open the case containing the brooch, grabbed it, and stuffed it into his pocket. The middle-aged woman shrieked, and the small nephew kicked him. 'Right,' said the King, 'move!'

But Arvarodd was gazing at his arm-ring, running his fingers over the beloved metal, his mind full only of the image of his first wolf, at bay on the hillside above Crackaig. The lecturer wiped the blood from his nose and staggered to his feet.

'*Your* arm-ring?' he said in wonder.

'Yes,' snapped Arvarodd, wheeling round. His hand tightened on his sword-hilt. 'Want to make something of it?'

'But it's eighth-century,' said the lecturer. 'And you're seventh.'

'Who are you calling seventh-century?'

'But your saga . . .' Heedless of personal danger, the lecturer grabbed his sleeve. 'Definitely set in seventh-century Norway.'

'I know,' said Arvarodd sadly. 'Bloody editors,' he explained.

Suddenly, the gallery was filled with large men in blue uniforms. Before Hildy could warn them, they ran towards the King. Glass cases crashed to the ground.

'Oh, no,' Hildy wailed, as a case of silver dishes was crushed beneath a stunned guard, 'not here.' Suddenly she remembered Arvarodd's magic charms. She fished in her pocket and pulled out the fragment of bone that made you irresistibly persuasive. Quickly she seized hold of the nearest guard.

'Not theft,' she said, 'fire.'

The guard looked at her. She tightened her hand round the fragment of bone. 'Fire,' she repeated. 'It's a fire alarm.'

'Oh,' said the guard. 'Right you are, miss.' He hurried off to tell the others. The battle stopped.

'Then, why did he break that glass case?' asked the chief guard.

'You know what it says on the notices,' replied Hildy desperately. 'In case of fire, break glass.'

The guards dashed away to evacuate the galleries.

Just as Hildy had feared, they had clamped the car. But the King was in no mood to be worried by a little thing like that. With a single blow of his sword, he sliced through the yellow metal and flicked away the wreckage. There were several cheers from passing motorists. The King and his company jumped into the car and drove away.

'That was quick thinking,' said the King, as Hildy accelerated over Waterloo Bridge.

'What was?'

'The way you got rid of those guards.'

'It was nothing,' Hildy said quietly. 'It was all down to that jawbone thing of Arvarodd's.'

'Nevertheless,' the King smiled, 'I think you've definitely done enough to deserve a Name.'

'A Name?' Hildy gasped. 'You mean a proper Heroic Name?' She flushed with pleasure.

'Yes,' replied the King. 'Like Harald Bluetooth or Sigurd the Fat, or,' he added maliciously, 'Arvarodd of Permia. Hasn't she, lads?'

From the back seat, the heroes and the wizard expressed their approval. In fact Arvarodd had been addressing himself to the problem of a suitable Name for Hildy for quite some time; but even the best he had come up with, Swan-Hildy, was clearly inappropriate.

'So from now on,' said the King, 'our sister Hildy Frederik's-daughter shall be known by the name of Vel-Hilda.'

'Vel-Hilda?' Hildy frowned. 'I don't get it,' she said at last.

The King grinned. 'The Norse word *vel*,' he said, 'as you know better than I, is short and means "well". The same, Hildy Frederik's-daughter, may be said of you. Therefore . . .'

'Oh,' said Hildy. 'I see.'

CHAPTER TEN

'Checkmate.'

Anyone looking through binoculars at the darkened windows of Gerrards Garth House would have thought that someone was signalling with a torch. In fact the little points of flickering light were Prexz, blinking in disbelief.

'Ninety-nine thousand, nine hundred and ninety-nine sets and nine games to you,' said Zxerp, almost beside himself with malicious pleasure, 'and *nine* games to me. All the nines,' he added, and sniggered.

'You're cheating,' Prexz muttered. But Zxerp only smiled.

'Impossible to cheat at Goblin's Teeth,' he said benignly. 'God knows, I've tried often enough. No, old chum, you've just got to face the fact that I'm on a winning streak. Mugs away.'

'Let's play Snapdragon, for a change.'

'Your move.'

'Or Dungeons and Dragons. You used to like Dungeons and Dragons.'

'Or would you rather I moved first?' Zxerp grinned broadly. 'For once.'

Angrily, Prexz slammed down the dice and moved his knight six spaces.

'"Go directly to Jotunheim",' Zxerp read aloud. 'Hard luck, what a shame, never mind. Six,' he noted, as he examined the dice he had thrown. 'Getting to be quite a habit. I think I'll take your rook.'

'I think it's something to do with that thing over there,' grumbled Prexz. He pointed at the computer banks.

'Could be,' said Zxerp. 'But . . .' He quoted Rule 138. Prexz muttered something about gamesmanship and tried to get his knight out of Jotunheim. He failed.

'And now your other rook,' chuckled Zxerp. 'That's bad, losing both your rooks. Remember how I always used to do that?'

Suddenly, the room was flooded with light. From somewhere down the corridor came the noise of confused shouting and the ring of metal. Zxerp looked up, and Prexz nudged his queen on to a black square.

'I'll see you,' he said.

But Zxerp wasn't listening. 'Something's happening,' he whispered.

'I know,' replied Prexz, 'I'm seeing you.'

'Shut up a minute,' hissed Zxerp. 'There's someone coming.'

The door to the office flew open. Five men in boiler-suits staggered into the room, beating vainly at an enormous bear with bunches of marigolds and tulips. With a swipe of his huge paw, the bear sent them flying into the computer bank, which was smashed to pieces. The bear stopped, nibbled at the tulips for a moment, then advanced on its terrified assailants, who took cover behind the spirits' tank. At that moment, the King, Hildy and the wizard came running in.

'Here they are,' shouted Hildy. The bear vanished, and was replaced by Brynjolf the Shape-Changer, spitting out tulip petals. 'What kept you?' asked Brynjolf.

The King looked down at the front of his coat, to make sure the Sutton Hoo brooch was still there, and drew his short sword. The men in boiler-suits covered their eyes and whimpered as he strode up to the tank, but the King paid no attention to them. With a wristy blow, he shattered the glass.

'Quick,' he said to the wizard. In the doorway Arvarodd appeared. He had a boiler-suited guard in each hand, and there was pollen all over his sleeves. 'All clear,' he said. 'The rest of them have bolted, but I don't think they're going to bother us.'

The wizard had disconnected the wires around the spirits' throats, and replaced them with wires of his own. Prexz struggled for a moment, but Zxerp was too busy bundling the pieces into their box to offer any resistance. All over the building, sirens were blaring.

'Right,' said the King, 'that's that done. Time we were on our way.'

At the end of the corridor, Thorgeir Storm-Shepherd crouched behind a fire-door and listened. He had been working late, trying to catch up on the Japanese deal. He had realised immediately what was happening, and had hurried down to see the King and his bunch of idiots being blasted back into the realms of folk-tale by the automatic weapons of Vouchers. From his hiding-place he had seen the guns turn into bunches of flowers, and Arvarodd and Brynjolf scattering the bemused guards. He had seen the Sutton Hoo brooch on King Hrolf's chest. It had reminded him that he never had tracked down the prototype of the Luck of Caithness.

He should have had two options, he reflected. One would have been to stand and fight, the other to run away.

The latter option would have had a great deal to be said for it, but sadly it was no longer available to him. He sighed, and glanced down at his crocodile shoes, his all-wool Savile Row suit, and the backs of his hands, which were now covered in shaggy grey fur. His nails had become claws again, and his dental plate was being forced out of his mouth by the vulpine fangs that were sprouting from his upper jaw. He pricked up his ears, growled softly, and wriggled out of his human clothes. Wolf in sheep's clothing, he thought ruefully. He lifted his head and howled.

'Jesus!' said Hildy. 'What was that?'

'Just a wolf, that's all,' said Arvarodd, tightening his grip on the two squirming guards. 'Hang on, though,' he said and frowned. 'I knew there was something odd going on, ever since I woke up in the ship, but I couldn't quite put my finger on it. No wolves.'

'There aren't any more wolves,' said Hildy, shuddering. 'They're extinct in the British Isles.' She had never actually seen a wolf, not even in a zoo; but she remembered enough biology to know that wolves are related to dogs, and she was terrified of all dogs, especially Airedales.

'No, you're wrong there,' said Arvarodd firmly. There was a hopeful light in his eyes, and he was fingering his newly recovered arm-ring. 'For a start, there's one just down the corridor. Here, hold these for me.' He thrust the two guards at Hildy and ran off down the corridor. Without thinking, Hildy grabbed the guards by the collar. They made no attempt to escape.

'Where's he gone?' asked the King. 'We haven't got time to fool about.'

'He heard a wolf,' said Hildy faintly.

'Him and his dratted wolves,' said the King impatiently. 'All he thinks about.'

'But there aren't any wolves,' Hildy insisted, 'not any more.'

'Oh.' The King turned his head sharply. 'Aren't there now?' He looked at the wizard, who nodded. 'That's awkward,' he said.

'Awkward?'

'Awkward. You see, our enemy had a henchman, Thorgeir Storm-Shepherd. Originally, Thorgeir was not a human being but a timber-wolf of immense size and ferocity, whom the enemy transformed into a human being by the power of his magic . . .' He fell silent.

'And the magic's been cancelled out by the brooch we took from the Museum,' said Brynjolf. He was looking decidedly nervous. 'So if Thorgeir's anywhere in the building he'll have changed back into a wolf.'

'Who is this person?' Hildy asked, but the King made no reply. 'Someone ought to go and tell Arvarodd that that isn't an ordinary wolf,' he said quietly. 'Otherwise he might get a nasty shock.'

As it happened, Arvarodd was on the point of finding out for himself. The excitement of the wolf-hunt had chased all other thoughts from his mind: the quest, the need to get out quickly, even his duty to his King. It did not occur to him that office-blocks are not a normal habitat for normal wolves until he rounded a corner and came face to face with his quarry. He drew his short sword and braced himself for the onset of the animal; as he did so, he noticed that this was a particularly large wolf, bigger than any he could recall having seen in all his seasons with the Caithness and Sutherland. The fact that its coat was so dark as almost to be black was not that unusual – melanistic wolves had not been so uncommon, even in his day – but the way that its eyes blazed with unearthly fire and the foam from its slavering jaws burnt holes in the carpet tiles marked it out as distinctly unusual. A collector's item, he muttered to himself, as he tightened his grip on his sword-hilt.

The wolf was in no hurry to attack. It stood and pawed at the carpet, growling menacingly and lashing its tail back and forth. In fact it was trying to remember exactly how a wolf springs, and regretting the second helping of cheesecake it had had with its dinner at the Wine Vaults that evening. It is difficult for a wolf to feel particularly bellicose on a full stomach, unless its whelps are being threatened; and Thorgeir's whelps, to the best of his knowledge, were quite safe in their dormitory at Harrow. He growled again, and showed his enormous fangs. Arvarodd stood still, just like the picture in the coaching manual: weight on the back foot, head steady, left shoulder well forward.

'Get on with it,' growled the wolf.

Arvarodd raised an eyebrow. Wolves that talked were a novelty to him, and he didn't think it was strictly ethical. 'Did you say something?' he said coldly.

'I said get on with it,' replied the wolf. 'Or are you scared?'

'If I was scared, I wouldn't be standing here,' said Arvarodd indignantly. 'I'd be running back down the passage, wouldn't I?'

'Not if you were too terrified to move,' said the wolf. 'Then you'd just be standing there mesmerised, waiting for me to spring. Rabbits do that.'

'But I'm not a rabbit,' Arvarodd pointed out. 'And I'm not mesmerised. Neither am I stupid. It's your job to attack.'

'Says you,' retorted the wolf. 'So let's have less chat and more action, shall we? Unless,' he added, trying to sound unconcerned, 'you'd rather scratch the whole fixture.'

'You what?'

'I mean,' said the wolf, relaxing slightly, 'you're not going to attack, and I'm buggered if I am. So we can wait here all night, until the sorcerer-king turns up and zaps you into a cinder, or we can go our separate ways and say no more about it. Up to you, really.'

'You're not really a wolf, are you?' said Arvarodd.

'Don't be daft,' said the wolf, and growled convincingly. But Arvarodd had remembered something.

'Our enemy had a sidekick called Thorgeir,' he said. 'Nasty piece of work. Used to be a wolf, by all accounts. Not a pure-bred wolf, of course.' The wolf snarled and lashed its tail. Arvarodd pretended not to notice. 'I seem to remember there was a story about his mother and a large brindled Alsatian—'

The wolf sprang, but Arvarodd was ready for it. He stepped out of the way and struck two-handed at the beast's neck (plenty of bottom hand and remember to *roll those wrists!*). But the wolf must have sensed that he was about to strike, or perhaps instinct made him twist his shoulders round; Arvarodd's blow overreached, so that his forearms struck on the wolf's back and the sword was jarred out of his hands. The wolf landed, turned and prepared to spring again. Arvarodd shot a glance at the sword, lying on the other side of the corridor, then clenched his fists. As he prepared to meet the animal's onslaught, he thought of what his coach had told him about facing an angry wolf when disarmed. 'Stand well forward and brace your feet,' he had said. 'That way, the wolf might break your neck before he has a chance to get his teeth into you.'

'Never believed that story myself,' he said. 'I hate malicious gossip, don't you?'

'No,' snapped the wolf, and leapt at his throat.

'Hell,' said the King. 'A wire's come loose on the brooch. Look.'

* * *

When the wolf turned back into a middle-aged stark-naked businessman in mid-air, Arvarodd was surprised but pleased. He made a fine instinctive tackle, and threw his assailant through a plate-glass door. Then he made a grab for the sword. But Thorgeir had the advantage of local knowledge. He picked himself up and ran. After a short chase through a labyrinth of offices, Arvarodd gave up. After all, his enemy might change back into a wolf again at any minute, and he was clearly out of practice. He retraced his steps, and met the King and his company by the lift-shaft.

'Where the hell have you been?' said the King.

'There was this wolf,' said Arvarodd, 'only he wasn't. I think it was Thorgeir.'

The King seemed to regard this as a reasonable explanation. 'We've got to go now. This brooch got unconnected from its batteries for a couple of minutes, and I'm not going to take any chances.'

'Good idea,' said Arvarodd. He was feeling slightly foolish. But not as foolish as Thorgeir. No sooner had he escaped from Arvarodd than he changed back into a wolf; and then, as he had gone bounding down the corridor to see if he could continue the fight where he had left it, he had turned back into a human being again, at the very moment when the King (and the Sutton Hoo brooch) had left the building. He gave the whole thing up as a bad job and went to look for his clothes.

As soon as he saw the smashed tank and the cowering guards, he guessed what had happened. He sat down on a wrecked photocopier and thought hard. He ought to go at once to the sorcerer-king and warn him, to give him time to prepare his defences. But something seemed to tell him that this would be a bad idea. What if the sorcerer-king should lose and be overthrown? Thorgeir bit his lip and forced himself to consider the possible consequences.

On the one hand, the boss's magic had preserved him, in human form, for twelve hundred years – without it, he would go back to being a twelve-hundred-year-old wolf, and wolves do not, even in captivity, usually live more than sixteen years. If the sorcerer-king's spell was broken, he would become, in quick succession, an extremely elderly wolf and a dead wolf; and if that had been the pinnacle of his ambition he would never have left the Kola Peninsula. On the other hand, King Hrolf's wizard was presumably competent in all grades of anthropo-morphic and life-prolonging magic, and his employer might just be persuaded to do a little deal. On the third hand, if the sorcerer-king won, which was not unlikely, and he found out that his trusty aide had betrayed him, being a dead wolf would be a positive pleasure compared to the penalty the boss would be likely to impose. Tricky, Thorgeir thought. He took a small slice of marrowbone from his pocket and chewed on it to clear his head.

Of course, in order for the sorcerer-king to win or lose, there would have to be a battle; if he could make sure that that battle took place, quickly and on relatively even terms, he could then have a claim on the eventual winner, whoever he turned out to be. Looked at from all sides, that was the safest course, but there was one deadly draw-back; he didn't have the faintest idea where King Hrolf was. He sighed, spat out the marrowbone, and put his socks back on. Just then, the telephone rang. He picked it up without thinking.

'Olafsen here,' he said. Who could it be at this time of night?

'Mr Olafsen?' It was the governor-presumptive of China Thorgeir groaned; he was not in the mood for young Mr Fortescue.

'I thought I should tell someone at once,' said young Mr Fortescue. 'I've just heard that the car that Our

Enemies are using,' and he mentioned the type and registration number, 'has been traced and seen by a police patrol in Holland Park. I'm there now, in fact. I'm talking to you' – there was a hint of pride in the young man's voice – 'over my carphone. What should I do now?'

Thorgeir muttered a quick prayer to Loki, god of villains, and said: 'Follow them. For crying out loud, don't lose them. And keep me posted on my personal number, will you?'

'Will do, Mr Olafsen. Do you think,' asked Mr Fortescue diffidently, 'I could have Korea as well?'

'Of course you can,' replied Thorgeir indulgently. 'So long as you don't lose that car, you can have Korea and Mongolia as well.'

'Thanks, Mr Olafsen.'

Thorgeir put the receiver down, and found an unbroken computer terminal. Within a few minutes, he had withdrawn the car from the police computer – the last thing anyone wanted was a cloud of bluebottles getting in the way. Then he sprinted down to the underground carpark and got out his car. Almost before he had closed the door, the phone buzzed.

'They're just moving,' said Mr Fortescue. 'Going up towards Ladbroke Grove.'

'Stay with them,' urged Thorgeir. 'I'll be with you shortly. And Tibet,' he added.

Just as the dial reached £11.65, petrol started to overflow from the tank, and Hildy put the filler nozzle back in its holder and went to pay. Just her luck, she reflected; another thirty-five pence worth of petrol, and she would have got two Esso tokens, which would have been enough for the trailing flex.

Had she been a true Viking, of course, she would have gone on filling, and to hell with the spilt petrol and the fire risk. Reckless courage was the hallmark of the warrior. She looked at her reflection in the plate-glass window of the filling station and, not for the first time, wished that there was rather less of her face and rather more of the rest of her. Short and means well. True. Very true.

As she waited her turn in the queue, it occurred to her that if she bought a couple of Mars bars, she could knock the grand total up over twelve pounds. Shrewdness and cunning are the hallmark of the counsellor, and you don't have to look like one of those creatures on the magazine covers to be clever. The cashier took her money and handed her one token.

'Excuse me,' she said assertively, 'my purchases were over twelve pounds. I should get two tokens.'

'Only applies to petrol,' said the cashier. 'Can't you read?'

Someone in the queue behind her sniggered. She scooped up her token and fled.

'What's up?' said the King. 'You look upset.'

For a split second, she toyed with the idea of asking the King to go and split the cashier's skull for her, but she decided against it. That would be over-reacting, and the wise man knows when to do nothing, as the Edda says. 'No, I'm not,' she replied. 'Where to now?'

'Somewhere nice and quiet,' said the King, 'where we won't be disturbed.'

Hildy nodded and started the engine. She drove for nearly an hour in silence, heading for no great reason for the Chilterns. The heroes were asleep, and the wizard was reading a spell from a vellum scroll by the faint light of Zxerp and Prexz.

'This'll do,' said the King.

Hildy stopped the car beside a small spinney of beech-trees and switched off the lights. The car which had been behind her all the way from London drove on past and disappeared round a corner. Hildy breathed a faint sigh of relief; she had been slightly worried about that.

'I don't suppose anyone's considered anything so prosaic as food lately,' said Brynjolf, stretching his arms and yawning. 'I had this marvellous dream about roast venison.' Hildy frowned and offered him a Mars bar.

'What's this?' he asked.

'You eat it,' Hildy said.

Brynjolf shrugged, and did as she suggested. Then he spat. 'No, but really,' he said. 'A joke's a joke, but—'

'Go turn yourself into a sandwich, then,' Hildy snapped. 'I'm exhausted, and I can't be doing—'

'All right,' said Arvarodd wearily, 'leave it to me. Only it'll have to be rabbit again.'

'If I have any more rabbit,' said Brynjolf, 'I'll start to look like one.'

'That's a thought,' replied Arvarodd. 'Decoy,' he explained. The two heroes got out of the car and wandered away.

'That, Vel-Hilda,' said the King, 'is heroic life for you. Rabbit seven times a week, and that's if you're lucky. Just be grateful you're not on a longship. Let's get some air.' He opened his door and climbed out, stretching his cramped limbs.

'Will the wizard be all right on his own?' whispered Hildy. 'I mean . . .'

'We won't go far,' said the King. 'You'll be all right, won't you, Kotkel?'

The wizard looked up from his scroll, nodded absently, and muttered a spell. On the seat beside him a giant hound appeared.

'Just a hallucination,' explained the King, 'but who's to know?'

Hildy shrugged, and strolled out into the spinney. It was a still night, slightly cold, and the wind was moving the leaves on the tops of the trees. The King spread his cloak over a stump and sat down. Across his knees he laid his broadsword in its jewelled scabbard.

'This sword,' he said, 'is called Tyrving. You're interested in the old days. Would you like to hear about it?'

Hildy nodded, and sat down beside him.

'One day,' said the King, in a practised storyteller's voice, 'the gods Odin and Loki were out walking far from home. Why, I cannot tell you. I always thought it was a strange thing for them to be doing, since by all accounts they hated each other like poison. However, they were out walking, and there was a sudden thunderstorm. Again, it seems strange that Thor should inflict a sudden thunder-storm on his liege-lord and best friend Odin for no reason, but perhaps it was his idea of a joke. Odin and Loki sought shelter in a little house, where they were greeted by a little old woman. She did not know that they were gods, so the story goes – and if you believe that, you'll believe anything; but she offered them some broth, although she had little enough for herself, and put the last of the peat on the fire so that they might be warm. All clear so far?'

'Yes,' said Hildy. 'Go on.'

'When the two gods had finished their broth and dried their clothes, they lay down to sleep. The old woman gave them all her blankets, and the pelts of otters for pillows. In the morning the gods woke up and it had stopped raining. "Old woman," said Odin, "you have treated us kindly." I don't know if Odin was given to understatement, but that's what the story says. "Learn that the guests you have sheltered are in fact the gods Odin and Loki. In return for your hospitality, I shall give you a great gift." And he drew from his belt his own sword, which the dwarfs had forged for him in the caverns of Niflheim, and gave it to the old woman, who thanked him politely,

no doubt through clenched teeth. Odin then put a blessing on the sword, saying that whoever wielded it in battle
should have victory. But Loki, who is a malevolent god,
put a curse on it, saying that the first man to draw it in
battle should eventually die from a blow from it. The old
woman put the sword away safely, and in due course she
gave it to her grandson Skjold, who went on to become
the greatest of the Joms-vikings. When Skjold was an old
man, and had long since given up fighting, he used to
laugh at Loki's curse. But one day he was teaching his
little son Thjostolf how to fight, and Thjostolf parried a
blow rather too vigorously. Skjold's sword flew from his
hand and struck him above the eye, killing him instantly.
Thjostolf went on to lead the Joms-vikings as his father
had done, and when he died his son Yngvar succeeded
him, and the sword brought him victory. But one day he
lost the sword when out hunting, and in the next battle
he fought he was killed, and all his men with him.
Eventually, the sword came into the hands of my grandfather, Eyjolf, who was Odin's grandson. That story is
supposed to prove something or other, but I forget what.'

Hildy sat still and said nothing. The moon, coming out
from behind a cloud, cast a shaft of light through the
trees which fell on the hilt of the sword, making it sparkle.
The King smiled, and with an easy movement of his arm
drew the sword from its scabbard. For some reason, Hildy
started to shiver. In the moonlight the blade glowed eerily,
and the runes engraved on its hilt stood out firm and
clear.

'Of the sword itself,' continued the King, 'this is said.
The blade is the true dwarf-steel, but the hilt and furniture was replaced by Yngvar with the hilt of the sword
Gram, which Sigurd the Dragon-Slayer bore. The blade
of that sword was lost, but the hilt was preserved as an
heirloom by the children of Atli of Hungary. In turn, my

grandfather Eyjolf had a new quillon added; that came from the sword Helvegr, which once belonged to the Frost-Giants of Permia. My father Ketil added the scabbard, which once housed the sword of the god Frey, and fitted to the pommel the great white jewel called the Earthstar, which fell from the sky on the day I was born, and after which I am named.' He smiled, and laid his hand gently on the hilt. 'It's not a bad sword, at that. A bit on the light side for me, but nicely balanced. Here.' And he passed the sword to Hildy. For a moment she dared not take it; then she grasped it firmly and lifted it up. She was amazed by how light it seemed, like a living thing in her hands.

'It's wonderful,' she said. As she gazed at it, blazing coldly in the moonlight, her eyes were suddenly opened, and she saw, as in a dream, the faces of many kings and warriors, and blood red on the blue steel. She saw the dwarfs busy over their forge in a great cave, vivid in the orange light of the forge, and heard the sound of their hammers, the hiss as the hot metal was tempered, and the scrape of whetstones as the edge was laid. She saw a tall dark figure muffled in a cloak, who watched the work and added to the skill of the smiths the power of wind, tide and lightning. She saw him take the blade in his hands, as she was doing now, and look down it to make sure that it was straight and true. Then, suddenly as it had come, the vision departed, leaving only the moonlight, still flickering on the runes cut into the langet of the hilt. As she spelt out the letters one by one, her heart was beating like a blacksmith's hammer.

Product of more than one country.

The moon went back behind its cloud.

'Very nice,' she said, and gave it back to the King, who grinned and slid it back into the scabbard.

'For all I know,' he said, 'the legends are all perfectly

true. True but largely unimportant. Like I said, that's heroic life for you. Like all heroes have magnificent bushy beards because it's difficult to shave on a storm-tossed longship without cutting yourself to the bone.'

'I see,' said Hildy.

'And this particular adventure,' said the King, 'is all heroic life, too; and you are a heroine just as much as we are heroes. It's incredibly dangerous, but you haven't been thinking about that. Just a game, a little reprise of child-hood – or why do you think that in the end all the legends of heroes and warriors end up as children's stories? When I was a little boy, I wanted to be a fisherman.'

'When I was a little girl,' said Hildy, 'I wanted to be a Viking.' She laughed suddenly. 'It's been fun,' she said, 'but not in the way I thought it would be. If we do get killed, will we go to Valhalla, across the Rainbow Bridge?'

'The Rainbow Bridge,' said the King, 'is something to be crossed when you come to it. If we fail, then we leave the world in the hands of its natural enemy. But, for all I know, nobody would notice except a few of the leading statesmen. Still, that's not a risk worth taking. Not only is our enemy very cruel and very evil, he is also very, very stupid. A good magician – the best ever – but I would-n't trust him with running a dog-show, let alone the world. And I don't think, for all his magic, that he could ever become ruler of the world; if he can't catch us, then he hasn't got the resources, and anyway I think the world has changed too much, though I don't suppose he's realised. But what he would almost certainly do is start enough wars to finish off the human race, one way or another, which would be rather worse. And he's certainly a good enough magician to manage that.'

'Don't let's talk about it,' said Hildy. 'We'd better go see how Kotkel's getting on.'

Just then, Arvarodd came hurrying up. Brynjolf was

with him, dragging along a man by the lapels of his jacket.

'Guess who's just turned up,' said Arvarodd.

'My liege,' said the man, bowing low to the King. 'I have come . . .'

'Hello, Thorgeir,' said the King. 'I was expecting you.'

'Thorgeir?' Hildy stared. 'You said he was a wolf or something.'

'Only sometimes,' said the man. 'It's a long story.'

'Shaggy-wolf story,' muttered Arvarodd. 'I found him snooping about in the woods back there. By the way, we couldn't find any rabbits, so it'll have to be squirrel.'

'I wasn't snooping,' said Thorgeir. 'I came here to tell you something that you might like to hear.'

'How did you find us?' The King's face was expressionless.

'Oh, that was easy,' said Thorgeir. He smoothed out the lapels of his jacket and sat down, his manner suggesting that he wouldn't mind at all if they all did the same. 'You don't suppose I haven't known all along, do you?'

'Of course you didn't know,' said the King. 'Otherwise we'd all be dead.'

'You'd have been dead if my lord and master knew where you were,' said Thorgeir patronisingly. 'I knew all along. He leaves things like that to me, you see, and a lot of trouble I've had keeping it from him.'

'And why should you want to do that?' asked the King.

'Guess.' Thorgeir smiled.

'For some reason, envy or fear or hatred, you want to betray him to us. Or you wanted to see which of us was more likely to win before you chose sides.' The King raised an eyebrow. 'Something like that?'

'More or less.' Thorgeir scratched his ear, where for some reason a little grey fur still remained. But the King's eyes were on him.

'I was born,' said the King, 'in the seventh year of the

reign of Ketil Trout. In other words, not yesterday. What you meant to say was that owing to your extreme negligence we were able not only to escape the notice of your lord and master, but also to recapture the two earth-spirits we need to overthrow his power. As soon as you realised that we had an even chance of winning, you decided to hedge your bets. By a stroke of good luck – I can't say what, but I expect I'm right – you found us. You decided to come to me and persuade me to attack at a certain time and place. If I win, you claim to have given me victory. If he wins, you can claim to have brought me to him. Correct?'

'Absolutely.' Thorgeir widened his smile slightly. 'Isn't that what I said?'

'More or less.' The King leant back and thought for a moment. 'What you will do is this. You will get in touch with your master and tell him that you have found us, that we are weak and unprepared, and that something has gone wrong with our magic. You will do this gladly,' said the King, 'because for all I know it may very well be true and, if I lose, you can take the credit, as you originally planned. While we are waiting for our enemy to arrive, you will tell me everything you know about his strength and, more important, his weaknesses. You will do this truthfully, firstly because if you do not my champion Arvarodd will cut you in half, secondly because it probably won't have any effect on the outcome, one way or another. Is that clear?'

'As crystal.' Thorgeir nodded approvingly. 'But what if he won't come?'

'He'll come,' said the King. 'Sooner or later there must be a fight, and I expect your master is as impatient as I am.'

'But he doesn't want to come out to you. He wants you to go to him.'

'Then, why,' said the King gently, 'did you imagine that

you could save yourself by tempting him to come and fight on even terms? Be consistent, please.'

Thorgeir shrugged his shoulders. 'And if I do what you ask,' he said, 'and if you do win, what will happen to me?'

'I have no idea,' said the King. 'It'll be interesting finding out, won't it? I could promise to spare you, or even give you a kingdom in Serkland, but you wouldn't trust me, now would you?'

'Of course not,' said Thorgeir. 'So that's settled, then, is it?'

'Settled.' The King clapped him on the shoulder. 'And to make sure, Arvarodd will stand one step behind you all the time with his sword drawn. Arvarodd is bigger than you, at least so long as you are in human shape, and I fancy he doesn't like you after your confrontation earlier this evening. Now, tell me all about it.'

So Thorgeir told him.

'But why there?' said the sorcerer-king for the fifth time. 'I thought we agreed . . .'

Thorgeir glanced over his shoulder at Arvarodd. 'Because it may be your last chance at anything like decent odds,' he said. 'It's worth the risk, believe me. Listen, Hrolf and his men have got those two spirits back. They broke into the office and rescued them.' He held the receiver away from his ear. Judging by the noises that come out of it, this was a wise move. When they had subsided, he said: 'I know, I'm sorry, it's not my fault. But I followed them here, and it'll be a couple of hours before they get the brooch wired up. There's still time.'

'Hold your water, will you?' Thorgeir waited breathlessly, and behind him Arvarodd patted the flat of his sword on the palm of his hand and made clucking noises. 'Even if you're right,' said the sorcerer-king, 'there won't be time to muster any force. It'd be suicide.'

'Balls,' said Thorgeir. 'I'm looking at them now. There's the King and that female, the wizard, Brynjolf and Arvarodd. You know,' he couldn't resist adding, 'the one who went to—'

'I know, I know. Shut up a minute. I'm thinking. Look, I could get together a portable set and some Special Effects, and there's the Emergency Kit all charged up, of course, and you could be a wolf. With that and the lads from Vouchers—'

'It'd be a doddle,' Thorgeir urged. Arvarodd was pressing his sword-point against the back of his neck. 'Get a move on, though, or they'll see me. God knows how I followed them so far without them spotting me.'

'If this goes wrong, I'll have your skull for an eggcup,' muttered the sorcerer-king. Thorgeir shut his eyes and offered a prayer of thanksgiving to his patron deity. 'Don't worry,' he said, 'it'll be no problem. Promise.'

'How long will it take me to get there?'

'The way you drive, forty minutes tops. It's just past the turning to Radnage. You got that?'

'The trouble with you, Thorgeir,' said the sorcerer-king, 'is that you combine stupidity with fecklessness. Be seeing you.'

There was a click and the dialling tone. 'Well,' said Arvarodd, 'is he coming or do I chop you?'

'He's coming,' said Thorgeir, straight-faced. 'Exactly like you wanted it. And he hasn't got any time to get his forces together; it'll be him and a couple of extras. You'll walk it, you'll see.'

Arvarodd shook his head and marched Thorgeir away. As he went, Thorgeir congratulated himself on his rotten memory. He had honestly forgotten all about the Emergency Kit.

CHAPTER ELEVEN

'I still think this is a bad idea,' whispered Danny Bennett. Angantyr nudged him in the ribs, expelling all the air from his body, and told him to be quiet. Utterly wretched, he lay still in the heather and turned the matter over in his mind.

On the credit side, he had persuaded them not to declare war. That had taken some doing, after such a conclusive victory. Hjort had already prepared the Red Arrow, to shoot over the battlements of Edinburgh Castle, and Angantyr was talking glibly of annexing Sunderland as well. It was the thought that they might conceivably win that had spurred Danny on to unimagined heights of eloquence, and in the end he had succeeded. But in order to do so he had had to make certain concessions, the main one being that they should all go to London and help the King. Although they would not admit it, some of the heroes were beginning to worry, and all of them hated the thought of missing the final excitement. So here they all were, lying in wait for the first suitable vehicle, and it was Danny's turn to be seriously anxious, although he had no qualms at all about admitting it. There was bound to be violence. There might well be blood-shed. If they did manage to get a van or a bus, he was going to have to drive it.

Round the bend in the road came a large red thing, with the number 87 displayed in a little glass frame above its nose. Danny closed his eyes and hoped that his companions wouldn't notice it; but they did.

'Here, Danny,' hissed Angantyr, 'how about that one?'

'Oh, no, I don't really think so,' Danny gabbled. 'I mean, it's probably too small.'

'Doesn't look it,' said Hjort on his other side.

'They're much smaller inside than out,' said Danny. 'Really.'

Hjort shook his head. 'No harm in trying,' he said cheerfully. 'What do you think, lads?'

Several heads nodded, the boar-shaped crests of their helmets visible above the heather like a covey of skimming larks. 'When you're ready, Starkad,' said Hjort.

'Hold it, hold it,' snarled Angantyr. 'And since when were you in charge of this, Hjort Herjolfsson?'

'Someone's got to do it, haven't they?' Hjort raised his head to glower at Angantyr.

Danny saw a gleam of hope. If he could start them quarrelling . . . 'I'm with you, Angantyr,' he said, and looked expectantly at Hjort.

But the hero simply shrugged and said, 'See if I care.'

'Here,' said Starkad, 'do I go, or what?'

'Yes,' said Hjort and Angantyr simultaneously. They glared at each other.

Starkad was on his feet. He could run like the wind if he didn't trip over something, and soon he had overtaken the bus. With a spring like a wild cat, he leapt at the driver's door, grabbed the handle and, bracing his feet against the frame, wrenched it open. The bus swerved drastically, mowed down a row of snow-poles and stopped dead.

The driver, his head spinning, pushed himself up from the steering-wheel and stared helplessly at the group of maniacs who had come running up out of nowhere. All save one of them were waving antiquated but terrifying weapons: swords, spears and axes. It could conceivably be a group of archaeology students staging a reconstruction of Culloden, but he wasn't hopeful. The one who was unarmed leant forward into the cab and cleared his throat.

'Excuse me,' he said, 'does this bus go to London?'

The driver dragged breath into the vacuum of his lungs. 'If it's the money you're after,' he gasped, 'there's three pound forty-two pence. Take it all.'

'Actually,' said the unarmed man, 'would you mind if we borrowed your bus? It's just for a day or a week or so.'

'Are you hijacking my bus, then?' asked the driver.

'Yes,' said the unarmed man unhappily. The driver went white, and Danny felt panic coming on. What if the man tried to resist and defend his passengers? Bothvar Bjarki would like that.

'It's all right, really,' he said, as reassuringly as possible, 'I'm with the BBC.'

'Is that right?' said the driver. He did not look reassured. 'Would you be the blokes who beat up all those coppers and soldiers at Farr the other day?'

'Yes,' said Angantyr. He stuck out his bearded chin impatiently and tapped his sword-blade with his fingers.

'The Army's looking for you,' said an old lady from the second row of seats. 'They're all over Strathnaver with armoured cars.'

'Really?' Angantyr's eyes lit up. 'Hey, lads,' he called out, 'did you hear that? They've come back.' The heroes began to chatter excitedly.

It was, Danny decided, a moment for action, not words. He grabbed the driver by the sleeve and pulled him out of his seat. 'Right,' he tried to shout (but the words came out as an urgent sort of shriek), 'I want everybody off the bus.'

'You must be kidding, son,' said the old lady. 'There's not another bus till Wednesday, and I've the week's shopping to do.'

Bothvar Bjarki climbed inside. 'You heard him,' he growled. 'Off you get, now.'

'Are we being taken hostage?' asked an old man in the fourth row.

'No,' said Danny. 'You're free to go.'

'Pity,' said the old man. 'That would have been one in the eye for George Macleod and his pigeons.' He shrugged his shoulders wearily and picked up his shopping-bag.

The passengers shuffled off the bus, all of them taking a good look at Danny as they went, and the heroes scrambled in. Danny took a deep breath and sat in the driver's seat. The driver raised an eyebrow.

'Do you know how to drive a bus then, mister?' he asked.

'I haven't the faintest idea,' Danny confessed. 'Is it difficult?'

'Yes,' said the driver. 'Very. Are you going far?'

'London,' Danny said.

The driver shook his head sadly, and deep inside Danny's soul something snapped. Perhaps he had Viking blood in his veins, or perhaps he was just fed up. 'All right,' he said quietly, 'you drive.'

'Me?' The driver stared. 'All the way to London?'

'Yes,' said Danny.

'Now, look here,' said the driver. 'The Ministry regulations say—'

'Stuff the Ministry regulations.' Danny wished he had accepted Angantyr's offer of a sword. 'Drive this bus to London or you'll be sorry.' Behind him, Angantyr nodded approvingly and clapped Danny on the shoulder.

'That's right,' he said, 'you tell him.' For some reason which he could never fathom, Danny glowed with pleasure.

'Right,' he said, giving the driver a shove. 'Let's get this show on the road.'

'What show?' asked Hjort, but Danny ignored him, for he had had a sudden inspiration. He leant forward and pointed to the roller above the driver's seat that changed the number on the front of the bus. 'Change that,' he ordered.

'What to?' asked the driver.

'"Special", of course,' Danny replied. 'Come on, move it.'

The driver did as he was told, and then started the engine. Danny stuck his head out of the window and waved to the ex-passengers.

'Never mind,' he shouted, 'there'll be another one along in a minute.'

The bus moved off, and Danny sat down in the front row of seats, feeling very surprised at himself but not at all repentant. He was, he realised, starting to enjoy all this.

'You realise,' said the driver over his shoulder, 'we'll run out of fuel before we're past Inverness.'

'Then, we'll get some more, won't we?' Danny replied. 'Now, shut up and drive.'

Angantyr came forward and sat down beside him. 'Have some cold seagull,' he said. 'I saved some for you.'

'Thanks.' Danny bit off a large chunk. It tasted good.

'You did all right back there,' said Angantyr Asmundson. 'In fact, you're coming along fine.'

'It was nothing,' said Danny with his mouth full.

'I know,' said Angantyr. 'But you handled it pretty well, all the same.'

'Thanks.' Danny chewed for a moment, then scratched his head. 'Angantyr,' he said, 'I've thought of something.'

'What?'

'When we get to London, how will we find them?'

'Don't ask me,' said Angantyr. 'Is it a big place?'

'Quite big.' Danny frowned. 'So you don't know where they're likely to be?'

'It was your idea we go,' Angantyr replied.

'Was it?'

'Yes,' said Angantyr. 'Don't you remember?'

Danny leant back in his seat. After all, it was a long way to London. He would have plenty of time to think of a plan.

'So it was,' he said, and yawned. 'You leave everything to me.'

Angantyr grinned. 'You've changed your tune a bit, haven't you?' he said. Danny shook his head.

'It just takes some getting used to, that's all,' he said. 'And you've got to start somewhere, haven't you?'

'That's very true,' said Angantyr.

'It was the same when I shot my first feature,' Danny went on. Angantyr nodded.

'Did you miss?' he said sympathetically.

Danny remembered the reviews. 'Yes,' he said.

'Same with me and my first wild boar,' said Angantyr. 'Nerves, principally. They all laughed.'

Danny sighed; he knew the feeling. 'The main thing is', he said, 'not to let it get to you.'

'That's especially true of wild boar,' Angantyr agreed. 'Tusks like razors, some of them. I remember one time in Radsey—'

He stopped short and stared. A great black cloud had appeared out of nowhere and was covering the sky. In a few moments it was as dark as night. From where the sun should have been there came a piercing cry; but whether it was pain or triumph no one could tell. A great wind rose up all around, and the air was filled with rushing shapes, like bats or small black birds. Then a great bolt of lightning split the sky, and hailstones crashed against the windows of the bus. The driver pulled over and hid under the seat, whimpering.

'Oh, well,' said Angantyr, 'looks like we're going to miss all the fun.'

King Hrolf staggered, tripped, fell and lay still. For a moment he could do nothing except listen to the beating of his own heart and the howling of the storm. Then he became aware of the blaring of the horns and the cries of the huntsmen and forced himself to rise. The savage music was too close. He commanded his knees to bear his weight, leant forward and ran.

Something had gone wrong, many hours ago now. A man whose face was familiar had driven up in a small black car. He had climbed out and walked forward, as if to surrender. Arvarodd had turned to look, and then Thorgeir had broken free from his grip. Before anyone could stop him, he had wrenched away the wires from the brooch, and then the storm had begun. However brave and strong he may be, a man cannot fight against lightning, or waves of air that strike him like a hammer. He had clung on to his sword and ran, and the storm had followed him.

That was all a long time ago, and he had not stopped running. He had passed through towns and villages, frozen and lifeless in the total darkness, across open fields and through woods, whose trees were torn up by the roots as he passed. Lightning had scorched his heels, flying rocks had grazed him, and the hailstones whipped and punched him as he ran. Sometimes his path had been blocked by strange shapes, sometimes human, sometimes animal; sometimes the ground had opened up before him, or burst into flames under his feet; sometimes the hail gave way to boiling rain that scalded his face and hands, or black fog that filled his lungs like mud. All these, and other things, too, he had run through or past, while all the time his pursuers were gaining on him; slowly, a yard or so each hour, but perceptibly closer all the time. So must the hour hand feel when the minute hand pursues it.

He stumbled again, and crashed to the ground. This time, his knees refused to obey, and the earth he lay on shook with the sound of many feet. King Hrolf raised his head and wiped the blood away from his eyes. In front of him the ground had fallen away on all sides. He was on a plateau, with a sheer drop all around him. Suddenly the wind dropped. Absolute silence.

King Hrolf drove his sword into the ground and used it to lever himself up to his feet. He filled his lungs with air and held it there.

'So.' The voice was all around him. 'This is where it must end.'

'This is as good a place as any,' said the King. The voice laughed.

'It is indeed. Was it worth it, Hrolf Earthstar?'

The King jerked his sword out of the turf and held it in front of him. 'That depends on the outcome,' he said.

The voice laughed again, and the skin of the earth vibrated like the surface of a drum. 'Well said, Hrolf Ketilson. If you wish, I will let you run a little further.'

'I am getting too old to run,' replied the King. 'I have lived long enough.'

'Too long.' The voice laughed a third time.

'I have only one favour to ask you,' said King Hrolf, raising his head and smiling. 'It is a small thing, but it would please me to know your name.'

'My name? That is no small thing. But because you have run well, and because when you are dead no one will ever be born again who would dare ask it, I shall tell you. Listen carefully, Earthstar.'

King Hrolf lowered his sword and leant on it. 'I am listening,' he said.

'Well, then,' said the voice, 'I am called Vindsval and Vasad, Bestla and Beyla, Jalk and Jafnhar. In Finnmark my name is Geirrod, in Gotland Helblindi, in Markland Bolverk, in Permia Skirnir, in Serkland Eikenskjaldi. Among Danes I was called Warfather, among Saxons Master; to the Goths I was Gravemaker, and in Scythia Emperor. The gods called me Hunferth, the elves named me Freki, to the dwarfs my name was Ganglati and to men . . .'

King Hrolf put his hands over his ears.

Hildy rolled over on to her side and opened her eyes. That meant she was still alive, for what it was worth. Through the gloom she could see Brynjolf lying on his face where the first gust of wind had blown him, and the wizard Kotkel, where Thorgeir had struck him down. Painfully she lifted herself up on one elbow and looked round. There was Arvarodd, or his dead body, and over it stood a great grey wolf. She remembered how they had fought until Arvarodd's sword had shattered into splinters in his hand, and his shield had crumpled like a flower under the impact of the wolf's assault. Then something had flown up into her face, and she had seen no more. Of the King there was no sign.

The wolf turned its head and growled at her, and licked blood off its long jaws. But Hildy was no longer afraid. She had reached the point where fear can no longer help, and anger offers the only hope of survival.

She hated that wolf and she was going to kill it. She looked around for a weapon, but could see none, except the hilt of Arvarodd's sword. The wolf was trotting towards her, like a dog who has heard its plate scraping on the kitchen tiles; she watched it for a moment, suddenly fascinated by the delicacy of its movement. Then, inexplicably, her hand was in her pocket. The little roll of cloth that Arvarodd had given her all that time ago had came loose, and her fingers touched and recognised the contents of it; the stone that gave mastery of languages; the splinter of bone that gave eloquence; the pebble that brought understanding; the pebble from the shores of Asgard . . .

If you throw it at something, it turns into a boulder and flattens pretty well anything. Then it turns back into a pebble and returns to your hand.

She threw it. She missed.

The wolf gave a startled yelp and galloped away. The pebble came whistling back through the air, stinging Hildy's palm as it landed, so that she nearly dropped it. She swore loudly and threw again. A loud crash told her that this time she had hit the car. By the time the pebble was between her fingers once more, the wolf was nowhere to be seen. She started to run after it, but stopped in mid-stride.

'Aren't you forgetting something?' said a voice.

She turned unsteadily on her heel and peered through the darkness. There were two tiny points of light . . .

'Instead of throwing things at us,' said the voice, 'you might get this contraption wired up.'

'Shine brighter,' said Hildy. 'I can't see.'

The lights flared up, and Hildy could make out the outline of the car.

'You could see well enough to throw that rock at us,' said the light. 'What harm did we ever do you?'

'I wasn't throwing it at you,' said Hildy. 'There was this wolf . . .'

'Pull the other one, it's got bells on it,' said the light. 'The brooch is just over there.'

The light flashed brilliantly on a garnet, and Hildy picked up the brooch. 'What do I do?' she said.

'Twist the ends of the wires round our necks,' said the light.

'Have you two got necks?' said Hildy doubtfully. All she could see was a pool of light. The pool of light flickered irritably.

'Of course we've got necks,' said the pool of light. 'You'll find them between our heads and our shoulders.'

Hildy grabbed at the light. 'Ouch,' it said, 'do you mind?'

'Sorry.' She grabbed again.

'Getting warmer,' said the light. 'Up a bit. That's it.'

With her other hand, Hildy took the end of one of the wires. 'Stay still,' she begged.

'Difficult,' said the light. 'It tickles.'

Hildy drew a loop in the wire and tied it. There was a spluttering noise and she apologised. She did the same with the other wire.

'Idiot,' said the light. 'That's my ankle.'

'Oh, for Chrissakes.' Fumbling desperately, she untied the wire and lunged. 'That's right,' gasped the light, 'throttle me.' She tied the second knot.

Suddenly, the sun came out.

The sorcerer-king froze. Something had gone wrong. He stared wildly at the sun, riding high in the clear blue sky, and the ground, inexplicably beneath his feet. He swallowed hard.

'But you,' he said, 'can call me Eric.'

'Right,' said the King, 'Eric. Shall we get on with it?'

He lifted his sword and whirled it around his head.

'I'm in no hurry,' said the sorcerer-king, backing away. 'As you know, I'm firmly opposed to needless violence.'

'What about necessary violence?' asked the King unpleasantly.

'That, too,' said the sorcerer-king. 'Besides, I seem to have come out without my sword.'

'What's that hanging from your belt, then?'

'Oh,' said the sorcerer-king, 'that.' Very unwillingly, he drew the great sword Ifing from its scabbard. The sun flashed on its well-tended blade.

'Ready?'

'No,' said the sorcerer-king.

'Tough.' Hrolf took a step forward.

'Toss you for it?' suggested the sorcerer-king. 'Heads I go away for ever, tails I disappear completely.'

'No,' said Hrolf. 'Ready now?'

'Best of three?'

'No.'

'Oh, have at you, then,' said the sorcerer-king wretchedly, and launched a mighty blow at the King's head. Hrolf parried, and the two swords rang together like a great bell. Hrolf struck his blow, first feinting to draw his adversary over to the left, then turning his wrist and striking right; but he was wounded and exhausted, and the sorcerer-king, who had always been his match as a swordsman, was fresh and unhurt. The blow went wide as the sorcerer-king side-stepped nimbly, and Hrolf fell forward. Quickly, the sorcerer-king lifted Ifing above his head and brought it down with all his strength, hitting Hrolf on the shoulder. The blade cut through the steel rings of the mail shirt and grazed the flesh, but that was all. The armourers of Castle Borve made good armour. In an instant, Hrolf was on his feet again, breathing hard but with Tyrving firm in both hands.

'Cheat,' said the sorcerer-king.

'Cheat yourself,' replied Hrolf, and lunged. The sorcerer-king raised his guard and parried the blow with the foible of his blade. Hrolf leant back, and the sorcerer-king swept a powerful blow at his feet. But Hrolf had anticipated that, and jumped over the blade. The sorcerer-king only just managed to avoid his counter-attack.

'Sure you wouldn't rather toss for it?' panted the sorcerer-king. 'Use your own coin if you like.'

Hrolf shook his head and struck a blow to the neck. His opponent stopped it with the cross-guard, and threw his weight forward, sliding his sword down Hrolf's blade until the hilts locked. For a moment, Hrolf was taken off balance, but just in time he moved his feet and drew his sword away sharply. The sorcerer-king staggered, lost his footing and fell, his sword flying from his hand as he hit the ground. Before he could get up, Hrolf was standing over him, and the point of Tyrving was touching his throat.

'Now we'll toss for it,' Hrolf said.

'Why now?' said the sorcerer-king bitterly. 'You could have done me an injury.'

'Heads,' said Hrolf, 'I let you have your sword back.' The sorcerer-king started to protest violently, but Hrolf smiled. 'What's up?' he said. 'Lost your sense of humour?' He lifted the sword and rested it against his shoulder.

'All right, Cleverclogs,' said the sorcerer-king, struggling to his feet, 'you've made your point. Can we call a halt to all this fooling-about now?'

Hrolf grinned and put his foot on the sorcerer-king's sword. 'Is your name really Eric?' he asked.

'There's no need to go on about it,' muttered the sorcerer-king. 'I tried spelling it with a K, but people still laughed.'

'I think it's a nice name,' said King Hrolf.

'You would.'

'Seriously, though,' said King Hrolf, leaning on his sword, 'I've got to kill you sooner or later, and I'd much rather you defended yourself.' He kicked Ifing over to the sorcerer-king, who scowled at it distastefully.

'I'm not really evil, you know,' said the sorcerer-king.

'You do a pretty good imitation.'

'Where I went wrong was fooling about with magic,' the sorcerer-king went on. 'Dammit, I don't even enjoy it. I'd far rather slop around in old clothes and play a few games of Goblin's Teeth.'

'Goblin's Teeth?'

'It's a sort of a game, with dice and—'

'I know,' said the King, with a strange expression on his face. 'So you play Goblin's Teeth, do you?'

'Yes,' said the sorcerer-king. 'Why, do you?'

The King inspected his fingernails. 'I used to dabble a bit,' he mumbled.

'Really?'

'Actually,' the King admitted, 'I was Baltic Champion one year. Pure fluke, of course.'

'I won the Swedish Open two years running,' said the sorcerer-king with immense pride. 'I cheated,' he admitted.

'You can't cheat at Goblin's Teeth,' said the King. 'It's impossible.'

The sorcerer-king smirked. 'No, it's not,' he said.

'Go on, then,' said King Hrolf, 'how's it done?'

'I can't explain just like that,' said the sorcerer-king. 'I need the board and the pieces.' He stopped, and gazed at Hrolf hopefully. 'You haven't got a set, by any chance? I lost mine back in the fifteenth century.'

'No,' said King Hrolf, his eyes shining, 'but I know someone who has.'

*   *   *

Brynjolf sat up and rubbed his head. It hurt.

'What happened?' he asked.

'No idea.' Brynjolf looked up and saw Arvarodd leaning against the car. 'But it's not looking too bad at the moment. Is it, Kotkel?' But the wizard shook his head, and made a sound like a worried cement-mixer.

'Pessimist,' said Arvarodd. 'Me, I always look on the bright side. Even when that perishing wolf was standing over me making snarling noises, I said to myself: Arvarodd, you've been in worse scrapes than this one.'

'Where?' muttered Brynjolf. 'In Permia?'

'I'll ignore that remark,' said Arvarodd coldly. 'And, sure enough, I just pretended to be dead and it went away. Saw a rabbit, I think. Then, I grant you, I passed out. But I'm still alive, aren't I?'

'Where's Vel-Hilda?' said Brynjolf.

'Here,' said Hildy as she came out from the spinney. 'I've been wolf-hunting. Look.'

On the end of the piece of rope she held in her hand was a sullen-looking wolf. 'Sit,' she said. The wolf glared at her, and sat.

'I'm going to call you Spot, aren't I, boy?' she said. The wolf growled, but she took a pebble from her pocket and showed it to him. He wagged his tail furiously and rolled on his back, waving his paws in the air.

'What are you so cheerful about?' said Brynjolf resentfully.

'I've just seen the King through the seer-stone,' she said. 'He's all right and I think he's captured the Enemy. In fact, they seemed to be getting on fine.' She leant forward and tickled the wolf's stomach. 'Who's got four *feet* then?' she asked. The wolf scowled at her.

'By the way,' said Arvarodd, 'in case you were worried, we're all alive.'

'I know,' said Hildy, apparently oblivious to all irony.

'I made sure of that before I went after the wolf. Lucky.'

'I dunno,' moaned Brynjolf. 'Women.' He turned himself into a statue of himself. Statues, especially stone ones, do not have headaches. Hildy tied the wolf's lead to his arm and sat down.

'I'm glad it's all worked out so well,' she said.

CHAPTER TWELVE

'This,' Hildy said, 'is for you.'

'Are you sure?' said the King gravely. Hildy nodded.

'Yes,' she said, and handed the decanter to him. She had finally traded in all her Esso tokens. 'Think of me when you use it in Valhalla,' she said.

'I shall, Vel-Hilda,' replied the King. 'What's it for?'

'You could put mead in it,' she said. 'But be careful. It's fragile.'

The King nodded, and with scrupulous care wrapped it up in his beaver-fur mantle. 'It is a kingly gift,' he lied.

The last rays of the setting sun shone in through the skylights of the Castle of Borve. It had not been easy getting there through the cordon of armoured cars, and in the end the wizard had had to make them all invisible. This had caused difficulties; in particular, Arvarodd kept treading on Hildy's feet, which he could not see, and it took the wizard several hours and three or four embarrassingly unsuccessful attempts to make them all visible again. Eventually, however, they had reached the castle, where the other heroes, located by Hildy through the seer-stone and warned by Brynjolf in corvid form to expect them, had prepared a triumphant banquet of barbecued seagull and seaweed mousse.

'Time to switch on the lights,' said the King. He nodded to Kotkel, who connected some wires up to the two chthonic spirits, who were sulking. They had just been playing a three-handed game of Goblin's Teeth with the sorcerer-king, and they suspected him of cheating.

'Don't ask me how,' whispered Zxerp to his companion. 'I just know it, that's all.'

Two great golden cauldrons, filled from the enchanted beer-can, were passed round the table, and Danny Bennett replenished his horn. It had been made by Weyland himself from the horns of a prize oryx, and the spell cast on it protected the user from even the faintest ill-effects the next morning. That was probably just as well. Nevertheless, he had reason to celebrate, for his career and his BAFTA award were now both secure; his interview with King Hrolf, complete with an utterly convincing display of magical effects by the wizard to lend credibility to the story, was safely in the can, thanks to a video-camera he had recovered from the spoils of the Vikings' most recent encounter with the forces sent to subdue them. Angantyr had been the cameraman; he had shown a remarkable aptitude for the job, which did not surprise Danny in the least. 'You're a born cameraman,' Danny had said to him, as they had played the tape back on the monitor. Fortunately, Angantyr was ignorant enough to take this as a compliment.

'I'll make sure you get your credit,' Danny assured him. 'Camera – A. Asmundarson, and the EETPU can go play with themselves.' He drained his horn and refilled it.

'Pity I won't see it,' said Angantyr.

'If only you were staying on,' Danny said. 'I could get you a job, no trouble at all.'

'Wish I were,' said Angantyr. 'The way you describe it, sounds like the life would suit me fine. But there it is.'

'Tell you what,' said Danny, putting his arm round his friend's shoulders, 'why don't you take the camera and the monitor with you to Valhalla? There's plenty of spare tapes. It'd be something to do if you got tired of fighting and feasting.'

'Good idea,' said Angantyr. He filled up his friend's horn. 'In return, I must give you a gift.'

'A gift?' Danny beamed.

'A gift,' said Angantyr, wishing he hadn't.

'Really?' Danny slapped him on the back, making him spill his horn. 'That's . . . well, I'm touched, I am really.'

'Oh, it's just heroic tradition,' said Angantyr, wiping beer off his mail shirt. He felt slightly ashamed of his previous reluctance, and considered what Danny might find most useful. An enchanted helmet? An arrow that never missed its mark, in case he ever went feature-hunting again? Somehow, such a gift seemed meagre. He braced himself for the ultimate act of generosity.

'I shall give you,' he said tight-lipped, 'my own recipe for cream of seagull soup.'

'Oh,' said Danny. 'How nice. Hold on while I find a pencil. Right.'

'First,' Angantyr dictated, 'catch your seagull . . .'

'Count yourself lucky,' said Arvarodd. 'It's a damn sight better than "Arvarodd of Permia".'

'I suppose so,' said Hildy sadly. 'Even so . . .'

'Even so nothing.' Arvarodd sighed. 'I had dreams, you know, once. Poet-Arvarodd, or Arvarodd the Phrase-Maker, was what I wanted to be called. And, instead, what am I remembered for? Bloody Permia. At least,' he said, brightening slightly, 'my saga survived. That's one in the eye for King Gautrek. I told him when he showed me his manuscript. Illiterate rubbish for people who move their lips when they read.'

Hildy nodded. She did not have the heart to tell him that *Gautrek's Saga* had made it through the centuries as well, and was regarded as the masterpiece of the genre. Men die, cattle die, only the glories of heroes live for ever, as the Edda says.

'But I was never satisfied with it,' Arvarodd continued. 'Needed cutting.' He fell silent and blushed.

'What is it, Arvarodd?' Hildy asked. He looked away.

'I don't suppose,' he said suddenly. 'No, it's a lot to ask, and I don't want to be a nuisance.'

'What?' Hildy leant forward.

'Well,' Arvarodd said, and from inside his mail shirt he drew a thick scroll of vellum manuscript. 'Perhaps, if you've got a moment, you might . . .'

Hildy smiled. 'I'd be delighted,' she said. She glanced at the scrawl of runes at the top of the first page. "Arvarodd's Saga 2", it read, "The Final Battle". Out of the bundle of sheets floated a scrap of fading papyrus. Hildy caught hold of it and ran her scholar's eye over it. 'Dear Mr Arvarodd, although I greatly enjoyed your work, I regret to say that at this time . . .' Hildy felt a tear escaping from the corner of her eye; then a sudden inspiration struck her.

'When did you write this?' she asked.

'Just before the battle of Melvich,' said Arvarodd. 'I was greatly influenced at the time by . . .'

Hildy thought fast. The manuscript was twelve hundred years old; carbon dating would verify that. No one would be able to doubt its authenticity. And if she was quick she would just be in time for the next edition of the *Journal of Scandinavian Studies*.

'What you need,' she said, 'is a good agent.'

'Checkmate,' said the sorcerer-king.

'Sod it,' said Prexz.

'That's nine games to us,' said King Hrolf, 'and none to you. Mugs away.'

'You're cheating,' said Zxerp angrily.

'Prove it,' said the sorcerer-king.

'What I still don't understand', said Starkad Storvirksson, 'is how it manages to move without oars.'

Hildy scratched her head. 'Well,' she said desperately, 'it's magic.'

'Oh,' said Starkad. 'Why didn't you say so?'

'Starkad,' said Brynjolf, 'why don't you go and get Vel-Hilda some more seagull?'

'Actually,' Hildy started to say, but Brynjolf kicked her under the table. Starkad got up and went to the great copper cauldron that was simmering quietly on the hearth.

'I'm very fond of Starkad,' said Brynjolf, 'but there are times . . .'

At the other end of the table, Danny was telling the sleeping Angantyr all about his President Kennedy theory. Hildy sighed.

'I wish you all didn't have to go,' she said. 'There's so much you haven't seen, so much you could do. We need you in the twentieth century.'

'I doubt it,' said Arvarodd. 'There aren't any more wolves to kill or sorcerers to be overthrown, and I think we'd just cause a lot of confusion.'

'Let's face it,' said Brynjolf, 'if it hadn't been for you, Vel-Hilda, I don't know what would have happened.'

Hildy blushed. 'I didn't do much,' she said.

'No one ever does,' said Arvarodd, smiling. 'What are the deeds of heroes, except a few frightened people doing the best they can in the circumstances? Sigurd had no trouble at all killing the dragon; it was a very old dragon, and its eyesight was starting to go. If he'd waited another couple of weeks it would have died of old age.'

'Or take Beowulf,' said Brynjolf. 'Weedy little bloke, got sand kicked in his face on the beach as often as not. But he just happened to be in the right place at the right time. It's not who you are that matters, it's what you do.'

'No,' said Arvarodd, 'you're wrong there. It's not what you do, it's who you are.'

'Whichever.' Brynjolf frowned. 'Or both. Anyway, Vel-Hilda, what I'm trying to say is that we couldn't have managed without you. Well, that's not strictly true,' he added. 'But you helped.'

'That's right.' Arvarodd nodded vigorously. 'You helped a lot.'

'Any time,' said Hildy. 'I'll miss you. It won't be the same, somehow.'

'Sorry, Vel-Hilda,' said Starkad Storvirksson, returning with an empty plate, 'but Bothvar Bjarki had the last of the seagull. There are still a few baked mice, if you'd like some.'

'No, thanks,' said Hildy, 'really. I couldn't eat another thing.'

Starkad breathed a sigh of relief and went off to eat them himself.

'I'm quite partial to a bit of baked mouse,' said Arvarodd, leaning back in his seat and pouring himself a hornful of beer. 'I remember when I was in Permia . . .'

'Checkmate.'

Zxerp glared at King Hrolf with deep hatred. 'You two,' he said at last, 'deserve each other.'

King Hrolf rose to his feet and banged on the table for silence. He poured a horn of beer from the decanter and drank it, then cleared his throat. Even Angantyr woke up. The company turned their heads and listened.

'Friends,' said the King, 'our work is done. Despite the perils that threatened us, we have overthrown the power of darkness and saved the world from evil.'

'Steady on,' said the sorcerer-king.

'Now our time in this world, which has been unnaturally long, is over, and it is time for us to go to feast for ever in Odin's golden hall. Roast pork,' he added before Angantyr could interrupt, 'and all the mead you can drink. At the head of the table sits Odin himself; at his right hand Thor, at his left Frey. With her own hands Freyja pours the mead, and the greatest of heroes are the company. There we will meet many we have known, many of whom we have sent there, in the old wars which are forgotten. They say that in Valhalla the men go out to fight in the morning, and at night all those who have fallen rise up again to go to the feast, and fight again the next day. There is also, I am assured, a swimming-pool and a sauna. Personally, I think it all sounds very boring being cooped up with a lot of dead warriors all day, but don't let me put you off. I intend to take a good book with me. Anyway, tomorrow we sail across the great sea. Long will be our journey, past Iceland and Greenland and into the region of everlasting cold, until we pass over the edge of the world and see before us Bifrost, the rainbow bridge.'

Hildy scratched her head. If they followed the route the King had described, it sounded to her as if they would end up at Baffin Island. But she had stopped doing geography in fourth grade, and only recently found out where Hungary is.

'Sorcerer-Eric and I have settled our differences,'

continued the King, 'and he will be coming with us to Valhalla.' A murmur ran round the table, but the King held up his hand. 'That is settled,' he said firmly. 'He has been an evil man and our and the world's enemy, but in Valhalla all earthly enmities are put aside, for all who go there, so it is said, are soon united in common hatred of the catering staff. Besides, there is always a place at Odin's table for men who are brave and have fought well, however misguided their cause, and who can play a good game of Goblin's Teeth.'

The murmur subsided. That, after all, was fair enough.

'Behind us,' went on the King, 'we leave one who has deserved a place in the company of heroes, our sister Vel-Hilda Frederik's-daughter. But for her . . . Well, she helped, and it is not by blows or good policies alone that battles are won.'

That didn't leave much, Hildy reflected, but presumably he meant it kindly. She blushed.

'In our day, the skalds would have sung of her deeds; but now, it seems, the skalds sing no more at the feasts of kings. In our day, her story would have been told by the fireside, when the shadows are long and children hear ghosts when the sheep climb on to the roof to eat the house-leeks. But of our last fight no songs will be made; no one will ever know that we have been here or done what we have done. So it will be for all of us at the world's end, we who thought to cheat death by living for ever in the words of men. Nevertheless.' The King smiled and made a sign with his hand. Arvarodd rose to his feet, and drew a harp out from under the table. 'I wrote it in the car coming up,' he whispered, as Hildy's eyes started to fill with tears. 'Hope you like it.'

'Vel-Hilda,' said the King, 'you have deserved a song, and one song you shall have. Arvarodd of Permia,' he commanded, 'sing us your song.'

'The name of this song is Hildarkvitha,' proclaimed Arvarodd. 'Any unauthorised use of this material may render the user liable to civil and criminal prosecution.' He drew his fingers across the strings, took a deep breath and sang:

> 'Attend!
> We have heard the glories
> Of god-like kings,
> Heard the praise
> And the passion of princes . . .'

Hildy stifled a sob and reached for her notebook.

The young lieutenant was excited. He had never been in this sort of situation before.

'We've found them,' he said. 'They're back in that fortified position on the cliffs above Farr. God knows why we didn't leave a unit there; they were bound to come back. Anyway, that's where they are. Do we go in, or what?'

The man in the black pullover scowled at him.

'Oh, go away,' he said.

Young Mr Fortescue stared in disbelief at the While-You-Were-Out message on his desk.

Message from Eric Swenson, Chairman and Managing Director, Gerrards Garth group of companies.

Expansion programme scratched owing to unforeseen difficulties, so no China for you. Consolation prize chair, managing directorship of entire shooting match, try not to cock it up too much, why am I saying this, that's why we've chosen you. Written confirmation follows, good luck, you'll need it, suggest you get out of electronics entirely.

Message at 10.34.

It would, of course, be a challenge, and it was nice to think that the boss had such confidence in him ('that's why we've chosen you'). Nevertheless, it would have been better if he had known he was being groomed for greatness rather earlier. He could have taken notes.

'All aboard,' said Danny Bennett cheerfully. 'Move right down inside please.'

The entire company was embarking. They were going on a long tour of the kingdom of Caithness and Sutherland, just for old times' sake and to fill in the hours before it was time to set sail; down Strathnaver to Kinbrace and Helmsdale, then up the coast to Wick and across to Thurso, and on to Rolfsness. The tank was full of petrol, magically produced by the wizard from peat.

'Danny's in no fit state to drive, you know,' Hildy whispered. The King smiled.

'For some reason he wanted to,' he said. 'Insisted that it was his bus, he'd captured it single-handed, so he was going to drive. The wizard's put a spell on him, so we should be all right.'

Hildy shrugged. 'Oh, well,' she said, 'if you're sure. I've done enough driving these last few weeks to last me, anyway.'

These last few weeks . . . How long had it been since her adventure started? She could not remember. It had been the same with holidays when she was a girl; week merged seamlessly with week, and soon she had not known which day of the week it was, or what month, or what season of the year, except that the sun always seemed to shine. It was, of course, shining now; strong orange evening light that made even the scraggy brown sheep look somehow enchanted.

'Hrolf,' she asked, 'what am I going to do once you've all gone?'

'As little as possible for at least a month,' replied the King. 'First, you're going to have to help Danny Bennett explain all this to the rest of the world – only for God's sake don't let him tell them the whole truth. Have you still got that bit of jawbone Arvarodd gave you? That ought to do the trick.'

'Shouldn't I give it back?'

'Certainly not,' said the King. 'It makes him insufferable. We'll see just how long his reputation as a wise counsellor lasts without it. Anyway, after you've done that, I advise you to go away for a while and persuade yourself that none of this ever happened. It'll be for the best, in the long run.'

'Oh, no,' Hildy said, 'I couldn't do that. Even if I wanted to.'

'And you don't.'

'No. I've had' – Hildy searched for the right words – 'the time of my life,' she said.

'Funny,' said the King. 'Oh, well, it takes all sorts. I'm not exactly overjoyed at the prospect of going to Valhalla myself, but I haven't got much of a choice.'

'Shall I see you there?' Hildy asked suddenly. 'Eventually, I mean?'

'I haven't the faintest idea,' said the King. 'But don't be in any hurry to find out.'

'I won't, don't you worry,' said Hildy, grinning. 'I guess I've had my adventure. And I know what I'm going to do. I'm going to publish the saga that Arvarodd gave me, and become the world's leading authority on the heroic age of Scandinavia. They'll make me a full professor before I'm thirty.'

'Is that a good thing?'

'Probably. Anyway, it's what I want to do, and I reckon I'll do it rather better now that I know what it was really like.'

'What was it really like, Vel-Hilda?'

'Just like everything else,' said Hildy, 'only there were less people, so what they did mattered more at the time.'

'You could put it like that.'

'I will,' Hildy assured him, 'only with plenty of foot-notes. Of course, I won't be able to tell them about the magic, so most of what I say will be totally untrue. You won't mind that, will you?'

'Nothing to do with me,' said King Hrolf.

'It'll be strange, of course. When I'm giving a lecture on Bothvar Bjarki and speculating on whether he was really just a sun-god motif imported from early Indo-European myth.'

'Is he?'

'Undoubtedly,' Hildy said. 'The parallels are conclusive.'

'I'll tell him that,' said the King. 'He'll be livid.'

'So are you,' she said, 'probably. Or you're an amalgamation of several pseudo-historical early dynasties, conflated by oral tradition and rationalised by the chroniclers. Your deeds are a fictionalised account of tribal disturbances during the Age of Migrations, and you have no real basis in historical fact.'

'Thank you, Vel-Hilda,' said the King. 'That's the nicest thing anyone's ever said about me.'

'What about me, then?' said the sorcerer-king, leaning over from the row in front.

'Oh, you're just a personification of bad harvests and various diseases of livestock,' said Hildy. 'No one's ever going to believe in you.'

'I believe in me,' said the sorcerer-king.

'And look where it's got you,' said King Hrolf.

'True,' said the sorcerer-king. 'But aren't I in Arvarodd's saga?'

'Like he said himself, it's heavily influenced by the

fornaldarsögur tradition. You're symbolic.'

'Allegorical?'

'Very.'

'Oh. Fancy a quick game, then?'

'Later,' said the King. The sorcerer-king leant forward again and scratched the wolf behind the ear. It growled resignedly.

'That's sad, in a way,' said King Hrolf. 'I wouldn't have minded being forgotten, but I'm not so keen on being debunked.'

'Men die,' Hildy quoted, 'cattle die, but the glory of heroes lives for ever. It's just that these days people hate leaving well alone. They can't bear anything to be noble and splendid any more. But who knows? In a couple of hundred years or so, they may start believing in the old stories again. That'd be nice, wouldn't it?'

'Like I said,' replied the King, 'nothing to do with me. There was a man at my father's court who had been a very great hero in his youth. He'd been with King Athils, and he'd killed frost-giants, and he'd wrestled with Thor himself. Unfortunately, he made the mistake of surviving all his adventures and becoming old. Nobody believed he was still alive any more, and when he used to tell stories of his youthful feats, people used to think he was wandering in his wits and either pretending or believing that he was one of the heroes out of the fairy-tales he'd heard as a boy. So he stopped telling his own stories, and had to sit still in the evenings when the poet sang songs about him, which were always inaccurate and sometimes downright slander. In the end he did go mad and started telling everyone that he'd created the world. Nobody took any notice, of course. It's a terrible thing to be a legend in your own lifetime.'

'What was his name?' Hildy asked. 'Maybe . . .'

'Can't remember,' said the King. 'It was a long time ago.'

Suddenly the King and the entire bus disappeared, and Hildy could see the ground moving below her at about forty miles an hour. She started to shriek, then realised that the wizard had made the bus invisible to get them past the soldiers. She started to laugh; she would never get used to magic, but she would miss it when it wasn't there any more. She said as much to where the King had been. He agreed.

'I've never given it much thought,' he said. 'It's like winter, or all these new machines of yours. You don't know how they work, but you accept them as part of life. We used to enjoy our magic rather more than you do. In fact, we enjoyed everything rather more than you do, probably because the conditions of life were rather more horrible then than now. I'm starting to sound my age, aren't I?'

'You don't look it,' said Hildy.

'That,' said the King, 'is because I'm invisible.'

The surveyer opened the door of his car.

'Hold on,' he said, 'I'm just going to take a leak.'

A still night on the Ord of Caithness, with only the pounding of the sea on the rocks below to disturb the silence. God, how he hated this place!

Suddenly, round the bend of the road came a number 87 bus. That was strange enough at half-past one in the morning, but what was stranger still was the fact that it appeared to be full of Viking warriors, plainly visible in the pale ghostly glow of two points of light that shone from inside. The warriors were singing, although he could not hear them, and passing a drinking-horn from hand to hand; and there, sitting on the back seat, was that female archaeologist he had taken up to Rolfsness just before she disappeared so mysteriously. The surveyor stared. The archaeologist – or her spectre – was waving to him. He shuddered, and remembered the old tales of the phantom coach taking the souls of the dead to Hell that he had always been so scornful of as a boy. The bus moved silently, eerily on, and suddenly vanished from sight.

Trembling, the surveyor returned to the car.

'I've just seen a phantom bus,' he said. 'An eighty-seven, with Rolfsness on the front.'

'Time you got a new joke, Donald,' said his companions, who hadn't been watching. 'That one wasn't even funny the first time.'

Past the new wind-generator high above the road ('Look, Prexz, electricity on draught!'). Past the turf-roofed houses of Ulbster and Thrumster, looking exactly as their predecessors had done when Hrolf's subjects had built them as Ideal Homes twelve hundred years ago. Past Gills Bay and Scarfskerry, where Bothvar Bjarki had watched the circling cormorants and given the place its name. Past Dunnet Head and Castletown, the slate fences with broom twigs tucked into them to frighten away the deer. Past Scrabster ('I could tell you a thing or two about Scrabster,' muttered Hring Herjolfsson), and the strange complex of buildings that Hildy said was a power station and which made Zxerp and Prexz suddenly feel thirsty. The flat coastal strip dwindled away into moorland and rock, and Ben Ratha was visible against the night sky. Across the little burn called Achadh na Greighe ('I never could cope with those damnfool Gaelic names,' said Angantyr. 'Why not call it something straightforward, like Sauthajarmrsfjall?'). Ben Ruadh. Rolfsness.

'It was nice to see it all again,' said King Hrolf. 'Godforsaken place, Caithness, but what the hell, it was my kingdom.'

'I like it,' said Hildy faintly. 'It's sort of—'

'You would,' said the King. 'Come to Caithness, they said to my grandfather, the Soft South. Agreed, it's a bit less bleak than Norway or Iceland, and there are bits of Sweden I wouldn't give you a dead vole for. It's all right, I suppose. In its way.'

The moon mirrored in the waters of Loch Hollistan. A rabbit scurrying for cover as the company approached. The sea.

'Well,' said Angantyr, 'here we all are again.' He slapped Danny Bennett violently on the back. 'It's been fun. Thanks for your help, and remember – you don't add the fennel until the meat is almost brown.'

'I'll remember,' said Danny. He suspected a bone was broken. 'Remember, if in doubt, stop down. Better to be a stop over than a stop under.'

The great mound, covered over and wired off, a slice cut out of it by the archaeologists. The King shook his head. 'I don't know what they're all so excited about,' he said, as he saw the signs of their scrupulous and scientific work. 'It's just a mound of earth, that's all.'

The ship. The moon flashed on the gilded prow, the gilded shields along its sides. As they stood and gazed at it, the west wind started to blow.

'I hate to mention this,' said the King, 'but how the hell are we going to get it down to the beach?'

'Same way we got it up, I suppose,' said Hjort cheerfully. 'Starkad, get the ropes.'

'Couldn't we all go in the bus instead?' pleaded Starkad. 'It's so nice and comfy.'

Patiently, Brynjolf explained that the bus wouldn't go over water.

'Why?' asked Starkad.

Brynjolf thought for a moment. 'Because it hasn't got any oars, Starkad,' he said.

'Oh,' said Starkad Storvirksson. 'Pity, that.' He disappeared into the hold of the ship and emerged with several huge coils of rope. 'They're all sticky,' he said.

'That's the preservative they've put on them,' said Hildy. 'Lucky they didn't take them back to the labs.'

Starkad passed ropes underneath the keel and called to the heroes, who took their axes and set about demolishing the mound and the trellis of oak-trunks. In a remarkably short time, the work was finished, and the heroes took their places at the ropes.

'Better get a move on,' said the King, looking at the sky. 'It'll be dawn soon, and I want to catch the tide.'

With a shout, the heroes pulled on the ropes and the ship rose up out of the ground. Starkad tied a line round the figurehead and, exerting all his extraordinary strength, dragged the ship off the cradle of ropes on to the grass. The other champions joined him, and, with a superhuman effort and a great deal of bad language, hauled Naglfar down the long slope to the beach. As the keel slid into the water, Starkad gave a great shout.

'Is that his battle-cry?' Hildy asked.

'No,' said Arvarodd, 'the keel went over his foot.'

The first streaks of light glimmered in the East, and the heroes saluted the coming dawn with drawn swords. The wizard stepped forward and, sounding like a hierophantic lawn-mower engine, blessed the longship for its final voyage. Bothvar Bjarki hauled on the yards, and the sail rose to the masthead and filled as the west wind grew stronger. On the sail was King Hrolf's own device, a great dragon curled round a five-pointed star.

'I told the sailmakers Earthstar,' he explained, 'but they had to know best. That or they couldn't read my writing.'

'So this is goodbye,' said Hildy.

'About my manuscript,' said Arvarodd. 'The middle section needs cutting.'

'I'm sure it doesn't,' said Hildy. There were tears in her eyes, but her voice was steady.

'I'm appointing you my literary executor,' Arvarodd went on. 'I know you'll do a good job. And I want you to keep those things I gave you – you know, the jaw-bone and the pebbles and things. I won't need them again, and . . .'

He turned away and went down to join the other heroes.

'Right, Vel-Hilda,' said the King, 'it's time we were going. Kotkel wants you to keep the seer-stone, and we both think you should hang on to these.'

He handed her a bundle wrapped in a sable cloak. She took it.

'That's the Luck of Caithness,' he said. 'After all, you never know. There may be new sorcerers one day. And we're letting Zxerp and Prexz stay behind; they've earned their freedom, and they've promised to be good.'

'We're going to go and live at the hydro-electric plant on Loch Shin,' said a faint light at Hildy's feet.

'But the condition of their freedom is that, if ever you need them, they'll be ready and waiting. Won't you?' said the King menacingly. 'Because if you don't, Kotkel has put a spell on you, and you'll end up in the National Grid so fast you won't know what's hit you.' The lights flickered nervously. 'Oh, and by the way,' added the King, 'thanks for the Goblin's Teeth set.'

'You're welcome,' snarled Zxerp. 'We were bored with it anyway.'

'Also in the bundle,' said the King, 'is the sorcerer-king's sword, Ifing. It's lighter in the blade than Tyrving, and easier to handle. That's also just in case, and he won't be needing it. He's a reformed character, I think. And this, Vel-Hilda Frederik's-daughter, is for you, in return for that lovely glass thing and all your help.'

From round his neck he took a pendant on a fine gold

chain. 'The kings of Caithness never had a crown,' he said. 'This passed from my grandfather to my father to me. Once it hung round the neck of Lord Odin himself. To wear it is to accept responsibility.' He hung the chain around Hildy's neck. 'I appoint you steward of the kingdom of Caithness and Sutherland, this office to be yours and your children's until the true king comes again to reclaim his own. Which,' he added, 'I hope will never happen. Look after it for me, Vel-Hilda.'

Hildy bowed her head and knelt before him. 'Until then,' she said.

'And now I must go, or they'll all start complaining,' said the King, and there were tears in his eyes, too. 'Think of us all, but not too often.'

He put his arms around her and hugged her. Before she could get her breath back, he was gone.

'There he goes,' muttered Zxerp, 'taking the game with him.'

'Cheer up,' said Prexz, softly. 'It could be worse.'

'How?' asked Zxerp.

'I could have forgotten to swipe their chess-set,' chuckled Prexz.

Hildy ran down to the beach. Already the ship was far out to sea, the oars slicing through the black-and-red water. As a dream slips away in the first few moments of waking, it was slipping away towards the edge of the world, going to a place that had never been on any map. Yet as she stood and waved her scarf, she thought she could still hear the groaning of the timbers, the creaking of the oars in their rowlocks, the gurgle of the slipstream as the sharp prow cut the waves, the voices of the oarsmen as they strained at their work.

'I don't suppose anybody thought to pack any food.'

Could it be Angantyr's voice, blown back by some freak of the wind? Or was it just the murmuring of the sea?

'You said you were going to pack the food.'

'I didn't.'

'You did.'

'I bloody didn't.'

And perhaps it was the cry of the gulls as they rose to greet the new day, or perhaps it was the voice of the King, just audible over the rim of the sky, telling the sorcerer-king about Rule 48. Hildy stood and listened, and the sun rose over the sea in glory. Then she turned, shook her head, and walked away.

About six months later, Hildy sat in her office at the Faculty of Scandinavian Studies at Stony Brook University. It was good to be home again on Long Island, thousands of miles away from her adventure, and she had her new appointment as professor to look forward to and the proofs of *Arvarodd's Saga* to correct. Around her neck was an exquisite gold and amber pendant; a reproduction, she assured all her colleagues, but she knew they had their suspicions. Still, she would continue to wear it a little longer.

She leafed through the day's mail. Three circulars with details of conferences, two letters from universities in Norway asking her to go over and give lectures, yet another flattering offer from Harvard, and a postcard with a stamp she had never seen before. She stared at it.

It had been readdressed from St Andrews and was written in Old Norse. She turned it over; there was a picture of a tall castle. Her heart started beating violently. She screwed up her eyes to read the spidery handwriting.

'Food awful, company worse,' it read. 'My window marked with X (see photo). Arvarodd sends his regards.

Hope this reaches you OK. See you in about sixty years, all the best, Hrolf R.'

She lifted her head and looked out of the window. 'Until then,' she said.

MY HERO

CHAPTER ONE

Against the background of a green sky, the two champions circled warily.

The arena was, incredibly, quiet. One hundred thousand spectators held their breath. In all of that huge multitude, nobody moved, nobody coughed, nobody was buying popcorn. More remarkable still, nobody was *selling* popcorn.

It was the culmination of the longest day of the year, and for the two men out in the middle – Regalian of Perimadeia, the reigning champion, and Gordian of Saressus, the challenger – it was the last day of one of their lives. That was, in fact, the only certainty; certain, because in their last nine bouts these two perfectly matched opponents had hammered each other to a standstill, until neither man had the strength to stand, and one thing the Perimadeian State Lottery couldn't permit was ten consecutive no-score draws.

The last round. From his box, the Emperor Maxen saw the first ray of sunset flashing a premonition of red off two swordblades, and shuddered.

Regalian struck first; a dazzling feint to the left, followed by a curling dropped-elbow backhand ('Reminiscent,' muttered the arena correspondent of the *Perimadeia Globe* under his breath, 'of Mazentius in his prime, if lacking the true finesse . . .') which Gordian met with a scrambled parry, only to find that the blade had somehow eluded him. For a fraction of a second both men froze, staring at the welling red gash on the top of Gordian's forearm—

(Desperately, the arena correspondent ransacked his brain for a lightning-flash of imagery, a drop of verbal amber in which to catch this mayfly moment. 'Sick,' he scribbled, 'as a parrot . . .')

—And then Regalian dropped his shoulder, put his weight behind it and committed himself to the final, irrevocable lunge.

Click.

The lights went out.

Jane tutted loudly, and swung the mouse up to the appropriate window.

Seventy pages still to go. There was no way she could afford to lose a central character now. Nothing for it but to erase the whole evening's work and start again.

'C'mon, you guys,' she sighed. 'Anybody'd think you *wanted* to kill each other.'

'Okay,' said a voice in the darkness, 'who forgot to bring the torch?'

'It's Dave's turn.'

'No it bloody isn't, it was my turn yesterday.'

'You forgot.'

'Okay, but it was still my turn yesterday. Somebody else's turn today.'

Somebody struck a match, and the eerie orange glow illuminated an empty lot, with five or six figures standing listlessly on the edge of the light. The arena, the circles of seats, altars and Imperial box had all vanished.

'We're definitely going to have to draw up a rota,' said Regalian, wearily. 'This is getting absolutely ridiculous.'

'It was Neville's turn, surely.'

'No it wasn't, it was my turn Thursday,' replied the tall young man who was standing in the centre, the hem of his cloak pressed hard against his forearm to staunch the bleeding. 'And besides, the batteries are flat.'

'Fine,' sighed his erstwhile opponent. 'So we need a batteries rota as well. And who's going to end up organising it, we ask ourselves? Muggins, that's who.'

'Pack it in, you two,' snapped the Emperor Maxen, then he yelped as the match burned down on to his fingers, and there was darkness once more. 'The hell with this,' he said. 'Last one down the pub gets them in. Mine's a Mackeson.'

Where they come from, nobody knows. Where they go to, afterwards, who cares? They are there to do a job. Provided the job gets done, what they get up to in their own time is nobody's business but their own.

Characters. As Tolstoy is reported to have said: some of my best friends are characters, but would you let your daughter marry one?

'For God's sake,' snapped Regalian, fishing the lemon out of his gin and tonic and discarding it into the ashtray, 'put a bit of sticking plaster or something on it, before you bleed to death. You're dripping all over my sandwiches.'

The young man (Gordian to the countless fans of Jane Armitage's *Circle In Chaos* trilogy, Neville to his mother, and That Tall Pillock, universally, behind his back) shook his head vehemently. 'I can't go on tomorrow with my arms covered in Band Aid,' he reasoned. 'Besides, they stick to hairs and when you pull them off it hurts like hell.'

'I've got some iodine in my bag,' Doris suggested, putting down her knitting. 'If you like, I'll . . .'

At the mention of the word iodine, Neville had turned a pale, blanched colour, and Doris (who specialised in minor Arthurian enchantresses and Celtic earth mothers with lots of silver jewellery) shrugged and went back to her matinée jacket. Regalian shifted his sandwiches ostentatiously to another table.

'It's your fault,' said Neville peevishly to his turned back. 'If you didn't get quite so carried away, I wouldn't have got cut in the first place. I knew you'd do somebody an injury with that thing one day.'

'Terribly sorry,' Regalian replied with his mouth full. 'I somehow got the impression we were having a sword fight, whereas in fact we were doing traditional Perimadeian folk dances. How stupid of me, I do apologise.'

'You two, save it for the show. We'll have the whole bloody thing to do over again tomorrow, don't forget.'

Names can be terribly confusing. The Emperor Maxen's real name was, in fact, Max; which shouldn't have been a problem, in theory. In practice, however, he generally found himself having to write down which one he was at any given moment on the inside of his wrist. As a result, he spent a lot of his time glancing down and thus failing to meet other people's frank and fearless gazes, which meant he usually got typecast as the wicked emperor.

'And whose fault is that?' Neville pressed on relentlessly. 'If someone who shall remain nameless hadn't got all over-excited and started lashing about with a whacking great sword . . .'

Regalian looked up. 'Come off it, Nev,' he said irritably, 'you're for the chop this time, and you know it.'

'Do I really?'

Regalian nodded. 'Yes,' he said. 'Not your fault, mind,' he added. 'It's just that the silly bitch has really written herself into a corner this time.'

'Typical,' commented Doris. 'She's about as much good at plots as Guy Fawkes.'

'Actually . . .' Linda (Lady Helionassa; dozy princesses and thick-as-two-short-dryads elf-maidens) furrowed her brow, that harbinger of the painfully obvious remark. 'Actually, Guy Fawkes must have been *quite* good at plots, or how did he get the gunpowder down in the cellars in the first place?'

Silence. Whenever Linda took part in a conversation, it generally tended to die shortly afterwards, rather like the three heavies leaning on the bar when Clint Eastwood first walks into the saloon. Regalian returned to his sandwiches. Neville dabbed at his arm with a bar towel. Max stared, pointedly but to no avail, at the bottom of his empty glass. Doris cast off the end of her row and consulted the pattern.

'Although,' Linda went on, 'I s'pose—'

'Gosh,' said Regalian, standing up. 'Is it that time already? Ah well, lines to learn, moves to block out. See you all tomorrow.'

He escaped quickly, to a chorus of 'Night, Reg,' into the relative safety of the beer garden. The time had been when he'd objected to being called Reg, on the grounds that Reg wasn't his name. Neither, it was pointed out to him, was Regalian; that was just what his character was called. Maybe; but he'd been Regalian so long that he couldn't remember what he'd been called before. These days he tended to answer to anything beginning with R, with the possible exception of Rover.

He was about to start the long trudge home when he stopped dead in his tracks, frowned and looked up. Nothing to be seen, of course, except the black sky; but there were times when he wondered . . .

'You're watching me, aren't you?' he said aloud. No reply, except for the soft snicketing of grasshoppers, the fidgeting whirr of a passing bat. For all her faults, Ms Armitage wrote a tolerable evening.

'If you *are* watching,' he went on, rather more self-consciously, 'do me a favour and don't write young Neville out quite yet. He may be two yards of undiluted pillock, but he needs the work.'

Cheep cheep, flutter flutter; and somewhere, over the page and far away, a sheep bleated softly in the velvet darkness. Regalian shrugged, stuck his tongue out at the vault of Heaven, and walked home.

Jane slept.

Australia, continent of superlatives, has produced many outstanding athletes over the years, in pretty well every discipline you can think of. Jane Armitage (born Perth, 16th June 1959) was to sleep what Don Bradman was to cricket, or Rod Laver to tennis. When she left the land of her birth for the Old Country, pundits across the world expressed grave reservations. Would the cold, damp climate suit her natural game? Would she find Pommy duvets too heavy? Would the change in conditions be the ruin of that fantastic natural talent, reducing the Ray Lindwall of the eiderdown to a mere nine-hours-a-night cat-napper? Their fears were groundless. After eight years in England, Jane still slept like a log marinaded in laudanum.

It was rare, however, for her to dream; and when she did indulge herself, it was usually light and trivial, the dreamer's equivalent of something glossy off the station bookstall. Five years of studying Jane would have sent Freud back into general practice.

Not so this time. She dreamed that she was lying on her back looking up at a glass roof, or perhaps a two-way mirror. There was a man standing over her looking down. He wasn't really the sort of man you'd welcome in a dream; you'd hope he had simply come to deliver something or read the meter, and then leave. Bald, fat and heavily built, he seemed to loom at Jane through the glass. His eyebrows would have made fairly exacting jumps in a high-class steeplechase.

'Hey,' he said. 'You.'

Who, me?

'Yes, you,' said the man. 'I know you can hear me. Look, you've got to get me out of here.'

Where's here? Who are you? And where are the fluffy rabbits? Usually by this stage I get fluffy rabbits.

'Have you got any idea,' the man went on, 'how long I've been here? Thirty-six years. Thirty-six *years* in this ghastly hole. You can't begin to imagine what it's been like.'

Gosh.

'And,' the man continued, glancing nervously over his shoulder, 'this time I really believe they're on to me. They've put a price on my head, you know, the bastards.'

Please don't swear in my dream. You'll frighten the rabbits.

'You know what it'll mean if they find me,' the man hissed. 'Especially that little sod LaForce. Why I didn't kill him off while I had the chance, God only knows.'

Gosh.

'Anyway,' said the man conspiratorially to the glass, 'I've got it all worked out. Even you shouldn't have any difficulty. You can keep the money, I'm not worried about that.'

What money?

'Ready? Right. Chapter One. A merciless sun beat relent-lessly down out of a cloudless blue Arkansas sky . . . Why aren't you writing this down?'

Sorry?

'You're supposed,' said the man unpleasantly, 'to be writing this down. Come on, for pity's sake. I haven't got all night.'

I'm sorry, I don't quite—

'Oh for crying out . . .' The man broke off, cast a hurried glance over his shoulder, and cringed. 'Oh Christ, it's LaForce and the posse. Look, I'll be back tomorrow night. For pity's sake, have a pen and paper handy. Better still, a dictaphone. Then it can be typed straight from the tape, and – shit, they're *coming*!'

Jane sat bolt upright, wide awake, sweating. Her mouth was as dry as a sophisticated cocktail, and her nose tickled.

It's all right, she told herself, it was just a dream.

Like hell it was, she told herself.

She switched on the light. The sight of her familiar environment immediately reassured her that it had been, after all, merely a collection of random electrical impulses flolloping round inside her subconscious, and nothing to worry about. It also reminded her, depressingly and with great force, that sooner or later she was going to have to do some ironing.

She drank a glass of water and went back to sleep.

Human beings are, of course, fools.

They spend hundreds of years of time, hundreds of thousands of man-hours of labour and research, devising means of near-effortless mechanical transport, and spend their holidays walking across wind-scoured moorland. They devote an infinity of resources to perfecting the hologrammatic fax, but don't understand about dreams. Still, what can you expect from a life-form that wears other animals' skins and deliberately burns all its food?

Having sent his fax, Carson Montague (born Albert Skinner; Montague being his *nom de plume*) ducked behind a large rock and closed his eyes tight. There was still a chance they hadn't seen him.

A bullet took a chip out of the rock and sang away into the air. Some chance.

'Well?' said a voice at his side.

'Well what?'

'Aren't you going to shoot back, then?'

Skinner growled quietly. 'Shut up,' he said.

In the holster on his hip, the Smith & Wesson .45 Scholfield wriggled and tried to cock itself. It had, many years ago, belonged to Wild Bill Hickock; and, although it had since fallen on hard times, it still had its pride.

'Chicken,' it said.

'Look, keep your voice down, will you?'

'CHICKEN!'

'Any more out of you and you get unloaded.'

'Bastard.'

One of the less important side-effects of Skinner's terrible mistake had been the Scholfield's acquisition of an immortal soul and a voice to go with it. Comparatively speaking, it was the least of his problems, but it was still a bloody nuisance, particularly as the wretched thing hadn't left his side for thirty-six years and he had nobody else to talk to.

'From here,' it muttered, 'I could get three of them, maybe four, no problem. That'd only leave six, and—'

'*Quiet!*'

Skinner's hissed command echoed alarmingly in the still, warm air of the canyon. One of the posse outriders lifted his head.

'Bill'd have gone for it,' the gun whispered reproachfully. 'Bill'd have had me out of the leather and blazing away before you could say . . .'

It wasn't even the fact that the gun's sole topic of conversation was human beings in their capacity as relatively straightforward moving targets that really got on Skinner's nerves. What irked him most was that the damned thing was so unceasingly chatty. He'd tried everything – cotton wool shoved down the chamber mouths, an old sock, even a silencer – and still it continued; a constant stream of bloodthirsty twittering, even when he was trying to sleep.

'For the last time,' he growled, in a voice like a file cutting hard brass. 'One more peep out of you and you go in the melt. *Capisce?*'

'. . . Best years of my life, and what thanks do I . . . ?'

With exquisite caution, Skinner ventured a quick glimpse round the side of the rock. The man who had fired at him was standing up in his stirrups, looking round. The others were spread out in a loose crescent formation, ready to deploy at speed. In the middle of the group, Jonah LaForce lounged in the saddle, his white Stetson pulled down over his eyes, a long Sharps rifle cradled in the crook of his left arm.

Shit, thought Skinner. All the running, the hiding, the living like a pig in this godforsaken wilderness of a potboiler, and it ends here. Shot to death by a goddamn cliché.

Slowly, unwillingly, he reached down and closed his fingers around the grips of the revolver.

'All right,' Regalian shouted, 'are we all agreed?'

Linda giggled. 'You do look silly,' she said, 'standing on that chair. I can see your socks.'

Regalian ignored her. 'The time has come,' he said, 'to stand up and be counted. For far too long—'

'Does that mean we all have to stand on chairs? Or can we be counted at floor level?'

Another day's work done, another night in the pub. That's fiction for you.

'For far too long,' Regalian persevered nevertheless, 'authors worldwide have been taking us for granted. Well, it's time we put a stop to all that. Characters united can never be def—'

'Time, ladies and gentlemen, please,' chirruped the landlord in the background. 'Come on, you lot, haven't you got plots to go to?'

'United,' Regalian said gamely, 'we can never be defeated, and until our perfectly reasonable demands are met I recommend that we work strictly to rule. Our demands are—'

'Put a sock in it, will you?' shouted Alf (Jotapian the High Priest; bad guys and Grand Viziers a speciality, no character too large or too small). 'I want to be out of here before the chip shop closes.'

'One: a say in the decision-making process. It's intolerable that in this day and age a character's destiny is still completely at the whim of some jumped-up little scribbler. Two—'

'Put a *sock* in it,' chortled Linda, rendered breathless by her own wit. Nobody else seemed to appreciate the joke, but she was used to that.

'Two: no character to be killed or married without his previous consent in writing. Three—'

The landlord switched the lights off. Slowly, with a long sigh, Regalian climbed down off his chair and felt his way to the door. Every night, for as long as he could remember, he had broached the subject of a characters' union, and the furthest he had ever been allowed to get was Demand Four.

A character's life is by its very nature nomadic, and for

the duration of the trilogy Regalian was living in a bedsit over a chemist's shop on the junction of Tolkien Street and Moorcock Avenue. It was so small that the sixty-watt bulb provided by the management produced more than enough light to illuminate the whole of it, but it was cheap (thirty zlotys a week, all found) and fairly central, and he only went there to sleep. His collection of dog-eared book jackets concealed the peeling of the wallpaper, and the fact that the whole building was so dilapidated that it only stayed upright through force of habit was no concern of his. He kicked off his shoes, poked his thumb through the foil on a bottle of milk, and sat down on the bed. Lines to learn for tomorrow, then sleep.

The lines were ready for him, neatly stacked on the chipped formica bedside table. He picked up the sheaf of papers and began to read.

It had never, in all his long career, occurred to him to wonder how they got there. Did they simply materialise, or did a trans-dimensional courier deliver them, silent and unobtrusive as the Milk Tray man, or did the landlady bring them in when she came in to hoover? He neither knew nor cared.

Fight Scene, he read. *Regalian fights with Gordian in the arena. One of them is killed.*

Marvellous, he thought. What the hell are we supposed to do, toss a bloody coin? He knew, in his heart of hearts, that it wouldn't be him, however; because he was the Hero, and nobody kills their Hero with seventy pages still to go. What it really meant was that the damnfool author had made yet another lash-up in the structure, which meant the big fight was happening on pages 180–3, instead of 241–4. In order to cover her tracks, she was going to have to leave the fight scene at the point where one of them (not specified) was killed, and then go trailing off into the subplot or do flashbacks or something for twenty pages or so before owning up and getting on with the story. The technical term is Agonising Suspense, and a surer indication of the pot boiling dry would be difficult to find. Regalian sighed. It meant a day or so off, at any rate, while some other poor fools (Linda, probably, and Doris) would have to work double shifts to cover. Not his problem, he decided. The milk was ever so slightly off.

The rest of the lines confirmed his suspicions so exactly that he simply skimmed through them; then he turned back and studied the details of the fight with a mixture of professional thoroughness and abject contempt. You couldn't do *that*, for a start, not with a six-pound, two-handed broadsword. You'd sprain your wrist.

He threw the pages on the floor, stretched out on the bed and felt for the light switch. What the hell, he said to himself, it's only work. More to the point, what was he going to do on his day off?

Jane sat down in front of her screen, flexed her fingers and put in the disk.

The usual green lines, beeps and facetious user-chummy comments; and then the screen went blank for a moment. Jane scowled and leaned forward.

Hi! My name's Hamlet, you may have heard of me. I was wondering, do you happen to have a job going?

Jane stared at the writing on the screen for a second or two and then reached out for the user's manual. A computer virus? she wondered. Hackers?

I know it's not quite the done thing to approach an author direct like this, but I've had it up to here working for Bill Shakespeare. I think you and I could be good for each other, you know?

'Really?' Jane said. 'What makes you think that?'

Well, read the screen, *I've been a fan of your stuff for ages now. I think you characters are, you know, neat. My kind of people.*

'Thank you.'

You're welcome. Your people, when there's someone whose head needs bashing in, they don't stand around agonising about it in blank verse, they just roll up their sleeves and get on with it. No wimps need apply. That's my kind of scene.

'I see.'

Say it myself as shouldn't, the screen read, *I do have a certain following. Just think how it looks to the boys and girls out there. Like for instance, there's the bit where I come up unexpectedly on the bad guy in the chapel?*

'I know the bit you mean.'

Well, I ask you. If it'd been one of yours, it'd be out with the whacking great knife, chippy-chop and on to the big love scene, no worries. And do you know what that ponce has me doing? Worrying that if I top the bastard, he'll go to Heaven. I mean to say, what're we doing here? A proper grown-up thriller, or Listen With Goddamn Mother?

'Um . . .'

And the women, the screen continued, the words flashing up like a huge flock of rooks startled off a ploughed field. *Don't get me wrong, but they're just not my type. Not like the birds in your stuff. I mean, you wouldn't dream of pairing your hero off with some droopy bit with tits like goosepimples who goes around talking to the flowers, now would you?*

'Thank you,' said Jane. 'I'll let you know.'

But . . .

'Goodbye.' She switched the machine off and pulled out the disk. As she did so, the printer suddenly screamed into life, shuttled the daisywheel a few times and went back to sleep. Jane pulled out the paper.

I ALSO DO COMEDY, it read. *AND BAR MITZVAHS.*

Having binned the page, switched on again and deleted yesterday's effort, Jane sat for a moment, wondering what the hell she was supposed to do now. A long time ago she had decided that writing was like the school holidays: a noisy cluster of whining voices, saying that they're bored and demanding that she find them something to do. That's the trouble with characters. No bloody initiative.

Skinner leaned back against the rock, feeling dazed and extremely foolish, as befits a man who's just shot his own villain.

'Told you,' crowed the Scholfield in his hand. 'Piece of duff, I said. Easy as falling off a—'

'Oh sure,' Skinner snapped. 'Nothing to it really LaForce shoots, nearly takes my head off; I stagger back in terror, accidentally jarring my hand against the rock; you go off; the bullet ricochets off his left stirrup-iron, his belt-buckle, the other guy's wooden leg and a flat stone, and ends up going straight through the back of his head, thus producing the only known instance of a man being shot from behind by someone standing directly in front of him. I do that sort of thing for a pastime.'

'Well,' sniffed the Scholfield, 'on page 86 of *Painted Saddles*, you have the hero shoot at the villain's reflection in a mirror, through two locked doors and a piano.'

'Yes,' Skinner shouted, 'but that's *fiction!*'

'So's this.'

Skinner sat down heavily and stared mournfully at the corpses littering the canyon floor. 'Yes,' he muttered soberly, 'I guess it is, at that.'

A revolver can't frown, but someone with an excessively vivid imagination might have thought he saw the trigger guard pucker slightly. 'I don't know why you've suddenly come over all droopy,' the gun said. 'Thought you'd be pleased, your worst enemy dead and all. Should make life a bit easier all round.'

A bullet sang off the rock, six inches or so above Skinner's head. He jerked sideways, tripped over his feet and fell behind a small, round boulder.

'You reckon?' he said.

'Who the hell's that?'

'This is pure conjecture on my part,' Skinner replied, 'but maybe it's one of the posse members who rode away when you started shooting.'

'And now you reckon they've come back.'

'Fits all the known facts, don't you think?'

'Yippee!'

An expression of revulsion passed over Skinner's face, and he glared at the pistol in his hand. 'You bastard,' he said. 'Don't you ever get tired of fighting?'

'No. I'm a gun. Think about it.'

Skinner sighed. 'Well,' he said, 'I'm a human, and I do. Any ideas?'

The gun was silent for a moment.

'You could try shooting back,' it said cheerfully.

'I thought you'd say that.'

CHAPTER TWO

The pigeons were restless tonight.

They shifted uneasily on their perches as blue fangs of lightning gouged the night sky over the huddled suburbs of Dewsbury. Occasional flashes of livid incandescence, bright and sudden as a flashbulb, threw their long shadows against the far wall of Norman Frankenbotham's pigeon loft, making them look for all the world like roosting pterodactyls.

In his shed, Frankenbotham gazed up at the fury of the heavens through the thick lenses of his Specsavers reading glasses. He didn't smile – he was from Yorkshire, after all – but in some inner chamber of his heart he was satisfied. Very soon now, perhaps even tonight, and it would all be over.

He turned over the small brown paper parcel in his hands, noticing with dour approval the Sheffield postmark, and then reached for a Stanley knife and started to cut through the packaging. It had taken him five years to find a lateral thermic transducer – five long years of combing the *Yellow Pages*, studying classified ads and newsagents' windows, enquiring in pubs and betting shops the length and breadth of the three Ridings. Oh, he could have had one from Geneva or Kyoto by return of post, but that wouldn't have done at all. It would have defeated the whole object of the exercise.

Nothing but genuine parts. Genuine *Yorkshire* parts.

Six years ago, Norman Frankenbotham had sat in the stands at Headingley, watching the once invincible Yorkshire cricket team suffering ignominious defeat at the hands of some pack of Surrey mercenaries, captained by a renegade New Zealander; and he had sworn an oath by all his gods that he, personally, would do something about it. He would provide his country with the fast bowler they so desperately required.

Had he been thirty years younger, it would have been easy. Early morning training runs, hours of relentless practice in the nets behind the Alderman Dewhurst Memorial Pavilion, early nights and a diet of raw red meat, and he'd have done the job himself. But that was out of the question; and a few cursory inspections of the earring-wearing, gaudily-clad youths purporting to play cricket in the local parks and recreation grounds had convinced him that there was no hitherto undiscovered Trueman or Old waiting to be identified and brought to the attention of the selectors. In short, there was only one thing for it.

He'd have to make one. Out of bits.

Frankenbotham shook his head at the memory, and reached for a small screwdriver. Outside, the sky groaned like a great oak splitting in a hurricane. Calmly, he unscrewed an inspection panel and studied a wiring diagram.

Locate connector A on terminal B and tighten retaining screws C. Be careful not to over-tighten. Insert resistor D using the tool provided.

Once the fateful decision had been taken, it had simply been a matter of applying himself and getting on with the job. Six years, a broken marriage and his life savings later, he could see before him the final consummation of his dreams. A little solder, a few minor modifications, a lick of formaldehyde and a bloody great big bolt of lightning, and he'd be home and dry.

With a dispassionate eye he studied his creation, stretched out on the workbench in front of him, and came to a decision. He would call it, he decided, Stanley. Stanley Earnshaw.

Neatly, deftly, without hurrying, he soldered the last connector in place and screwed down the small metal plate to the back of Stanley's head. Five minutes with the formaldehyde bottle, a few last touches with the neutronic lancet – was he dawdling, he asked himself, finding things to do so as to postpone the moment of truth? – and a last systems check, ticking off each entry on the back of the dog-eared envelope that bore the master schematic; and he was ready. Slowly, his heart pounding, he taped the electrodes in place and waited.

A flash of lightning whitened out the world, and he counted – two, three, four – for the thunder. It was headed this way, getting nearer. Soon, soon. To occupy his mind, he checked the central neural directory one last time, flicking the feeler gauges in and out with the ease of long practice. *Flash!* one, two. The next one, he promised himself. The lightning was coming!

Steady, Norman lad, don't get carried away. With exaggerated care he armed the secondary relief circuits and engaged the main console. The air hummed and crackled.

First God, and now me, he thought. But God hadn't had to get all his supplies out of the back pages of the *Exchange and Mart.*

Now! He could feel the lightning strike through the soles of his boots. With a quick, frantic movement he threw the central switch, and was nearly thrown off his feet by the incredible surge of power running through the system. Fat worms of blue fire crawled up and down the wires connecting Stanley's wrists to the transformer. There was a sickening smell of burning.

'Live!' he screamed. 'Stanley, live! Stanley, tha daft bugger, get on wi' it!'

And God created Man in His own image.

God's image had been skilfully crafted for Him by Kraftig & Stein, public relations consultants to the *really* important (established -1). It had been a tricky assignment.

'Sure,' the original Mr Stein had said, 'we want omniscient. Sure, we want omnipresent and omnipotent. That's good. That's *you*. But is that going to be enough?'

ENOUGH?

'Yeah.' Mr Stein put his fingertips together and leaned back in his chair. 'Think about it. What I ask myself is, what does omnipotent *say* to me? What sort of aura has it got?'

AURA?

'Exactly,' interrupted Mr Kraftig, nodding. 'Just what we were thinking. Which is why we think you should be more . . .'

The two image consultants exchanged the most fleeting of glances. They were, they knew, taking a risk here, but if you want to be known as daring and innovative, it goes with the territory.

'More, kind of, *caring*,' cooed Mr Stein. 'Compassionate. Accessible.'

'Lovable.'

'Cuddly.'

The burning bush arched two incandescent branches.
I SEE.

Mr Kraftig took a deep breath. 'Omniscient and omnipotent and omnipresent and stuff as well, of course. No question about that. We think you should be very big in all the omnis. But, at the same time . . .'

'Cuddly.'

The bush crackled thoughtfully. This was, of course, probably the most significant pause in history.

I LIKE IT.

'That's great,' said Mr Stein, as the cosmos breathed a sigh of relief. 'Now, as a first step . . .'

All that was, of course, a long time ago; to be precise, the breakfast meeting at 7 a.m. on the first day. The problems associated with creation have not, however, changed all that much since. In a sense, each subsequent act of creation has been a sort of rerun of the very first; a random dip into the Scrabble bag of potentiality, a wild guess in Destiny's endless game of Twenty Questions. The problem is, of course, that creation is irrevocable. Once a thing has been created, it's there, somewhere, for ever. No matter what you try and do about it subsequently, there'll always be some interfering bastard with an ark and a dove to make sure it survives.

Jane switched on and emptied her mind. Here, with nothing between her and her characters but a thin plate of glass and a few glowing green letters, she was once more alone and with nobody to turn to.

Well now, she thought. What the hell can I find for these idiots to do next?

She could feel the screen staring at her, like an over-efficient secretary waiting to take dictation from an unshaven, hung-over boss. She frowned.

What sort of book do you want this to be?

Where the question came from, and what it was doing in her head in the first place, she had no idea. It ran around inside her brain like an escaped dog, yapping and trailing its lead.

Profitable, she replied. I want this book to outsell David Eddings and Storm Constantine and Dragonlance *put together*. And that's all there is to it. Now, can we stop this nonsense and get on with some work, please?

Yes, but think. When you were a little girl, you wanted to be a writer. You wanted to create a magical world that people could go to, full of wonder and magic and deep, powerful resonances. You wanted to make a world fit for heroes to live in. And have you?

Shut up, she replied. Instead of all that bullshit, tell me how I'm going to get Gordian out of there alive *and* get Maldezar to Perimadeia before Dunthor notices the Weirdstone's gone missing.

Silence.

That, Jane mused, is just typical of mystic voices in one's brain. No practical help whatsoever. Understand that fact, and you won't go far wrong. If Joan of Arc had stopped for a moment and asked, 'Drive the English out of Aquitaine, yes, fine. How, exactly?' she'd probably have lived to be ninety.

Something clicked in the back of her mind. That's a thought, she considered, I could have a vision. Regalian is standing over Gordian's recumbent form, sword raised for the coup de grace, and a vision could suddenly appear and tell him not to.

Yes? And?

Jane shook her head. One step at a time.

She lit a cigarette, swigged a mouthful of cold, clammy tea and started to type. Meanwhile, Central Casting started auditioning for the part of A Vision.

'Not you again.'

Hamlet scowled. 'There's no need to take that attitude,'

he said. 'I'll have you know I'm dead good at visions. In Act One, Scene—'

'Seeing them, maybe. Being them's something quite other.'

'Shall I do my bit, or are we just going to stand here chatting all day?'

Central Casting sighed. 'In your own time, Mr Hamlet.'

'Oh dear,' said Skinner cheerfully. 'I seem to have run out of bullets.'

'There's plenty more in the saddleba—'

With a quick, firm movement, Skinner jammed his gun into its holster, fastened the strap and stood up. In the distance, the last survivor of the posse rode like a bat out of hell across the skyline. Only forty-eight hours before, he had been filling in time waiting tables and parking cars, poised for his lucky break into the big time. Get me out of this alive, he muttered as he leaned down low over his horse's neck, and first thing in the morning I'll enrol for medical school like they wanted me to.

Alone at last. With a sigh, Skinner picked up his saddlebags, settled them on his shoulder and started to talk, musing as he did so on how all his characters, when stranded in the middle of the desert after a savage gun battle, had managed to find their way to the Lucky Dollar saloon in time for the start of the next scene without so much as a blistered toe. He must have written them very comfortable boots.

He eventually stumbled into town, dog tired and footsore, seven hours later – just in time to be told that the last room in the hotel had been taken twenty minutes ago but he was welcome to sleep in the haybarn for just three dollars fifty. For a few dollars more, he could have a blanket.

Three dollars fifty, he reflected bitterly as he kicked

the straw into something resembling a mattress, for a night in a lousy barn. He sat down, opened the saddle-bag and counted his money; running low on that, too. When, in Chapter One, he'd envisioned twenty thousand dollars in hidden Confederate gold stashed away in the deserted mineshaft at Las Monedas, he hadn't anticipated that it would have to last him thirty-six years.

I have to get out of here, he thought, and soon. Which means I've got to get the message through. Which means . . .

Bright and early next morning – the proprietors of Finnegan's Hotel provide a highly efficient early morning call service to their guests in the form of a large rat, which bites their toes at six thirty-one *precisely* – Skinner packed his bags and set out for his next destination. If he'd been in the mood for company, he'd have found it hard to come by. Volunteers for a trip into the heart of the Blackfoot nation were as rare as thousand-dollar bills, and rather more expendable.

An arrow, passing through the crown of his hat and neatly parting what little remained of his hair, informed him that he'd arrived. He reined in his horse – bought that morning from Hank's Cheap 'n' Cheerful Livery & Hire, and worth every cent of a tenth of what he'd paid for it – sat perfectly still and waited.

About thirty seconds later, a group of warriors mounted on small ponies burst over the skyline out of nowhere and rode round him in a circle, yelling and whooping. Trying his best to look bored, Skinner took out a nail file and attended to a troublesome hangnail, until the leader of the war party broke off from the main group and trotted over to him.

'How,' he said.

Skinner put the nail file away and smiled. 'Quite,' he replied. 'Look, I just want a quick word with your chief, okay? So if we can just skip a few of the formalities . . .'

'How.'

Skinner frowned. 'Hey,' he said, 'save it for the customers. I know for a fact you can speak English, so why don't we just—?'

'Paleface come from far away bearing stick-that-speak-like-thunder . . .'

'Look.' Skinner leaned forward in his saddle and scowled. 'I know you,' he said. 'I wrote you for Chapter Six of *Last Stage to Tombstone*, nearly forty years ago. Before that, you were a clerk in a shipping office. Take me to the big guy and your secret is safe with me.'

As they rode in silence towards the village, Skinner had time to reflect bitterly on the way things worked around here. Forty years since he'd created the character of Dances With Pigeons; forty years during which time had stood still, or rather lounged about with its feet up. Just think, this was supposed to be 1878. He'd been here for thirty-six years. By rights, it should now be 1914, in which case all he'd have to do was take a train to Chicago, walk to 354 Paradise Street and warn his seven-year-old self that under no circumstances should he take up writing Westerns for a living; or, if he did, never on pain of death to start writing one called *Painted Saddles*, in which the hero—

'How.' A familiar voice woke him from his reverie, and he saw that he'd reached the village. In front of him stood an aged and unbelievably dignified Blackfoot chief, flanked by an escort of tall young warriors. He nodded politely and said, 'Hi.'

'Me Chief Three Blind Mice,' said the Indian. 'You smoke pipe of—'

'Later.' With an effort and a certain amount of pain, Skinner eased himself off Hank's Special Offer Eezi-Go deluxe saddle, straightened his left knee with his hand,

and rubbed some circulation back into the leg. 'Good to see you again, Mice, you're looking well. Now, there's a little job I'd like you to do for me. Okay?'

Three Blind Mice's expression was so impassive, his bearing so rigid, that Skinner instinctively glanced to the chief's left in the hope of catching sight of the cigar store. 'It's only a little thing, Mice, won't take you a minute. Or do you want me to tell the boys and girls about the scene in *Ride Down the Whirlwind* which we cut out of the final draft? The one with the buffalo skin and the pot of—?'

'Paleface follow me.'

'Delighted.'

In Three Blind Mice's teepee, the two men sat on either side of a smouldering fire.

'You crummy bastard,' snarled Mice. 'Where d'you think you get off, turning up like this and threatening me in front of the whole goddamn nation? I oughta have your ass stuffed down an anthill for that.'

Skinner shrugged. 'Nice to see you too, Mice. Been keeping well?'

'Well?' Mice sneered. 'Thanks to you and that lousy fight scene at the end of *Five Rifles For Texas* I can only eat liquids and I gotta go to the john three times every hour. And you ask me if I'm keeping—'

'Hey, calm down,' Skinner replied amiably. 'Most guys'd be thrilled to bits at a chance to meet their Creator face to face. People have been burnt at the stake for less.'

Mice grimaced. 'Most guys have a Creator they can respect, Skinner,' he replied unpleasantly. 'Not me, though. I gotta have you.'

'At least you know I exist, Mice.'

'Yeah. So does small-pox.'

Skinner spread his arms in a gesture of magnanimity. 'Be that as it may, Mice. I need a favour. Now, it's like this . . .'

★   ★   ★

Jane sat bolt upright, groped for the light switch, and then realised she was still asleep. In the circumstances, this was a pity.

Hi.

'You again.'

Me again. Look, thinking back over our previous conversation, it occurs to me that maybe you haven't got my letter yet.

'What letter?' Jane's eyes moved under their closed lids. 'And who are those people behind you?'

The dream grimaced shamefacedly. *They're medicine dancers of the Blackfoot nation, if you really want to know. They're helping me. Some goddamn snake-oil king of a medicine man has sent my spirit out of my body so's I can talk to you.* He paused, glanced over his shoulder and went on. *Actually, I'm not at all convinced they know what the hell they're doing, so if we could make this snappy . . .*

Jane tried to open her eyes, but for all the good that it did she might just as well have tried to open a soft drink can off which the little aluminium loop has just snapped. 'Who are you?' she said.

My name's Skinner, said the dream, *I'm a writer and I'm in terrible trouble. And only you can help me. Okay so far?*

Jane nodded. Virtually all the writers she knew, herself included, were in terrible trouble of some sort, usually with their spouses or the credit card companies. The beak of sympathy started to tap against the inside of the shell of bewilderment.

Right, where do I start? Basically it's quite simple. I used to write Westerns, under the name of Carson Montague. Maybe you've heard . . . ?

Jane shuddered slightly. 'Sorry,' she said. 'Doesn't ring a bell.'

Oh. The dream looked slightly wistful. *Oh well. Never mind. People were just starting to say I was going to be the next Zane Grey . . .*

'Who's Zane Grey?'

The dream gave her a cold look. *Anyway,* it went on, *as a result of an unfortunate accident, the details of which I won't bore you with right now, I got stuck in one of my own books.*

'Stuck?' Jane tried to blink, closed eyes notwithstanding. 'In one of your own . . .'

Yeah. Painted Saddles. *Not one of my best, at that. And I've been here ever since. Thirty-six years come June sixteenth.* The dream swallowed hard and passed a finger round the inside of its collar. *It hasn't been fun, I'm telling you.*

'I can imagine.'

Which is why, the dream continued urgently, *I need your help. You gotta get me out of here, before I'm killed or I go crazy.*

'How can I help?'

For an instant, the dream almost smiled. *That's my girl,* it said. *It's very simple. All you have to do is rewrite the book.*

'Hang on.' Jane licked her lips, which were as dry as very stale bread. 'You want me to write a Western?'

The dream nodded. *Nothing to it, I promise. Any fool can do it. I used to do it, for Christ's sake, and Dostoevsky I ain't. If it'll make it any easier for you, I can tell you where my manuscript is. Or where it was. I guess in the last thirty-five years, someone might have moved it.*

Sadly, Jane shook her head. 'Sorry,' she said, 'I can't do that. I'm hopeless at pastiche.'

Hey! The dream pressed its nose against the reality interface and scowled at her. *Don't give me that. Look, it doesn't have to be any good. Jesus, Westerns are supposed to be crummy. All you have to do is write something in which I get out of this dump, and . . .*

Jane shook her head again. 'You don't understand,' she said. 'I really am terrible at everything except mainstream fantasy. I'd probably only make things worse for you. I don't know the first thing about horses, and I'm not even sure where Arizona is, let alone what it's like, and I haven't a clue whether a Winchester .45 is a rifle or a pistol, so . . .'

The dream looked thoughtful. *Maybe you have a point,* it mused, *at that. I hadn't actually thought it through, I guess. Okay, just a second, let me just . . .*

The dream stepped back out of the interface, and for two minutes or so Jane dreamed unpleasantly of Blackfoot warriors dancing doggedly round a smouldering fire making peculiar noises with no apparent enthusiasm whatsoever. Then the dream reappeared.

Got it. All you have to do is send your hero. He'll find a way to get me out.

'I beg your pardon?'

Your hero, the dream said impatiently. *You have got a hero, haven't you?*

For a few moments, Jane's mind was blank. 'Oh,' she said, 'the hero of my books. But he's a fantasy hero, I'm not quite sure he'd—'

So? The dream shrugged. *I'm no bigot. So what if he dresses in dumb clothes and talks like a cross between Grimm's Fairy Tales and the Bible? All he needs to do is get me out of this book and across the county line into one of your books, and then you can write me home from there. What could be simpler than that?*

'But . . .'

Look, he's a hero, right? Which means he's brave, resourceful, cunning, altruistic, noble, good with horses and weapons, all that shit. Well, isn't he?

Jane paused, thinking of her central character. 'Well,' she said, 'sort of. I mean, he tries his best.'

Jeez! You mean to say you've got a wimp for a hero?

'No,' said Jane, thoughtfully, 'not a wimp. Not,' she added, 'as such. I mean, he's a deep and really quite complex character.'

Fuck.

'I'm sorry?'

Look, that's all right. Anything's better than nothing. If he can ride a horse and read a map, he'll do just fine. So long as you get him here quickly, I'm prepared to take my chances. You are going to help, aren't you?

'I . . .'

Beside Jane's bed, the alarm clock went off.

Livid sheets of blue fire rolled through the shed, flickering hideously. Oblivious, Albert knelt beside the workbench and howled at his creation.

'*Stanley! Stanley lad! Live! Wake up, tha bloody great pillock!*'

The body on the workbench twitched; then, as another bolt of lightning seared through the already crackling air, it jerked convulsively, snapping the D-clamps as if they were made of porcelain, and sat upright.

It was alive. Heart beating. Lungs drawing. Tendons flexing.

All it needed now was a soul.

Mr Hamlet?

'Yeah. Whoosat? Look, have you any idea what time it—?'

This is Central Casting. We've got a job for you, if you'd be interested.

'Be with you in a jiffy.'

CHAPTER THREE

Slowly, it turned its head and stared at its Creator; who, for the very first time, began to wish he'd paid just a little bit more attention to the aesthetic side of things. True, when you're putting together a fast bowler out of whatever you can lay your hands on, you take what you can get and are thankful. Nevertheless . . .

'Now then, Stanley lad,' muttered Norman, backing away and finding that the shed was rather smaller than he remembered. 'Stay ont' workbench until I tell thee otherwise. Stanley! Be told!'

With an eerie grinding noise (*Oh bugger*, thought Norman, *forgot to oil t'eyelid bearings*) its eyes opened. And – graunch graunch, grind grind – blinked twice. Its lips mouthed noiselessly, as if it had suddenly discovered in mid sentence that it had forgotten how to speak.

'What about,' squeaked Norman, 'a nice cup of tea?'

A shudder ran through the Thing, and it made a little gurgling noise at the back of its throat. Norman tried walking backwards through the shed wall, ineffectually.

'. . . And, by a sleep, to say we end, The heartache and the thousand natural shocks. That flesh is heir to, 'tis a consummation Jesus bloody Christ where the fucking hell am I?' it said.

'Dewsbury,' Norman replied.

'Dewsbury?'

'In Yorkshire.'

'Yorkshire.' Slowly, the Thing raised a hand, rubbed its eyes and yelped. Specially roughened palms, for obtaining better purchase on a wet cricket ball, had been one of Norman's more satisfying design modifications. 'That's in England, isn't it?'

Ordinarily, Norman would have had something to say about a remark like that. In this context, however, he simply nodded.

'Ye gods,' snarled the Thing, swinging its legs off the workbench and getting unsteadily to its feet, 'they did it! The slimy little sods actually did it! Just wait till I get my hands—'

'Tha what?' Norman queried.

'Rosencrantz and Guildenstern,' the Thing replied. 'This time they actually did get me to England, all that crap with the pirates notwithstanding. I'll . . .' Something seemed to dawn on it, and it looked down. 'Hoy!' it said. 'That's not my body. What bloody practical joker's been mucking about with my body?'

That, as far as Norman was concerned, was it. With a terrified squeal he jumped back and hid himself behind the draught-excluder curtain that hung over the shed door. The Thing sighed.

'Oh for crying out loud,' it said wearily. 'Not another one. Not another ruddy ponce who thinks that sneaking round the back of the soft furnishings makes him invisible. Come out of there, you clown, I can see your blasted shoes poking out under the hem.'

The curtain twitched slightly, but that was all. The Thing shook its head sadly (*And the neck swivels*, muttered

Norman's subconscious. *Ah well, too late now*), selected a rubber hammer from the toolrack and applied it with modest but palpable force to where it calculated the kneecaps ought to be. Norman fell forwards through the curtain, barked his shin on the corner of the workbench and sat down clumsily in a big cardboard box full of offcuts.

'Strewth,' continued the Thing, looking round the shed. 'This is a bloody odd book we're in, if you ask me.'

'Book?'

The Thing nodded. 'Yeah,' it said. 'You know, the book we're characters in. What's it about, by the way? Nobody saw fit to tell me before I left. Sorry if I startled you earlier, by the way, but it all took me a bit by surprise. Didn't know where I was for a moment back there. Still don't,' it added.

'What's tha mean, book?' Norman mumbled. 'This in't a book, tha daft ha'porth. This is like I said. Dewsbury.'

The Thing frowned, making a sort of crinkling noise in the process and causing Norman to make a mental note never again to use cheap glue on a job like this. 'Is that some sort of play or something?' it said. 'Because if it's not a book, then . . .'

'Tin't a book,' yelled Norman frantically. 'Don't tha understand? This is real bloody life!'

The Thing's jaw dropped (although, thanks to Norman's years of practice with the soldering iron, not off completely). 'Real life?'

'Of course it's flamin' real life.'

'Oh.' The Thing's brows contracted again. 'That can't be right, surely. Are you pulling my leg?'

Norman, who had a pretty good idea of what would happen if anyone tried pulling the Thing's leg (at least before the epoxy resin had a chance to dry), repressed an involuntary shudder. 'Straight oop,' he replied.

'But that's crazy. I'm a character. I can't come into real life.'

In the middle of all this, something occurred to Norman that made him turn white as a sheet and loosened the joints on his knees. Something he should have noticed before – immediately, in fact – if only he hadn't been sidetracked . . .

'Here,' he said. 'Tha doesn't sound Yorkshire.'

The Thing frowned. 'What the hell are you blathering on about now?' it demanded.

'Tha doesn't sound *like tha comes from Yorkshire*,' Norman screeched. 'Tha sounds,' he ground on, articulating a fear that was beginning to gnaw his brain like worms in a rotten carcass, 'like one of t'buggers on t'telly.'

The Thing shook its head. 'Of course I don't sound Yorkshire, I'm a Dane,' it said. 'Of all the damnfool . . .'

Norman's grip on sanity, which had been at the fingernails-slipping-off-tiny-ledge stage for months now, finally gave way; as was only reasonable, in the circumstances. To have devoted his life to the project, sacrificed everything, finally pulled it off – only to discover he had in fact created an *overseas player* . . . With a yowl like a banshee suddenly realising that its parking meter has just run out, he wrenched open the shed door and fled screaming into the night.

Hamlet scratched his head, trying to ignore the fact that doing so made large bits of it come away in his hand. 'Be like that, then,' he said. 'See if I care.'

He stood down and looked about him. In the corner of the shed, he noticed a biscuit tin lid, the shiny inside of which, he realised, would probably do service as a mirror . . .

'Oh my *God*!' he said.

Nor (let's be honest about this) was he over-reacting. When a blunt, straightforward Dewsbury man builds a human being, he doesn't muck about with frills and decorations. Function, rather than form, is his primary consideration. Where Leonardo or Benvenuto Cellini would have put in a few hours with the polyfilla, the palette knife and the 000-grade wire wool, Norman had made do with a lick of paint and a dab with the coarse sandpaper. The result was something that would have had the model-making team from *Alien* hiding under the bed calling for their mummies.

Hamlet sat down heavily and buried his face in his hands. Then, feeling slightly sick, he unstuck his hands and wiped them carefully on a bit of rag. He wasn't vain, not exactly; but when you're used to looking like Olivier, Gielgud, Richardson and Mel Gibson you do acquire a certain self-image. Looking in a mirror and seeing something that bears a close resemblance to the contents of a vulture's Christmas hamper will therefore come as something of a blow.

'Great,' he muttered. 'Marvellous. Now what the hell do I do?'

Hi, this is Cheryl from Central Casting. Do I get the impression you're not thrilled with the part?

Hamlet looked up angrily. 'You bloody well bet you do. What the hell am I doing here anyway? It may have escaped your notice, but this is real life.'

Well, yes . . .

'In addition to which,' Hamlet raged on, 'I seem to have ended up in something that could pass for Burke and Hare's bargain discount warehouse. Please get me back to where I belong immediately.'

No can do. Sorry.

'What?'

There's a reason, apparently. It's just coming over the wire to me now, if you'd care to hold.

'All right.'

Yes, here we are. 'Serves you right.' Um. You got that?

Hamlet's jaw set in a grim line. Not straight, exactly, but grim. 'I would like to speak to your supervisor, please,' he said. 'At once.'

Sorry, she's at lunch. Look, we'll call you back as soon as—

'Oh no you don't. Just tell me how I can get out of here and we'll say no more about it.'

How can I put this? You're stuck.

'Stuck?'

Marooned. We don't actually know how you got there, but we're one hundred per cent certain sure you can't get back. Well, there is a way, but it's impossible. So we suggest you, er, make the best of it and try and enjoy yourself. Um, get a job, marry, settle down, that sort of thing.

'Look . . .'

You really have just the two basic alternatives, Cheryl went on, with just a hint of something in her voice. *Either you can suffer the slings and arrows of outrageous fortune, or you can take arms against the sea of troubles and, by opposing, end them. Okay? Ciao.*

'Look . . .' Hamlet waited for a moment, and then breathed a long sigh. Cheryl had broken the link and gone. He was stuck.

A few moments later, he found a paper bag, in which he punched two eyeholes. With that, Norman's frayed old Gannex mac, a packet of sandwiches he found on the bench, twenty pounds in change liberated from the electricity meter and a bare bodkin, he set out to explore Reality.

He had the feeling he wasn't going to like it much.

It wasn't as if Jane didn't like doing book-signing sessions. Perish the thought. Any opportunity to get out there and mingle with her public was, by definition, a rare treat. It's the interface with the guys and gals who actually read the stuff that makes it all worthwhile.

It was just, she considered, as she gazed out of the bookshop window at the falling rain, that in her case it didn't seem to work like that. She was painfully aware that her ability to clear a bookshop of all sentient life forms except the people who worked there had earned her the nickname Bomb Scare Armitage; and having to get up at six in the morning and sit through a four-hour train journey in order to do it struck her as a wee bit much.

Just as she was considering making herself a little nest out of copies of her book and going to sleep, a shadow fell across the signing table and she looked up.

A customer.

True, he was wearing an old coat that would have scared the most lionhearted of crows and he seemed to have a paper bag over his head; but since this was a specialist bookshop catering to the fantasy and science fiction trade, that wasn't in itself surprising. What did disconcert her rather was the powerful smell of formaldehyde. Nevertheless . . .

'Hi,' she said. 'Who shall I sign it to?'

The paper bag twitched a fraction. 'Just put *To Hamlet*, please.'

She had written *To Ham* when the celebrated cartoonist's light bulb switched on in her mind. 'Hamlet?' she said.

'Yeah.' The eyes, visible through the holes in the bag, glowed dangerously. 'We spoke only the other day. Or at least, you spoke. I sort of printed. On your screen, remember?'

Jane nodded. 'Hi,' she repeated. 'Well, hope you enjoy the book.'

'It was just come wonder,' Hamlet went on, sitting

down on the edge of the table. 'There I was, passing the door, and I saw this poster. And I thought, now there's just the person who could help me out of this mess.'

Screaming Jesus, Jane thought, not another one. 'You're in a mess?' she asked, as calmly as she could manage.

'Figuratively and literally,' Hamlet replied. 'You wouldn't want me to take the bag off, I promise you. Look, how soon will you be through here?'

As a variant on the old when-do-you-finish-work line, Jane reckoned, it lacked sparkle. 'Actually,' she said, 'I am in rather a hurry today, so . . .'

Hamlet laughed grimly. 'This isn't a chat-up,' he said, 'believe me. Look, you really have got to help me, okay? I'll do anything you like to make it up to you, if you'll only—'

'You could start by buying a copy of the book.'

'Wait there. I'll be right back.'

Jane had hoped that the diversion would have given her time to disappear into the stockroom and hide behind the piles of Stephen Donaldsons until he'd gone away; but in the event he was quicker than she'd expected at the cash desk, and the strap of her handbag had got hooked round the leg of her chair. As he waved the book and till receipt under her nose, all she could do was sit down again and smile weakly.

'Now,' said Hamlet. 'It's like this.'

'I'm listening.'

'I could a tale unfold,' said Hamlet, 'whose lightest word would harrow up thy soul, freeze thy young blood, make thy two eyes, like stars, start from their spheres, thy knotted and combined locks to part, and each particular hair to stand on end, like quills upon the fretful porpentine.'

'You could?'

'Yeah. No sweat. Listen.'

*   *   *

In the beginning . . .

Was the Word? Not quite. To be strictly accurate, in the beginning was the Screen; and the screen was with God and the screen was God. And, admittedly, the Word moved upon the face of the screen, was put into pitch ten, italics, bold, right margin justify, macro/WORD and all the rest of it, but that came later.

Nowadays, the screen just *thinks* it's God, particularly when you want to print out. In the intervening time, creation has become a routine, a simple task that anybody can perform, given (as a bare minimum) a sheet of paper and a pencil.

One small but energetic sect somewhere in Nevada believes that when people die, they are reincarnated as characters in books. Good people become heroes, bad people become villains, and people who have led wasted, pointless lives come back as the characters in unpublishable first novels written by accountants on the office WP. The members of the sect, convinced that they are God's elect, firmly believe that they will be reborn as characters in the works of Jackie Collins. Admission to their prayer meetings is by ticket only, and there is a substantial waiting list.

They exaggerate, slightly. It is very nearly impossible for a human being to become a character, or vice versa; and on the rare occasions when it happens, it represents a serious fuck-up somewhere in the system, leading to quite forthright inter-office memos and the occasional departmental enquiry.

The vast majority of characters are, in fact, small slices of the life-force, ranking in the hierarchy some way below men and angels, but several notches above ghosts, poltergeists and things that go bump in the night. Although they have the potential for eternal life, their chances of immortality depend entirely on the skill of their creators and the commercial acumen of their creators' publishers. They are nominally subject to the ordinary laws of physics and rules of causality, but if the copy editor and the reader don't notice, they're perfectly capable of wearing a green shirt on one page and a red jumper on the next page without even having to step into a telephone box to change.

Where they come from is largely a mystery. Some experts hold that they are parthenogenetically conceived in the mind of the author. Others maintain that every human being carries around with him millions of unfertilised character eggs, simply waiting for a stray experience or turn of phrase to float in through the eyes or the ears and set the whole process in motion.

A third body of opinion believes (correctly, as it happens) that the stork brings them.

Regalian had been Regalian for so long that he could barely remember being himself.

This is an occupational hazard of heroes of fantasy fiction, a genre which tends to come in eighteen-hundred-page trilogies, and the syndrome is usually referred to in the profession as 'good steady work'. Nevertheless, it has its drawbacks, principally the disorientation effect when a hero comes off duty. It is disconcerting and often humiliating to come home after a day of strangling dragons with your bare hands to find you can't get the lid off the pickled onion jar.

Regalian's main problem was with doors. His character in the trilogy was three inches shorter than him, with the result that he was forever nutting himself on low doorframes.

A rather more insidious side-effect was the severe personality crises he tended to suffer when he was off work for more than forty-eight hours. The longer he was out of character, the more his own submerged personality tried to reassert itself; but since he was no longer entirely sure what it was, this caused various problems which he usually resolved by staying in bed with the radio on.

Jane's four-day book-signing tour was, therefore, something of a trial for him – a cross between ice-cold turkey and a fortnight in a decompression chamber. By the end of the second day, his landlady had forced him to switch the radio off, he wasn't really convinced he knew where he was, and he felt an unaccountable craving at the back of his mind to telephone someone called Valerie and explain that the whole thing with the budgerigar had been nothing but a silly misunderstanding. It was accordingly a relief when his bleeper went, indicating an urgent message from his Creator.

Even so, the decencies have to be observed.

'This had better be bloody important,' he snarled into the telephone. 'Disturbing me on my day off. Aren't you supposed to be in Stockport?'

'I am in Stockport,' Jane's voice replied defensively. Because of the trans-dimensional shift and its peculiar effect on telephone signals, Jane's voice had an echo on it like God saying, *Testing, one-two-three, can you hear me at the back there?* 'Look, I need your help, something odd's come up.'

The phrase *something odd*, magnified, echoed and distorted by being shoved backwards through the fabric of reality, can be very disconcerting indeed. Regalian raised an eyebrow and put his hand on his left temple to stop his head reverberating.

'Could you,' he asked pleasantly, 'keep your voice down?'

'Sorry. Really, I hate to bother you, but this could be rather important.'

'Fire away.'

'Right, it's like this. There's – oh nuts, my money's run out. Could you call me back on 0167—'

The line went dead.

Regalian frowned. Jane was, by and large, a reasonably considerate author, and it was very unusual indeed for her to call her characters at home – probably, so the consensus ran, because she was sick to the teeth with them during working hours anyway. *Rather important* in this context could be anything from nuclear war to a firm offer for the film rights. He needed to know more.

Five minutes later, the phone hadn't rung again, and Regalian decided it was time to show a little initiative. Here again, the dislocation effect took its toll. Regalian the hero had more initiative than a busload of management trainees on an encounter weekend, and knew he'd think of something. The other Regalian scratched his head and wondered precisely what something might turn out to be.

Let's think this through. What would *I* do in this situation?

Well. I'd know she was in Stockport.

Concentrate. I'd ride up into the hills, probably in the middle of the night during the worst electric storm in living memory, and consult some old crone who'd summon up spirits of the dead, and they'd say where she was. Piece of duff.

Regalian had been Regalian longer than it's safe to be anybody, but even he had the notion that real life isn't quite like that.

The part of him which wasn't Regalian whispered, *Phone the publishers.*

So he did. 'Publicity department, please,' he said. 'Quick as you like. Hello? This is the Benighted Realms bookshop in Stockport. Where the bloody hell has she got to?'

There was a confused buzzing at the other end of the line, from which Regalian was able to deduce that Jane was due at Dillons at half past twelve and Waterstone's in Cheadle at two. He glanced at his clock, did the necessary mental arithmetic (his clock, of course, worked in Overtime, which is three hours plus one minute for each phase of the moons of Saturn ahead of Greenwich) and called directory enquiries for the number of Dillons, Stockport.

'Hello, could I speak to Jane Armitage, please? Yes, she's there doing a signing session. Yes, *that* Jane Armitage. Yes, I'll hold. Regalian. Um, Harvey Regalian. Thank you.'

There was a long pause, during which Regalian could visualise bookshop staff looking under piles of books and in the dark corners of the stockroom; and then Jane came on, saying, 'Yes?'

'It's me.'

'Gosh.' An impressed pause. 'How did you know I'd be here?'

'Call it heroic intuition. Look, what's the problem?'

There was a long silence at the other end of the line, which Regalian charitably put down to Jane being asked to sign a book. 'It's a long story,' Jane said at last. 'And you might find it a bit difficult to believe. Are you ready?'

Regalian frowned. On the one hand, he badly wanted to know what was going on. On the other hand, it was his phone bill.

'Call me back,' he said. 'You've got the number.'

This is America.

This is, to be precise, Chicopee Falls, Mass., and the year is 1959. *Rifles for Cochise* is playing at the Roxy, in gentle competition with *West of the Pecos* at the drive-in. In back yards all over town, small boys wave wooden tomahawks and shoot each other with diecast sixguns drawn from cardboard holsters. And in a nice house on the edge of town, a man who once wanted to be a writer but now does Westerns scowls at his typewriter and tries to think of some even vaguely original way for the good guy to outdraw the baddie.

Crack! Crack! Crack! The heavy Colt bucked in Slim's hand like a Rio Pueblo bronc as his left hand brushed the hammer . . .

Oh for Christ's sake. He stood up, ground out the twelfth cigarette of the day, and stared out of the window. In the glass he saw his own face; and, as he gazed at it in his distraction, it seemed to change into that of his hero. His useless, whisky-sodden, two-left-footed geek of a hero.

Howdy, partner.

'Go play with yourself,' Skinner growled.

Only being sociable, partner. Seems like you're mighty cross-grained this fine April morning.

'And whose fault is that?' Skinner replied. 'Just for once, why don't you do like you're frigging well told?'

I got my public to think of, bud.

Skinner's eyebrows huddled together like frightened sheep. 'One of these days,' he said, 'I'll let you get on with it, and we'll see just how fast you really are. What am I saying? Probably you'll shoot your damn foot off just trying to get the gun out the holster.'

You sayin' I ain't fast?

The idiot in the window was giving him the eye, and it suddenly occurred to Skinner that he'd been making a mistake all these years. The sonofabitch character was in fact a villain, somehow miscast as a hero. That would account for his habit of running away from showdowns on Main Street, and wearing a black hat.

'You? Fast? I've seen faster things climbing walls with their houses on their backs.'

You wanna put your iron where your mouth is?

Feeling incredibly foolish, Skinner reached out and opened the drawer where he kept the Scholfield. He'd bought it as a publicity thing, eight years ago, out of his advance money for *Geronimo's Nephew*, and had tried to have as little as possible to do with it ever since. Firearms made him nervous, and rawhide brought him out in a little pimply rash. He was absolutely terrified of horses.

Nevertheless. The face in the window had got to him, somehow, and it was time he showed the evil sucker who was boss around here. He strapped the gunbelt round his waist – it took some doing; Wild Bill evidently didn't believe in regular meals and starchy foods – lifted the gun out, lifted the catch to check it was empty, and slid it back into the holster.

'You're slow, Slim,' he said quietly. 'You're so slow I could call you, listen to the third act of *Lohengrin*, and still blow your fucking head off. Okay?'

Sheer hatred flickered across the eyes in the window, and suddenly Skinner was very afraid, although what of, exactly, he didn't know. Of its own accord, his hand went to the gun on his hip. The reflection in the glass did likewise, as reflections are wont to do . . .

BANG!

There was a hole in the glass, surrounded by concentric circles of shatter-marks, like the web of a slovenly spider. The reflection was looking down at his shirt-front.

Reckon you've killed me, Skinner. You gonna be sorry you done that.

Skinner looked at the window, and then at the gun in his hand. A little curl of grey smoke drifted out of the tiny gap between the cylinder and the barrel.

'Hey!' he said. 'The gun wasn't loaded.'

The hell it wasn't, pard. Leastways, this side of the glass it was loaded pretty darn good.

'Gee, Slim, I'm sorry. I didn't think . . .'
Like I done said, Skinner. You gonna be real sorry.
The figure in the glass slumped and slid down under the windowsill. Instinctively, Skinner stepped forward, and . . .

And fell over a body.

'Neat draw, mister.'

Skinner looked down at the corpse at his feet, and then realised. The voice had come from the gun.

'Did you just say something?'

'I said, neat draw. I exaggerated.'

'Hey . . .'

'I thought, it's the guy's first time, he needs his confidence boosting. Actually, if it hadn't been for me you'd have blown a hole right through the five-day clock.'

Skinner looked round. He was on Main Street; not Main Street, Chicopee Falls, but generic, industry-standard Main Street; and, as the specification requires, a man in a black hat on a second-floor balcony across the way was aiming a rifle at him.

BANG!

And, as the specification insists, the man in the black hat, now deceased, fell forwards through the balcony rail, which collapsed like balsa wood around him. The sound he made as he hit the ground was a sort of lazy thump, like a windfall apple.

'Now that was a neat draw, I gotta hand it to you.'

'Hey, you!' Skinner screeched. 'Cut that out, you hear me?'

'That's gratitude for you,' grumbled the Scholfield. 'Now, if you wouldn't mind taking your finger off my trigger, you're choking me.'

It occurred to Skinner that at this juncture it might be politic to run away and hide behind something.

Having done so (something turning out to be the door

of the livery stable; there were horses in there somewhere, but they didn't seem inclined to bother him), he sat down on a pile of hay and did a bit of violent trembling. It didn't help much, but he knew what was expected of him.

'Are you planning on sitting there all day? Because I don't know about you, but I need a good clean and a shot of oil. You'd better put the kettle on.'

'Kettle?'

'You have to flush me out with boiling water, otherwise I rust. I'd have thought you'd have known that.'

'Hey.' Skinner closed his eyes. 'Have you got any idea what's happening to me?' he asked.

'Sure.'

'Well?'

'Boiling water. A drop of Rangoon oil, if you've got it And you use a feather or something to get the bits of dust and crap out of my works. Then I might consider explaining.'

Skinner hadn't the faintest idea what Rangoon oil was when it was at home, but he found a coffee pot and an iron stove with a broken leg, and there was water in the horses' troughs. He scalded his fingers painfully trying to dribble water out of the pot down the Scholfield's barrel.

'That's better. You've missed a bit down in the forcing cone, but you can do that later. Right then, why are you here?'

Skinner shook his head. 'You tell me,' he said.

'You shot your hero. You're not supposed to do that.'

'But that's crazy,' Skinner replied. 'People kill off their heroes all the time. Look at Shakespeare, for Chrissakes.'

'Ah, but not personally. They get other characters to do it for them. Actually taking a gun and shooting them yourself is against the rules.'

'What rules?'

'Which means,' the Scholfield went on, 'you have to

take his place. That's only if he insists, of course. I guess
Slim insisted. Probably he didn't like you very much.'

'But . . .'

'And who can blame him? You really made life hell for
that sucker, believe me. How could you fail to notice he
was meant to be a villain, for God's sake?'

Skinner shook his head. As a method of field testing
the maxim 'Truth is stranger than fiction', it was certainly
thorough; but he couldn't help wishing someone other
than himself had got the job.

'All right,' he said wearily. 'So what do I do now? And
how do I get back home?'

There was silence for a moment as the Scholfield
considered its reply. Tact comes as naturally to full-bore
handguns as, say, ice-skating to African elephants, but
there comes a time when an exceptional individual is
prepared to stand up and break the mould.

'In answer to your second question, you can't. Turning
to the first question . . .'

'Yes?'

'Assuming you're looking for a nice, simple, relatively
painless answer to all your problems . . .'

'Well?'

'You could always try shooting yourself.'

'. . . And he's still there,' Jane concluded. 'Thirty odd
years later.' She paused. 'Isn't that *awful*?'

She waited for a reply. Eventually, she heard the sound
of Regalian heaving a long sigh.

'Sunny up where you are, is it?'

'No, not particularly.'

'Right, so we can rule out sunstroke. And it isn't April
the First, though it might conceivably be some forward-
thinking individual getting his joke in early to avoid the

seasonal bottleneck. Otherwise, I can only imagine you've been drinking.'

'But . . .'

'In which case,' Regalian went on, 'jolly good luck to you, I can see the merits of your chosen course of action. Still, I'd prefer it if the next time you ring me up to breathe gin fumes at me you don't choose my day off. Goodbye.'

'Hang *on*, will you?'

His author's voice. Unwillingly Regalian paused, then put the receiver back to his ear.

'Look,' Jane said, 'I know it all sounds a bit cock-eyed . . .'

'Cock-eyed!'

'. . . But I'm convinced. I don't know why, but I am.'

'You're the fantasy expert.'

'Yes,' Jane replied. 'But that's got nothing to do with it. I swear to you, I believed him. I still do.'

'Listen,' Regalian said, 'I'm holding my watch close to the phone so you can hear the ticking. Fifty-seven, fifty-eight, fifty-nine – there, another gullible idiot's just been born, you have company.'

'Look . . .'

Regalian sighed again. 'I know what you're going to say,' he said. 'You're going to say you're the writer and I'm just a poor bloody character, so why don't I do like I'm damned well told.'

'No,' Jane said. 'Actually, I wasn't going to say anything of the sort.'

'Weren't you? Going to rely on innuendo and the unspoken threat, were you?'

'I was going to say,' Jane went on, 'that that wasn't all.'

'You mean there's more?'

'Yes.'

'Dear God,' Regalian exclaimed. 'Don't you think there's a risk of you wearing your imagination out if you carry on like this? I mean, you need it for work.'

'*Look . . .*'

'Go on.' Regalian propped his feet on the table and unwrapped a toffee. 'I'm listening.'

CHAPTER FOUR

Having extracted from Jane her solemn promise of assistance and ten pounds in change, Hamlet went in search of something to keep body and soul together. After weighing up the available alternatives, he decided on sellotape.

They were due to meet again at four in Cheadle, under the station clock. Until then, all he had to do was stay out of trouble and try not to shed too many component parts. Easy enough, he reckoned, for someone who had spent the last four hundred years wrestling with insoluble moral dilemmas and stabbing people. A change is, after all, as good as a rest.

He found a public lavatory with an empty booth, and sat for ten minutes or so taping himself up, until he resembled a transparent mummy or, if you prefer, a sausage in a skin. Provided that he avoided sudden movements and it didn't rain, he was all right for the time being.

He left the lavatory and strolled down the street. Up till now he had been too preoccupied with his problems to pay much attention to his surroundings, and it suddenly hit him that here he was, in Real Life.

Gosh.

Oh brave new world, that has such people in it. Hitherto, he had spent his life in the company of characters. Now characters aren't like people in many respects, and appearance is one of them. Characters, like film stars, are invariably strikingly handsome, meltingly beautiful, or at the very least charmingly ugly. You don't tend to get many ordinary-looking characters. Even First Citizen and A Courtier tend to look as if they've just stepped out of an underwear advertisement. It was only when passersby started giving him odd looks and crossing the street that he realised that he was staring.

Another thing that struck him forcibly was the total aimlessness of everything they did. Where he came from, all the world was a stage and all the men and women merely players; they had their exits and their entrances, and everything they did or said either advanced the plot, developed character or filled in the gaps with jokes. It meant that life was initially hectic and, once you'd been in the play a few times, mind-gnawingly repetitive. Out here, there was absolutely no way of knowing what anybody was going to do next. It was intoxicating.

'God,' he said aloud (he was, after all, Hamlet, and old habits die hard), 'this is absolutely amazing! I want to stay here for ever and ever.'

He turned, and smiled winningly at a small child, who was prodding its mother in the ribs and drawing her attention to the fact that there was a man over there with a paper bag over his head. Because of the bag, the smile didn't achieve much, and in any event the mother whisked the child away with the practised speed of a waiter on piecework; but Hamlet didn't mind. It was all really *fun*. It was so much nicer than work.

Work, he thought. Let's see, it's half past three. Matinée time. Right now, I'd be starting that dismal bloody scene with the Players. Bugger that for a game of soldiers.

(And just then, at the theatre in Stratford on Avon, a very bemused actor playing Polonius was explaining to the Players that if Hamlet had been there, instead of having been called away to a vitally important business meeting, he'd have been urging them to hold, as it were, a mirror up to nature . . .)

He stopped in his tracks. Did he really have to go back? Why didn't he just stay here, settle down, enjoy himself for once? Get a job in a building society and become the Relatively Cheerful Dane?

A stray atom of pollen drifted into his nose, and he sneezed.

It's a sad fact of life that good noses are hard to come by; and in spare-part surgery, more than anything else, you get what you pay for. Norman Frankenbotham, struggling to make do on a pension, had had to settle for a job lot of nasal gear that had seen better days, and plenty of them. He'd done his best with polyurethane varnish and suture, and the result was fine for ordinary everyday breathing. Sneezes, however, are another matter; and if he'd had the chance for a quiet chat with his creation, Norman would have impressed upon him the vital importance of avoiding dust, pollen and similar irritants if he didn't want to end up with a face like something dreamed up by Stephen King after a late night snack of extra mature Cheddar.

Hamlet froze; then, having looked round to make sure nobody was watching, he stooped quickly, feeling a few coils of sellotape giving way as he did so, retrieved the nose and sidled into a shop doorway, where he could examine the damage in the glass.

'Oh *budder*!' he exclaimed. 'By doze!'

Having replaced the bag, he stepped back into the street, breathing through his mouth and walking very carefully. He had reached a decision. He was going home, whatever it took. The spirit may have been willing, but the flesh was just a smidge too weak for his liking.

'Forget it,' Regalian said. 'There is absolutely no way . . .'

'Please.'

Regalian drew a deep breath, intending to let Jane know, with map references, where she could put her suggestion. He hesitated.

'Did you say,' he whispered, 'cowboys?'

'That's right.'

'Like, um, John Wayne and, er, Gary Cooper and, you know, um, thing?'

'Thing?'

'Audrey Murphy.'

'It's Audie, not Audrey. Yes, just like them. Why?'

'Oh, nothing.'

Like a fisherman detecting the faintest twitch on the line, Jane suddenly became alert. 'There's something, isn't there?' she asked. 'You like the idea, don't you?'

'It's the most stupid suggestion I've ever heard in all my—'

'Clint Eastwood.'

'Of all the hare-brained crazy schemes I've ever . . .'

Jane smiled into the telephone. 'Admit it,' she said, 'you're interested. You're a secret Western buff, right?'

'Absolutely not. We can't get films over here. The inter-dimensional interface buggers up reception, you just get snowstorms.'

'What is it, then? Books?'

'I have better things to do with my time. For example, being sick, or falling out of trees, or catching diphtheria . . .'

Jane's grin widened. 'I know!' she said. 'It's the music, isn't it? You're a country and western fan.'

'No!' There was a pause. 'Not a *fan*, God forbid. Never in a million years.'

'But?'

'Occasionally,' Regalian said defensively, 'we do get the odd country song on the jukebox in the pub here. Once in a blue—'

'You sing along, don't you?'

'I do not.' Another pause. 'I may hum, sometimes, but—'

'There you are, then. Go on, be honest. You're dying for an excuse to wear your cowboy boots.'

'I do not possess a pair of—'

'*And* your ten-gallon hat. *And* your buckskin shirt.'

'Nor do I possess a buckskin shirt. They bring me out in a rash.'

'So you've tried one, have you?'

The voice at the other end of the line became stiff with coagulated dignity. 'I owe it to my craft to sample as many out-of-the-way experiences as possible, I grant you. I still draw the line at—'

'I can write you a pair of Colt forty-fives.'

'No, thank you.'

'With pearl handles.'

'Anachronism.'

'Pardon me?'

'Bone,' Regalian replied. 'Ivory, even. But not pearl.'

'How do you know that?'

'Um. Common knowledge. Read it in a magazine in a dentist's waiting room somewhere. Look . . .'

'You can have,' said Jane enticingly, 'any name you like. Kansas City Zeke. The Lightning Kid.'

'Do you mind? I've only just eaten.'

'All right then, you can be Jedediah Something. That authentic enough for you?'

'I really wouldn't know,' Regalian replied sternly. 'As I

say, a mere fleeting acquaintance with some of the less painfully embarrassing examples of a certain popular musical genre—'

'You'll do it, then?'

'Escapist ephemera, the opium of the masses—'

'I'll get on to it,' said Jane, 'straight away.'

There was a long silence, during which Jane held her breath. A customer came up to the desk with three copies of the hardback for her to sign, but she ignored him.

'If you absolutely insist,' Regalian sighed. 'But I demand a full written indemnity, together with—'

'Ride 'em, cowboy.'

'Oh drop dead.'

'Whad the hed,' Hamlet demanded, 'kebt you? I'be been waitidd here for hours.'

Jane raised an eyebrow. 'Why are you talking in that funny voice?' she asked.

'Nud of your biddined. Now, I need a needuw and some thread, and—'

'Later. We've got a train to catch.'

'Slow dowd, will you? Do you wabt my ledz to fall off too?'

Regalian strode into the bar, a character with motivation.

There was a moment of stunned silence, during which you could have heard a pin drop on deep satin cushions, followed by the first snigger, followed by laughter, freestyle, at will.

Regalian ignored it. He stopped at the counter, placed a pointed toecap on the brass rail, and called for whisky.

'I beg your pardon?' asked the barmaid. Her name was Trish, and when trade was slack she knitted for her niece's baby.

'You heard me,' Regalian growled. 'Whisky. And keep

it coming.' He slapped a silver dollar down on the counter-top, spilling a small plate of peanuts.

'There's no need to take that tone with me,' said Trish. 'And watch what you're doing, will you? You'll scratch the formica.'

After the novelty of Regalian making an idiot of himself in a different way had worn off, the other occupants of the bar drifted away, leaving him alone with his drink, his rather uncomfortable clothes (the shirt itched) and his thoughts.

It posed an interesting technical problem. In theory it's impossible for a character from one writer's books to get into someone else's book (that would be plagiarism). In practice it happens all the time, but usually by accident, or at least unconsciously. Doing it on purpose is one of the hardest tasks an author can undertake. When it's attempted, in ninety-nine cases out of a hundred, a new character is created in a totally new book. Both the book and the character strongly resemble the originals, but with subtle differences that generally sabotage the attempt.

Over a second glass of whisky, Regalian did his best to recall what he had learnt in Theory class at character school. This didn't come easily (he'd spent most Theory lessons trying to analyse the motivation of the girl sitting opposite) but, with the third, fourth and fifth whiskies, things began to come back to him, albeit rather bedraggled and with several days' growth of beard. He considered.

Authorship theory, he remembered, is a subdivision of basic creation theory. Creation theory is easy.

In an infinite, curved universe, everything is possible. One needs only to recognise the possibility of a particular set of circumstances, and it then exists, somewhere, in some form. This is creation theory. Let there be light; and there is light. Let, by the same token, there be huge single-cell life forms called greebles who inhabit ventilation shafts and eat the smell of cheese, and there are greebles. The difference is that light is a fairly sensible, practical concept which can fit into virtually all reality systems; whereas greebles can only subsist in the really low-rent backstreets of reality where nobody gives a damn any more, and where no one with any sense ever goes except as the result of a horrible accident.

Fine, said Regalian to himself, that's basic creation theory. He found a half-eaten packet of smoky bacon crisps in his jacket pocket and started to chew.

Authors do to creation theory what highly paid accountants do to the tax laws; without breaking the rules, they contrive to bend them to such an extent that they might as well be made of Plasticine.

Authors take untrue things, people who don't exist, events that never happened, and make other people believe in them. Belief is water poured on the blazing chip-pan of creation. A fictional thing which people believe in can never be real, but it can exist far more vehemently than any number of real things which are too boring for anybody to be interested in. The shipping forecast is real, but *The Archers* live because people want them to.

Basic authorship theory.

'More whisky.'

'That'll be one pound forty, please.'

'Here.'

'Sorry, we don't take foreign money here.'

'Hey, this is a saloon, ain't it?'

'Well, it says saloon bar on the door.'

'Right. Well, in any saloon this side of the Rio Bravo, a silver dollar buys a bottle of raw drinkin' whisky. Or are you callin' me a liar?'

Trish's brows furrowed. On the one hand, the better

part of her intellect advised her that she was going to have fun and games persuading them to accept silver dollars at the bank in the morning. On the other hand, an influential minority of her could see the logic; and besides, a big coin made of pure silver's got to be worth a lot of money, hasn't it?

'Right you are, then,' she said.

Basic authorship theory, as amended by the publishers' lawyers, goes on to say that characters can exist without being real, on the strict understanding that they stay inside their books and don't ever get loose, because of the damage they would inevitably cause this side of the screen.

Basic authorship theory, as further amended by the writers' agents, goes further and states that in any event a character belongs to his author body, soul and merchandising rights, and has to do exactly what he's told on pain of editing.

Basic authorship theory, as further amended by the characters' agents, adds the proviso that characters can only believably do things which are in character, and any attempt to get out of their allotted book would be a breach of credibility, resulting in immediate implosion.

Basic authorship theory, as amended by inserting a crowbar into a weak seam and leaning on it, states that there are loopholes. These range from the well-known minor technicalities, which make it possible for tired and overworked authors to carry out the occasional discreet cattle-raid into an adjoining author's stock of ideas, to the celebrated and entirely mythical airlock in the cellars underneath the west wing of the Library of Congress.

There is no known loophole that allows a character from one book to hop into another book whenever he likes. By the same token, there is no way of getting into the vaults of the First State Bank of Idaho without first going past the security; but only because to date nobody has stacked a wagonload of dynamite up against the wall and lit the fuse.

Coincidentally, in a dimension long ago and far away, the senior partner of Messrs Shark, Shark and Shark, a firm of lawyers with a very specialised but extremely lucrative practice, was advising a client.

'Now then,' said Mr Shark. 'I don't suppose you've given any real thought to constructive inheritance tax planning. Well, have you?'

King Lear bit his lip. 'Now you mention it,' he replied, 'I can't say I have.'

Mr Shark shook his head sadly. 'It's about time you did, don't you think? What I would advise you to do is to gift over your kingdom to your two eldest daughters. Then, provided you survive the gift by seven years, there'll be no tax to pay whatsoever.'

'Really?'

'Really.'

King Lear rubbed his chin thoughtfully. 'Sounds like a good idea, then. Only – well, it's a bit drastic, isn't it? Just sort of giving it to them like that with no strings attached. What if . . .'

Mr Shark frowned. 'Can't make an omelette without breaking eggs, now can we? I mean, do you *want* to be stuck with a massive great tax bill?'

'No, no, of course not. But couldn't I keep a little something back? A hundred knights, say, something like that?'

Mr Shark sighed. 'Sorry,' he said, 'but that would constitute a gift with reservation, which is caught by the anti-avoidance provisions and that would render the whole scheme void. And if a thing's worth doing—'

'Yes, you're right, I suppose. But why only my two

eldest daughters? Isn't that a bit rough on the youngest? She's a good kid, and—'

'True,' interrupted Mr Shark wearily, 'but she's married to the King of France, isn't she? Which makes her non-UK resident, and the statutory provisions about taxation of offshore interests would just make a mockery of the whole scheme. You do see that, don't you?'

'Yes. Yes. If you say so, I suppose . . .'

'Right, I'll get on with drawing up the papers and I'll let you know when they're ready. Thanks for dropping in. Bye.'

No sooner had the door closed than the phone rang. 'Yes?'

'Two callers holding for you, Mr Shark,' said his assistant. 'I've got Macbeth asking for advice about this proposed takeover bid. He says he can see your point about why it's a good idea, but he can't help thinking it's a bloody, foul and unnatural merger and he reckons he'd have problems sleeping nights. And then there's Hamlet on the other line, won't say what it's about.'

'I see. Tell Macbeth to be bloody, bold and resolute, and we're sending him an interim bill. I'll take the Hamlet call.'

Buzz. Click.

'Hello. Mr Shark?'

'Shark here. How's things? Look, about your inheritance claim—'

'Actually,' said Hamlet, 'I wasn't calling about that. What I—'

'I think,' said Mr Shark firmly, 'that you have ample grounds for contesting your father's will, and if I were you I'd crack on and have a damn good go. Now I know you're fond of your uncle and you don't want to upset your mother, but really, it's the principle of the thing. I feel sure that if your father knew what was going on, he'd turn in his grave.'

'Okay,' said Hamlet, 'whatever you think's best. What I actually wanted to talk to you about—'

'I mean,' Mr Shark continued, 'yes, your scruples do you credit, obviously you're a very conscientious young man, and I know you'd really prefer to carry on with your academic career rather than go into the family business anyway. Nevertheless I put it to you—'

'Mr Shark.'

'Yes?'

'Shut up,' said Hamlet, 'and listen. Through no fault of my own, I've somehow managed to get myself trapped in the real world. How do I go about getting back?'

There was a long pause – at Mr Shark's charging rates, about six hundred pounds' worth. 'Mr Shark?'

'It's an interesting problem you've got there,' said Mr Shark. 'Yes, certainly very interesting. All sorts of possibilities for creative tax planning, for a start.'

'Fine. What can I actually *do*? I mean, not to put too fine a point on it, I'm falling to bits down here. My nose is currently glued on with Araldite and every time I move my right arm there are little tearing noises.'

'I sympathise,' replied Mr Shark, 'believe me, I do. Unfortunately, we're into a rather grey area of the law here. I think this may take some time.'

'Time? How much time?'

'Immigration law is tricksy stuff,' Mr Shark replied. 'The last thing we want to do is rush into anything. We could come badly unstuck if we do.'

'Mr Shark,' said Hamlet, controlling himself with difficulty, 'I'm going to come badly unstuck any bloody minute now. Have you got any suggestions, or would you rather I took my business elsewhere?'

'Now then,' said Mr Shark, 'calm down, let's not say anything we might later regret. You have my word we'll start looking into this thing right away, and as soon as there's any progress I'll let you know. Happy now?'

'I suppose so.'

'And,' Mr Shark went on, 'in the meantime we will of course need a small payment on account, say twenty thousand to be going on with, so if you'd just send a cheque—'

'Ah. That might be a problem. You see, I haven't actually got any money over here. Not as such.'

'I see.' Mr Shark leaned back in his chair and scowled at the ceiling. 'You know, you're putting me in a very difficult position here.'

'Really? Your toes have just fallen off too, have they?'

'I'm sorry,' said Mr Shark. 'I'd love to help, really I would, but our policy as a firm is very strict. Unless we have money up front, there's very little we can—'

The line went dead. Mr Shark shrugged and replaced the receiver.

'I don't know,' he sighed. 'Bloody clients.'

The literary equivalent of stacking dynamite against a wall:

'Hello?'

'Hello, this is Jane Armitage, I'm afraid I'm not in to take your call right now but if you'd care to leave a message . . .'

'Hey!' Regalian shouted into the receiver. 'Cut that out! I know you're there, because the line's been engaged for the last half hour. Hello?'

'. . . as soon as I return. Thank you. Beeeep.'

Regalian swore under his breath. He hated talking into the bloody machines.

'Right,' he said, 'now listen carefully. This is what you've got to do . . .'

Mr Prosser, of Prosser and White Funeral Services Ltd, drew his dressing gown tight around his waist and peered round the door.

'Yes?' he said.

'Excuse me,' said Jane, 'but it did say twenty-four-hour service in the phone book, and it's rather an emergency.'

Mr Prosser suppressed an inner sigh. Twenty years in corpse disposal had taught him that people who are dead today are almost invariably still dead tomorrow, and frequently still dead the day after. The term 'emergency' should not, therefore, have any meaning within the parameters of his profession. Still, bereavement does funny things to people, and the golden rule of bespoke gravemaking is, be sympathetic, even to the nerks and the time-wasters. 'Of course,' he said. 'Do please come in.' He removed the chain from the door, and refrained from mentioning the fact that 'twenty-four-hour service' was in fact a reference to his answering machine.

'Thank you ever so much,' Jane said, having refused a cup of tea. 'To get straight to the point, I need someone embalmed.'

'I see,' said Mr Prosser. 'And the identity of the sadly departed?'

Jane pointed. 'Him.'

There is another golden rule of bespoke gravemaking, if anything, even more fundamental than the first. Never be shocked, never allow yourself to be sickened or revolted, never let the punter see that you want to throw up. 'Quite,' said Mr Prosser. 'Might I just point out that the sadly departed would still appear to be alive?'

'Yes, I know,' Jane replied wearily. 'And we did try the hospital first but they threw us out.' She shuddered from head to foot. 'I was all right, but he landed sort of awkwardly. We've got all the bits in this plastic bag here. Actually, while you're at it, you might just see if you can't sort of sew them back on, if that's all right with you.'

Golden rule, Mr Prosser muttered to himself under his

breath, golden rule. 'Perhaps I'm not explaining myself clearly enough, miss,' he said. 'We really do prefer to specialise here in, um, dead people. That's basically what we're all about, you see, and your, er, friend here isn't really all that dead, now is he? Not as such, I mean.'

'All right,' said a voice from under the paper bag, 'let me talk to him. Listen, creep.'

'Um—'

'Don't interrupt. Now, unless you make with the suture and the embalming fluid pretty damn quick, I shall be back here tomorrow. And I shall take this bag off, and I shall strut up and down in front of your shop window stopping passers-by and saying, You don't want to go in there, the service is absolutely terrible, I mean, just *look* at me. Now, are you going to co-operate?'

Mr Prosser sat down, closed his eyes and swallowed a couple of times. Then he stood up again. He was twitching slightly, but, apart from that, he was his usual professional self once more.

'That won't be necessary, sir,' he said politely. 'Now, if you would care to follow me into the, er, if you would care to follow me.'

'I shall be watching what you do,' Hamlet went on. 'And don't you dare cut any corners, or you'll regret it. The first suggestion of a bolt through the neck, and I phone Esther Rantzen.'

'Quite,' said Mr Prosser. 'This way, please.'

'Yes? Wassawant?'

'It's Jane here. I got your message. Are—?'

Regalian growled, and switched on his bedside light. 'For crying out loud, it's half past two in the morning.'

'I've only just got in. Look, if you're ready, I can start immediately.'

'Alternatively, you could go to bed and we could make

a start in the morning. Have you considered that line of
approach in any significant detail?'

'I . . .'

'Yes, I know, it's a tricky decision to have to make, and
I don't want to rush you. Tell you what, you sleep on it
and call me back tomorrow. Goodnight.'

'I think,' Jane said, 'we should start right away, if it's
all the same to you. It's really a question of how long
things are going to hold together at this end.'

'Hold together?'

Jane glanced at the figure stretched out on her sofa,
reeking of preservatives and muttering softly about the
pain in his seams. 'Yes,' she said. 'I don't think we've got
much time. So I'm going to make a start at my end. I'll
be about twenty-five minutes, okay?'

'Okay,' Regalian sighed. 'Don't use too many technical terms.'

Jane replaced the receiver and tottered wearily through
into her workroom, where she plugged in the machine
and slipped in the disk.

'Inspiration, please,' she said.

And, either by coincidence or some unaccountable
cross-dimensional telepathy, inspiration came. It wasn't
particularly high-class inspiration; it bore the same degree
of resemblance to the good stuff that works canteen coffee
bears to the finest Arabica. But it did the job, in the
circumstances, as far as the situation required.

Jane began to type.

Regalian slept, she typed. And, as he lay on his crude
couch of z'myri hides, his bronzed limbs stretched out in
slumber, he dreamed . . .

. . . Of a strange landscape, of a kind he had never
seen before. It seemed to him as if he was walking down
a dusty and deserted street, between rows of tall wooden-

framed buildings with weird shiny squares set into their sides, like sheets of crystal. And he noticed that he was wearing some outlandish costume: a buckskin shirt fringed with strips of hide, a large, broad-brimmed hat, strange wide-legged trousers and long boots, and around his waist a thick, wide belt, from which hung a scabbard. But there was no sword in the scabbard; only a small, heavy iron object that looked something like a hammer.

He stopped walking. There were three men barring his way. They too wore the same outlandish garb, and the same strange instruments hung by their sides. Their swarthy faces were grim.

'Howdy, stranger,' cried the tallest of them . . .

CHAPTER FIVE

'H owdy, stranger,' said the tall man. Regalian blinked twice.

'Sorry?' he said.

'I said,' said the tall man, 'howdy. You deaf or somethin'?'

Regalian smiled ingratiatingly. 'I do beg your pardon,' he replied, 'I was miles away. My, what an attractive and pleasantly situated township you have here.'

Confused, the tall man turned to his colleagues and conferred briefly in whispers. 'Yeah,' he said eventually. 'We reckon it's kinda cute ourselves. Trouble is, we don't take too kindly to strangers in these parts.'

'Quite right, too,' Regalian replied, nodding. 'It's always better to be cautious at first when meeting new people. A certain initial diffidence frequently proves to be the bedrock on which a lasting relationship of mutual support and trust is constructed, don't you find?'

The tall man looked at him; rather as you'd expect a sentry to look when he's issued his time-honoured challenge and been told, 'Foe'. He didn't seem entirely sure what he should do next, but he was a tryer. He cleared his throat nervously.

'Reckon so, stranger,' he said. 'So why don't you jes' turn yourself round and head straight back out of town the way you jes' done come?'

He hesitated, as if aware that he was laying it on just a bit too thick. Too late now, however, to do anything about it.

'I quite agree,' Regalian said. 'What an eminently sensible suggestion, if I may say so. If one of you gentlemen would be kind enough to point me in the way of the next settlement down the line, I should be eternally obliged to you.'

This time, the tall man refused to be drawn, and there was an embarrassed silence; during which Regalian offered the three of them a peppermint. Eventually the man in the red shirt, who gave the impression of having learned his lines and being extremely loath to waste them, expressed the view that the town wasn't big enough for the both of them.

'Excuse me?'

'You heard.'

'Yes,' Regalian answered, 'but might I just briefly trouble you for a few words of explanation? You referred to "the both of us", but, in point of fact, between us we number four. Which particular two did you have in mind?'

That, as far as the three men were concerned, put the tin lid on it. Without taking their eyes off Regalian, they started to back slowly away, and in due course backed right into the town watering-trough, fell over their feet and landed in a small, confused heap on the ground.

'Hey,' whined the tall man, from underneath his two associates, 'that ain't fair. That's cheatin'.'

Regalian shrugged, drew his revolver and thumbed back

the hammer. 'You could say that,' he replied. 'Now, get up slowly, or I'll blow your fucking heads off.'

The three men relaxed. Admittedly, they were being held at gunpoint at the mercy of their enemy, but at least they knew where they stood, or rather sprawled. Any minute now, one of them would try and go for his gun, there'd be some nice, familiar shooting and . . .

Quite so. For the record, the man in the red shirt went for his gun first, but he was so flustered that he dropped it on his foot. The tall man followed his lead, however, and was all poised for the nauseating sensation of hot lead punching holes in his body when he noticed that Regalian hadn't moved. In fact, he wasn't even looking in the right direction.

'Hey!' he shouted.

'With you in a minute,' Regalian replied over his shoulder. 'Gosh,' he added, 'that really is a stroke of luck.'

The tall man froze, his revolver in his hand and levelled at Regalian's heart. 'Luck?' he repeated helplessly.

Regalian nodded. 'Absolutely amazing,' he replied. 'Look, you see that big white building with the horse and cart standing outside?'

'The livery stable, yeah. What—?'

'Well,' Regalian went on. 'Follow the line of the roof about seventy yards to the left and you'll come to a low tree. Look over the top of that and you'll see another tree, sort of roundish with a bald patch halfway up. Got that?'

'Sure thing. What—?'

'Now then,' Regalian said. 'Look closely at the lowest branch on the right-hand side, and if I'm right, and I'm pretty sure I am, the small green bird perched there is in fact a Jackson's warbler. Now, according to Audubon . . .'

The tall man narrowed his eyes and stared; and just when he thought he could make out a small green blob, someone standing behind him fetched him a terrific crack with a pickaxe handle, and he fell unconscious on to his nose beside his two similarly concussed associates.

Regalian sighed, holstered his gun, and wiped a little oil ostentatiously off his hands. Then he nodded to the man with the pickaxe handle.

'Not bad,' the pickaxe-handle user said. 'Against the rules, but who cares a damn, anyway?'

Regalian nodded, and then extended his hand.

'Mr Skinner, I presume?' he said.

Everybody knows that characters in books can do things that ordinary people can't.

They can jump off tall buildings and survive. They can remember, word for word, conversations they had sixteen years ago. They can fire ten shots from a six-shot revolver without reloading. They can encounter historical figures who haven't actually been born at the time the book is set. They can get from Paris to Marseilles faster than it would take a mortal just to get to the front of the checking-in queue, and still arrive cool, refreshed and without a splitting headache. They can even fade out at the end of Chapter Five hanging by their fingernails from a precipice and stroll on at the beginning of Chapter Seven in immaculate evening dress without a word of explanation.

This is called Dramatic Licence. If you want to be a character, you apply for one at your local Editing Station by lodging the appropriate application form in triplicate, five passport-sized photographs and the administration fee.

Woe betide the character whose licence is revoked, because he'll never work in the business again. They don't even tell you when they do it, so that the first you know is when you jump from the speeding train, hit the deck and go SPLAT!

The grounds for revocation are Byzantine in their complexity, but the gist of them seems to be that characters aren't allowed to cheat; in other words, they can do impossible things, but only if they're in character and appropriate to the situation and the general world-view of the book. Accordingly, James Bond can get away with things that would get Tom Sawyer struck off instantaneously, and the hero of a fantasy can do pretty well what he pleases provided that they're the sort of thing he ought to be doing anyway. This, of course, begs the question; but, since there's a fair chance that by the time a fantasy novel is past its first hundred pages only twenty per cent of the readers (not necessarily including the author) have the foggiest idea what's going on anyway, the authorities are usually prepared to be flexible.

There's flexible, however, and there's being taken for a sucker; and if there's one thing the Editorial Department can't be doing with, it's being taken for a sucker. If you anticipate trying that, make sure you have a real parachute handy before jumping, even if only to a slightly far-fetched conclusion.

For the record, there is an appeal procedure if you disagree with the revocation of your licence, and one of these days it'll undoubtedly be tried out, just as soon as a disenfranchised character survives long enough to contact his lawyer.

'So?' Skinner asked. 'What's the plan?'

Regalian wiped whisky off his chin and shook his head. 'There isn't one,' he said. 'There's only a plot.' He gestured to the bartender for another, and sighed. 'And that may be something of an overstatement,' he added. 'She's absolutely bloody hopeless at plots. Usually we get to page three hundred and fifty and stop. When we're absolutely stuck, she gets all mystical, which is a real drag, let me tell you. Millions of bloody adjectives. I try to ration her to three a sentence, but it's an uphill struggle.'

'I see,' Skinner said. 'That's going to make things awkward, isn't it?'

'Probably.' Regalian sipped his whisky and shuddered. 'Still, we can only give it a go, can't we? We're probably going to die in the attempt, but that's the writing business for you.'

Skinner's head dropped. 'I don't know,' he said. 'Maybe I was hoping for too much. I thought you might know some sort of back way out or something; where the loose bricks are in the wall, if you see what I mean.'

'There aren't any,' Regalian replied. 'Except for the Library of Congress, of course, and that's just a myth.'

'Library of . . . ?'

The hero shrugged. 'Old character's tale,' he explained. 'According to literary tradition, there's a weak spot in the fiction/reality interface somewhere in the cellars of the Library of Congress building in Washington. You know, where they have a copy of every book ever written, or something along those lines? The theory is that the concentration of so much fiction in one place has sort of rubbed a hole, and if you can find it you can get into any book you like, and out again too, presumably. But like I said, it's just a legend.'

'Pity.'

'It is, rather. No, what I had in mind was something a bit more practical.'

Skinner finished his drink and propped his elbows on the bar. 'Go on,' he said.

'*Alice in Wonderland*,' Regalian said.

'Come again?'

'*Alice*,' Regalian repeated, '*in Wonderland*. Now according to something I read in one of the technical journals, there's a sporting chance that there's an airlock in there somewhere, if only we could find it.'

Skinner raised an eyebrow. 'Just a second,' he interrupted. 'Let's just get this straight. You're saying that if we could somehow get into *Alice in Wonderland*, there may be a way of getting home?'

Regalian shrugged. 'Depends,' he said, 'on what you call home. If you're lucky and there is an airlock in there, you'd probably find you'd come out again somewhere in the nineteen nineties. Still, at least it'd be the real world and you wouldn't have people trying to kill you all the time.'

Skinner thought about it for a second or so, and then nodded. 'What've I got to lose?' he said. 'All right, how does it work?'

'Like this.' Regalian leaned forward. 'Now, you've read the book?'

Skinner nodded. 'A long time ago, mind,' he added. 'On a train, I think.'

'Wherever, it doesn't matter. Now, do you remember the scene with the bottle marked DRINK ME and the cake marked EAT ME?'

'Vaguely.'

'Fine. That's the stuff we need. One of them, haven't the faintest which, makes you grow smaller. And it's a known fact that if you're small enough, you can get out of the system by crawling out the back of the word processor and down the electric flex. You'd have to take some of the other stuff with you so you could get back to normal size, but that's no problem.'

'I see,' said Skinner, who knew as much about computers as, say, Orville and Wilbur Wright knew about flying a Boeing 747. 'And this is known to work, is it? This crawling down flexes stuff, I mean?'

Regalian made a wry face. 'Not exactly,' he said. 'On account of there not being any characters small enough to fit in a cable or daft enough to try. But the theory's one hundred per cent rock solid. Well, maybe eighty per cent, say mud solid. It's the best offer you're going to get.'

'Then we might as well try,' Skinner replied. 'Since we're going to get killed long before we get there . . .'

'Quite,' Regalian said. 'Better to travel hopefully, as the saying goes. The real problem, of course, is getting out of this book and into *Alice.* That's,' he added with a sad smile, 'one hundred and ten per cent impossible.'

'Is it?'

'Yes. No question about that whatsoever.'

'Oh.'

'Which means we'll have to cheat.'

'I see. Is that possible?'

Regalian stood up and laid a dollar on the bar. The bartender picked it up without looking at it and wandered away. 'Oh yes,' he replied. 'Cheating's easy. Provided, of course, you follow the rules.'

The sun shone. Sheep bleated respectfully in neatly hedged fields on the hillside overlooking the old stone manor house, while carriage-wheels crunched on the gravel of the drive. Mr Darcy put on his hat and set out for his morning stroll. Another fine day in the works of Jane Austen.

BANG! Suddenly, the air in front of him grew thick, and out of it stepped a terrifying apparition. Horrified, Darcy started to back away, as the cloud of sparkling fuzz grew slowly more solid and resolved itself into two human shapes . . .

One tall and lean, one shorter, fatter and older; both dressed in crude working clothes of a design that Darcy had never seen before; both uncouth and desperate looking, with a wild gleam in their eyes.

He was just about to drop his stick and run when the taller man smiled, tipped his hat and said, 'Good morning, Mr Darcy. Exceedingly clement weather for the time of year, is it not?'

And then, with a feeling of great foolishness and no little bewilderment, Darcy saw that the two men were in fact dressed in the latest London fashion, in long tailcoats and knee-breeches and tall black hats, and he recognised them as Mr Skinner and Sir Humphrey Regalian, the two gentlemen who had taken Ardleigh Manor for the summer.

'Exceedingly clement,' he agreed. They all tipped their hats again, and parted; Darcy to continue his stroll, Skinner and Regalian wandering at no great pace towards the house.

'How the fuck,' muttered Skinner, 'did you do that?'

Regalian grinned. 'I cheated,' he said. 'It's a piece of cake, like I said. Whether it actually gets us any further forward is another matter entirely.'

By way of explanation, he reached in the side pocket of his coat and produced a small, leather-bound book. Skinner opened it and nearly fell over.

'Dear God,' he said. 'It's my goddamn book!'

Regalian nodded. 'More or less,' he said. 'We call it a monitor. It's like a sort of teleprompter. You'll see the pages in the second half of the book are still all blank.'

'But it's the book I was writing when I got into this mess,' Skinner said, pointing to the first page. 'I can remember every word of it.'

Regalian nodded. 'Quite,' he said. 'And if you read on, you'll find all your adventures over the last thirty-odd years, described in your own distinctive brand of uniquely vile prose. Now,' he went on, 'look up the last page with any printing on.'

Skinner did so; and read:

As Kid Regalian sat in the noisy bar of the Lucky Strike Saloon, his hand strayed to his pocket and he found himself looking at the book he had taken from the body of his first wife, the schoolmarm, on the day all those years ago when he had come home to find the place had been raided by Ragged Bear's renegade Comanches. He glanced at the spine and made out, despite the charring and the bloodstains, the words 'Pride and Prejudice'. Almost of its own accord the book fell open in his hands, and he began to read.

'Mr Collins was not left long to the silent contemplation of his successful love,' he read, 'for at that moment the arrival of Mr Skinner and Sir Humphrey Regalian was announced, and he rose at once to greet them . . .'

'Oh for Chrissakes,' Skinner exclaimed. 'We'll never get away with this!'

'You'd be amazed,' Regalian replied, raising his hat and nodding affably to some large woman in a big puffy dress. 'The only problem is that you can only go backwards. Logical, really; a character can't read a book that hasn't been written yet. Also, to be perfectly frank with you, it's completely arbitrary which book you end up in.'

'Is it? But I thought . . .'

Regalian smiled sheepishly. 'Depends entirely on the book the character happens to be carrying in his pocket at the time,' he said. 'And that depends on who the character is, and his motivation and stuff like that. For some reason, it was dramatically right I should be reading—' He indicated his surroundings with a broad, encircling gesture. ' — this drivel while sitting in the Lucky Strike waiting for Butch Donovan to turn up for the big showdown. Just count yourself lucky. Given the circumstances, it might very easily have been the Bible, and then we'd really be in the smelly.'

All this was a bit much for Skinner, who basically wanted a quiet life with regular meals and a radio tuned in to the baseball. Instead of making any comment, therefore, he shrugged his shoulders and smiled.

'Fine,' he said. 'Thank you for explaining so clearly. What do we do now?'

Regalian returned the shrug. 'I believe the phrase is, Go with the flow. Of course, it would help tremendously if we had access to a library.'

'They've probably got a library in there,' Skinner said, pointing with his cane at the big house. 'That sort of library?'

'It'll do for now, I expect,' Regalian answered. 'Look, how about this? We go in, you keep them talking and I'll try and sneak into the library and see if anything suggests itself. Okay?'

Skinner was about to reply when a voice inside his coat said, 'Yeah, sounds fine. And if anybody tries anything, we'll just blast our way out. In fact, we could save time and go in there shooting to start with.'

Skinner groaned. 'Oh for Pete's sake, you're not still here, are you?' he said. 'Why didn't you stay behind? I expect you'd have found some nice, compatible psychopath you could have teamed up with if only you'd looked hard enough.'

'Yeah,' agreed the Scholfield. 'The thought did cross my mind. Still, stand by your man, that's what being a personal sidearm is all about.'

Before Regalian could ask for footnotes, Skinner smiled weakly at him and said, 'Don't worry, it's only my gun. Long story. It's no bother really so long as you ignore it.'

'Hey!'

Regalian nodded. 'I know the feeling,' he said. 'I got lumbered with a magic sword once. Nattered away nineteen to the dozen when I was trying to sleep. As soon as the book was over I chucked it in a bush somewhere.'

'*Hey!*'

*   *   *

The bounty hunter should have been played by Jack Palance; but, since Skinner's works had never attracted the interest of a producer, he just looked like Mr Palance. Rather more, in fact, than Mr Palance ever did himself.

About twenty minutes after Regalian and Skinner left the Lucky Strike, he barged into it, accompanied by five heavies armed with rifles. He marched to the bar and attracted the bartender's attention by poking a cocked .44 Frontier in his ear.

'Okay,' he purred. 'The two guys who came in here earlier. One tall and thin, the other short and kinda fat, not much hair. Where are they?'

'You just missed them, Mr O'Shea,' the bartender replied. 'Say, would you mind being a bit careful with that thing?'

'Yes,' O'Shea replied. 'Now, you gonna tell me which way they went, or do I get careless?'

'Um,' said the bartender. 'You're asking something there, boss.'

'Am I?'

'Yeah.'

O'Shea nuzzled the barrel of the gun a little further into the bartender's ear. 'You're right there,' he said. 'I'm asking where those two sons of bitches got to. I'm waiting.'

'You ain't gonna like this.'

'Try me.'

Slowly, trying not to move his head at all, the bartender pointed at a small, leather-bound book lying open on the bar top.

'They went thattaway,' he said.

Jane switched off the screen and sat back in her chair. From the spare bedroom came the disturbing sound of

Hamlet snoring through a nose held on with Copydex and fishing line. No point in trying to sleep, even if she'd felt in the mood.

She had a bad feeling about all of this. All right, she had spoken blithely about bringing the boys home by Christmas, but she couldn't help worrying about all the things that could go wrong. Regalian hadn't exactly stressed these points, but he had dropped large hints; particularly about the risks involved in moving from one book to another. The theory alone was terrifying.

The main risk, according to Regalian, was snap-back. Because, when you broke into another book, you were simultaneously still in the book you came from, there was a material danger that you could be whisked back into your own book without any warning, simply because it was artistically right. The more books you broke into, the greater the risk became, obviously; although there was apparently a break-even point you could reach if you managed to jump far enough, by which stage you were so far removed from where you'd started that you were into the avant-garde and nobody would dare to presume to say what was aesthetically correct. This was, apparently, known as the Booker Effect.

The other nasty one was the principle whereby you could only go back, to a book written earlier than the one you were breaking out of. There was a loophole in this rule, Regalian had assured her; but it had never been tried in practice, and to make it work, it sounded as if you had to be one hell of a novelist. Jane had always been profoundly realistic about her talent, and the thought of the kind of writing she was going to be called upon to do made her feel distinctly uncomfortable.

Although she was ashamed to admit it, the part that really got to her was the thought that she was doing all this writing with no prospect whatsoever of anybody publishing it. Not that she was mercenary or anything; but the man at the bank who wrote her the letters with the word 'unless' in them undoubtedly was, and she did of course have a book of her own to finish. Added to which, there was a danger that if something went wrong, she was going to lose her hero; which would leave her in an embarrassing position, to say the least. It wasn't that she was *fond* of him exactly, because he was only a character in a book – one that she'd dreamed up herself, at that – but she didn't want anything nasty to happen to him, or at least not unless it got her out of a hole with her plot.

She glanced at her watch; half past five in the morning, that godforsaken hour of the day when you really, really want to go to bed, but you know in your heart that if you do, you'll only lie there staring at the ceiling and listening out for the dripping tap and the milkman playing xylophone concertos with the milk bottles.

There was also the problem, she compelled herself to remember, of him next door. True, Regalian had mumbled something about fitting him into the plan somewhere along the line and maybe being able to do something with the Law of Conservation of Anti-Matter, whatever that was. In the meanwhile, however, she had as an indefinite house guest a tragic hero who was largely held together by blind faith and force of habit, and who smelt depressingly like the biology lab at school. And he wasn't the least bit like Laurence Olivier in the film; not the film of *Hamlet*, anyway.

She made a cup of strong tea, ate four digestive biscuits and sat down in front of the screen again. By the time she'd logged in, and the machine had finished saying © *Copyright DataZap Corporation 1995 All rights protected* at her, she was fast asleep.

The machine, however, was on, and the last page of

text was sitting there on the screen, winking its cursor and looking for mischief. And there's a certain well-known author, a prolific writer under a wide variety of pseudonyms, who finds work for idle screens to do.

The keyboard started to type.

Having walked as far as the folly, Mr Darcy stopped for a moment to admire the view, and turned to return to the house.

BANG! There it was again. Being a product of the Age of Reason, and knowing full well that the peculiar visual effect he had experienced only a short while before was simply a product of his imagination, he forced himself to look straight ahead and walk on by.

The peculiar visual effect (who was, incidentally, a dead ringer for Jack Palance) coshed Mr Darcy on the back of the head with the butt of a .44 Frontier and stole his watch. Then, grinning evilly, it strolled on down the hill towards the house.

'It is a truth universally acknowledged,' observed the younger Miss Bennet pointedly, 'that a single man in possession of a good fortune must be in want of a wife.'

She waited for some appropriate response, but none came. The visitor, she observed, was looking out of the window.

'Would you not agree, Mr Skinner?' she said.

'Yeah,' the visitor replied, and Miss Bennet made a mental note that she was probably wasting her time. Nevertheless, she persevered. Mr Skinner might be middle-aged and fat and have the manners of a dung-beetle but even so he was a young Greek god compared to the curate.

'The young gentleman who has taken Netherfield Park . . .' she started to say; but before she could develop the theme, Mr Skinner exclaimed loudly, using a word she wasn't familiar with but whose general meaning she could deduce from context, threw himself under the big mahogany table and drew from inside his coat something that looked like some sort of gun. Miss Bennet edged forward slightly on her chair, intrigued. This sort of thing, she couldn't help feeling, rarely happened at Longbourn.

'The young gentleman who has taken . . .' she repeated; and then the door flew open and the tall, better-looking one burst in, a book in one hand and Papa's fowling-piece in the other. He seemed flustered, and Miss Bennet's first instinct was to offer him tea.

'Get down, for Chrissakes,' screamed Mr Skinner. A moment later, the glass in the window shattered. Mr Regalian (a foreign-sounding name, Miss Bennet reflected, although the gentleman didn't seem particularly out of the ordinary) hurled himself under the table, waited for a moment, stood up and fired the gun out of the window. Probably, Miss Bennet said to herself, he's seen a partridge or something. Gentlemen, she knew, take sport very seriously and sometimes act unaccountably while under its influence.

'The young gentleman who has taken Netherfield . . .' she said.

'This is more like it,' said a small, metallic sounding voice from under the table. Miss Bennet raised an eyebrow. She was certain that the voice emanated from neither of the two gentlemen, and yet she had heard it quite distinctly. Would it, she wondered, be polite to ask for an explanation?

'Shut up, you,' snapped Mr Skinner irritably. 'And this time, do as you're damned well told.'

(His language, Miss Bennet said to herself, was not quite the thing; but no worse than some of the things she had overheard when the foxhounds had met at Netherfield the year before last. Gentlemen, she told herself, have a certain licence in these matters when indulging in sporting pursuits.)

'Can I offer either of you gentlemen some refreshment?' she volunteered. They ignored her.

'How do you load these things?' Mr Regalian said, staring at the gun in his hands.

'Right,' replied the metallic voice. 'First, take your powder flask . . .'

'What's a powder flask?'

'Oh for crying out loud.'

There were footsteps on the stairs. Goody, said Miss Bennet to herself, more visitors. This is turning out to be quite an eventful day.

'They're coming,' Mr Regalian hissed. 'Oh my God!'

'I thought you were supposed to be a hero?'

'There's heroism,' Mr Regalian replied, 'and there's getting killed sitting under a table. I'm afraid I've always specialised in forms of heroism where getting killed wasn't obligatory.'

'Here,' replied the metallic voice, 'grab a hold of my grips. You'll soon get the hang of it. *He*'s useless.'

Mr Regalian reached over and took the peculiar-looking gun from Mr Skinner, who didn't seem to mind in the least. Then the door opened again. It was not, as Miss Bennet had feared, the curate. Instead she saw a large, swarthy man with a grin on his face and another peculiar-looking gun in his hand. Gosh, thought Miss Bennet, perhaps the partridge has got into the house, like the time the fox ran into the drawing-room at Arnscot and the hunt chased it three times round the room before it escaped through the window.

There was a very loud bang.

The new arrival – could this, she wondered, be the mysterious Mr Derwent, who was supposed to have bought the Shirefield estate and have four thousand a year from his uncle in the West Indies? – ducked down behind the chaise longue, and shortly afterwards there was another loud bang. The teapot – best Wedgwood – disintegrated into small pieces. But there was no sign at all of any partridge.

'The young gentleman who has taken . . .' said Miss Bennet, but the rest of her sentence was drowned out by further loud bangs. A French clock, a mirror and the portrait of Sir Joshua Bennet over the fireplace went the way of the teapot.

The door opened yet again, and Miss Bennet saw, with an involuntary flutter of the heart, that Mr Darcy had entered the room. He didn't, she noticed, look his usual immaculate self. In fact, his clothes were crumpled and muddy, and he was holding a bloodstained handkerchief to the side of his head and looked pale as death. Oh dear, thought Miss Bennet, he's fallen off his horse again.

Displaying an impressive turn of speed, the swarthy man (who Miss Bennet had decided probably wasn't Mr Derwent) jumped up, grabbed Mr Darcy round the neck and poked the muzzle of his gun in his ear.

'Okay,' he said. 'Lose the iron or the dude gets it.'

Mr Regalian swore loudly, stood up and threw his gun to the ground. He must have forgotten to uncock it first, however, because it immediately went off, and a moment later the man who wasn't Mr Derwent was hopping round the room on one foot shouting horribly, while the metallic voice was saying something about if you want a job done properly you might as well do it yourself. Grabbing the gun with one hand and Mr Skinner's ear with the other, Mr Regalian rushed out of the door, and Miss Bennet heard the sound of running footsteps on the stairs. She turned to Mr Darcy and the stranger, who was now sitting in the coalscuttle holding his left foot and moaning.

'The young gentleman who has taken Netherfield Park,' she said, 'seems little inclined towards society. Yet I have not altogether given up hope of our seeing him shortly at Longbourn.'

She paused. Nobody seemed to be paying her the least attention. As the youngest of five daughters, however, this was something she could easily relate to. She decided to stay with it and see what happened.

'It is a truth universally acknowledged . . .' she said.

The laws of reality are bad enough. The laws of fiction are downright terrible.

In reality, things generally get worse, nothing ever goes entirely right, there is no free lunch, people fall out of love, pay taxes and die.

In fiction, right triumphs over wrong, long-lost brothers are united in improbable circumstances, everything works out all right in the end, and boy meets, loses and finally gets girl. Whether the participants like it or not.

The laws of fiction are unbendable, and there are no loopholes. Furthermore, even the timetable is beyond the control of the people involved, because things happen at the aesthetically correct time; not a page early, not a paragraph late. There are some things even the author can do nothing about.

One of them is about to happen to Skinner.

'Talk,' whined the Scholfield, 'about a goddamn shambles. I was so ashamed I didn't know what to do with myself. You guys had better get your act together, or—'

'Shut up,' Skinner said, 'or I'll saw your barrel off. Now then,' he went on, turning to Regalian, 'what do we do now?'

Regalian scowled. 'How the bloody hell am I supposed to know?' he replied, sitting down heavily under a chestnut tree, taking his left boot off and shaking it. 'You think I do this sort of thing all the time?'

'You're a hero. Heroes are supposed to know these things.'

'Get stuffed,' replied the hero.

'You're formulating a plan of campaign, aren't you?'

'Get real. I'm trying to get this poxy chunk of gravel out of my – ah, that's got it. Right, where were we?'

Skinner sat down beside him. 'The next step.'

'That's what I wanted the book for,' Regalian said. 'Not that I'm admitting for one second that I have got a plan, mind. It's just that, the moment I saw it in the library there, I thought it might come in handy.'

'What book?'

'This one,' Regalian said, and held the volume out to Skinner. It was a first folio Shakespeare. Skinner recoiled as if he'd been handed a toad.

'Absolutely no way,' he said vehemently. 'I absolutely refuse to set foot in there. It's full of lunatics with damn great swords talking blank verse. The life expectancy of the guys in Shakespeare's about on a par with the first day of Ypres.'

'Actually,' Regalian replied quietly, 'I was thinking we could take it to a bookshop somewhere and sell it. It's a first edition, and I gather they're quite valuable.'

'Oh.'

'I thought some money might come in handy, you see. For food and things.'

'Yes, quite. Sorry.'

'Don't mention it.'

Idly, Skinner opened the book. Shakespeare had always bored him silly, but a first folio isn't something you come across all that often, and . . .

Idly, Skinner opened the book and began turning the pages, his mind slanting back to those days long ago when he had sat in the little timber-framed schoolhouse in Dalhoxie County and listened to Miss Withers, the school-marm, reciting her favourite speeches. He could almost hear her high, shrill voice dwelling on the metre and the cadences, bringing to that small, remote building a faint echo of the wooden O, and beyond it, the field of Agincourt, the ramparts of Dunsinane, the wood near Athens . . .

'Oh *shit*!'

That, by the way, isn't the horrible, inevitable, artistically necessary thing that happens to Skinner. That comes later. Soon, but later.

CHAPTER SIX

'Of all the woods,' said Skinner, 'in all the plays in all the world, we have to end up in this one. Thanks a heap.'

'Not my fault,' Regalian snapped, lashing out at the brambles with a heavy stick. 'I didn't say open the bloody thing. I didn't say start reading. If you had as much common sense as a bloody lemming, you'd have known better than to open the . . .'

Not far away, they could hear strange, disturbing sounds, half-animal, half-human. Possibly it was just lemurs, but somehow Skinner doubted it. He had a horrible feeling he knew exactly what was making that noise.

'There may,' Regalian went on, between grunts of effort, 'be an advantage to be had here, if we use our brains. Fantasy setting. Could be any time, anywhere. If only we could find some jumping-off point, we should be able to go anywhere from here.'

'We should live so long,' Skinner snarled back. 'Listen to the noisy sons of bitches. They're following us, you realise.'

'You're paranoid.'

'No I'm not. Why are you trying to make out I'm paranoid all of a sudden?'

Regalian glanced up at what was visible of the sky though the branches of the trees. 'I reckon it's about four-thirty in the afternoon, so assuming it stays light till say ten . . .'

'What are you drivelling on about?'

'Midsummer Day,' Regalian replied. 'The one thing we can be sure of is which day of the year it is.'

Skinner stopped in his tracks. 'Hang on,' he said. 'Midsummer *Day*.'

'Exactly,' Regalian replied, gently bending a low branch out of his way. 'It's still day. Which means the play hasn't started yet. Which means we're probably safe until dark. So if we get a move on and find our way out of this bloody wood, we can get to Athens and find a library, and then—'

'Safe? Are you sure?'

Regalian scowled. 'Well, I'm not about to swear any affidavits, but it could be worse. One thing I do know about fairies is, they don't come out during the day.'

'How do you know that?'

'I work in fantasy, remember? I know fairies from nothing, and they're strictly nocturnal, trust me. Which means that apart from bears and wolves and outlaws and quicksands and the like, I think we're fairly—'

He vanished. Skinner froze in his tracks, which was probably what saved him. He looked round.

'Hello?' he said.

'Up here.'

Skinner looked up. Regalian was hanging upside down about fifteen feet up in the air. A rope, attached to his ankle, connected him to the top of a thick, tall green sapling.

'I think,' he said, 'I stepped in some sort of trap.'

'Looks that way,' Skinner agreed.

'Fine. Look, do you think you could see your way clear to getting me down? Or do you want to wait until autumn and see if I come down with the apples?'

'Sorry.' Skinner looked round. 'What we need,' he said, trying to keep his head, 'is something like an axe or a saw.'

'Left them in my other jacket,' Regalian snapped. 'Can you hurry it up, please? I think my brain's trying to get out of my ears.'

'You could shoot through the rope,' suggested the Scholfield helpfully. 'At this range, if you rested on something, with a bit of luck—'

'I've warned you already.'

'I'm just trying to be positive,' the gun replied, hurt. 'Nobody else has come up with anything, have they?'

'Be quiet.'

'I—'

'I said be quiet.'

'But—'

'QUIET!'

It was then that Skinner registered the feel of a very sharp pricking at the back of his neck. Very slowly, he turned his eyes hard right, and caught sight of something luminous directly behind him, at the absolute limit of his vision.

'I was just trying to tell you,' said the Scholfield smugly, 'that there was this guy with a knife creeping up behind you. But you appear to have found that out for yourself.'

'Okay,' said the fairy. 'Which one of you scumbags is the weaver?'

'Look, fellas,' protested Skinner, some time later, 'don't

get me wrong, I sympathise with what you're trying to achieve here and I'll be delighted to do anything I can to help. I don't have a problem with any of it, I promise. But are the ears absolutely necessary?'

'Yes.'

'Are you sure you're not just erring ever so slightly on the over-literal side here? I mean, we're into some pretty deep symbolism here, the donkey motif and all that, I mean, it's a common element in Western European literature right through from Apuleius, so couldn't we just take it as read and let the metaphor kind of do its thing without hammering it into the ground and having actual physical donkey's ears?'

'No.'

'I really don't want to seem in any way obstructive here, but the words "hopelessly jejune" are sort of hovering about over our heads, and you've got such a wonderful situation going here, I'd hate for you to spoil it by—'

'Co-operate,' growled the fairy, 'or I cut your nose off. Okay?'

'Okay.'

Bloody marvellous, Skinner thought as they stumbled their way through the wood in unhappy convoy. The one time when a bit of initiative from that poxy gun might come in handy, and it just sits there in the holster, rusting. Now if only . . .

'And if you're expecting your friend to help you,' said the fairy, 'forget it.'

'Friend?'

'The metal guy with the long nose,' the fairy replied. 'The one you carry around with you. We've put a hex on him so strong it's taking him all his time not to turn into a bunch of daffodils.'

Skinner shrugged. 'Oh well,' he said, 'dark cloud, silver lining. In fact, if you could just jot the spell down on a scrap of paper sometime, I have a feeling it could well come in very useful in the future.'

'Shut up.'

'Okay.'

They had reached a clearing; well, more than a clearing. One tries to avoid the expression whenever possible, but there are times one has to call a glade a glade.

'Right,' said the fairy. 'Puck.'

'Stub your toe, did you?'

'Puck,' continued the fairy, 'you hide in that tree there. I'll just hunker down behind this bush. You lot, make with the music.'

The fairies vanished, leaving Skinner standing in the middle of the glade with his hands in his pockets, feeling extremely conspicuous. Well, he consoled himself, at least they were only joshing when they said about the donkey's . . .

He felt a curious sensation, which reminded him of the time when he was a boy and had voluntarily swallowed a live worm in order to join Lumpy Flannagan's gang. If the worm had been made of burning mercury and coated in sugar, there would have been a striking resemblance.

And suddenly he could hear. Not just hear, but really *hear*. For example, half a mile away a rabbit sneezed. The shock nearly knocked Skinner over.

Unwillingly, he put a tentative hand to the side of his head, and felt fur.

'You ba—' he started to say; and then the pile of leaves in front of him quivered slightly, and turned somehow into a tall, slim, scantily dressed young woman with silver skin.

'What angel,' she said, rubbing her eyes, 'wakes me from my flowery bed?' She rolled on to her side and squinted. 'Just a minute,' she went on, 'you're not the usual chap.'

Skinner realised that he was staring. Either she was extremely absent-minded and had forgotten to put on the rest of her clothes, or she didn't feel the cold at all. He looked away and made a sheep-clearing-its-throat noise.

'Um,' he said. It came out different to the way it had sounded in his head; more a sort of guttural honk. Of course, he realised, completely different bone structure on a donkey, larynx in a different place. He smiled feebly. He felt like Cyrano de Bergerac in the distorting mirrors booth at the fair, and his ears itched like buggery.

The girl was staring too, and it suddenly occurred to Skinner that whoever usually did this job must look really *ghastly*, because it was the sort of stare that has a hidden agenda of pink hearts and gypsy violins. A fly landed on his nose and began to buzz.

'Hi,' he said. 'My name's Skinner, and I'm not really stopping, we don't really have to go through with this, so . . .'

'Hi,' replied the girl, in a voice you could have iced a cake with. 'I'm Titania, but my friends call me—'

'Quite. As I was saying, I'm sure you're only too aware by now that you're being made the victim of a cruel practical joke, and since I have no wish to participate in this degrading exhibition, perhaps you'd—'

'Take the weight off your hooves, why don't you?' She giggled. 'You've got the cutest mane I've seen in a long, long time.'

'Please,' said Skinner, 'madam. I'm old enough to be your father.'

'Really?' Titania raised an immaculate eyebrow. 'Funny, you don't look ten thousand and thirty-eight years old.'

'No, but I feel it sometimes.'

'I can probably do something about that,' Titania replied, with a smile that would have grown roses on the dark side of the moon. 'Come here and try me.'

Before he could formulate a reply, Skinner felt his legs collapse, as completely as if he'd been robbed by an international gang of high-class tibia thieves, and he found himself sitting on the leaves, with his head resting on an expanse of disconcertingly-contoured silver flesh. Christ, he speculated, what the hell could the other guy possibly have looked like?

'Relax,' Titania said. 'Now, then.'

Hamlet slept.

He was having a dream (one of his usual repertoire, in which he was standing on the stage in front of twenty thousand people, and he was being played by Kenneth Branagh, and he'd forgotten to put his trousers on) and snoring mildly through what was left of his nose, producing the sort of noise a New Orleans trombonist achieves by putting his bowler hat over the bell of the trombone. It had been a long day.

The window opened.

Hamlet grunted, turned over on his side and brayed softly. A shadow, a semitone or so darker than the ambient darkness, flitted through under the window sill. There was a soft bump, as of skull against timber, and a muffled oath.

The shadow advanced. It was whistling, very softly and tunelessly, under its breath. Probably it didn't even know it was doing it.

From the pillow a mild grunting noise, followed by a few lines from the rogue-and-peasant-slave speech. Hamlet was one of the few people in history who soliloquised in his sleep.

A stray moonbeam flashed on the hair-thin needle of a hypodermic, which the shadow was holding up and preparing for use. A dewdrop of colourless liquid slid down the needle as the shadow expelled the surplus air from the chamber before stooping over the bed. As the syringe went home, Hamlet may have stirred slightly, but nothing more. The shadow withdrew the needle, stood back and waited for perhaps two minutes, until the breathing sounds became slower, flatter and more regular.

Satisfied, the shadow packed the syringe away in the small toolbox strapped to his waist, and turned to the bed. And stopped.

There is, of course, no soundtrack to this scene, and both participants were mere silhouettes in the darkness. The shadow, however, had extremely expressive body language, and he communicated his next emotion with perfect clarity. If he'd been an actor in the days of silent movies, he'd have been banned for life for swearing on screen.

Yes, his gestures said, fine. We worked out how to get in here and how to administer the tranquilliser drug. Only thing we didn't consider was getting the tranquillised body out through the window. Pity, that.

Having apparently formulated his plan of campaign, the shadow began stripping sheets off the bed and tearing them into strips. There followed an interval of undignified heaving, shoving and dropping of sleeping bodies, which resulted in Hamlet being lowered out of the window on a cat's cradle of improvised ropes. Then the shadow left by the way it had come. A dull thump from the ground below suggested that the makeshift harness had almost lasted out, but not quite.

Darkness seeped back, like penetrating oil in a rusty hinge.

Hamlet woke up, opened his eyes, and screamed.

He was strapped hand and foot to what appeared to be an operating table. Shining directly in his eyes was a very big, bright light, of the sort you get in up-market dentists' surgeries. Somewhere in the background a piece of machinery hummed ominously.

'Here!' Hamlet yelled. 'What the hell do you think you're doing? And what the devil have you done with my left foot?'

'Now, now,' said a voice, coming from somewhere just outside his line of vision, 'there's no need to get excited, so just pull yourself together, will you?'

'Easier said than done,' Hamlet replied savagely. 'Look, who are you, and what's going on?'

'Now,' the voice went on, 'this isn't going to hurt you one little bit, so please keep perfectly still.'

'But . . .'

'If it's your foot you're worried about,' the voice continued, 'I've got it perfectly safe, packed in some ice. I'll put that back on for you in just two ticks, after I've finished this.'

'This? What's this?'

'Absolutely still, please. Igor, the forceps.'

'Actually, Doctor Rossfleisch, my name's Tracy.'

'What a pretty name. Thank you, now the soldering iron, please.'

A pair of gloved hands materialised in the far periphery of Hamlet's vision. A moment later, frantic signals of pain scurried up and down the two cocoa tins and bit of string he called a nervous system.

'Sorry,' said the voice, 'I should have warned you that that might smart just a little bit. The electric drill, please, Tanya.'

'Tracy.'

'Thank you.'

Oh spiffing, Hamlet thought. Not only is this lunatic the mad scientist, he's the absent-minded professor as well. Pausing only to wish he was safely back in Elsinore with the ghosts and the poisoned swords, he passed out.

When he came round, he was still strapped to the table; but the light had gone away, and there was something strange about his body. It was a bit like turning the ignition key in the lock of your clapped-out old Triumph Dolomite to find that during the night some practical joker had fitted it with the latest model of Cosworth racing engine. The whole outfit seemed to growl with vitality. He clenched his fists, and the thick webbing straps around his wrists snapped like wet paper-chains.

'Yeah!' he breathed.

He sat upright, breathed in deeply, and was hit on the back of the head with a three-pound lump hammer.

The bounty hunter reached the edge of the glade, stopped and peered round a tree trunk.

It takes something pretty far out of the ordinary to disconcert a trained, experienced bounty hunter. It's a line of work that attracts the cool, level-headed type, and people who worry about having left the gas on when they go on holiday generally tend to leave the profession at a fairly early stage; frequently on a stretcher.

There are, however, limits; and the sight of his target lounging on a sea of cushions wearing a donkey's head, surrounded by flickering blue lights and heavily entangled with a gorgeous, silver-skinned woman was enough to make him pause, just for a moment, and cast his mind back over the last few days to see if he could recall receiving any sharp blows to the back of the head.

Even Butch Cassidy, he reasoned, never went this far.

Having given the matter some thought, he stepped back into the undergrowth. This one, he reckoned, would probably keep for the time being. The sensible thing to do would be to round up the other one and then come back and take another look.

* * *

At that particular juncture, the other one was sitting under a lime tree, chewing hard and reflecting on the fact that the rope in these parts tasted damned odd.

You get to chew a lot of rope if you're a hero, because people are always tying you up. True, you always manage to free yourself, beat the pudding out of the inoffensive little nerk they've left behind to guard you, and find your way to the secret hideout/sacrificial altar/grand vizier's palace where you're due to effect the timely rescue; but that's only because it's aesthetically right. The powers that be appreciate these things, and they aren't particularly cruel or vindictive. The ropes in heroic fiction, therefore, tend to be either toffee or sherbert flavoured, and generally saliva-soluble.

This rope, on the other hand, was thick, tough and tasted of hemp and fairy's armpit; all of which taken together gave Regalian the feeling that something wasn't quite right about any of this. Maybe it wasn't aesthetically right that he should get out of this one; in which case, he was in deep trouble.

Maybe chewing through the rope wasn't the answer, at that. Looking round, he noticed Skinner's gunbelt lying about a foot from his big toe. Perhaps this was one of the cases where the hero gets hold of the gun, holds up the guard, is untied and *then* escapes and gets on with the job. Regalian shrugged. Only one way to find out.

'Pssst!'

If the gun had heard him, it showed no sign. Fair enough, he reasoned; they have to make these things difficult, because heroes thrive on difficulty. If any fool could do it, it wouldn't be heroic; and wandering minstrels whose repertoire consisted of such works as 'The Chores of Hercules' or 'The Saga of Sigurd the Doer of Ironing' would probably end up doing more wandering than minstrelsy. He wiggled his foot towards the gunbelt and finally managed to get his heel on to the buckle.

From the glade opposite came sounds of hawing and female giggling. As he drew the gunbelt towards him, Regalian found himself wondering whether he'd completely misunderstood the situation after all. All his finely honed character's instincts were shouting to him that this was the stage in the narrative where he rescued Skinner. The question was, did Skinner know that?

He had just managed to manoeuvre the gunbelt into a position where, with a bit of energetic wriggling and at the cost of taking all the skin off his wrists, he ought to be able to reach the gun, when a lean, dark figure who looked depressingly familiar (Jack Palance in green tights and sequins) stepped out of the shadows, flipped the Scholfield out of its holster, pointed it at him, and grinned.

'Reach for the sky,' he said.

Regalian, with whom the penny had just dropped, obeyed. The bounty hunter drew a knife from his boot, slit the ropes and said, 'On your feet.'

'No,' Regalian replied.

'You heard me. On your feet.'

'Piss off.'

The bounty hunter's grin widened. 'The poster says dead or alive, mister,' he said. 'Guess you just made my mind up for me.'

He thumbed back the hammer, levelled the gun at Regalian's head, and squeezed the trigger. There was a brief whirring noise, a flag inscribed BANG! popped out of the muzzle of the gun, and a small flame appeared on the top of the frame in which, had he been a smoker, the bounty hunter could conveniently have lit a cigar.

'You see,' Regalian explained, springing to his feet and kicking the bounty hunter savagely in the nuts, 'the fairies put a spell on the gun which stops it working. That meant that at some stage in the adventure—' The bounty hunter dropped to his knees, moaned and rolled over on to his side. '—it was inevitable, dramatically speaking, that someone would try and turn my own gun on me, only for it *not* to go off at the crucial moment. I think it's one of the lesser isotopes of dramatic irony. Should've seen it coming,' he added, stamping on the bounty hunter's hand and retrieving the gun. 'Silly of me. Ah well, never mind.'

He buckled on the belt and, with the air of a man who once again knows exactly what's expected of him, strolled off towards the glade to do the rescue.

When Hamlet came round the second time, he'd learned his lesson. Instead of sitting upright and flexing his muscles he lay where he was, still as death, and waited for someone to hit him.

'Ah,' said a voice above his head, 'you've woken up. And how are we feeling?'

Idiot, thought Hamlet. Up till then, the Golden Lemon award for the daftest question he'd ever heard had always been reserved for To be or not to be. Now, he reckoned, it had competition.

'Give you three gue . . .' he began to say; and then stopped himself as status reports from the various parts of his body began to filter through to his brain. 'Marvellous,' he said, bemused. 'Never felt better in all my – well, never felt better.'

'Splendid,' replied the voice, which he recognised as that of the mad scientist chap. Rossfleisch? Something like that. 'I'm so glad.'

'If I sit up, is anything going to happen to me?'

'Happen to you? In what way?'

'I mean, is anybody going to thump me, or anything?'

'Certainly not, my dear fellow. Please, do feel free to sit up as much as you like.'

'Thank you.'

From a sitting position, Hamlet saw that he was still in the – operating theatre? Something like that. Maybe he just had theatres on the brain. Standing over him was a tall, straggly-looking man with big round glasses, a bald head, a white coat, carpet slippers and a little wispy grey beard; suggesting that either he was going to a fancy dress ball as an absent-minded professor, or he was one. A moment later, he introduced himself as Doctor Sebastian Rossfleisch.

'Pleased to meet you,' Hamlet lied. 'Look . . .'

'Remarkable.'

'Pardon?'

'The way the isothermic membrane has taken,' Rossfleisch explained (at least, presumably it was his idea of an explanation, just as the grey fluid you get in styrofoam cups at railway stations is somebody's idea of tea). 'I was so afraid there would be a positive reaction with the selenium nitrate. That would have been most unfortunate.'

'Would it?'

'Profoundly disappointing,' the Doctor replied. 'One never really knows where one is with polymers, does one?'

'Tricksy buggers,' Hamlet agreed, striving to be polite. 'Look . . .'

'Yes?'

'Where am I, and what am I doing here?' Gosh, he reflected as he spoke, sounds like old times, me asking that. This time, though, I could really do with a sensible answer.

Rossfleisch shook his head, setting the wisp on his chin dancing. 'Perhaps I had better put you in the picture,' he said. 'You see, I'd been hearing rumours for quite some time.'

'Rumours?'

'About Mr Frankenbotham's experiments.'

'You mean that strange chap in the shed? My, um, creator.'

'Precisely. A remarkable fellow, some quite astounding intuitive leaps, and with the facilities he had available it was quite incredible that he was able to achieve as much as he did. Nevertheless, the whole project was basically ill-conceived.'

'You mean me?'

'Exactly. To put it bluntly, you were not well made. Without a thoroughgoing overhaul and some substantial rethinking of a number of fundamental aspects, there was a severe risk of terminal dysfunction.'

'Oh, that this too, too solid flesh would melt, thaw and resolve itself into a dew, you mean? I think I get the picture.'

'Indeed. Well, it would have been a tragedy to have let that happen. So I, er, stole you.'

'I see.'

'And,' continued the Doctor cheerfully, 'I've done the necessary work, and I'm delighted to say it would appear to have been completely successful.'

'Golly.'

'Quite. In fact, rather more so than I had anticipated myself. For example, the superhuman strength.'

'What superhuman strength?'

'In the original design,' said Rossfleisch, 'you were intended to have the strength of ten men.'

'Gosh.'

'As it turns out, that would appear to be a material underestimate.'

'Blimey.'

'The invulnerability, too. That seems to be . . .' The Doctor blinked twice. 'Very satisfactory. Very satisfactory indeed.'

'When you say invulnerable . . .'

'Allow me,' said the Doctor, producing a huge revolver from inside his lab coat, 'to demonstrate.' He raised the gun, aimed it at Hamlet's forehead, and fired. There was an ear-splitting noise, and Hamlet felt just the very faintest tickle.

'Hey!' he protested. Then he caught sight of something lying on his knee; a flat disc of lead, about the size of a twopenny bit. 'Neat,' he said, impressed. 'People always told me I was too thin-skinned for my own good,' he added.

'Kevlar-reinforced synthesised plasma,' commented the Doctor proudly. Although Hamlet had the feeling that the technicalities were so far above his head you could have bounced radio messages off them, he nodded.

'Pretty slinky stuff,' he said. 'Probably saves you a fortune in sun-tan lotion, I bet. Next time you're down the cash and carry, order me a bucketful.'

'There are, of course,' the Doctor continued, 'a number of minor incidental sub-reactions which I hadn't quite anticipated, but I feel sure that in the fullness of time, when we've had an opportunity to study them in depth, we shall be able fully to assimilate the ensuing data and adjust the methodology accordingly.' He beamed encouragingly. 'After all,' he added, 'you are, if I may say so, only the beginning.'

There was something about that remark which didn't taste very nice. In fact, Hamlet reckoned, if that statement had been a piece of haddock he'd be picking bones out of his mouth right now. 'Come again?' he queried.

'What I mean is,' the Doctor continued, 'the rather – how shall I put it? – hit and miss manner of your construction does mean that there are certain very basic design flaws which I really can't put right in you, but which I will rectify in, let us say, Marks Two and Three. You, of course, being Mark One.'

Hamlet frowned. He had lost the thread rather by now, and his name was Hamlet, not Mark, and he had a funny itching feeling that seemed to be coming from inside his head, which made him want to poke a six-inch nail through his ear and wiggle it about. 'You mean,' he hazarded, 'like a guinea pig.'

'A fine metaphor. Yes, certainly.'

'I'm not sure I like that.'

He was about to expand on this theme when something made him put his hand to the side of his neck. His fingers touched metal.

'You bastard,' he hissed. 'There's a bolt through my neck!'

The Doctor nodded. 'I know,' he said, with a slight deprecating shrug. 'Terribly crude, I know, but effective nonetheless. I'm working on a carbon-fibre version, but that won't be ready until the third generation prototype at least.'

Hamlet wasn't listening. He was looking at his feet. Just as he'd anticipated; bloody great big square boots. 'Hey!' he objected, 'that's not on. Get me a mirror, now. I want to see what else . . .'

It was the Doctor's turn to frown. 'With the very greatest respect,' he said, 'I really fail to see what business it is of yours.'

'You . . .' Hamlet felt his fists clench, and there was a cracking sound as his knuckles popped. 'Just what the hell are you playing at, anyway?'

The Doctor gazed at him, mild as lamb stew with lentils. 'My agenda, you mean? I would have thought that would be obvious by now.'

'I'm thick, you'll have to explain. I think my brain came free with twelve litres of lawnmower oil.'

'It's very simple,' said the Doctor. 'I'm going to rule the world, and you and your, um, subsequent models are going to make it possible.'

'Really?'

'Absolutely. I shall build an army of invincible artificial humanoids, seize absolute power and reform human society on strictly scientific principles. It's my life's work, you know. Or at least,' he added, 'my life's work for the last twenty-three years. Before that, of course, I worked for the soap powder people.'

Hamlet stood up, and as he did so he began to realise the extent of the changes that had been made to him since he was last on his feet. It was a strange and somewhat awkward feeling, but exhilarating, like taking a Challenger tank for a joyride. 'Sorry, mate,' he said, 'but no thanks. Don't bother to show me to the door, I can probably walk out through the wall.'

The Doctor gave him a look, woolly but stern, like a cross between Judge Jeffreys and a sheep. 'I really wouldn't advocate that,' he said. 'Really, I wouldn't.'

'No?'

'Quite. You see, I've planted a bomb in your chest.'

'Oh.'

The Doctor nodded. 'Only a small bomb,' he went on. 'Powerful, but small. There's no danger unless I operate the remote control.' He fished in his pocket and produced a small handset.

'We'll see about that,' Hamlet replied; then he made a grab for the little plastic box, secured it and ate it. 'All right?' he said.

'Actually,' the Doctor answered, unfazed, 'it doesn't matter in the least about that one. The device is harmonically regulated.'

'Huh?'

'The bomb will go off,' the Doctor translated, 'in response to certain sounds. To be precise, a specific piece of music.'

'Get away!'

The Doctor nodded. 'A pleasing refinement,' he said. 'Anticipating a potentially hostile reaction, I thought it best to take sensible precautions.'

'Which specific piece of music?'

The corners of the Doctor's mouth twitched ever so slightly. '*Buffalo Girl*,' he replied.

Hamlet frowned. 'You what?'

'Oh, you'd recognise it as soon as you heard it,' the Doctor said. 'It's what's always being played on the pianola in the saloon in Westerns. I'd hum it for you now, only . . . Anyway, it was a particular favourite of my late wife. I have the melody in question loaded into the intercom system here. If you make any further untoward movements, I can set it playing by using the remote control device built into the ring on my left hand.'

Hamlet sat down on the table he'd been strapped to when he came round. 'I see,' he said. 'Clever sod, aren't you?'

'You are too kind.' The Doctor shrugged. 'In any event,' he said, 'for your own good I really can't advocate your leaving this particular environment. At least, not until the side effects I mentioned a moment ago have had a chance to stabilise.'

'Side effects? What—?'

'Ah,' said the Doctor. 'I was coming to that.'

'Excuse me,' Jane said. 'I'd like to report a missing person.'

The desk sergeant was a tall man, but he slouched, which meant he was six foot two (gross), five foot nine (net); and the only reason his knuckles didn't trail on the ground was that he had his hands on the counter. He would have reassured Charles Darwin, but he didn't inspire Jane with overwhelming confidence.

'Uh?' he said.

'A missing person,' Jane said. 'I've lost a person and I'd like him found, please.'

'Jussa minnit.'

'Sorry?'

'Jussa minnit. Finda pen.'

Jane opened her handbag and produced a biro. 'His name,' she said, 'is Hamlet, he's a Danish citizen, I think, but he speaks *very* good English, some of the best there is, in fact, and he's about five foot eight, slim build, I don't know what his face looks like because he wears a paper bag over his head all the time, but you'll know him when you see him because he smells of embalming fluid. He was wearing an old raincoat. I think he's been stolen.'

'Name.'

'I just said, Hamlet, that's H–A—'

'Your name.'

'Oh. Armitage. Jane Armitage.'

'Address.'

Jane gave her address, and the policeman wrote it down in slightly less time than it would have taken to do a page of the Lindisfarne Gospels. 'Right,' said the policeman. 'What can I do for you?'

'I'd like to report a missing person, please. Preferably,' she added, 'before he dies of old age and the whole thing becomes academic anyway.'

'Name.'

'Whose?'

'His.'

'Right, it's Hamlet, that's H—'

'How do you spell that?'

'H-A-M-L-E-T.'

'Just the one T?'

'Yes, please. And two sugars.'

'You what?'

'Nothing. Look, can you get a move on, please? I'm worried.'

The policeman turned his paper over. 'And when did you see him last?' he asked.

'Last night. Well, about half past two this morning, actually. Like I said, I think someone's stolen him.'

'You want to report a theft?'

'I suppose so . . . Look, can I just—?'

'Name?'

Jane drew a deep breath, thanked the policeman nicely, and left. Probably just as well, she reflected as she drove home again. She was no expert on immigration law, but she had the notion that it might have something to say about buckshee imaginary Danes occupying home-made bodies. She parked the car, let herself in and switched on her screen.

There was, she realised, rather a lot more there than she remembered.

Her first reaction was annoyance. Many a time she'd gone to bed in the early hours of the morning secretly wishing the writing fairy would come while she was asleep and knock off ten or so pages for her; and now, apparently, it had, and it wasn't a publishable book.

Then she read what was on the screen.

Regalian stared.

He was not, all in all, a happy character. He'd just crawled three hundred yards, noiselessly, through thick brambles, right under the noses of a number of very fierce-looking fairy guards, and he was currently lying flat on his stomach in a bed of the most virulent stinging nettles it had ever been his misfortune to encounter. He was observing Skinner, the man he had been sent to save. He was wondering why the hell he bothered.

In fairness, the mortal wasn't doing anything he wouldn't be doing himself if he were in Skinner's position; but that, he felt very strongly, was beside the point. It was aesthetically right that Skinner had to be saved, PDQ. And it was artistically inevitable that he, Regalian, was going to have to do the saving; which was a pity. Left to himself, the most he'd be inclined to save would be green shield stamps, and then only if there was something in the catalogue he actually wanted.

Skinner, of course, was a mortal, and so he had no instinctive knowledge of what was and wasn't right. More than that, he was an author; and any character will tell you that those dozy buggers wouldn't know an aesthetic necessity if they found one in their breakfast cereal.

Ah well, Regalian muttered to himself, publish and be damned. He looked around, and started to put together his plan of campaign.

What I need right now, he told himself, is a good diversion.

. . . Such as might be caused by an angry, still partially concussed bounty hunter crashing through the undergrowth on the edge of the glade, clutching a Winchester rifle and not looking where he's going. And, talk of the devil . . .

The bounty hunter, too, was not happy. As he entered the glade, tripping over a root as he did so and very nearly shooting himself in the foot, he looked like Jack Palance waking up to find the freezer had defrosted itself in the night and flooded the kitchen floor. The fairy who tried to impede his progress got the butt of the Winchester in his solar plexus, together with a very unfriendly look.

'You,' he snapped at Skinner, who was on his knees

scrabbling frantically for his trousers. 'On your feet, or the broad gets it.'

There was a screech at his right elbow, and he found himself confronted by a beautiful, scantily clad, silver-skinned female holding a very sharp-looking knife. He reassessed his priorities.

'You,' he snapped at the female. 'Back off or the donkey gets it.'

The female backed off, snarling. 'Peaseblossom, Moth, Mustardseed,' she growled, 'stomp the bastard!'

This complicated matters. He was covering Skinner with the rifle and the female with his revolver, and he only had one pair of hands, for Chrissakes. He resolved the problem by booting Moth savagely in whatever fairies have due south of their navels, and stepping back towards the presumed safety of the trees.

A mistake. As the immortal Kurt Lundqvist says in Chapter Nineteen of *Bounty Hunting For Pleasure And Profit*, never presume. Just as he was within arm's length of the edge of the glade, he felt a depressingly familiar cold, metallic something pressing in his ear, and heard the sound of a hammer being cocked.

'All of you,' said a voice behind him, 'freeze or the bounty hunter gets it.'

There was a moment of puzzled silence.

'So?' demanded a fairy. 'What of it?'

'You're quite right,' Regalian said apologetically. 'What I meant to say was, freeze and nobody's going to get hurt.'

'Oh. Right. Why didn't you say so before?'

'Now then, the knives. Drop them slowly, where I can see them.'

There was a clatter of falling cutlery. 'It's confusing enough as it is,' the fairy continued, 'without you fluffing your lines.'

'Look, I said I'm sorry. And you, the one with the big log. Thank you.'

'Yes,' complained the fairy, 'but who's he meant to be threatening? The other one's in the way, I can't see what's going—'

'Hoy!' It was Skinner, waving his arms. 'Just what in hell is going on?'

'Don't you start,' Regalian snapped. 'Now, get yourself over here and we can be on our way.'

'Not damn well likely,' Skinner replied. 'I like it here.'

'Get over here or I'll blow your stupid head off!'

'Hey, *he's* threatening *him*,' wailed a fairy. 'I thought *he* was on *their* side.'

'No, *he's* on *our* side, that's why *he's* threatening the other one, and—'

'No, you're wrong there, because otherwise they'd both be threatening us.'

'Surely not.'

'HEY!' Regalian shouted, and there was silence. 'Get this straight, will you? I'm threatening all of you, so if you'll just . . .'

He tailed off in mid sentence. Titania had stepped in front of Skinner, who was now trying to step in front of her. She was holding him back with one slim but obviously very strong arm. Meanwhile Mustardseed was trying to step in front of both of them, and Peaseblossom was trying to barge him out of the way. It was, Regalian said to himself, all so utterly *depressing* . . .

'Please yourselves,' he said, and, for want of anything better to do, he belted the bounty hunter across the back of the head with the barrel of the Scholfield, dropping him to the ground. That, at least, simplified matters to some extent.

'NOW!' yelled a voice from the bushes, and suddenly the glade was full of fairies in black pullovers and balaclava helmets. Regalian recognised the leader as the chap who'd ambushed them in the forest and fitted out Skinner with the big ears. That, presumably, was Oberon, whose practical joke all this had been.

The arrival of Oberon's people didn't do much to simplify the position. There were now so many fairies trying to stand in front of each other that the far end of the glade looked like the queue for night-of-performance tickets for *The Phantom of the Opera*. The bounty hunter, having recovered from his nasty knock in excellent time, had lunged forward towards Skinner, tripped over his own feet, and was being fought over by two separate contingents of Oberon's lot. Titania, meanwhile, had grabbed hold of Oberon himself and was giving him a fearful shellacking with an empty champagne bottle. Regalian stepped back into the vegetation at the edge of the glade, picked up a stray apple from the picnic, and holstered his gun. Let someone else do the running around for a change, he thought.

When he'd finished his apple he put the core tidily in the hollow of a dead tree and strolled forwards through the heaving tumult of fighting elves, muttering the occasional, 'Excuse me, please,' and, 'Mind your backs, please, coming through.' Pleasingly enough, the fight seemed to eddy round him, and he got the distinct impression that the participants had other issues to resolve besides the detention/rescue of Skinner. They had even stopped kicking the bounty hunter, except occasionally in passing.

When he reached him, Skinner was kneeling over a rather battered-looking Oberon, brandishing a small fork in his face and yelling something about ears. With a sigh, Regalian grabbed him by the scruff of his neck, hauled him to his feet and said, 'That'll do. Time we were leaving.'

'Not,' panted Skinner, 'without my ears, I want my goddamn ears back, and I'm not . . .'

Enough, Regalian said to himself, is enough. Pausing only to knock Skinner silly with a large veal and ham pie, also left over from the picnic, and fireman's-lift him on to his shoulders, he turned and started to walk away; only to find the dratted woman blocking his path.

'Can I come too, please?' she said.

'No. Bugger off.'

'I can fix your friend's ears for him if you'll let me come too.'

Regalian scowled. 'Miss,' he said, 'my job is to deliver this idiot to the real world, preferably alive. Nothing was said about ears. Now get out of my way before I thump you with this pie.'

Titania didn't move. 'You want to get out of here?' she said. 'Back to real life?'

'Yes. Now I warned you . . .'

The pie twitched in his hand, and turned into a white rabbit. With a shudder of distaste, Regalian opened his fingers and let it go. 'Was that you?' he asked.

Titania nodded. 'I'm good at that sort of thing,' she said. 'I could be a lot of help getting you out of here.'

Regalian was about to try pushing past when an unpleasant thought occurred to him. Letting Skinner slide gently off his shoulder on to the ground, he turned to Titania and folded his arms. 'Why exactly are you so damn keen to tag along?' he asked.

Titania prodded the recumbent Skinner with her toe. 'Him,' she replied. 'I think he's cute.'

'You're the love interest, aren't you?'

The Fairy Queen nodded. 'That's right,' she said. 'It's a lousy job, but someone's got to do it.'

They stood for a moment; two professionals, each with a job to do. They understood each other.

'All right, then,' Regalian sighed, 'if you must. But I'm warning you, the moment you sprain your ankle or get kidnapped by the bad guys, you're on your own, got it?'

'You don't mean that.'

No, Regalian sighed to himself, I probably don't. Who'd be a hero, anyway?

'All *right*,' he said grumpily. 'But you get to carry him until he comes round.'

'But he weighs a ton!'

'True. But I'm a strictly equal opportunities hero, and I refuse to conform to outmoded stereotypes. Come on, we haven't got all day.'

CHAPTER SEVEN

Hamlet sat and stared into the darkness.

Had he been feeling his usual self – the self who saw ghosts, went mad, stabbed government officials through curtains and eventually got killed – he would undoubtedly have thought of something pretty pungent, not to say quotable, to say about all this; although since it would have had to be a soliloquy, nobody would have been any the wiser for it. As it was, he merely sat with his elbows on his knees, occasionally muttering, 'Bugger!'

It was, he decided, a sorry state of affairs, slice it how you like. On the positive side, admittedly, instead of having a body like a clapped-out Skoda, he had the corporeal equivalent of an armoured car. On the negative side, according to Dr Rossfleisch, he had a number of fairly major side effects to look forward to, at some unspecified but probably not too distant point in the future.

Among the more palatable of these were sudden uncontrollable fits of violent rage, a dual personality oscillating between diabolical malevolence and whimpering remorse, murderous headaches, adrenalin rushes, catatonic trances and extra-special heartburn. There was also the prospect of a stray snatch of music from a car radio, a supermarket muzak tannoy or a whistling postman blasting his intestines out through his ears at half a second's notice. To make matters even worse, it seemed that he no longer had the choice of to be or not to be. He was, and that was that.

To help pass the time, he got to his feet, groped his way to the door and tried battering it down with his head; but it didn't get him very far. The good Doctor had evidently had that in mind when he'd designed the room, and all he did was make his headache slightly worse.

It would be nice, he said to himself, to get my hands on whoever's responsible for this, and pull his head off. No, dammit, he corrected himself, that's what the bastard wants you to think, he's planning to use you as a sort of para-human Dobermann, don't give him the satisfaction. Think nice thoughts. Peace. Love. Spring flowers. Wee lambkins.

It didn't work. After about four seconds, all he could see in his mind's eye was himself, chasing wee lambkins across flowery dells with a bloody great cleaver.

All right, then, he urged himself, harness that aggression and hostility, make it work for you. Try giving the door another damn good hiding.

It was a palliative, nothing more; and as soon as he stopped, the bad thoughts started again. World leaders, he found himself thinking, heads of state, I bet a lot of this is their fault. If I could just get my boot behind some of those suckers . . . Dear God, he said to himself, this is *bad*, I'm definitely going round the bend here. Put a hawk and a handsaw in front of me right now, and I'd be lucky to get it right four times out of ten.

Well now, he ventured, what would Hamlet do in this situation? Well, he'd agonise. He'd speak lots of blank verse, prance around a bit scoring verbal points off anyone who didn't get out of his way fast enough, and end up dragging everybody around him down into a cock-up of monolithic proportions. Not exactly ideal, admittedly, but better than running around the place scragging people.

He left the door alone, sat down in the middle of the floor and tried very hard to remember who he was. It didn't come easy. He no longer felt the slightest inclination to think of himself as a rogue and peasant slave, and the thought of his too, too solid flesh melting and resolving itself into a dew just made him want to find the guy who looked after the air conditioning and bash him into a pulp. With an effort, he throttled back on the adrenalin and made a conscious effort to face up to the moral dilemmas his situation posed.

Moral dilemmas, as is well known, are like policemen; there's never one about when you need one. He was just turning over in his mind the moral ambivalence of ripping the guts out of total strangers when the door started to open. At this point instinct took over, and he sprang at the doorway like a tiger.

'Only me,' said Rossfleisch's voice, and Hamlet froze in his tracks. All the Doctor had to do, he knew, was whistle. He subsided into a growling heap.

'I thought you might be feeling a bit peckish by now,' the Doctor said, 'so I've brought you some nice raw meat and a cup of hot blood.'

Hamlet snarled. He'd wanted to say thank you, politely, but somehow he couldn't manage it. He had the unpleasant feeling that the nicest thing he'd currently be capable of saying would be, 'GrrroARRRR!'

'And when you've had that,' the Doctor went on, 'we must have a little chat about what I want you to do next. I think,' he added cheerfully, 'it's something you'll enjoy very much. Very much indeed.'

*　　*　　*

Jane looked up from the screen, lit a cigarette, and thought hard.

Plots, she was always ready to confess, really weren't her thing. The broad outlines ('Well, there's this prince sort of person and he finds this magic ring, and he's got to take it to this sort of temple place before the bad guys catch him, and that's sort of it, really') she could just about manage, given time and encouragement; but when it came to what actually happened, the running around and toing and froing that one needs to fill in the awkward gap between the opening paragraph and the last page, she tended to find herself going with the flow; or, to be more accurate, the trickle.

That approach, however, wasn't going to cut much ice in this case. She leaned back in her chair, closed her eyes and tried to think . . .

So, we're in *A Midsummer Night's Dream*, and we want to get out of that and into *Alice in Wonderland*. This is, essentially, a continuity problem, and we need a link of some sort.

She breathed in, inhaled a mouthful of smoke the wrong way, choked and stubbed out the dog-end. A link, between the two. Shouldn't be too hard, surely.

Twenty minutes later, she came to the conclusion that it was probably a bit harder than she'd anticipated, but not completely insoluble. She got up, made a cup of tea, and sat down again.

Fifteen minutes later, she remembered that she hadn't drunk her tea.

Eight minutes later, she reviewed her progress so far. It consisted of the one word, Wonderland.

In Wonderland, there is no here or there, only wherever and another part of the forest. In the kingdom of the imagination, the cock-eyed man is king.

Let there, then, be a rabbit hole.

*   *   *

'If she thinks I'm going down there,' Regalian observed angrily, 'she's got another think coming.'

Titania looked at him quizzically. 'I think we're meant to,' she replied. 'Otherwise, it wouldn't be there, would it?'

'Not necessarily,' Regalian said. 'More to the point, did you see the size of that thing?'

'Oh come on,' Titania objected. 'It was a big fluffy white rabbit with a comical hat and a big pocket-watch. You aren't going to tell me you're afraid of fluffy white rabbits, are you?'

'I am when they're five feet ten inches tall,' said Regalian unhappily. 'Must have teeth like large chisels. If you think I'm scrabbling about down a long dark tunnel with those buggers roaming about . . .'

Titania shook her head. 'It's only a character,' she said, 'like you and me. I'm sure it means us no harm. It's from a children's book, after all.'

'You read any children's books lately? Your average child is about as bloodthirsty an animal as you can find this side of a piranha colony. They have dragons in children's books, for God's sake, and wolves that eat grandmothers. No, I think I'll go the long way round, if it's all the same to you.'

Titania was about to reply when there was a scuffling sound and the rabbit reappeared. Its big top hat was rather muddier than you see in the illustrations, and it had torn the sleeve of its frock coat on an underground root.

'Are you two clowns going to stand around gossiping all day?' it demanded. 'Because if so, you can damn well find your own way. Oh my ears and whiskers,' it added dutifully, and vanished back down the hole.

'All right,' Regalian conceded, 'maybe it's not exactly a *wild* rabbit. That doesn't alter the fact that we've got him to lug about with us.' He jerked a thumb at the recumbent Skinner. 'Sheer dead weight, he is.'

'You shouldn't have hit him so hard, the poor lamb.'

'That's beside the point. I say we wait till he wakes up, at the very least. Or else we find some rope to lower him down with.'

Titania nodded. 'Rope,' she said, and there was rope. Regalian scowled.

'Smartarse,' he said.

There is a tide in the affairs of men, muttered Hamlet to himself as he balanced the chamber pot on the lintel, that, taken at the flood, leads on to fortune.

Stepping back gingerly so as not to disturb the delicate equipoise of the chamber pot, he reflected bitterly that that was about the only quote from Shakespeare that wasn't in *Hamlet*, and it was the only one he had ever had the slightest use for. Would he, he mused, nevertheless be entitled to his staff discount?

As befitted a graduate of the University of Wittenberg, he had calculated the physics of the thing to a nicety. He backed against the far wall, took a deep breath and started to bellow.

Thanks to Dr Rossfleisch's unquestionable design flair (lung capacity increased by 27%) it wasn't long before somebody came. The inspection hatch in the door shot back, leaking light into the cell like a breach in the Dutch sea wall, and then slammed shut. There was a rattle of keys in the door. The door opened.

Poetry in motion. The chamber pot, supported on a stiff piece of leather ripped out of Hamlet's left boot and jammed into the door frame, tottered and fell from its perch just exactly at the moment when Dr Rossfleisch's assistant walked under it, holding a portable cassette player and a torch. A thud and a crash and it was all over.

Pausing only to tread heavily on the cassette player,

Hamlet scooped up the keys, bundled the assistant into the cell, locked the door and stood for a moment, the temporary victim of his own success. Since he hadn't imagined for one moment that such a hare-brained scheme would succeed, he hadn't wasted any mental energy on thinking what he would do after he'd broken out. He scratched his head, snagging a fingernail on a slightly proud rivet.

Up the corridor, he asked himself, or down the corridor. That is the question.

Oh for crying out loud, don't let's start all that again. He turned left and started to run.

As he turned a corner, he could hear running footsteps coming up behind him. Bad *déjà vu* here; this was about the point in the proceedings when he generally got caught and sent to England. Ha, he said to himself, fooled you, I'm already in England. Talk your way out of that one if you're so damned clever.

He gripped the torch he'd liberated from the assistant, flattened himself as best he could against the wall and waited. A few seconds later two men in white coats came flying round the corner, also clutching portable cassette players. They never knew what hit them.

Cripes, thought Hamlet, this is so *easy*. If ever I get back to Elsinore, certain people are going to have to watch out, because there's a whole different way of going about things I never even dreamed of.

Catching his breath, he ran on down the corridor, pausing only to smash any PA speakers he passed on the way. There didn't seem to be anybody about, and the way his luck was going, this tunnel would pretty soon end in a door leading straight out on to the street. And to think, he mused as he ran, how most characters make such a song and dance about breaking out of nick. A doddle. Kids' stuff. Any fool can—

He stopped dead in his tracks. He had reached the end of the tunnel and it was a wall. A dead end.

There were footsteps down the corridor behind him; not so fast this time. It was probably safe to say that whoever his pursuers were, they had passed by the two men in white coats and were determined to learn by their mistakes.

Think. Why go to all the trouble of building a corridor, just to end it with a blank wall? Architectural error? Job creation scheme? Fifty thousand bricks left over from the main job, waste not, want not? Improbable. There had to be something here he hadn't seen.

Like, for instance, a secret passage.

One of the drawbacks to secret passages, however, is that they're secret. If they weren't, they'd be painfully obvious passages and the builders couldn't charge nearly as much for them. An educated guess told him he had about forty-five seconds to work out what the secret was before the heavies arrived.

Not for the first time, Hamlet found himself wishing he was back where he belonged. Where he came from, in fiction, the hero always finds the knob and lever that operates the hidden door, usually by stumbling against it or trying to hang his hat on it. Success is guaranteed, or else why the hell did the author put it there in the first place? In real life, there are no such guarantees. For all reality cared, he could spend the rest of his life down here biffing the walls and prodding the floor, and be none the wiser.

Something inside him, probably one of those goddamn side effects, told him that this was the wrong attitude; that what he should do in the circumstances was turn, face his attackers and beat the pulp out of as many of them as he could before one of them managed to switch on his tape recorder and operate the bomb. Who knows, continued the insidious little voice, you might get an opportunity to put your hands round Dr Rossfleisch's scrawny little neck. Now, wouldn't that be worth getting your liver blown out for?

Briefly urging his inner voice to put a sock in it, Hamlet turned to the wall and tried running against it with his shoulder. To his pleasant surprise, it didn't actually hurt despite the terrific wallop when he made contact. That aside, however, there wasn't much to be said for it.

He tried again, and again. Waste of bloody time.

The footsteps were very close now. It was time, Hamlet conceded, to give it best, hold his hands up, go back to his cell and try again tomorrow. Obviously the rules of dramatic necessity didn't work here, and the sooner he accepted that fact the better. Accordingly, he stood back, put his hands behind his head in a gesture of submission and waited.

Not for long. A split second later, a gaggle of five men in white coats came haring round the corner—

—Saw him, tried to stop sharply on the smooth concrete floor, failed and piled up in a confused, high-velocity heap against the wall—

—Which swung open, revealing a spiral staircase descending steeply into the darkness, down which they all fell, with much bumping and use of profane language; after which, the door slowly swung to behind them, and shut with a loud clunk.

'Oh come *on*,' Hamlet said disgustedly to the heavens. 'There's no need to take the mickey.'

Then, without any real urgency, he started on the long trudge back up the corridor.

'No,' insisted Titania, 'it went this way.'

Regalian stayed where he was. Quite apart from the fact that he was never at his best when down long, dark tunnels, scrabbling about on his hands and knees among rabbit droppings the size of pigeons' eggs and towing behind him a heavy, insensible body, he was beginning to feel ever so slightly sick of Titania's company. Four centuries of being the queen of the fairies had left its mark on her character, and he never had liked bossy women.

Thank God, he murmured to himself, she's not *my* love interest; at least, not yet. There was plenty of time for the plot to demand an eternal-triangle situation. The very thought made him shudder.

'Are you sure?' he asked.

Titania clicked her tongue. 'Of course I'm sure. Besides which,' she added, 'if you hadn't been dawdling we wouldn't have lost the damn rabbit in the first place.'

Regalian toyed with the idea of pointing out that he had been dawdling only because he was lugging along with him two hundred and forty pounds of sleeping novelist, which by rights was her responsibility anyway; but decided against it, on the grounds that life is too short, even if you're technically immortal. 'Sorry,' he mumbled.

'Well, come on then, if you're coming.'

'I'm right behind you.'

A certain time later, he observed that this seemed to be a very long tunnel.

Some time after that, he pointed out that this appeared to be a very long tunnel indeed.

A bit later, just as he was about to bring to Titania's attention the fact that this tunnel was, horizontally speaking, extensive, they came to a dead end.

'Oh,' Titania said.

'Quite.'

'There's probably a door of some kind somewhere,' she continued, 'if only we knew where to look.'

'You reckon.'

'It's artistically right that there's a secret door.'

Matter of opinion, muttered Regalian to himself. As far as he was concerned, poetic justice demanded that half a mile up the wrong tunnel, which she had insisted on following in the teeth of his advice, should end in a blank wall. On the other hand, he didn't exactly fancy retracing his steps, particularly as there wasn't enough room to turn round, which meant that instead of pulling Mr Skinner he'd have to push. On occasions like this, he was prepared to concede, there's no particular shame in admitting you were wrong.

'In that case,' he said, 'we'd better find it, hadn't we?'

They were still searching when Skinner finally woke up. It took them some time to calm him down and convince him that he was not, in actual fact, in his grave. They asked him if, by any chance, he could see anything that looked like a door.

'No, sorry,' he replied; and then he remembered something, and his hands shot to the sides of his head.

'It's all right,' Regalian assured him. 'I made her take them off.'

'Thank God for that.' Skinner lowered his voice. 'Look,' he said, 'just what exactly is she doing here?'

'She's the lo— I think she just wanted to come along for the ride,' Regalian answered. 'You know, a change is as good as a rest.'

In the flickering light from a match clutched between his thumb and forefinger, Skinner glanced round. 'Funny sort of place to come for a holiday,' he observed.

There was a cry of triumph from the wall face, and the two men craned their necks to look at the spot Titania was pointing at.

'Look,' she said, 'it's a letter box.'

'Get away, so it is. Any doors in the vicinity, did you notice? Only, all due respect, both of us are a bit chubby to be getting through letter boxes.'

'Yes, but don't you see?' Titania demanded. 'Where there's a letter box . . .'

'I don't like the way this conversation is headed,' Skinner said loudly.

'And,' Titania went on, 'here's a sort of brass plate thing, you know, like you get on the outsides of offices and old-fashioned houses . . .'

'I really am getting a bad feeling about this.'

'And – yippee! Hey, guys, there's a bell-pull. Where there's a bell-pull, there must be a bell. All we have to do is—'

'Whatever you do, don't touch that bell . . .'

'—Ring it and see who answers.'

There was a moment's silence, which Skinner broke by saying, 'She didn't pull it, did she? Tell me she didn't pull it.'

From behind the wall came the sound of bolts being shot back and chains removed; and then the tunnel flooded with light.

'Oh crap,' mumbled Skinner. 'I thought it was.'

Silhouetted in the doorway was an outlandish, disturbing figure. Generally humanoid in overall appearance, it was dressed in a sort of dowdy Edwardian style. Instead of a human head, a black rodent's snout poked out of the creased wing-collar and sniffed at them. In the backlight from the open door, they could see the glow reflected on two sharp, pointed front teeth.

'Hang spring cleaning,' it said.

'It could have been worse,' Skinner said a little later. 'It could have been *Winnie the Pooh*.'

Regalian didn't bother replying. He was saving all his strength and concentration for his next attempt to chew through the ropes round his wrists.

'It's a fair point,' agreed Titania loyally. 'I mean, yes,

maybe we are stuck in *The Wind in the Willows* and maybe Mr Mole does have a pathological hatred of human beings and a gun, but at least we're in the right area, classic children's fiction. There may well be a connecting door or a—'

'Don't tell me,' Regalian sighed. 'A looking glass. As in *Through The*. No, thank you very much. I've had enough to put up with as it is.'

'Look . . .'

'And the same goes,' he added savagely, 'for wardrobes. Got that?'

Titania wriggled angrily against the ropes. 'Well, that attitude's really going to help, isn't it?'

'Helps me,' Regalian replied. 'Surly truculence. Can't beat it, in my experience.'

'Nuts,' Titania replied. 'Instead of just sitting there making comments, you ought to be doing something. I mean,' she added scornfully, 'I had assumed you were meant to be the *hero*.'

'You're expecting me to gnaw through ropes, aren't you?'

Titania considered. 'It's a thought,' she said. 'It'd be better than lounging about practising your repartee.'

'You people have no idea,' Regalian snapped. 'Did you know that there's more cholesterol in six inches of rope than four cream doughnuts?'

'Spit it out, then. Honestly, if all you're going to do is complain—'

'And,' Regalian went on, 'there's my teeth to consider. A fine hero I'd be, mumbling my way through the rest of the trilogy in a dental plate.'

'Shut up and chew.'

'Yuk,' said Regalian, with his mouth full. 'Liquorice again. I can't be doing with bloody liquorice.'

* * *

Hamlet had been walking for hours, and his feet hurt.

The enormous boots didn't help. Why Rossfleisch had seen fit to equip him with them, given that his actual feet were more or less normal size (he'd checked), was quite beyond him, unless it was just tradition or something. He felt like a circus clown in them, although he was prepared to concede that most circus clowns don't have bolts through their necks.

Quite some place the Doctor has here, he mused, must have set him back a bob or two. Most of it, admittedly, seemed to consist of mile after mile of identical-looking tiled corridors, none of which appeared to lead anywhere, but maybe that was all the architect was good at.

Nobody had tried chasing him for some time now. That could have been because there were too few people to patrol all these miles of tunnel, or because he'd thumped all the staff who could be spared from duty for patrol purposes (he'd rather lost count, but he must have clobbered upwards of twenty of the poor devils by now); or maybe the good Doctor had other things on his mind and knew there was no way out of here anyhow. On reflection, the third alternative seemed the most likely. Sooner or later he'd collapse from exhaustion, whereupon they'd send out a crew with a small truck and bring him in.

How tiresome, he reflected, as he pulled down and crushed yet another PA loudspeaker (seventy-three; he had been counting them), and, in the final analysis, how pointless. For all he knew, this was all part of some complex research programme, to see how he would react under certain circumstances; white mouse job. Depressing, he concluded, turning a corner into yet another half-mile-long straight of tiled corridor. I could easily spend the rest of my life trolling about down here.

He stopped. Far away in the distance he could hear a gentle buzzing sound, like a hive of bees. As he stood, the noise came nearer and grew louder, and he concluded it was probably some sort of machine. A robot, perhaps. Rossfleisch was just the sort of man who would have robots; probably big silver ones with square heads and lots of flashing lights that went beep. He waited, and eventually just such an artefact wheezed round the corner at the far end of the straight. It was about five feet tall, chrome plated, vaguely human-shaped, and carrying a mop and a bucket.

It wasn't in any particular hurry; and about five minutes crept by before it clanked past him, apparently oblivious to his presence. As soon as it was level with him, he reached out, grabbed it round what passed for its throat with both hands and lifted it off the ground. He was rewarded with a massive electric shock, and let go as quickly as he could. There was a loud thump and a frantic outburst of beeping; and then the machine shut up and lay still.

Great, Hamlet reflected bitterly, I've killed it, that really does help a lot. There was an outside chance it might have been going towards an exit of some kind. I could have followed it.

He was just about to vent his rage on the gadget when a couple of green lights, mounted on the side of its head where its ears should have been, switched themselves on and started to hum. Bemused, Hamlet stood back and waited to see what would happen.

Don't just stand there, said the robot in an electric monotone, *help me up before my batteries go flat.*

'Why?' Hamlet demanded. 'You're just a machine. And besides, you aren't safe to touch. You nearly fried my kidneys back then.'

Automatic defence system, replied the robot, *which I have now deactivated. It is perfectly safe, repeat, perfectly safe. Come on, help me up. Or are you training to become a stalagmite or something?*

'I'll help you up,' Hamlet said, 'if you show me the way out of here.'

In your dreams, buster.

'Alternatively,' Hamlet suggested, 'I could jump up and down on you till you're nothing but a heap of scrap. The choice is yours. Personally, I'd prefer option two. I'm just in the right frame of mind for smashing up something fragile and expensive.'

How do you know, asked the robot cagily, *that I won't lead you straight back to the labs you've just escaped from?*

'You try that,' Hamlet replied, 'and I'll make sure you give Humpty Dumpty a bloody good run for his money in the jigsaw puzzle stakes. The more of Doctor Rossfleisch's property I damage, the better I shall be pleased, so don't tempt me.'

Big bully, the robot grumbled. *All right, you win. Help me up and—*

'Not so fast. Switch yourself off again while I pick you up. And make sure you keep your nasty volts to yourself.'

The robot obediently bleeped into immobility, and Hamlet manhandled it back on to its feet. 'Ready,' he said. 'Lead on, Macduff.'

Here, I thought you were the other one, you know, the one with the skull and the poncy black tights.

'And shut up.'

The robot was aggravatingly slow, like the milk tanker you always find yourself behind in a winding country lane; but eventually it puffed and bleeped its way to a closed brushed-steel-finished doorway with a panel with buttons on it. Hooray, thought Hamlet, a lift shaft. Now we're getting somewhere.

This is as far as I go, muttered the robot. *I have an idea it leads to Up, but I've never actually been there. My life is extremely boring.*

'Just as well you're not a sentient life form, then, isn't it?'

But the robot had switched itself off, and was standing to attention on a humming metal disc set into the floor. Recharging itself, Hamlet assumed, the cybernetic equivalent of a sit down with a cup of tea and a smoke. Now then, let's see where this lift goes to.

He examined the panel and pressed the button marked G. A moment or so later, the door slid back and Hamlet stepped in.

It is, of course, entirely true that G stands for Ground. It also stands for a lot of other things as well.

The door slid open.

Maybe it was only in Hamlet's over-productive imagination that, as it swished back to let him through, the door sniggered. It certainly shut again pretty damn quick as soon as he was through; and before he could do anything about it, he heard the lift scurrying back down the shaft as fast as its cable could carry it. He fumbled for buttons to press to bring it back, but there weren't any.

G. G stands for ground, garage, gourmet, guano, gelignite, goldfinch, general, Guatemala, guild and gimcrack. And graveyard. This, Hamlet realised, was where Doctor Rossfleisch kept his spare parts.

It was a huge open space, like a gigantic ballroom, and it looked like a body-snatcher's car boot sale. There were bits of people everywhere; laid out on tables, stacked in piles, spilling out of tea-chests or just lying about. Most of them had little labels attached – stock numbers, presumably, or use-by dates – and some had been bolted together in an apparently haphazard manner, giving the impression that these were the bits of old junk the Youth Opportunities lads were allowed to practise on.

There was an unpleasant smell.

It must have taken him years, considered the part of Hamlet's brain that wasn't yet completely traumatised by horror, to put this little lot together; years, a lot of money, and thousands and thousands of pairs of rubber gloves. Gosh, it added, bits of me probably came from here. Then it, too, switched off.

Stairs. There must be stairs here somewhere, or a window or a fire escape. There's got to be some way out, unless everybody who comes here ends up joining the stock. Trying not to look where he was going, Hamlet stumbled about, bumping into things, knocking things over. He put his foot on something round, and fell over.

He opened his eyes. Hell fire, he said to himself, I know that face.

'Yorick?' he said. 'What the hell are you doing here?'

A bloody silly question, if ever there was one. He scrambled to his feet, removed a hand from his trouser pocket and tried going back the way he had come, with a vague idea of battering down the lift door and jumping down the shaft.

'Ah,' said a voice he knew, 'there you are. I was wondering where you'd got to.'

Rossfleisch, portable cassette player in hand, stepped out from behind a palletful of knees and smiled indulgently. Hamlet froze.

'This . . .' he said, and ran out of words. The Doctor nodded graciously.

'A life's work,' he cooed. 'Tread carefully, for you tread on my dreams.'

Hamlet wasn't so sure about that, because he had the idea that dreams didn't go squish when you trod on them in heavy boots. He wasn't, however, inclined to argue the point. He made a sort of general purpose gesture with his hand.

'Actually,' the Doctor continued, advancing a pace or

two, 'it's extremely fortuitous, you finding your way here like this, because I did want to see if we haven't got something a bit more suitable for you in the way of brains. I'm beginning to suspect that the one I put in is just a bit too high-powered for the job. So if you wouldn't mind stepping over to the freezer cabinet there on your left . . .'

But Hamlet, tragically indecisive though he might occasionally be, had decided that that wouldn't be a terribly good idea. With a movement so swift that it did enormous credit to Dr Rossfleisch's skill with nerve-endings and a soldering iron, he stooped, grabbed the first object that came to hand, and threw. Then he ducked, rolled and came to rest behind a large wooden crate of left feet.

He peered round the edge of the crate. Rossfleisch was lying on his back, out cold, half buried under a pile of assorted bits that presumably he'd backed into and knocked down on top of himself. The cassette player lay on the ground beside him. Hamlet managed to jump on it fairly comprehensively on his way past to the lift; which, as he'd hoped, was standing open. He found the controls, pressed a button at random, and stepped back out of the way of the door.

As the door closed, he had a feeling he was not alone.

It was a rather irrational feeling, given that the lift measured four feet square. If there was someone else in there with him, he felt sure, it ought to be fairly obvious. For a start, given the size of his boots, he'd be standing on the poor bugger's feet.

Unless, of course, the other person happened to be a ghost.

Hamlet, said the shimmering pillar of ectoplasm that now materialised in front of him, *I am thy father's spirit, doomed for a certain term to walk this lift, and for the day confin'd—*

'Er, yes, hi there, Dad,' Hamlet replied, frowning slightly.

'Actually I'm a bit tied up right now, could I possibly get back to you a bit later on?'

As he spoke, he sensed that the lift had slowed down. The ghost flickered irritably.

I could a tale unfold, it said crossly, *whose lightest word would harrow up thy soul, freeze thy young—*

'Sure, only not now, okay? Look, when this is all over it'd be really good to have lunch, have a really good talk about all the things we never seemed to find the time to talk about when you were, um, alive, uncurl a few locks together, stuff like that. Right now, though . . .' He stopped, his inner ear ringing with the sound of a big penny dropping. 'Just a minute,' he said, 'what the hell are you doing here anyway? This is the real world, there's no such thing as ghosts in the real world.'

My hour is almost come, snarled the ghost in that reproachful, I-told-you-not-to-play-with-that-ball-near-the-French-windows tone of voice that Hamlet knew so well, *when I to sulphurous and tormenting flames must render up myself.* It paused, clicked its tongue and then went on. *Pity me not, but lend thy serious hearing to what I shall unfold. But soft! methinks I scent the morning air—*

'Dad, it's half past four in the afternoon.'

The ghost flickered wildly, mouthed, *Remember!*, buzzed and snapped out of sight, leaving behind only a few spangles of blue light. Hamlet stared for a moment, shrugged and banged on the wall with his fist. The lift started to move.

It was going back up.

Regalian nibbled through the last remaining strand of the rope, shook his hands free and spat out a mouthful of liquorice-flavoured fibre. He felt sick.

'Right,' said Titania. 'If you've quite finished stuffing your face, can we please get a move on?'

'I was not stuffing my—'

'Please?'

'All right, just hold your water a minute, will you? I've only got one pair of hands.'

(And just as well, he added mentally, since scarcely five minutes seems to go by around here without some bugger tying rope round them. One set is plenty enough for me, thank you very much. You can get seriously ill eating too much liquorice.)

'Excuse me,' Skinner interrupted, 'but when you two have quite finished bickering . . .'

Regalian frowned. Quite right. Unprofessional. A hero acts, he does not bicker. As he traced his way through the Labyrinth, spinning out the golden thread, Theseus didn't bicker with Ariadne about who forgot to bring the torch.

'Sorry,' he said. 'I think we're ready now. This way, I think.'

'Hey,' yelled Titania. 'What about us?'

Regalian bit his lip. 'Actually,' he said, 'if it's all the same to you, I think I'll leave you both tied up just for now, and come back for you both later after I've sorted out what we do next. I mean, you'll be perfectly all right there, and I'll know where you are. No chance of anybody spraining an ankle or being used as a hostage. Cheerio. Won't be long.'

He took advantage of the brief stunned silence and departed. At least, he mused, this is business sort of as usual; crawling through pitch-dark underground tunnels on a desperate mission to seek out and fight with a giant rat. The fact that the rat wears a straw boater and a pink blazer and is known to generations of small children as Ratty is neither here nor there.

His hand went instinctively to his side. He would have preferred a sword; a sword is long and sharp and has only one moving part, which does not require lubrication or frequent cleaning in order to make it work. Likewise, generally speaking, a sword doesn't answer you back. Nevertheless, he told himself, it's better than nothing. 'Aren't you?' he asked aloud.

'I'm not talking to you.'

'Oh? And why not?'

'Because,' replied the Scholfield, 'you let them put a spell on me. Honestly, I've never been so embarrassed in all my—'

'But you're cured now, aren't you?'

'That's beside the point,' the revolver snarled. 'Back in 1875, I'll have you know, I was the state of the art. Competing manufacturers packed it in and went into the bicycle business once they'd seen my improved patent frame latch. And now, at my age, to have a flag come out of my barrel with BANG! written on it . . .'

'It must have been terrible,' Regalian said soothingly.

'It was.'

'If I were you, I'd want to get my own back on those bastards.'

'I do.'

'Or if not them, then some other lot of bastards.'

'I'd settle for that, certainly.'

Regalian nodded. 'Tell you what I'll do,' he said. 'First lot of bastards we come across, they're yours.'

'Really?'

'Promise. Provided of course,' he added quickly, 'that they start it, not us, and that armed response can within the context be classified as reasonable and a minimum-force position within the scenario as a whole, holistically speaking.'

'Come again?'

'In other words,' Regalian explained, 'don't shoot till I pull the trigger, or it's in the furnace for you. Got that?'

'Rotten spoilsport.'

Regalian shrugged, squared his shoulders in the orthodox manner and set off down the corridor. It was dark, and damp, and there was a faint smell of toasting crumpet that spoke eloquently to his trained character's senses of classic Edwardian escapist literature. He felt depressingly out of place. In fact, if it hadn't been for the fact that he knew as an absolute certainty that he was the hero, he could have sworn he was the villain.

He turned a corner; and froze, rooted to the spot in sudden terror. In front of him, filling the tunnel, was an enormous rodent.

Yes, it was indeed wearing a straw boater; and too true, it had on a pink blazer and a little silk cravat round its thick, coarse-haired throat. But its small, red eyes and villainously sharp teeth sent clear, unequivocal messages down every nerve in Regalian's body. Okay, so perhaps this little fellow liked messing about in boats; but so did his ancestors, the big grey buggers who brought the Black Death from Constantinople to Europe. Regalian backed away and reached for his gun; and, at the same time, the right words found their way spontaneously to his lips.

'You dirty rat,' he growled. 'I'm gonna fill you full of lead.'

At which point, Jane reached for the keyboard and started to type furiously.

God knows, she thought, I'm not all that fussed about what posterity says about me. Let them say I was derivative, and my plots lacked sparkle. Let them, even, not remember me at all. But don't let me go down in the annals of literature as the woman who killed Ratty. They'd probably dig me up and hang my bones in chains from Tower Bridge.

Think seamless, she commanded herself. All you have to do is steer the dialogue away from filling people full of lead and point it in the direction of the pointlessness of spring cleaning and the general desirability of rowing up and down the river in little boats. Doesn't matter how you do it so long as it gets done.

Which was why, suddenly and without warning, Regalian found he had been turned into a beaver.

It was nearly two hours before Regalian was able to get back to his friends in the cellars of Mole End. He had been having such a jolly time with his new friends Mr Rat and Mr Toad, cruising lazily down the river in Ratty's little boat and eating cucumber sandwiches, that he had quite lost track of the time.

'Where the fuck have you been?' Titania snapped, as he put his soft, hairy nose round the doorway and smiled. 'I've got cramp in both knees, and I've had to put up with his incessant whingeing as well. Get me out of here before I start screaming the place down. And why are you dressed as a beaver?'

'I'm not dressed as a beaver,' Regalian answered quietly. 'I *am* a bloody beaver, and it looks like I'm stuck that way till we get out of this madhouse. Hold still while I nibble through these blasted ropes.'

'Oh, so that's why you're a beaver.'

'No,' said Regalian with his mouth full, 'actually I think it's just a coincidence. Christ, this stuff tastes awful.'

'And what,' Titania said a little while after, swinging her arms round to restore a little circulation, 'have you been doing all this time? Lounging about feeding the ducks?'

'Actually, I've been fixing up our way out of here.'

'About time too.'

'The rat,' Regalian continued, with dignity, 'claims he knows where there's a sort of fault-line we might be able to use to get straight into *Alice*. Mind you, I wouldn't normally trust him as far as I could sneeze him when the pollen-count was low, but this time I think he's telling the truth.'

'Oh? Why?'

Regalian closed his eyes. 'He wants me to deliver a package,' he replied.

'A package? What sort of package?'

'Oh for God's sake, woman, use your bloody imagination. It's a squarish sort of parcel about a foot long, it's wrapped in brown paper and weighs about five kilos. You don't think you get to write books about disappearing white rabbits and jabberwocks and mirrors you can walk through just by closing your eyes and using your imagination, do you?'

'Ah. I see.'

Regalian nodded and twitched his whiskers. 'Apparently,' he went on, 'it's quite a regular traffic. The weasels and the stoats bring it downriver from Toad Hall in big crates marked Tractor Spares, and Ratty and Mole handle the distribution from this end. I think they launder the proceeds through a holding company at Pooh Corner. Anyway, something nasty happened to the regular courier and they need a replacement. That's us.'

'Dear God.' Skinner looked up, dazed. 'I always thought there was something weird about your goddamn limey children's books, but I didn't think it was as bad as that. What a country!'

'You can wipe that grin off your face,' Regalian snapped. 'Next time you see Brer Rabbit, ask him how he paid for his bright pink Mercedes convertible. Now, are you two coming or do you want to stay here and argue the toss with Mister Badger?'

Jane looked up, and blinked twice. That wasn't what she'd had in mind at all.

On the other hand; if it worked . . .

* * *

Slowly, inch by inch, the bounty hunter edged his way along the river-bank.

His calling had taken him to some odd places, and brought him into contact with some strange people; this, however, looked set fair to establish new parameters of meaning for the word 'kooky'.

Jesus, the place was full of goddamn *animals*.

He found what he was looking for; and sat behind a bramble bush for five minutes or so, waiting to see if anyone came in or out of the little round painted door in the side of the bank.

Just when he'd concluded it was safe to proceed, he was tripped up neatly from behind and thrown on to his face in the mud. As he tried to rise, someone put a clawed foot in the small of his back and prodded his ear with the barrel of a gold-plated Uzi.

'I say, Moley,' said Mr Rat. 'It seems we have another visitor.'

CHAPTER EIGHT

The lift stopped.
     The doors opened.

Hamlet shut his eyes, left a prayer on God's answering machine, and stepped out. Into the street.

The doors shut behind him. In fact, if he had been inclined to be thin-skinned and oversensitive, he could have imagined they ostentatiously dusted off their hands, like a night-club bouncer who's just thrown out a couple of drunks. Not that Hamlet minded one little bit. Of all the places in the world he was most keen to get thrown out of, Dr Rossfleisch's cosy little establishment headed the list by quite some way.

On further inspection, the street turned out to be nothing but a back alley, designed as a repository for dustbins and a playground for tattered-eared cats. Hamlet picked up his enormous feet and ran, filling the narrow way with the echoes of his clopping.

At the end, the alley opened on to a broad, crowded street, into which Hamlet turned right. He was clearly in a big town or a city somewhere, although he had no idea which one. He had an idea that it wasn't anywhere in

Denmark, because he remembered something about Denmark being an unweeded garden, and there were no weeds to be seen anywhere.

Trying to mingle unobtrusively with the crowd – difficult, since he was a foot taller than anybody else within sight, and his head stuck up above the throng like a giraffe feeding on treetops – he strolled as nonchalantly as his big clumping boots would allow him towards the southerly end of the street. It would all, he knew, be wonderfully simple. In a moment or so he would find a telephone box. He would call Jane Armitage. She would come and pick him up, or at the very least tell him what to do. Then they would work out how he could get back into his play, where he belonged. If things went well, he might even get back home in time to be murdered.

At the end of the street, sure enough, stood a phone box. He smiled and pulled open the door . . .

'Hey, do you mind?'

'Sorry.' Hamlet stepped back. 'I didn't mean—'

'There's another one just round the corner,' said the occupant of the box quickly. Hamlet couldn't help noticing that he was half in and half out of a red and blue leotard, and that a plain charcoal-grey suit was lying discarded on the phone box floor. 'And next time, look before you go barging in.'

'Sorry,' Hamlet repeated, and closed the door. He had got about ten yards down the street when there was a sharp crack and a whooshing noise above his head. He looked up to see a tiny figure in blue and red disappearing into the sky. All around him, people were staring after it.

'My God,' someone said, 'I didn't know he was real. I thought he was just in comics.'

Hamlet turned back, entered the now empty phone box, fumbled in his pocket for a coin and dialled Jane's number.

Hello, this is Jane Armitage. I'm sorry there's no one here to take your call but if you'd care to leave a message . . .

Hamlet replaced the receiver, briskly, with an oath. The bloody woman, he said to himself, how dare she go swanning off when I'm missing? Typical bloody author. About as reliable as a petrol station watch.

Never mind, he reassured himself, I'll use my initiative. No problem at all finding out where I am and how to get out of it. His head held high (or as high, at least, as it would go without unseating the main neck bearings), he strolled down the road in search of somebody to ask.

There is a stubbornly entrenched streak of bigotry in all of us. We may have made some progress towards flushing out prejudice on grounds of race, gender, creed and sexual orientation; but troll down the street with staring red eyes, big shoes and a bolt through your neck, and don't be surprised if no one wants to know you. All Hamlet got for his efforts at communication were twelve funny looks, a muffled scream and an offer to share with him the glad tidings of Our Lord Jesus Christ; all of which, he found, wasn't getting him anywhere. He caught sight of a big sign saying POST OFFICE and headed towards it.

Before he reached his objective, however, he found his path blocked by a girl, fourteen years old or thereabouts, in school uniform and carrying a satchel. She was staring at him. He stopped and frowned.

''Scuse me,' said the girl, 'but you're him, aren't you? The bloke in the film.'

Am I? Gosh, yes, of course I am. Laurence Olivier, Mel Gibson and a tall Russian bloke with a name that seemed to go on for ever, to name but three. Hamlet smiled, and nodded.

'Can I have your autograph?' The girl rummaged in

her satchel and produced a grubby exercise book and a pen. Hamlet accepted both as graciously as he could manage, signed with a flourish and handed them back.

'Here,' said the girl. 'I thought you said you were Frankenstein.'

'I . . .'

'That's bloody marvellous, that is. Now you've gone and written all over my geography book.' She scowled at him, stuffed the book back in the satchel and flounced off; which was probably just as well for all concerned. Hamlet had never struck a woman, but only really because the ones he most wanted to thump were able to get out of the way in time.

He sighed, pushed open the post office door, and joined the queue.

'On air in fifteen seconds,' said the continuity girl. 'Fourteen, thirteen . . .'

Jane gave the camera a worried frown. It was bad enough that she had to do things like this, she reflected, but of all the inopportune moments in history, this one was in a class of its own. She caught sight of herself in the monitor, realised that the horrible, scowling woman was her, and hitched up the corners of her mouth. She had just realised that that made her look like an opium addict when the interviewer took a deep breath and started to speak, leaving her stuck like it, just as her mother had warned her all those years ago.

'Hi,' said the interviewer, 'this is Cable South West's Afternoon Show, I'm Danny Bennet, and we're lucky to have with us this afternoon none other than Jane, um, Armstrong, author of the bestselling Zarmanico trilogy. Tell me, Jane, where exactly do you get the ideas for your characters from?'

As she mouthed the usual pleasantries, Jane let her

mind wander. Wherever they were now, whatever they were doing, there was nothing she could do to help until she got back home; at which point, she added remorsefully, I've also got to do something to find out where Hamlet's got to. Another stray bloody cat to worry about, another whale to save, another rain-forest to preserve; but there was something more to it than that, something rather more immediate forcing her to get involved, although she couldn't really say what. Why, she demanded of herself, am I doing all this anyway? I must be out of my . . .

'I expect,' the interviewer was saying, with the air of a man drowning in tapioca, 'that sometimes you find your characters almost seem as if they have a life of their own, don't you find? Almost as if they know what they want to do, and you're just there to help them do it.'

Jane laughed; and there was a tiny sliver of hysteria in there somewhere, like the metal strip in a banknote. 'Oh, I wouldn't say that,' she said. 'No, I generally find they do what they're told. If they know what's good for them, that is. Anyway, my lot are usually so damned idle they wouldn't get out of bed from Easter to Michaelmas if I didn't put my boot behind them.'

Was that it? she wondered. Was it because they were her characters, wholly dependent on her, like a mother and her children? No, probably not. She'd never worried about them before. She could kill any of them without a second thought if the plot required it. Often, she recalled, with great pleasure.

'Now then.' The interviewer was finding it difficult to keep afloat. 'Perhaps you can tell us about what you're working on at the moment.'

'Yes indeed.' Oh Christ. 'It's a bit of a new departure for me, really. It sort of starts off as a western, goes on as a pastiche of a couple of classics of English literature, and I don't know what happens after that. But,' she added firmly, 'it does have a happy ending. I mean, they do all get home safely in the end.'

'Quite,' said the interviewer, sourly. 'Well, we have to take a short break now for the news headlines, but we'll be back with Jane in a moment, when I'll be asking her more about her fabulous new book. And now it's coming up to five o'clock, and here's the latest from the Cable South West newsroom. The main story this afternoon is the armed siege in the Birmingham post office, and I think we now have some pictures for you . . .'

Images of a deserted street flashed on to the monitor, and Jane turned her head and cast a jaundiced eye over them. She was just about to look away when the camera zoomed in . . .

. . . On Hamlet, his face pressed against a window, waving frantically. Behind him stood a tall, dreamy looking man with a portable cassette player in one hand and a revolver in the other. Cut back to the street outside . . .

Jane sat on the edge of her chair, doing goldfish impressions. She was sure, she *knew* that it was Hamlet in there, even though he looked completely different. In fact, she realised, she hadn't got the faintest idea what his face looked like, because she'd never seen him without his paper bag. But even so, she *knew*; just as a mother always knows her child, perhaps. Unimportant why. What mattered was that her Hamlet, a character of hers by adoption, was in trouble and she had to go to him. Only she couldn't, because she was on telly.

She wrenched her mind away and tried to listen to what the interviewer was saying.

'The man holding the hostages,' he said, 'has been identified as a Doctor Rossfleisch, a world-famous scientist working in the field of genetic engineering. The siege is apparently the result of a botched kidnapping attempt. Dr Rossfleisch has so far demanded a helicopter to fly him to Tripoli, a plate of jam sandwiches and a tape of *50 All-Time Pianola Greats*. A spokesman for the Performing Rights Society has declined to comment.'

She was wrong, Jane realised. It was because they were hers that she cared. All right, so occasionally, when it was necessary, she killed them or had them paralysed in devastating accidents; but that was for her to do, not anybody else. Because if she did it, it was because it was right and she would know that that was what the character was there to do. If it simply happened, there could be no reason or justification for it; it would be just like Life. And that wasn't something she'd wish on her worst enemy, let alone a character she had deliberately called into existence.

Come *on*, you silly man, let's get this over with so I can go and protect my baby.

'And there'll be more from the newsroom at six o'clock. Now then, this is *The Afternoon Show*, I'm Danny Bennet and I have with me this afternoon the novelist Jane, um, Armitage. Tell me, Jane, do you write in longhand or do you use a word processor?'

Got to get out of here. Find a pretext. Got it. Right.

'Honestly!' she snapped, rising to her feet. 'How dare you! I've never been so insulted in all my life.'

'But,' flummoxed the interviewer, 'I only asked if you—'

'That does it.' Livid with synthetic rage, Jane tore off the microphone, threw it on the chair and stalked out of the studio. As soon as the door closed behind her, she picked up her feet and started to run for the car park.

Down this mean river-bank a man must walk.

After half an hour's stroll beside the pleasantly lapping waters, with Skinner peering anxiously into every bush in case it contained narcotics agents or the Mob, and the

Scholfield observing from time to time that if he was going to ambush anyone in these parts, *here* was as good a place as you could hope to find, they reached a small boat-shed.

'Right,' said Regalian, his hand resting as if by coincidence on the butt of the revolver, 'this looks like the place.' He sighed. It was a hot day, he was uncomfortably warm inside the beaver's skin and he had a headache. The thought of having to do anything heroic seemed positively distasteful. 'I suppose,' he went on mournfully, 'I'd better lead the way.'

Nobody contradicted him. He took a deep breath, pushed the door open and waited. After what seemed to him a decent interval, he dropped on to all fours and scuttled through the doorway.

'It's all right,' he called out after a moment. 'Looks like we've got the place to ourselves.'

Titania and Skinner walked through the door, each doing their best to follow the other. It was dark inside, and there was a strong smell of mould, stagnant water and decomposing boat. So far, in fact, so reassuringly normal.

'Well?' Titania demanded.

'It's somewhere,' said a voice from under a low table, 'over here, if only I can find . . .'

There was a muffled clinking noise, followed by a bump; and a moment later the beaver reappeared, looking dusty but triumphant, with a small green bottle clutched between its front paws.

'Now then,' Regalian said. 'Let the dog see the . . . Ah yes, right. Here goes.'

He uncorked the bottle, which was inscribed DRINK ME, took a mouthful and wiped his muzzle on the back of his front left paw. Then he passed the bottle to Titania, who accepted it with the same degree of enthusiasm she would have exhibited had she been given a large, hairy spider.

''Sorlright,' Regalian mumbled. 'A bit nutty, perhaps, with maybe a slightly over-long aftertaste, but—'

He vanished. Titania and Skinner exchanged glances.

'And I thought things were a bit over the top where I come from,' Titania commented. 'Well, if he thinks I'm going to drink this stuff after what—'

She stopped and looked down, to see a very small man jumping up and down on her foot and pointing excitedly to what she had assumed on a previous cursory inspection to be a mousehole.

'I think,' said Skinner, 'he wants us to go through there. It's a proper doorway, with a doorbell and a handle and everything.'

'Just because it's a door doesn't mean we've got to go through it,' Titania replied, backing away a step or two. 'There's millions of doors I've never been through, and they were all the right size, too.'

Skinner shrugged. 'He's the hero,' he said. 'You gotta trust the hero, or where are you?'

'Where aren't you, more to the point,' Titania replied. 'And high up on the list, I've put *crawling about down mouseholes*.'

'I'm game if you are.'

Titania winced. 'An odd expression, that,' she commented. 'As far as I'm concerned, game is dead furry things hanging up in butchers' windows. Mind you, in this particular instance, I can see where the expression might acquire a certain relevance . . .'

'Time I was going,' Skinner said, taking a long swig. 'You don't have to come if you don't want to.'

'Oh yeah, I can stay here and wait till we come out in paperback. No thanks.' She took the bottle, finished it off and then held it up to read the label.

'Hey,' she said, 'this stuff's got riboflavin and permitted food colouring in it. I heard that stuff makes you go—'

Skinner vanished; and a moment later, so did Titania. Another moment later they were all three standing at the entrance of the mousehole, which had turned out not to be a mousehole after all.

'It looks bigger like this,' Titania conceded.

'I thought this sort of thing was all in a day's work for your lot,' Skinner said, impatiently. 'Or else how come you're called things like the Little People and the Wee Folk?'

'All right,' Titania admitted, giving the door a tentative prod, 'on our own turf we have a certain flexibility in these matters. Doesn't mean I have to like it, though. I always feel distinctly jumpy whenever I'm in a situation where I have to look up to a cat.'

They looked at each other.

'Oh well,' said Titania, remembering that she was, after all, the Erl-King's daughter and, par excellence, a thing that goes bump in the night, and therefore presumably afraid of nothing, 'here goes. Last one through the door's a cissy.'

'After you, then.'

'Shut up quibbling and get through that door.'

'Fine love interest you turned out to be.'

Regalian, having screwed up what remained of his courage, opened the door with a flying kick and went through the doorway in a low gunfighter's roll, as recommended by the Israeli secret service.

The advantage of this manoeuvre is that you come out the other side with your weight nicely balanced on both feet, shoulders square, gun at the ready in a textbook Weaver stance in position to engage targets within a forty-five degree arc of fire. It's about as good as you can get, but it still doesn't provide for all eventualities.

Like, for example, there being a table in the way. When Regalian regained control of his movements, therefore, he found himself sitting in the middle of a white table-cloth, surrounded by smashed crockery and spilt tea, pointing his gun right up the nose of a strange-looking individual in a top hat.

For a brief moment, he was at a loss, then the correct explanation registered, and he looked round for confirmation. He found it.

'Terribly sorry,' he said. 'You must be the Hatter, and you're the March Hare.'

'Yes,' replied the Hatter. 'What the bloody hell do you think you're playing at?'

'Just passing through.' Regalian started to inch his way off the table, trying his best to cause as little further damage as possible. There was a sharp crunch as he knelt on a plate of cucumber sandwiches.

'This really isn't on, though,' complained the Hare. 'I mean, yes, we are supposed to be off-the-wall, kooky characters from the back lots of the human subconscious. We're quite prepared to hold our paws up to that one, sure. Still doesn't give you the right to come bursting in here trashing our crockery.' It sighed, and pointed at what was left of the teapot. 'I mean, how the hell are we supposed to get the Dormouse in that?'

'Can't stop,' Regalian muttered. 'Send me the bill for the damage, okay?' He rolled off the table, holstered the gun and stopped. 'Hang on,' he said. 'Just one thing. Am I human or a beaver?'

The Hare and the Hatter looked at each other. 'Is this one of those wordplay gags,' asked the Hare wearily, 'like the treacle-well and the best butter and so on, because if so, we really aren't in the mood.'

'Nope. Just a simple request for information.'

'Fine. You're not a beaver. Whether you're human or not is a matter between you and your author, in which I have no wish to get involved. Now piss off.'

'Obliged to you. Goodbye.'

After he had gone, the Hatter and the Hare exchanged long, significant looks.

'And we're supposed to be the goofy ones,' said the Hatter.

'That's the trouble with this business,' the Hare agreed. 'Too much amateur bloody competition. Come on, let's get this lot cleared away.'

They lifted off the tablecloth, shook it free of Wedgwood shrapnel, replaced the cups, saucers and plates, and made a fresh pot of tea. In doing so the Hatter got tea-stains on his shirt-cuffs and the Hare cut his paw. The Dormouse stayed fast asleep.

'Okay,' said the Hare, 'that's all right, then. Now, where were—?'

There was a crash.

'Oh for crying out loud,' said the Hatter.

'Enough,' agreed the Hare, dodging a fast-spreading tea-slick, 'is enough. From now on it's paper plates and a disposable tablecloth.'

'Excuse me.'

'Alternatively,' suggested the Hatter, 'we could try moving the table.'

'Excuse me.'

The Hatter scowled. 'What do you want?'

Titania stood up, brushing bits of broken china off herself. 'Sorry about this,' she said. 'We didn't realise you were here.'

'Evidently.'

'Did you,' Titania persevered, 'see a man come this way a few minutes ago? Big chap, tall, probably holding a gun?'

The Hare gave her a long look. 'We did just happen to notice him, yes. Friend of yours?'

'Yes.'

'Figures.'

'Which way did he go?'

The Hare rubbed its chin. 'Let me see,' it said. 'If memory serves me correctly, he came in where you did, landed on the teapot, crawled all over the sandwiches, stood on the sugar bowl, kicked over the cakestand and went off that way.' It pointed vaguely at a house behind them. 'What is it you people are going to, anyway? Some sort of Hell's Angels convention?'

Titania turned to Skinner, white-faced. 'Are you going to let him talk to me like that?' she demanded.

'Yes. Look,' he added, 'it wasn't my idea to have a love interest. Nobody asked me.'

'Nor me,' Titania snapped. 'Believe me, I was much happier with the damn donkey.'

Skinner nodded. 'More your type,' he said.

The Hare banged on the table with a spoon. 'Look,' it said, 'would you two clowns mind having your argument somewhere else? We're five pages behind schedule as it is.'

'Sorry.' Titania crunched her way to the edge of the table and dropped to the ground. 'We'll pay for the damage, of course. Just send the bill to—'

'Get out of here, both of you, before I call the flamingoes.'

'We're just going.'

This time, the Hatter and the Hare waited ten minutes before clearing away the breakages and re-laying the table. They also moved the whole shooting match ten feet to the right. Then they sat in brooding silence, not eating or drinking, just in case. There were bits of broken china in the sugar, and the Victoria Sponge would never be the same again.

After a while, the Hare looked at its watch.

'I think,' it said, 'we're probably safe now. Right, you pour the tea and I'll see what can be done with this blasted cake.'

At which point, Alice came hurrying in, ran full-tilt into the table (which was, of course, ten feet out of position) and landed face-down in the black forest gateau. There was a long silence.

'Stuff it,' said the Hare, resignedly. 'I turned down a part in *Our Mutual Friend* for this. I'm going home now, and if anybody tries to stop me I'll break their bloody neck. So—'

He stopped. Someone was prodding a gun in the small of his back.

'Okay,' growled the bounty hunter, emerging from behind a bush. 'Nobody moves, or the rabbit gets it.'

'I would strongly advocate,' said Rossfleisch, rather self-consciously, 'that everybody remains exactly where they are. Otherwise . . .'

(This, of course, is the entirely legitimate literary device of drawing parallels. One character unconsciously echoes another, setting up a resonance that crosses over the divisions of situation and form.

In all fiction, there is a tendency to symmetry and balance. Particularly balance. For every cue, a reply. For every entrance, an exit.

And for every exit, an entrance.)

The siege had lasted three hours.

Outside the building, the usual muster of police cars,

vans, men with flak jackets, men with megaphones, men with television cameras. Another day, another melodrama.

Inside the building, two men – well, two humanoids – facing each other.

Not quite in and not quite out of the building (to be precise, wandering around in the sewers underneath the building with a torch, a portable word processor and a very wry expression, because of the smell), a novelist.

Gee, mused Hamlet, but life can be a right bugger sometimes. Now if I was really Hamlet, *the* Hamlet, I could launch into a bit of impassioned oratory and talk this idiot into letting me go, or at least send him to sleep, which would amount to the same thing. A bit of blank verse, a few slices of heavy-duty industrial-grade imagery, and Bob's your uncle. But no. All I can think of to say is, *Gosh, this is silly, isn't it?* and that doesn't quite have the necessary voltage to do the job.

Nevertheless, one can but try.

'Gosh,' he said, 'this is silly, isn't it?'

The mad scientist nodded. 'I quite agree, my dear fellow,' he said. 'Ludicrous. It only goes to show how low scientific research is in some people's scale of priorities. Still,' he added, drumming his fingers on the casing of the cassette player, 'the remedy is in your own hands. You're completely bulletproof. All you have to do is lead the way, and we could be out of here in no time at all.'

'Yes, but—'

'In fact,' said Rossfleisch, glancing at his watch, 'if this goes on much longer I may have to insist. I really can't afford to waste much more time in here. I have experiments that need constant monitoring.'

Hamlet edged closer to the window. With luck, he might just be able to jump through it before the doctor had time to switch on the tape.

'All the same,' he said, 'it's a bit thick, don't you think?

I mean to say, all this fuss and bother and sirens going and men with rifles and things. Have you seen—?'

'Please come away from the window.'

Hell! 'But like you said, I'm bulletproof, there's no danger—'

'In case you should get the urge to jump. That wouldn't do at all, you know.'

'Ah. Right.'

He was just about to try another line of argument, something involving the bearing of fardels, although if anyone asked him what a fardel was he'd have to admit he hadn't a clue, when his high-performance ears picked up a strange noise. A scrabbling sound, coming from under the building.

'Hey . . .' he said, and checked himself quickly. Best not to let the loony know about it, he reasoned. After all, it might be help.

'I beg your pardon?'

'Hey,' Hamlet improvised, 'did you realise you can see right across the city from here?'

Jane pushed.

Whatever it was she was pushing against, it lifted; and she found she was looking up into a room. A boiler room, by the looks of it, or something similar.

She was, of course, hopelessly and irretrievably lost. When she'd been standing at the edge of the police cordon, staring at the building in which she knew Hamlet to be trapped, and wondering what her hero would do if he were here, it had seemed the most logical thing in the world to head for the nearest manhole cover and drop in.

That had been some time ago.

Since then, she had reassessed her priorities. Yes, she still wanted to find Hamlet and rescue him. But more than that, more than anything else in the world, what she really wanted to do was get out of the drains and have a long, scented bath lasting maybe three months.

She hauled herself up out of the sewer, closed the cover behind her and sat down on a wooden crate to rest and think about what to do next. While she was thinking, she switched on the WP and waited for it to warm up.

It started to beep.

It wasn't the ouch-you're-hurting-me beep she got when she did something wrong, or the hurry-up-I-want-more-paper beep. It was somehow more friendly; no, that wasn't the word. More positive. It was a come-on-don't-dawdle-it's-this-way sort of beep, and it gave her the impression that the machine wanted to tell her something. If it had been a dog, she realised, the WP would be rushing round her feet with its lead in its mouth.

'All right,' she said, 'which way?'

Beep. Beepeepeepeepeep. BEEEP!

'Sorry?'

Beepeepeepeeepeepeepeeepeeeeep!

'I'm terribly sorry, I don't under—'

BEEEEEEEEEEEEP!

'Oh, right, up the *stairs*. Got you. And then what?'

Beep. Beep. Beep.

'You mean a fire door.'

Beeeeeep. Beepeep. Beep.

'What, because of the snipers? Yes, good point.'

Beep.

'Yes, all right, I'm coming as quick as I can.'

She scrambled to her feet, hefted the word processor and started to jog up the iron spiral staircase that led out of the boiler room. Halfway up she stopped and frowned.

'Just a minute,' she demanded. 'Who the hell are you and how come you can—?'

Beep.

'Oh I see. Sorry. You did say left at the top, didn't you?'
Beeeeeeeeeeep.
'No, I haven't the faintest idea what a fardel is, but I promise I'll look it up as soon as we get home. Now, is it left or isn't it?'
Beep.

Hamlet held his breath. Any moment now. Then straight through the window, hit the deck, remember to roll, and . . .

'Who were you talking to just now?' the Doctor asked quietly.

'Me?' Hamlet swallowed hard. 'Oh, nothing, just soliloquising. You know, thinking what a rogue and peasant slave I've been all these years.'

The Doctor glowered at him. 'There's someone coming, isn't there?' he said accusingly. 'Someone you can talk to without actually speaking.'

'Gosh,' said Hamlet, 'you *are* clever, aren't you? I wish I was as brainy as you, it must be wonderful to be so—'

'Behind the curtain, quickly,' the Doctor snapped. 'Come on, jump to it. I'm afraid I'm in no mood for silly games.'

Behind the curtain. Oh joy! 'Must I? What about the snipers? You said just now—'

'Do as you're told!' the Doctor growled, and he brandished the cassette recorder significantly. Masking a grin the size of Yorkshire, Hamlet nodded and stepped behind the curtain . . .

A hint for aspiring character-nappers. Stop and think what a curtain is. Reflect for a moment what happens when a character steps out in front of a curtain, and what also happens when he goes behind one.

Some curtains are better than others. The best sort are fireproof and required by law to be raised and lowered in the presence of five hundred empty seats and the ice-cream queues. Next best are the thick, dusty red velvet jobs with gold tassels. At a pinch, though, any curtain will do. Or even, if the worst comes to the worst, an arras.

Suddenly, Hamlet knew exactly who he was and what he was supposed to do next. With a brave flourish he drew the sword that was now hanging by his side, identified the bulge in the curtain and lunged with all his might. The correct line was, *'A rat! A rat!'*, but he was in a hurry.

The sword-blade bent like a bow and snapped, just as Hamlet winked out of existence and dematerialised in a shower of golden sparks.

On the other side of the curtain, Dr Rossfleisch stared in complete bewilderment at the filing cabinet, which had six inches of rapier blade protruding through the side of the drawer marked 'N – P', and so entirely failed to notice the door opening, Jane coming through, or the torch landing hard and square on the back of his head.

Hamlet opened his eyes.

He expected to see the ramparts of Elsinore. He expected to hear the sound of frantic voices and running feet, the flicker of torches in the courtyard below, the confused echo of shouted orders.

No such luck.

What he did see was a dark, rather cluttered room, furnished in the late Victorian style, with dark, solid furniture, gaslamps and VR picked out in bulletholes on the far wall. In the corner, some obscure scientific apparatus hiccupped quietly to itself. The walls were lined with leather-bound books. There was a healthy fire crackling in the grate, and on the mantelpiece a slipper stuffed with tobacco.

'Remarkable,' said a voice from the armchair.

He looked up, and saw a long, thin man with a sharp nose and a high forehead, wearing a silk dressing gown and smoking a big, curved pipe. He had a horrible feeling he knew who it was.

'From your appearance,' said the man, 'I deduce that you are somehow connected with the theatrical profession. The traces of makeup just below the hairline and the rather eccentric boots are conclusive on that point. From your general demeanour, I gather that you left the place you have just come from in something of a hurry, probably,' he added, after a moment's consideration and a puff of blue smoke, 'in fear of your life. The colour of your hair and the set of your cheekbones imply Scandinavian descent, and I would venture to suggest that you are a Dane. The manner in which you arrived here is also,' the man said, and smiled crookedly, 'most suggestive. However, the hilt of a broken sword in your right hand puts the matter beyond any semblance of doubt. Your Highness,' he added, with mock deference. 'And how stand matters at Elsinore?'

Despite his other preoccupations, Hamlet was impressed.

'Cor,' he said. 'You worked all that out just by looking at me?'

The man nodded. 'Elementary, my dear Hamlet,' he said.

In the hallway of the house there was a looking-glass.

Regalian, out of breath from running fast, stood in front of it and stared. Yes, he said to himself, a great big mirror with an ornate frame hanging over a mantelpiece. I remember now. This is exactly what it looks like.

'Your hair needs combing,' observed the Scholfield.

'Apart from that, what's the big deal? I thought we were meant to be—'

'Shut up,' Regalian ordered. 'We're here.'

'Yes, I know we're *here*,' the gun replied. 'But I thought we wanted to be somewhere else.'

Regalian smiled thinly and pointed. 'Somewhere else is that way,' he said.

'Don't be silly, that's just a wall,' the gun said. 'Maybe you're thinking of ghosts. In case you weren't aware, you're not a ghost. Trust me, I know about these things.'

Regalian thought for a moment, and then started to unbuckle the gunbelt.

'Here,' whined the gun, 'what the hell do you think you're—?'

'I've got to go back and get the others,' Regalian replied, laying the belt on the mantelpiece. 'You can stay here. Won't be long.'

The gun squirmed in its holster. 'Here, you can't do that. What are you doing that for?'

'Because,' Regalian snapped, 'I've had enough of you to last me a trilogy, that's why. Now shut up or we'll leave you behind.'

'Eek!' The gun wriggled and, with a frantic effort, managed to slide out of the holster, edging its way in millimetre stages towards the mirror. 'You can't leave me here on my own,' it wailed, 'they're all nutcases in this book, I'll end up as a paperweight.'

Regalian reached out to replace the Scholfield in its holster but somehow it eluded him and made a phenomenal spasmodic leap, two inches at least, towards the surface of the glass. It miscalculated, hit the frame and cocked itself. Regalian grabbed again – it was like trying to catch a goldfish in a bowl – missed and connected with the trigger. There was a loud bang.

'Strewth!' Regalian exclaimed.

The recoil must have edged the gun right up against the glass, because the gun wasn't there any more. But its reflection in the mirror was.

'Hey,' Regalian shouted, 'how did you do that?'

Just this once, the gun made no reply. Cursing under his breath, Regalian reached into the looking-glass, scrabbled for the revolver and flicked it back through the glass . . .

And found himself looking at his reflection in a mirror. But his reflection was holding a Scholfield revolver and he wasn't. And then there was just the Scholfield, lying on the mantelpiece on the other side of the glass.

'Oh *hell*,' Regalian whispered.

He reached out and put his hand on the surface of the mirror. It felt smooth, cold and depressingly solid. Which is, of course, exactly how mirrors do feel, in the real world.

'Marvellous!' he growled. 'Oh that really is completely fucking marvellous. What the hell am I supposed to do now?'

He turned and looked around, examining the room. It was large, well-furnished and cosy. A glass-fronted book-case by the fireplace housed a complete set of the works of Carson Montague, also known as Albert Skinner. *Oh Christ!*

For every entrance an exit. For every exit an entrance.

He turned back, but the mirror was gone. In its place was a window, with a bullet-hole in it, and in his hand he noticed the Scholfield, with a little wisp of smoke drifting out of the gap between the cylinder and the barrel; and, beyond the window, a man in dungarees shaking his fist and pointing at a shattered cucumber frame.

'Freeze!'

Skinner did as he was told. In the big looking-glass

directly in front of him, he could see the bounty hunter's face; not to mention the long, black Colt revolver in his right hand.

Christ, he said to himself, *I know you. Goddammit, yes!*

'Okay,' the bounty hunter continued. 'Turn around, real slow, and keep your hands where I can see them. And if you was having any fancy ideas about making a grab for that gun on the mantelpiece . . .'

'The thought,' said Skinner truthfully, 'never crossed my mind.'

'Hoy,' Titania hissed under her breath. 'Who is this idiot?'

Skinner sighed. The only thing that puzzled him was why he hadn't thought of it before.

'Titania,' he said wearily, 'I'd like you to meet my hero. Slim, this is Titania, Queen of the Fairies.'

'Pleased to make your acquaintance, ma'am.'

'I last saw Slim,' Skinner went on, 'in a mirror. Well, a window, to be precise, but it was being a mirror at the time. I shot him. I think that's why I'm here. Isn't that right, Slim? I have the horrible feeling,' he went on, 'that he's my alter ego. You know, the part of me I don't like. In fact,' he continued, 'he's probably the reason why I used to find it difficult to look myself in the eye in the shaving mirror every morning.'

'Gosh,' Titania said. 'It's a funny thing, but when people give me these simple, logical explanations I always end up more confused than I was to start with. What does he want, exactly?'

Skinner shook his head. 'Whatever it is,' he said, 'I don't want to know about it. Hey, Slim.'

'Yeah, partner?'

'What the hell *do* you want anyhow? I mean, there's got to be a reason, hasn't there?'

Slim laughed, briefly and without humour. 'Reckon so,'

he said. 'Now why don't you-all just use your brains while you still got them?'

'Hell, Slim, you know me,' Skinner answered. 'Never was any good at plots.'

'Sure enough,' the bounty hunter replied. 'It's 'cos I ain't through with you yet, bud. Not by a long way.'

He raised his hand, pointed the Colt and fired.

It would be an exaggeration to say that the whole of Skinner's life flashed before his eyes, because he'd had a long and interesting life and there simply wasn't time. He'd got as far as his sixth birthday party, when Jenny Mason ate too much jelly roll and was sick on Mom's new carpet, when he realised he was still alive.

He turned round. The bullet had hit the looking-glass dead centre, and all that remained of it was a few splinters of glass tucked into the edge of the frame.

CHAPTER NINE

Jane let herself in through the front door, dumped her portable WP and sagged into an armchair. It had been a long, long day.

In retrospect, the police had been quite reasonable considering the fact that she had offered no explanation at all for her presence in the building apart from saying that she'd been researching for a book down in the sewers and had got lost. They had left her with the distinct impression that she'd been suffered gladly, but they'd let her go. Eventually.

As for what had happened to Hamlet, she had a theory about that, and she was horribly afraid it was correct.

Still, she reassured herself as she put the kettle on, if I'm right it does mean he's back more or less where he belongs; or at least, back with his own kind. Kind of his own kind. In any event, beyond her help, which was all that mattered as far as she was concerned.

When the coffee was made, she broke into a new packet of chocolate digestives, curled up on the floor in front of the fire and reached into her bag for the book she'd been reading on the train. Not exactly her usual thing, Sir

Arthur Conan Doyle; but it had been the only book on the bookstall that didn't have a naked female on the cover, and she had to admit, she'd forgotten how readable the old things were, once you'd got into them.

The book fell open at the place she'd left off. She read:

'One moment,' said I. 'You have, no doubt, described the sequence of events correctly, my dear Holmes, but there is one point you have left unexplained. What became of the hound when its master was in London?'

Before Holmes could reply, the young stranger leaned forward, his face a mask of the most intense emotions. 'Hey, Jane,' he cried, 'is that you? For fuck's sake, woman, where the hell have you been all this time, I've been trying to reach you for bloody hours. Look, you've got to get me out of here, they're all a bunch of raving nutcases and there's this bloody great dog, you would not believe the size of this sodding dog, and it jumps up and puts its horrible paws on your chest and licks your damn face off, so get your bum in gear and find some way I can— By all that's marvellous, Mr Holmes,' he exclaimed, 'I can scarcely believe . . .'

Jane closed the book with a shudder. Her first reaction was, No, the hell with it, it's out of my hands now. Let the little creep find his own way home; or he can stay there, get a job and a mortgage, just like the rest of us. She threw the book into a corner, folded her arms and tried to think of something else.

Tried, and failed. But somehow, in some weird system of logic that she couldn't hope to understand, he was her responsibility. Because, if she didn't help, nobody else would. Because . . . Because.

Hell!

Later, though. First, she was going to have a bath, a toasted ham sandwich and a good night's sleep, and that wasn't negotiable.

And, in due course, she slept.

There you are. Where have you been, for Chrissakes? You think it's easy getting through on this frigging thing?

Still fast asleep, she sat bolt upright in bed and swore. 'Not you as well,' she shouted. 'Go away!'

The dream of Skinner clenched its fists in rage. *You goddamn lazy bitch,* it ranted, *I'm stuck in this lunatic asylum and you want to go back to sleep? Jesus, lady, if you don't get me outa here, I will personally make sure you never sleep again. You hear me?*

'Hold on, now,' Jane mumbled. 'I thought all that was under control. Haven't you been through the looking-glass, then?'

Oh sure. I'm just haunting your dreams for something to do. Of course I didn't. That lousy stinking wimp of a hero of yours . . .

'Don't you talk about Regalian like that.'

Why not? The spineless little geek just pissed off and left us here. Just . . .

'Us?'

Yeah, us. Titania and me. And now we're . . .

'What, *the* Titania? As in ill-met by moonlight, proud? The one with the donkey?'

Yeah. Why don't you listen when people tell you things?

'What's she doing there, for God's sake?'

I don't know, do I? Skinner exploded. *It's your goddamn book!*

Jane lay down again, turned her face to the pillow and growled like a tiger. The dream stretched out an incorporeal hand towards her shoulder, but he was, after all, only a dream.

'Look,' Jane snarled into the pillow, 'get this straight, you third-rate hack. This – is – not – my – *book*. Understand?'

The hell with you too, sister. Just get me out of here, okay?

Look, I gotta go, there's a queue of goddamn chessmen outside this booth and they're getting impatient. You know where I am. Now get on with it.

The dream faded; but before Jane could wake up, another face floated in front of her mind's eye. It was vague and hard to make out, and somehow it wasn't the face it should have been, because it looked uncannily like Skinner, only it wasn't. To be precise, it looked like Skinner's reflection in running water.

Hello? Can you hear me?

'Regalian! God in heaven, you gave me a start. What are you—?'

Listen, I'm in trouble. You've got to find some way to get me out of here.

This time, Jane laughed so loud she woke herself up.

The theory about the US Library of Congress in Washington DC, which nobody seriously believes, states that, because the library holds a copy of pretty well every book there is, it's theoretically possible to break out of the real world and into fiction through a fault-line somewhere in the boiler room; the argument being that:

(a) truth is stranger than fiction

(b) there's a lot of fiction about nowadays which is so weird that even Aleister Crowley would have to stop halfway through, go back and read the first chapter again before he could work out what's supposed to be happening; which is a pretty tough act to follow

(c) the idea of there being a hole in the reality-fiction interface in the basement of an American public building is so profoundly kooky that it must, *a fortiori*, be true.

It should be added that no university, even in California, has ever been persuaded to fund further research into the theory, and there is therefore no published data; and the theory's proponents have to rely on anecdotal evidence of maintenance engineers meeting strange, unreal people wandering about when they go down to fix the heating system. These tales can, of course, be easily explained by the fact that it's quite normal to meet strange, unreal people in the basements of government buildings. Who do you think works in these places, after all?

Above all, you wouldn't catch a sane, rational person like Jane Armitage believing a cock-eyed theory like that in a million years. Absolutely not. No way.

'Excuse me,' said Jane. 'Can you tell me the way to the boiler room, please?'

'Sure, no problem. You go down this corridor until you come to a turning on your left. Follow that down about, oh, two hundred yards, and you'll see a door on your right. Go through that, down a flight of stairs and you're there. Okay?'

'Thanks,' said Jane. 'Um . . .'

'Yes?'

'Can I have your autograph, please?'

'Huh?'

'It's not for me, you understand, it's for my cousin's nephew.'

The helpful man frowned for a moment; then he took the pen and paper Jane had thrust at him, scribbled 'James T. Kirk' and handed it back. Then he sauntered away down the corridor, turned right and was gone.

And sure enough, there it eventually was; or at least there was a door marked:

BOILER ROOM

and underneath in smaller letters:

Authorised personnel only
No smoking
For every entrance, there must be an exit; and vice versa.

Jane hesitated, her hand half an inch from the door-handle. She had, she knew, done many bloody silly things in her life, but never before an *impossible* bloody silly thing, and she was a great believer in sticking to what she knew best.

On the other hand; for every entrance there must be an exit, and vice versa, and she'd just seen a character walking away down the corridor. Was he, she wondered idly, an exit or an entrance? Depends which side of the door you're on, presumably.

She turned the handle and pushed open the door.

There are agents – people who find you a job, take their ten per cent, and then move on to something else – and there are agents.

Into the latter category fall the superagents, who feed your cat while you're away, insist on being present at the birth of your child and talk you down off the windowledge when the *Boston Globe* points out the fact that you appear to fall asleep halfway through the second act.

Beyond the superagent is the hyperagent, and there is only one of these. Her name is Claudia, she is extremely selective in who she represents, and above all she gets results. If it wasn't for Claudia, the showbiz legend runs, Jesus Christ would have lived to a ripe old age doing stand-up, weddings and the occasional Bar Mitzvah.

In the course of an extremely long career – other agents never seem to find the time to take a holiday; Claudia keeps promising Death they'll do lunch just as soon as her schedule allows – she has represented a few select characters, most of whom have gone on to become the focal points of major religions.

One of these is Polonius.

Polonius? Yes, Polonius. And she's working on it right now. When Bill Shakespeare originally wrote the play, her client was one of the bit players who come on at the end and say nice things about Fortinbras. By the year 2140, if everything goes to plan, they're going to be forced to change the name of the show to *Polonius, Home Secretary of Denmark*. Watch this space.

En route, however, there are bound to be hiccups. For example . . .

'Then find him!' Polonius yelled into the receiver. 'Now!'

'Hey, Pol, cool it, will you?' Claudia cooed. 'We're doing everything we can. It's only a matter of time . . .'

'Yeah,' snarled the courtier, 'sure. Meanwhile, I'm the one who's being made to look a complete idiot. You've no idea how embarrassing it is, standing behind that bloody curtain and *nothing happening*.'

'Okay, right. Now . . .'

'I have to pretend to have a heart attack just to get off the stage. You've got to do something about it. The rest of them are starting to get depressed as well. The night before last, in fact, there was only me and the ghost who bothered to turn up at all. And I do my best, but you try keeping a packed house at Stratford entertained with four hours of I Spy With My Little Eye Something Beginning With G, and see how you get on.'

'Point taken, Pol. And as soon as we've got anything, I promise you, I'll let you—'

'Yeah. Well, mind you do. Goodbye.'

The line went dead. Claudia replaced the receiver, chewed the end of her pencil thoughtfully for a moment and reached for her address book.

One of the good things about having a first-class quality clientele is that, when necessary, you can get one client to do a favour for another. She found the number, picked up the phone and dialled.

'Hi, Sherlock, it's me. Look, I need a . . . You've got him with you now? That's absolutely wonderful, Sher, but how did you know . . . ? Yes, of course, you would, wouldn't you. Yes, elementary, quite. Okay, Sher, keep him there, I'll be right over. Ciao.'

Jane blinked.

Oddly enough, what disconcerted her most of all was the smell. Not that it was unpleasant; in fact she rather liked it. It reminded her of second-hand bookshops, the sort of establishment where the proprietor drifts around the place in an old cardigan and carpet slippers mumbling to himself and can never quite bring himself to believe you want to buy a book. It was, she realised, the smell of old paper.

Which was odd, because she wasn't in a library, or a paper mill, or even a second-hand bookshop. In fact, she appeared to be standing in the middle of a . . .

Yes. Let's not pussyfoot. The whole essence of being a writer is the ability to select the exactly appropriate word. A battle.

A battle, what was more, in the freezing cold snow. About three feet from her ear, a whacking great cannon went off, making the earth shake. The noise hit Jane like a hammer, and she felt her knees sag. Before she could recover, another cannon exploded on the other side of her, and the shock pushed her back on to her feet again.

Nobody seemed the least bit interested in her, and this came as something of a relief, since she had no right to be there whatsoever and explanations are always so embarrassing.

The battlefield was occupied by two opposing forces, as is often the way with battlefields. The part she was in was swarming with men in blue coats, tall black hats shaped like chimney-pots, and fancy white leggings that looked excruciatingly uncomfortable. They seemed to be talking in French. In fact, they were swearing a lot. The main topic of conversation appeared to be how, once they got to Moscow, they were going to drink a great deal of alcohol and try and make friends with the local women-folk. There was also a lot of technical stuff about the loading of cannons, which was beyond the limits of Jane's schoolgirl French and was probably only of interest to artillerymen anyway.

Right, Jane thought. The Napoleonic wars. Snow. Eighteen twelve. Moscow. Oh *bugger*.

War and Peace. A fine short cut this had turned out to be.

This is the police. We have the wood surrounded. Throw out your gun and let the Piglet go, and nobody's going to get hurt.

The electronically amplified voice died away on the gentle breeze, and all that could be heard in the Hundred Acre Wood was the twittering of songbirds and the gentle humming of the bees. Skinner cringed.

'It's all my fault,' he muttered. 'How could I have been so goddamned stupid?'

'There, there,' Titania replied soothingly through a mouthful of acorns and honey, 'don't blame yourself, we all make mistakes.'

'Sure.' Skinner nodded miserably. 'And the biggest mistake I ever made in my whole life was listening to you.'

'But . . .'

'"Tell you what," you said. "Let's retrace our steps," you said. "Let's go back into the river-bank, and see if we can't get into *Winnie the Pooh* from there, I bet there'll be a way out there somewhere," you said. And now look . . .'

Titania frowned dangerously. 'I admit,' she said, 'that was my idea. I don't seem to remember anything about breaking into Piglet's house and taking him hostage.'

In the corner of the dark, circular room, the Piglet favoured them both with a stare of pure, blind hatred. Since he was three feet tall, however, and bound hand and foot with sticking plaster, he could safety be described as the least of their problems.

'I never meant for this to happen,' Skinner protested. 'All I had in mind was, let's break into an empty house somewhere, find something to eat. How was I to know the little bastard would be waiting for us with the goddamn poker?' He rubbed his upper arm gingerly.

'You shouldn't have shot the bear, though.'

'Shot *at* the bear,' Skinner corrected her. 'I missed, remember? And I didn't mean to fire in the first place. The poxy gun just sort of went off . . .' Skinner checked himself, and scowled. 'Hey,' he added. 'You did that on purpose, didn't you?'

There was a short pause.

'You talking to me?' asked the Scholfield innocently.

'Of course I'm talking to you, you frigging psychopath. He's only four foot six and stuffed with kapok. Are you trying to say you didn't overreact just a little?'

'Hey,' replied the Scholfield, its voice heavy with reproach. 'You said, *Oh look, there's a bear.* Where I come from, bears are big and hairy and they eat you. How was I supposed to know—?'

'All right, you two,' Titania interrupted. 'This isn't getting us very far, is it? What we need to do now,' she added hopefully, 'is think of a plan of campaign.'

Skinner sighed. 'Such as what?' he asked. 'Demand a

helicopter to take us to the North Pole? Float down the river disguised as a poohstick?'

'We could shoot our way out,' suggested the Scholfield cheerfully. 'There's only about ten of them, I could do it standing on my hammer.'

Skinner closed his eyes. 'One more suggestion like that,' he muttered, 'and you go down a rabbit-hole. You think we're in trouble now, you try to imagine what they'd do to us if we waste Eeyore!'

'We could negotiate,' Titania said. 'Explain what's happened, tell them we didn't mean any harm. After all, it's a children's book. I'll bet you anything you like they aren't really armed.'

Skinner raised an eyebrow; then he found a small biscuit tin, balanced it on a broomhandle and pushed it out through the window. When he brought it back in again a moment later, it had twenty-three bullet holes in it, all of them within a three-inch circle of the middle of the tin.

You in the tree-house. This is your last chance. Let the Piglet walk or you'll leave us no alternative.

'Those idiots,' said Titania firmly, 'are starting to get on my nerves.'

'Mine too,' Skinner agreed. 'All right then, suggest something.'

Titania thought for a moment; then an evil smile crossed her face, like on oil-slick on an ornamental pond.

'How about . . . ?' she said.

Basic authorship theory.

Take an author (you'll need to wake him up and pour three pints of black coffee into him first), park him in front of a microphone and ask him how he designs his characters, and chances are he'll pretend he made them up from scratch. Lies.

Characters are built, like Frankenbotham's Hamlet, out of bits and pieces of real people more or less cobbled together. A friend's mannerisms, an aunt's squint, an employer's unsightly facial blemishes are fed into the subconscious, reconstituted and come out the other end as a character.

Therefore, there are bits of all of us in all of them. Do you know an author to speak to? Then there's a substantial risk that there's a character up there wandering around wearing your nose.

The real problem arises when an author, consciously or not, bases a character on himself. The old maxim *you can't take it with you* suddenly acquires a whole new set of macabre resonances.

Think about that for a moment.

On the one hand, Jane has gone into fiction. At almost exactly the same moment, her hero has popped into real life. There are likely to be serious consequences for the fabric of reality. Imagine a man standing in the dead centre of the aisle between the seats on an airliner fifty thousand feet up when two windows on opposite sides of the plane smash simultaneously, and you might begin to get the general idea.

While we're on the subject, consider this.

1. For every exit there must be an entrance.

2. Jane Armitage, a writer of sensational popular fiction, was born on the same day that Albert Skinner, a writer of sensational popular fiction, became marooned on the Other Side.

It might, of course, simply be a coincidence. By the same token, the stars might just conceivably be the holes in the sky that the rain comes through. Neither proposition, however, is one you'd be advised to bet next month's rent on.

* * *

Having looked round to make sure the coast was clear, Hamlet rolled up his sleeves, took a firm hold on the pickaxe handle, and swung.

Indecisive and vacillating? He'd give the smug bastards indecisive and vacillating. Most other characters of his acquaintance, stuck in this ghastly position, would just roll up in a ball like a hedgehog and wait to be rescued. Not Hamlet.

He was digging a tunnel.

Where exactly he was digging it to, he wasn't quite sure. What he knew about multi-dimensional spatio-temporal physics could have been written on the back of a postage stamp with a thick-nib marker pen, but that was neither here nor there. Isaac Newton, he argued, knew bugger all about gravity until the apple hit him. It was probably something you could pick up as you went along.

More to the point; what was he going to do with all the earth?

Sherlock Holmes, fortunately, was out on a job some-where, which did at least mean he had the run of the place until he got back. Investigations in Holmes' bedroom had produced a significant number of socks, each of which (Hamlet estimated) would hold at least a pound and a half of soil. Once the socks were full, he could hang them up with clothes pegs from the curtain rail, and nobody would be any the wiser.

There were times, he realised, when his own ingenu-ity quite frightened him.

Another slight problem was the fact that 221B Baker Street was on the first floor.

Who was it (Hamlet asked himself, as the pickaxe blade hurtled downwards) who described a problem as a good idea just waiting to happen? Not Shakespeare, for a start. That dozy old windbag never ever said anything practical, just a lot of dreary waffle about Life and things. All he had to do was to break through the ceiling into Mrs Hudson's sitting room and then carry on vertically downwards after that. Piece of cake. Obviously, he'd have to find some cunning way to conceal what he was up to, but that ought not to be difficult. How many people look up at their ceilings more than once a year anyway?

The pickaxe blade connected with the floor, hit something hard and bounced back, nearly skewering Hamlet's head with the other end. Puzzled, Hamlet bent down and prodded at the place under the carpet he'd struck at. Sure enough, he felt something under there; something flat and smooth. Curious.

With infinite care and a pair of scissors, he began prising up the carpet tacks, keeping each tack safe for the time when he'd have to put the carpet back. Since Holmes appeared to be a fairly observant sort of chap, it would be vitally important not to leave any clues as to what he'd been up to, such as the carpet rolled back and a gaping hole in the floorboards.

What on earth could it be? As he plied the scissors, he tried to call to mind the various categories of article that people usually stash under the floorboards. Tin trunks full of gold coins. Illegal arms caches. Dismembered corpses. None of these seemed to fit in with Holmes' public image, but on the other hand, if you go to the trouble of shoving something away under the rug, the chances are that you don't want people to know about it. Maybe the only reason why nobody usually associated the name Sherlock Holmes with suitcasefuls of detonators and Semtex was that nobody as yet had thought to prise up his floor.

It was a manhole cover.

Hamlet sat back on his heels and scratched his head.

Yes, he muttered to himself, quite. Why *would* a world-famous detective living in a first-storey apartment have a manhole cover in the middle of his floor? Only one way to find out. He grabbed the handle, braced his feet and pulled.

There was a hole. Not an unreasonable thing to expect to find under a manhole cover, at that. Hamlet knelt beside it and peered down.

Instead of the bird's eye view of Mrs Hudson's sitting room he'd expected to see, there was what looked for all the world like a steel-lined ventilation shaft; the sort of thing, in fact, that Our Hero always finds, conveniently situated behind a flimsy chicken-wire grating, in the makeshift cell the villains leave him in after he's been captured, and which always and without exception comes out in the control room of the chief villain's underground command centre. Hamlet sighed. Welcome, he said to himself, to Thrillerland.

Just because it's there, Hamlet thought, doesn't mean I have to go down it. I could put back the cover, replace the carpet and make myself a nice strong cup of tea.

On the other hand, he mused, stroking his chin, someone's obviously been to a lot of trouble to put it there. And this is, after all, fiction, where everything has a purpose. Whoever built this ruddy thing is probably waiting for me at the other end right this very minute, tapping his foot and looking at his watch.

As he knelt and pondered, a vision floated into his mind of a crowded auditorium, a proscenium arch and a spotlit figure in black centre stage with a skull in his hand. Indecisive and vacillating. Well, quite. The sort of man, in fact, who'd uncover a perfectly good ventilation shaft and then sit on the edge of it agonising for half an hour until the villain came back again and caught him. Not ruddy likely.

'Here goes,' he said aloud; and then, a moment later, 'Down the hatch.' He stayed where he was.

Who the devil would want to build a ventilation shaft slap bang in the middle of Sherlock Holmes' living room floor?

Good question. There is a difference, after all, between being dynamic and positive, and not looking both ways before stepping out into the road and getting run over by a passing truck. Perhaps we should just hold our water and think this one through a little longer . . .

He froze. From the stairwell came the sound of footsteps: the heavy clunk he recognised as Holmes' size eights, and a sharper, more clopping noise that suggested high heels. With an economy of movement that would have done credit to the proverbial drain-ascending rat, Hamlet jumped to his feet, swung himself into the mouth of the shaft, braced his knees against the sides and let go.

By a dramatically permissible coincidence, at that very moment in a cellar under a warehouse in Rotherhithe, Professor Moriarty was writing a cheque.

The cheque was for sixty-two pounds, drawn in favour of Jas. Harris & Co., Builders, Baker Street. The invoice that lay beside the cheque book on Moriarty's desk read:

To supplying and installing at 221B Baker Street while the tenant thereof was otherwise engaged a steel-lined ventilation shaft connecting directly with your secret underground lair; to include drawing plans, furnishing materials, all incidental works and making good; prompt settlement will oblige.

Moriarty blotted the cheque, folded it and slipped it into an envelope. That, he muttered to himself, was the easy part.

★　　★　　★

Claudia closed her eyes and counted up to ten. Then she opened them again.

'Just run that past me one more time, Sher,' she said. 'And this time, don't bother explaining how you know, because it makes my head hurt.'

If Holmes was offended, there was no indication in his dark, enigmatic face. An eyebrow may have quivered for a fraction of a second; a corner of a lip may have twitched. Nothing more.

'Very well,' he said. 'To recapitulate, then; the man Skinner – who, as is painfully apparent, is the key to this whole rather intriguing conundrum – is presently "holed up", as I believe the expression is, in Piglet's house at Pooh Corner. I suspect that he is in company with a female person, quite possibly Titania the Queen of the Fairies. I trust,' he added sardonically, 'that you had already reached that conclusion. The evidence admits, after all, of only one possible interpretation.'

Claudia nodded impatiently. 'The other guy,' she said. 'The he-man type with the beard.'

'Regalian?' Holmes leaned back in his chair, his fingertips touching. 'I suggest you look for him at Skinner's last-known address in Chicopee Falls, Iowa, at some point circa June 1959. Quite elementary, of course.'

'Fine. And the writer, whatsername.'

'Jane Armitage.' Holmes shrugged. 'I scarcely imagined you would wish me to insult your intelligence by pointing out that she is to be found somewhere in the Retreat from Moscow in Tolstoy's epic masterpiece.' He allowed himself a visible smirk. 'Do you wish me to name the novel, or are you—?'

'All right,' Claudia snapped. 'So cut to the chase. Where *is* he?'

'You mean Hamlet?'

'Yes.'

'Ah.'

'Well?'

The great detective shifted in his seat. 'You know my methods, my dear Claudia. Apply them.'

'You mean you don't know.'

'The precise location,' Holmes said slowly, 'may perhaps still elude me . . .'

'He was here only a few goddamn hours ago. You can't have lost him *already*.'

Holmes' brows twitched like curtains. 'The crude mechanical details,' he said, trying to sound bored, 'I prefer to leave to the official police. Once the underlying cause has been uncovered—'

'Wonderful.' Claudia got up and snapped her fingers round the handle of her organiser bag. 'I hire the so-called best detective in all fiction to find someone, and he says, *Have you tried the cops?* Next off, you'll be suggesting we phone round the hospitals.'

'My dear lady,' Holmes growled ominously. 'Had you been listening while I explained to you the precise sequence of events . . .'

'Yeah,' Claudia snapped. 'If I'd wanted a history lesson I'd have called in Harvard. I want to know where the schmuck is *now*.' She paused. 'Do you happen to know that, Sher?'

Holmes pursed his lips. 'When one has eliminated the impossible . . .' he began.

'Save it for the customers,' Claudia snarled from the doorway. 'I'm disappointed in you, buster. They told me you were good. I'm going to find this sucker myself, and I don't expect to receive a bill. So long.'

The door slammed. After a few moments of complete stillness, Holmes opened his eyes, leaned his head back, and shouted.

'Watson!'

The doctor's head appeared through the doorway. 'Yes, Holmes?'

'Get me an aspirin.'

Moriarty drew the collar of his coat close to his cheeks and shivered; unaccountably, since it was a warm night.

'All there, I trust?' asked his companion, politely.

Moriarty nodded, and shoved the thick sheaf of Treasury bills into the side pocket of his coat. 'In the coach,' he muttered, trying not to catch the other man's eye.

'Undamaged?'

'I believe so, yes,' replied the Professor, trying his best to keep the distaste out of his voice.

The other man reached out a hand and took Moriarty's shoulder between forefinger and thumb. His grip was like ice and steel.

'For your sake,' he said, 'I do hope so. I know where you live, Professor. Good evening.'

With a swirl of a black cloak, the man seemed to vanish into the fog. A moment later, Moriarty heard the clop of hooves on cobbles, and earnestly thanked God that he was alone. He started to walk briskly in the direction of Whitechapel.

Back in his secret lair, he pulled out the big bundle of money and opened his safe. As he counted the notes through, he noticed something he'd previously overlooked. An envelope.

His hands trembled as he tore it open. But, on closer inspection, it turned out to be completely innocuous. Train and steamer tickets; a hotel reservation; guide books, even. As he cast his eye over the accompanying letter, his face relaxed into a gentle, amused smile.

He had not, as he had feared, incurred the wrath of his awesome customer; quite the reverse. As a token of esteem and thanks for a job well done, he was being treated to the winter holiday of a lifetime, all expenses paid, in the romantic splendour of the Swiss Alps. First class travel and accommodation in Interlaken, followed by three weeks of luxury at an internationally-acclaimed hotel a mere stone's throw from the awe-inspiring natural grandeur of the Reichenbach Falls.

Gosh, thought Professor Moriarty. Things are looking up.

Regalian threw back the curtains and stared uncharitably at the sunrise.

It was, he admitted, the real sun. All the same, to someone brought up on the sunrises of heroic fiction, it was damned unconvincing.

Where I come from, he muttered to himself, sunrises are retina-scorching coruscations of vivid red fire boiling tumidly out of cloudy crucibles, not something like a motorway service station version of a poached egg. We, of course, only have sunrises when the dramatic situation requires them. The rest of the time we just switch on the lights.

He picked up his coffee cup and his plate of toast and sat down on the window seat, looking out over Main Street. Another day, he reflected, and nothing is going to happen unless I make it happen. What a depressing prospect.

He had, after thirty-six hours of patient argument, threats and blatant disregard of the rules of chronological physics, managed to patch through a telephone call to Jane's number in 1996, only to get the answering machine; which suggested, in the circumstances (she had a deadline for her new book which she could now only possibly hope to meet by writing it while orbiting the planet at light speed), that Jane had gone charging off on her own to mount some sort of amateur rescue bid; which was silly. She had no qualifications for that sort of work whatsoever. True, by virtue of being a writer of fantasy fiction she wasn't exactly a stranger to weird and dangerous experiences – he recalled vividly her description of the time her publishers had sent her to a science fiction convention in Congleton, where she'd spent a harrowing weekend surrounded by four hundred and sixty-two self-proclaimed representatives of the Klingon Empire – but there's a material difference between boldly going and making a complete bloody fool of yourself. And there are some things which really do have to be left to the professionals.

Such as heroism.

Being a hero isn't something anybody can do. True enough, once in a lifetime a quiet, mild-mannered newspaper reporter can save a child from being run over by a negligent steamroller. If on the strength of that the reporter buys himself a cape and a pair of tights and tries jumping off tall buildings, however, he is likely to find out two things in pretty short order; the second of which is the folly of pushing one's luck.

It's different, of course, for heroes.

Heroes have nine lives, rubber kneecaps, diplomatic passports, an uncle on the board of magistrates, an exercise book permanently in place down the back of their trousers and a sick note signed by God. In a cosmology where everybody knows his place, it is immutably ordained that the guards the hero has to stalk and silently kill before scaling the castle wall are the only two in the whole brigade who happen to be stone deaf and crippled with arthritis. Even the most lacklustre hero has available to him resources on a scale which would put Spielberg into immediate bankruptcy, while the household names have more doubles and stunt men than Napoleon had

Old Guards at Waterloo. The only sure-fire way to kill a hero is to lock him up for six months in a room with no mirror.

For the first time, he noticed in the corner of the room a big cabinet radio, the kind that hums for thirty seconds and then plays Glen Miller, regardless of where the dial is pointing. Perfectly normal thing to find in a house of the period.

In the bicycle shed of Regalian's subconscious mind, an idea stirred. At that particular moment, it bore as much resemblance to a workable plan of action as the first ever single-cell organism to a Nobel prizewinner, but everything has to start somewhere.

Basic authorship theory; the hero rises to the occasion. The grottier the occasion, the more outstandingly brilliant and innovative the hero's response; and the laws of physics, generally speaking, are happy to come along for the ride. Set a hero a sufficiently nasty problem, and there's virtually no limit to what he can achieve. Provided, of course, that the odds are sufficiently stacked against him.

The difficulty is, therefore, not that the task confronted is impossible; but whether it's impossible *enough*. Luck, like a Russian car, generally only works if you push it.

It's basically the same inverse feasibility matrix that you find when you want to borrow money. Try and borrow fifty quid from your bank to pay the rent, and you're a no-good loser. Ask to borrow fifty million to take over a moribund company, and you're a respected financier. Raise a forced loan of five hundred billion to pay the interest on the fifty zillion you borrowed last week, and you're a Chancellor of the Exchequer.

Having made himself a strong cup of coffee, Regalian sat back and thought hard . . .

★   ★   ★

Jane paused, knocked a substantial quantity of compacted snow off her left boot, and stared at the signpost. It depressed her.

She wasn't obsessive about her art, God knows; you can't afford to be, if you're a professional. But there were some things that did offend her sense of basic craftsmanship, and this was one of them.

The sign read:

MIDDLE BIT BYPASS
Characters for Chapters 23–47 are advised to leave at
Junction 12

CHAPTER TEN

'Igor?'

No reply.

'Igor?'

The howl of the wind in the fir trees. The rippling crash of the thunder. The pecking hammer of the rain on the shed roof, like a spectral Fred and Ginger doing the Tap Danse Macabre.

'Igor, tha daft booger, what's tha playin' at?'

The bounty hunter flickered.

Imagine a double-sided mirror. He was on both sides simultaneously.

Half of him, during this strange moment of transition, was in Fiction, half in Reality. He'd never been in Reality before, in whole, part or instalments. A less completely focused individual might have paused to look around, admire the scenery, take an interest. He didn't. Understandable; when the SAS are parachuted in miles behind enemy lines to blow up a bridge or rescue a hostage, they don't make detours to take a look at interesting old churches or unusual rock formations. Likewise with the bounty hunter, only more so.

Go in, do the job, get out again. Yes. Absolutely.

He was looking for a doorway . . .

'IGOR!!'

In the distance, an unfastened gate banged eerily. The woodwork of the shed creaked under the insistent malice of the storm. Somewhere far away, maybe as far out as Halifax, a forked tongue of lightning flicked at the wet, chill earth.

'Hold tha water, Norman lad. Ah'm coomin' as fast as ah can.'

And about time too. Having an assistant was a mixed blessing, Frankenbotham reflected. True, it had meant that Stanley Earnshaw #2 had been assembled in only a fraction of the time it had taken to piece together the prototype; before his retirement, Igor Braithwaite had been one of the five most respected TV repair men in all Yorkshire, and he could do things with a soldering iron that no mortal man should be capable of. The flipside was that Igor was eighty-three years old, and ever since his operation the intervals between his trips to the little boys' room were shortening like daylight in December.

'Hurry *oop*, tha daft old sod, there's bits leaking all over t'shop.' Which was true; and with black market AB negative standing him at close on a fiver a pint (and when I were a lad, you could get ten pints, a bucket of jellied brains and still have change out of half a crown . . .) that was no laughing matter. More to the point, the lightning was headed this way, and who could say where their next major electric storm was coming from?

Stanley Earnshaw #2 lay motionless on the workbench before him. If you overlooked the damp patches and the messy bit where Igor hadn't quite finished connecting up the main relay circuits just over the right ear, he was a fine figure of a man; six foot eight, massive of bone and sinew, and (a marked improvement over the first model) proper organic outer dermatic membranes instead of insulating tape, brown paper and treacle. It had been Igor who had pointed out the amazing properties of the skin that forms on stagnant cold tea; Frankenbotham had taken the idea one step further in using the exterior surface of works canteen rice pudding for the hard-wearing areas such as the palms of the hands and the soles of the feet. A direct hit from a Rapier missile might cause problems; otherwise, his creators felt sure, Stanley Earnshaw #2 was proof against anything Fate had to chuck at him.

Igor hobbled in, still fumbling with his fly buttons. With an impatient gesture, Frankenbotham shooed his assistant back to work, and for the next half hour there was no sound but the fizz-crackle of the Mig welder, the buzz of the sewing machine, the low drone of Igor muttering to himself, and the ping of the occasional small component dropped on the floor.

And then . . .

'Reckon that'll do, Norman lad.'

Just in time, too. A fraction of a second after Igor's gnarled fingers tightened the last retaining screw on the inspection panel, a livid fang of searing blue light arced down through the wire coathanger that connected Frankenbotham's jury-rigged lightning conductor to the primary pulse electrodes in Stanley's ears. There was a flash, a sizzle, a repulsive stench of burning . . .

'Igor! More power! Ig— Oh for cryin' out loud, tha prawn, can't tha wait five minutes?'

The distant clank of a chain and surge of a cistern were faintly audible in the distance. Frankenbotham took a deep breath, spluttered as his lungs filled with smoke, and threw the main switch . . .

The smoke cleared.

'IGOR!'

On the workbench, something stirred.

As he dragged himself up from the floor and wiped matted sawdust and shavings out of his eyes, Frankenbotham hardly dared look. If, after all this, he had failed . . . But something told him he hadn't. He turned to face the bench. Suddenly, it was very quiet.

'Stanley?' he breathed.

'Howdy, partner.'

Igor, framed in the doorway, gave a strangled gasp. His eyes met those of his colleague, reflecting the same horror.

'Norman, lad,' whispered the older man, 'tha's only gone and built a bloody Yank!'

'No,' said Skinner firmly. 'Absolutely not. No way.'

Titania clicked her tongue impatiently. 'It might work,' she said. 'Not a new idea, genre splicing. Entirely possible, in theory.'

Skinner stopped pacing, turned and glared at her. 'All sorts of things are possible,' he growled, 'including artificially generated plague viruses and nuclear holocausts. Just because something's possible doesn't mean we actually have to do it. The same applies to—'

'Chicken.'

Before he could reply, Skinner caught the Piglet's bewildered, terrified stare and his heart sank. 'For the last time,' he said, 'we are not going to kill the pig. Over my dead body.'

Titania considered for a moment. 'No,' she said. 'Good of you to offer, but just one corpse ought to be enough. Look, it's only a dratted pig. Or are you trying to tell me you've never eaten roast pork?'

'Hey . . .'

'Or bacon? Ham and eggs? Frankfurters? Listen, buster, that's the way it is with pigs. They don't herd them

into the abattoir and wait for them to pass away peacefully in their sleep, you know.'

'Watch my lips, you bloodthirsty bitch. We are *not*—'

The gun went off.

With a terrified squeal, Piglet wriggled on to his chest,
scrabbled with his tiny paws (ropes notwithstanding) and
burrowed under the rug like an agoraphobic mole. Before
Skinner could swear at it, the gun fell off the table, landed
on its hammer, cocked itself and fired again. A small fur-
fabric donkey wobbled on the mantelpiece and fell with
a soft thud into the fireplace.

'Jesus!' Skinner screamed.

Titania jumped up, retrieved the toy and poked her
finger through the bullet-hole. 'That'll do,' she said
happily. 'Now then . . .'

'That maniac's just shot Eeyore!'

The Queen of the Fairies shook her head. 'This isn't
Eeyore,' she replied patiently. 'This is just a kid's soft toy.
The real Eeyore's down there with the rest of them. I saw
him. He's got a Remington sniper's rifle with infra-red
sights, he's tied his tail round his head like a headband and
smeared camouflage paint all over his nose and ears. Guess
he's finally found a role in life he can be happy with.'

Skinner stared at the perforated object in Titania's
hand. 'What do you mean, just a toy?' he demanded.
'They're all frigging toys, that's the whole *point*.'

'No, you're wrong there,' Titania said. 'This is a toy's
toy. Like, you know, subtext. Here, even the cuddly furry
animals have cuddly furry animals. Now then, we've got
work to do.'

Shaking his head, Skinner took the limp object and
laid it on the ground. Titania picked up the Scholfield
(guns can't smirk, but, by the same token, they can't of
their own volition shoot stuffed donkeys, can they?) and
laid it artistically beside the body, one stuffed paw on the

grips. 'That'll do,' she said. 'Now we wait and see.'

Genre splicing theory. Set up a classic stock situation from one genre in another genre and see what, or who, happens. So; a body on the hearthrug, apparently suicide, except that that would be too simple. Two obvious suspects, nobody else could have entered or left the room. But if it wasn't suicide, what possible motive could there have been? And what about the third witness, the seemingly innocuous Piglet, who, at the time the fatal shot was fired, was supposedly cowering under the rug?

'This isn't going to work,' Skinner said, with gloomy satisfaction.

'Give it a chance, miseryguts.'

'Waste of everybody's—'

The scene changed.

Genre splicing theory. Set up a situation that obviously, painfully obviously, belongs in one sort of book and one sort only, and you might just build up enough dramatic tension (what reviewers call a critical mass) to bust out of one genre into another, regardless of the laws of artistic physics. Nice idea, but you wouldn't want to try it. Even if it worked, you'd have absolutely no control over where you ended up.

The scene *had* changed. Same basic layout; hearthrug, corpse, gun, chairs, table. But the walls were now oak-panelled and lined with books, the rug had once been the outside of a tiger and the corpse had somehow changed from a stuffed donkey into a tweed-clad, white-haired man with a bristling moustache, probably a retired Indian army colonel. Closer inspection revealed a clock that had stopped the first bullet, its hands now frozen at 12.15; a scrap of paper in the fireplace that looked suspiciously like the remains of a compromising letter; a small glass bottle lying under the writing desk, very probably containing the last dregs of a dose of an undetectable poison known only to the Bushmen of northern Natal; a footprint from a size nine walking shoe with a built-up heel . . . One could go on for ever. It was like one of those newspaper puzzles where you have to find thirty-six tropical birds hidden in unlikely places all over the picture. Skinner made a peculiar noise.

'There,' said Titania. 'Piece of cake.'

. . . Oh yes, and a half-eaten slice of seed cake on the window-ledge. No prizes for guessing that, once analysed, the cake will turn out to be marinaded in enough arsenic (the white variety, as opposed to the brown variety commonly used in rat poison and weedkiller) to kill half of Bradford . . .

And the door opens, and a fussy little man with an egg-shaped head and enormous moustaches trots in, beams and introduces himself . . .

'I think,' said Skinner, 'I'd like to be sick now, please.'

The bounty hunter sat up.

So, he said to himself, this is Reality. Could have fooled me.

True, he wasn't seeing it at its most convincing. The electric storm still raging outside was every bit as melo-dramatic as one of its fictional counterparts. He'd heard one of the funny little old men who were gawping at him call the other one Igor. And there was something disturbingly familiar about the look of his feet.

Big shoes they wear in Reality. Almost like old-fashioned diving boots.

Very big . . .

'Hey,' he said. 'What's the big idea?'

One of the funny men took a step backwards. 'How were I to know?' he stammered in a peculiar voice. 'It were all genuine Yorkshire parts. Maybe he just sounds like a bloody Yank.'

'Ask him, then. Go on, ask him.'

'Tha ask him.'

'He's thy bloody fast bowler.'

The bounty hunter was reassured. Maybe there was a passing similarity, but nobody ever talked like that in Fiction. He smiled.

'Howdy,' he said. 'Say . . .'

('That's never Yorkshire, young Norman.'

'I dunno. Could be Harrogate. They talk bloody funny in Harrogate.')

'Say,' continued the bounty hunter, reaching out a hand towards a large piece of ironmongery with a view to pulling himself upright, 'can you folks put me on the right road for Chicopee Falls? Reckon I'm kinda out of my way here—'

'Don't touch that!'

The bounty hunter raised an eyebrow. As he did so, something tore . . .

('It's them Co-op tea bags. Told thee they were weak as buggery.')

. . . but he ignored it. Instead, he inspected the curious gadget he was holding on to. He had no idea what it was.

'Don't touch that! It's t'random particle accelerator. If t'lightning shorts through that and tha's holding on to it—'

'Hey up, Norman lad, tha never said tha'd got a random particle accelerator.'

'Didn't ah? Well, tha knows Chalky Wainwright, as used to live across t'way from t'canning factory? Well, his dad—'

There was a blinding flash, as enough power to run Scotland for twenty minutes crackled across an inch of empty air and leapt joyfully towards the bare terminals of the random particle accelerator. The windows blew out in a shower of razor-edged confetti. Quite a lot of things caught fire.

Chalky Wainwright's dad, whose superior Yorkshire intelligence had graduated from cat's whisker radios in the 'twenties into a staggering new vista of One Hundred and One Things A Young Man Can Make, had rigged up the particle accelerator out of cannibalised transistors, used HT leads, electric fire elements, a broken telly and twelve square yards of tinfoil, round about the time Harold Wilson had been enthusing about the white heat of technology. It had always been Chalky's dad's ambition to travel backwards in time; and there was a small but enthusiastic body of opinion which held that he hadn't simply walked out one day on the pretext of buying an evening paper and never returned, but had in fact achieved his aim and somehow made it back to Huddersfield, circa 1109, where he was currently running a thriving jellied eel concession in what would one day be Palmerston Street. All pure speculation, of course.

'Igor.'

'What?'

'Where's he gone?'

'Who?'

'T'Yank, tha dozy pillock.'

Igor looked round. 'What Yank, Norman lad?'

'T'one we were building . . . .'

'Talk sense, Norman,' replied the older man sharply. 'Who with any sense'd be building a bloody American?'

For a moment, Frankenbotham surmised that all the lightning they'd been having recently must have fried his assistant's brain. Then it occurred to him that, in order to reach an advanced age in the TV repair business north of Wakefield, you probably had to have survival instincts which would make the average gazelle look like a kamikaze pilot.

'Tha's right, Igor,' he said slowly. 'Nobody in their right mind'd be building an artificial Yank. Not,' he added, 'in Dewsbury.'

Igor nodded conclusively. 'Flamin' daft idea, if you ask me.'

'Fancy a brew?'

'Now tha's talking, Norman lad. Now tha's talking.'

Damn, thought Jane.

It was all very well to say, I know, I'll use the interface fault under the Library of Congress to slip into Fiction; but Fiction, she was beginning to realise, is big. Ever so much bigger than, say, Carlisle. This one book she'd wandered into, a single book out of countless hundreds of thousands (how many books were there? A million? Ten million? Apart from the guess that ISBN stands for Incredibly Seriously Big Number, she hadn't a clue) was easily as big as the human imagination, if not bigger. Every book can be that big, with the possible exception of *Teach Yourself Thumb-Twiddling* and the works of Jeffrey Archer. Accordingly, wandering into Fiction by the back door and expecting to fall over Regalian was rather like standing on the platform on Fulham Broadway station and expecting to come face to face with your second cousin from Toronto. Only somewhat less likely.

Oh well, she said to herself. Nothing for it but to go back again.

She turned round. One good thing about trackless wastes of snow is that you tend to leave footprints. All she had to do was follow them, and she could retrace her steps.

There were no footprints.

Odd.

Sure, if you wait long enough, the snow and the wind

will cover up your tracks. But that doesn't happen *instantaneously*. She had stopped walking, oh, about two seconds ago; and there were no footprints to be seen. A disturbing thought occurred to her.

Maybe the white stuff wasn't snow. Maybe it was paper.

As she entertained the thought, a thoroughly unpleasant but nevertheless familiar panic started to flow into her, filling her up like a kettle under a tap. Every author's everyday nightmare, the blank sheet of paper with no words on it, grinning horribly up at her from the jaws of the typewriter.

Blank white everywhere; featureless, virgin, without cardinal points or signposts. Stare at it long enough and you hallucinate watermarks. This, Jane had always believed, is where very wicked authors go when they die. This was what it was like in the Beginning, before there was the Word.

Indeed. Or the Middle. Or the End.

Welcome to the Columbus Experience. Sail too far across the ocean, and you fall off the edge. Go too far into Fiction, and you come to the edge of the page, the unimaginable void, the empty pages nobody has written on yet. As she stared at it, Jane reflected with a shudder that pre-Columbian mariners probably had the easy end of it. For them it was just a case of splosh-whoops-aaaaaagh-THUMP. Here, the rest was silence.

She sat down. The whiteness was making her snow-blind. If she stayed here too long, she'd forget everything. After that, she'd become invisible herself, and quite simply cease to be.

All in all, she'd rather be in Milton Keynes. This place had a lot in common with Milton Keynes, but at least Milton Keynes was a sort of pale grey, and some of the hard, flat surfaces had things written on them, usually in aerosol paint by people with limited vocabularies. Hey, she thought, maybe if I can write something on this, I can get out of here. She rummaged in her pockets for a pen, lipstick, eyebrow pencil, bit of stick, nailfile; nothing. Not even the inevitable unwrapped, furry boiled sweet that lives in all pockets everywhere, provided you burrow deep enough.

'Oh,' she wailed. The word seemed to drift away and seep into the vast whiteness, like water draining away into sand. Very apt metaphor, in the circumstances.

Woof.

Jane lifted her head. Either she was imagining things, or something had just said Woof. As an unkind but truthful reviewer had once pointed out, imagining things wasn't exactly her strong point. Accordingly, the other theory, however improbable, must be the truth.

'Woof. Woof.'

She narrowed her eyes against the blinding white glare and looked around. In the very far distance, she thought she could see a tiny dot. After she'd been looking for thirty seconds or so – this space reserved for substantial migraine – the little dot seemed to grow four legs. And a tail.

'Woof. Woof. Woof.'

Jane tried to stand up; but that presupposed the existence of an Up to stand into, and there no longer seemed to be one. Imagine floating in an isolation tank of fairly thick custard; or rather, if you value the ability to sleep at night, don't.

It was a dog; a hairy, bouncy, chunky, substantial sort of a dog, with a fringe that came down over its eyes and a friendly pink tongue hanging out of the side of its mouth. It was the sort of dog you'd visualise curled up in front of the roaring log fire of your dreams; a Dulux dog, the kind you want to take for bracing walks through the virgin dew and throw sticks for. You could call it Rover without feeling guilty.

It trotted up, sat on its back legs, and said, 'Woof.'
It had a barrel hanging from its collar.

Bloody odd ventilation shaft, Hamlet mused, as he hurtled downwards.

Admittedly, he could only spare about four per cent of his mental capacity for the task of analysing the problem – ever since he'd lost his footing and started to fall, the other ninety-six per cent had been fully occupied with thoughts of the *AAAGH! SHIT! I'M GOING TO DIE!* variety – but he had to admit that he was baffled. On the basis of the observational data he'd been able to accumulate so far, the shaft was very long, smooth-sided, and more or less spiral, like the slide at a fairground as conceived of by a very disturbed mind. As part of an integrated ventilation design concept, it left a lot to be desired.

It was very, *very* long. He hadn't been keeping a scientific record of how long he'd been falling down it (why is it that you never have a fully-calibrated chronograph handy when you most need one?) but he reckoned it was safe to say that this shaft didn't just connect 221B Baker Street with 221A Baker Street, or even the main drain. Bearing in mind that his calculations were unlikely to be all that precise, his best guess was an ETA in Australia in about two seconds.

Nope. This service, apparently, doesn't stop in Australia. Must be the through-drain. If you'd wanted to get off at Australia, you should have waited for the Super Shuttle.

Not for the first time, Hamlet regretted that he hadn't been born a thoroughbred action adventure hero. Your action adventure hero, falling down a shaft or drain, somehow manages to wedge himself against the sides, using his shoulders and feet, and then creepy-crawl back up again to safety, the quintessential human spider coming back up the plug-hole. The more intellectual and introspective class of hero to which he belonged just keeps on falling, passing the time with complex analysis of his mental state and carefully worded commentaries on Life, Fate and stuff like that. And, when he finally hits the deck and goes flump, it's all cosmically significant and Means Something. Bloody cold comfort for a chap who, by this point, presumably looks like a dollop of strawberry jam, but there you go. We can't all be Arnie, can we?

Well, quite.

FLUMP.

After a pain break and a brief pause for status checks, Hamlet crawled to his hands and knees and looked up. Directly above him, he could see a horrible, nightmare, cheese-just-before-bedtime vision, a huge reptilian head with gaping jaws and about twelve rows of inward-facing teeth. A thin ropelike tongue drooped from the lower jaw. It was forked.

Above the head, the serpentine body spiralled away upwards into the darkness for as far as the eye could see. The whole thing was huge; about the thickness of an Underground train.

And I, he realised, am kneeling on a thick, bouncy mattress.

I just fell down the snake.

Thinks . . .

Down the snake.

Puerile . . .

After that, it didn't take him long to find the foot of the ladder. It took him rather longer to climb back up to the top of it, and by the time he crawled, raw-handed and bloody-kneed, over the lip of the hole and back once more into Sherlock Holmes' comfortable bachelor apartment in Baker Street, he was feeling rather tired and sorry for himself. All in all, he wasn't in the mood for the big framed notice inscribed:

SERVES YOU RIGHT

which was the first thing he set eyes on as he emerged. Once he'd caught his breath, however, and had a chance to relieve his feelings by use of colourful and vulgar language, he was able to get a grip on himself and read the small print at the bottom of the notice; which read:

BASIC HEROISM THEORY: so you wanna be a hero? Forget it. The ease of the escape is in direct proportion to the stature of the hero. James Bond and Jim Kirk can shin down ventilation shafts and get away with it. You can't. Next time, there won't be a mattress. Unfair? One law of gravity for the big guys and another for the small fry? That's fiction for you. Be told.

Ripping the notice out of its frame and tearing it into tiny pieces was, objectively speaking, a futile gesture and didn't prove anything, but Hamlet found it helped. A bit.

'Woof,' said the dog.

Because her hands were numb, it took Jane an embarrassingly long time to unbuckle the dog's collar, pull the lid off the barrel and shake out the little foil-wrapped sachet inside. There was writing on the outside, as follows:

Emergency Plot
Get Out Of Trouble Free

Jane sat back on her heels and stared at the dog in wonder.

'Hey,' she breathed. 'Where have you been all my life?'

A sparkling shower of bits, like a shotgun cartridge loaded with glitter and fired by starlight. A dappled twinkling coruscation of tiny flickers, scrapes and flakes of colour, drifting and swirling. A glass snowstorm paperweight, based on an idea by Magritte, Dali and Bosch.

Reality is stranger than fiction. It can afford to be. Reality doesn't have to worry about getting letters that start off, *Dear Sir, Are you aware that on page 153 . . . ?*

A million or so bits came together and formed the bounty hunter, all seven feet two of jury-rigged, solder-it-together-and-hope DIY genesis. The big boots. The crudely hand-stitched seam on the forehead. And, yes, the bolt through the neck. God, but every bit of him *hurt*.

Travelling through time by science fact, as opposed to science fiction, is rather like going by rail, in the guard's van, in the bottom of a big tea chest full of rusty lumps of iron, instead of flying, first class, Air Canada. It gets you there, and that's about all you can say for it.

The bounty hunter sat up. He was on Main Street; except that it was slightly different from all the Main Streets down which a man must walk where he came from. No horses tethered to rails outside saloons. No manly men and womanly women bustling about their everyday chores. No distant gunfire as the cowpokes celebrated reaching the end of the Lone Star trail. The houses were still timber-framed and the shops were dusty and board-fronted, but there were a handful of cars parked out in the street, and here and there a few TV aerials were sprouting through, like the first green shoots of spring. Across the way, a man in dungarees was putting a new pane of glass into a cucumber frame; apart from that, he had the place to himself. Welcome to the nineteen-fifties, dateline Chicopee Falls, Iowa.

The bounty hunter grinned.

Temporal displacement theory: a time and a place for everything. If you take something out of its time and place, it leaves a hole, the kind of gap that Nature proverbially abhors. If you then disperse that something into its component physical and temporal particles, for example by bringing it into contact with an overloaded random particle accelerator, the extremely powerful natural phenomenon known as Force of Habit ought to return it to its proper place and time, just as the string jerks back the yo-yo, or the subliminal guidance system directs the racing pigeon. Doesn't always work, but the same goes for computers, lifts and expensive electrical appliances of all kinds. The effect had brought the bounty hunter back to the place and time where he had been created, Realside, by the pulp novelist Albert Skinner.

More or less. The margins of error weren't bad; he'd overshot the house by about seventy-five yards, and the time by a few days, maybe a couple of weeks. Doubtful whether it would make any difference, practically speaking. All he had to do was find the mirror window and go through, and he'd be back where he wanted to be. There's a special providence which looks after villains, particularly when they're needed in the last reel. It's like having a combination safe-conduct and bus pass, or being seeded through into the quarter-finals.

The body, he reflected as he trudged up the street, was a bit of a pain, but that was likely to be nothing more than a temporary problem. Thanking his lucky stars he wasn't really Real, he opened the gate and walked up the short path to Albert Skinner's house.

★   ★   ★

The second law of heroism, briefly stated, is that whereas all engineers are heroes, not all heroes are engineers. To put it another way, there's no correct answer to the question *How many heroes does it take to change a light bulb?* for the same reason that there isn't one to *How many elephants are there in the average can of giraffes?* It's a non-question. Heroes don't change light bulbs. Shoot them out, swing from them, unscrew them for use as improvised weapons, yes; change them, no.

Confronted with the problem of how to get back into Fiction, therefore, Regalian had to admit that he wasn't quite sure where to start. Jumping through the broken window had a certain specious attraction, but his basic common sense told him that it wasn't as simple as that; and he had enough on his plate without bruises, concussion and bits of broken glass embedded in his kneecaps.

Think.

Half an hour of rummaging through cupboards, drawers, the bottoms of wardrobes, trunks, chests and old orange boxes produced as diverse a collection of junk as you could possibly hope to find, but none of it produced the intuitive spark in Regalian's mind that would lead to a brilliantly innovative solution. Apart from the thought that he could hold a garage sale and live comfortably on the proceeds for quite some time, he was no better off than before.

Item: a hammer.

Item: a screwdriver, bent, rusty.

Item: a reel-to-reel tape recorder.

Item: two saucepans with the bottoms burnt out.

Item: a hundred and six dog-eared paperback detective novels, long-distance rail travellers for the use of.

Item . . .

Some people, for example Leonardo da Vinci, James Watt and the Wright Brothers, must have felt this way all the time. For Regalian, however, it was a novel experience; the weird, slightly hallucinatory feeling of being on the sharp end of a really spiffing idea. As he stood in Skinner's kitchen, staring at the heap of junk he'd piled up on every available surface, Regalian could hear the words *character bomb* throbbing away in the back of his brain like a sore tooth.

(CHARACTER BOMB: Regalian was, of course, reinventing the wheel™. Character bombs have been around for a very long time; but they live in those big concrete underground playpens out in the desert where the military hoard their toys, so it's hardly surprising that Regalian wasn't familiar with the concept.

Consider the neutron bomb, which kills people but leaves buildings standing. The character bomb takes out derivative characters without wrecking the mainframe.

Confused? Try this. A vampire-dedicated character bomb would eliminate every vampire in literature, up to and including the works of Anne Rice, with the exception of Bram Stoker's original Dracula. Let off a spy-dedicated bomb, and once the smoke had cleared there would be holes in the works of Deighton, Le Carré, Forsyth, Clancy etc. through which you could drive a Mercedes lorry, with only *The Thirty-Nine Steps* remaining intact. The devastation that would ensue outside of Tolkien if someone exploded an elf-bomb defies even the most lurid imagination. And so on. Even the thought of such a device would have publishers queuing up to jump from upper-storey windows.

To make a character bomb, take the two most extreme and opposite divergences from the norm that you can think of, put them together, and hide under something solid.)

★   ★   ★

Character bomb . . .

Well, Regalian said to himself, it might work. He set up the tape recorder on the kitchen table, placed two piles of paperbacks on either side of the microphone, and drew up a chair. He took a book from the left hand pile, opened it at random, switched on and began to read into the mike.

'Ouch!'

The emergency plot or novelist's escape capsule is one of the few truly revolutionary breakthroughs in the fiction industry since the self-calibrating flashback. Simply tear open the foil sachet, and a fully-fledged storyline whisks you up and away, high above any ghastly standstill you may have written yourself into. Suffering from a writer's block that makes the Maginot line look like a sandcastle? Just open the packet, close your eyes and grin.

As far as she could tell, Jane had landed in a large-capacity metal wastepaper basket. To be precise, she was sitting in it, with her legs hanging out over the side like fuchsias in a wilted hanging basket. So thoroughly was she wedged, in fact, that she wasn't quite sure how she was ever going to get out of it.

'Ouch,' she repeated. She looked round. At first glance, she seemed to be in an office. A foot or so to her left was a big old-fashioned desk; behind that, a veteran filing cabinet, one drawer of which was open and filled with empty whisky bottles. There was a weary-looking chair behind the desk, also of antiquated design. Beyond the chair was a door with a frosted glass panel, on which was written:

P MARLOWE
PRIVATE INVESTIGATOR

The problem with emergency plots is that there's only a very limited number of them. This will, of course, change. As with every epoch-making new invention, the first generation products are heavy, cumbersome, gawkish things, the ugly ducklings which will eventually morph into swans shortly after you've bought one of the original models. Think of the early prototype photocopiers, video cameras, personal computers, CD players. Compare them with the sleek, compact, self-confident triumphs of design you get nowadays. The same will be true, one day, of the emergency plot. Until then; well, there are snags to be ironed out, minor technical difficulties to be dealt with and – here comes the relevance; all stand – only three basic storylines to choose from. These are:

(a) the adultery-in-Hampstead plot
(b) the disaster movie
(c) the gumshoe plot.

They were out of stock of the other two. They usually are.

'Help!' Jane observed.

'"The garden is not looking at all as it should," said Miss Marple, but still speaking absent-mindedly. "Doctor Haydock has absolutely forbidden me to do any stooping or kneeling – and really, what can you do if you don't stoop or kneel? There's old Edwards, of course – but so opinionated. And all this jobbing gets them into bad habits, lots of cups of tea and so much pottering – not any real work."'

Regalian paused, his eyes closed, his face wrinkled as if with pain. Did they have this much trouble out in the New Mexico desert, he wondered; Oppenheimer and all that crowd, when they were building that other potentially quite dangerous bomb? If so, they had his sympathy.

'Freeze.'

What?

Oh. Oh for crying out loud.

'You again,' Regalian sighed, without turning his head. 'How in hell's name did you get here?'

'Reckon I might just ask you the same thing, partner,' replied the bounty hunter softly. 'Now, boy, if it's quite convenient, unbuckle your gunbelt and stand up.'

'I haven't got a gunbelt,' Regalian said, as if someone had just implied he had some unsightly skin disorder. 'Sorry.'

'No gunbelt?'

'Not even to please you.'

The bounty hunter shrugged. 'No derringers in the vest pocket?'

'No vest pocket. Ergo, no derringers.'

'Bowie knife slipped inside your sock?'

'Negative. The same goes for Gatling guns cunningly stashed under my dental plate. I do have a paperclip somewhere in the lining of my trouser pocket, but perhaps you could see your way clear to trusting me with that.'

'On your feet then, pard.'

Regalian stood up and turned his head through twenty-five degrees or so until he had a clear view of the doorway. By a substantial effort of will, he managed not to register surprise at what he saw there.

'Fancy dress, huh?' he said.

The bounty hunter frowned (rip rip, crinkle crinkle). 'Reckon you should keep your smartass remarks to yourself, buster,' he said, now with twenty per cent added extra menace, absolutely free. 'Reckon a guy could take offence real easy, if he had a mind to.'

A tiny cog or gear engaged in Regalian's mind. He gave the bounty hunter a long, considered looking over.

'Excuse me,' he said, 'but have you got a gun?'

'Not on me,' the bounty hunter replied.

'Thought not. Then why the hell am I doing what you tell me to?'

The bounty hunter thought for a moment. 'Because I'm seven feet tall and I got superhuman strength?' he hazarded.

Regalian shook his head. 'Wouldn't have thought so,' he replied. 'I mean, the height, yes; I can see for myself you're pretty tall. And I take your word for it about the strength. But if you want to overawe people with your sheer physical presence, I should do something about the stuffing coming out of the split seam under your armpit, if I were you. It lets the side down.'

In the split second it took for the bounty hunter to glance under his arm, Regalian grabbed a heavy object – an old-fashioned, cast-iron, crank-operated coffee mill, to be exact – drew back his arm like a baseball pitcher and let fly. His aim wasn't spot on; he was trying for the centre of the bounty hunter's forehead, but he failed to allow for the sheer weight of the projectile, and the shot landed twenty-seven inches low. It's results that matter, however, and certainly Regalian had no cause for complaint as the bounty hunter moaned horribly, buckled at the knees and sank to the floor, his hands cupped over his groin; a testament to the thoroughness and attention to detail of his creators. When a Yorkshireman builds an artificial human, he doesn't cut corners and leave bits out, arguing that his artefact would never in a million years find any use for *those*. While the bounty hunter was thus occupied, Regalian had plenty of time to rootle around in the kitchen drawers until he found Skinner's rolling pin, walk round the back of the bounty hunter and bash him nine times very hard until he fell over and went, apparently, to sleep. A few turns of washing line around the arms and upper body, a singularly repulsive duster wedged between the jaws to ensure the peace and quiet so necessary when one is engaged in creative work, and another problem solved, under budget and ahead of schedule.

That was easy. Beating the crap out of large, savage enemies is to heroes what filing pink pro-formas in triplicate is to civil servants. Now, back to the difficult stuff. He sat down in front of the tape recorder, switched it back on and cleared his throat.

The door opened.

'Hello,' Jane said. 'Who's there?'

Whoever it was didn't believe in switching on the light. Easy enough to think of several perfectly good reasons why he shouldn't; cost of electricity, place is an awful mess, bulb gone again (how many private investigators does it take to change a light bulb?) – all manner of perfectly rational, non-bloodcurdling explanations. Why do I feel sure, Jane asked herself, that none of them is likely to be the truth in this sentence?

'Hello?'

Shunk-shunk. Courtesy of SFX Unlimited, the sound of well-oiled metal parts moving together. Could be someone adjusting the settings on a washing machine. No earthly reason to assume it's the slide of a .45 automatic being racked. Good grief, Jane, you *will* jump to these absurd conclusions . . .

She made one final effort to extract herself from the wastepaper basket; in vain. Death with dignity? Ah, shucks.

'Okay,' said a deep, grating voice. 'Ditch the hardware, hands where I can see 'em.'

'Excuse me.'

'Don't get wise with me, kid,' the voice growled. 'Try any funny business and you're going home in a box.'

'Excuse me,' Jane repeated, 'but could you possibly help me get out of this wastepaper basket?'

'Huh?'

'If it wouldn't be too much trouble.'

There was a heartbeat of silence. 'Did you say waste-paper basket?'

'Yes.'

And then there was light. 'Hot damn,' said the man in the doorway, 'you're right. You *are* sitting in the waste-paper basket.'

'Mr Marlowe?'

The man narrowed his eyes. 'How'd you know my name?' he demanded.

Jane paused before answering. The trenchcoat, with the collar folded up. The dark brown fedora. The shiny black automatic looking like a natural extension of the right arm. The hard lines of the face, the weary blue eyes.

'It's written on the door,' she said.

'Oh. Yeah. Right.'

Marlowe pocketed the gun, bent down and put one arm under Jane's knees, the other behind her head, and lifted. The bin came too, like a drip mat stuck to the bottom of a beer glass.

'It's all right,' Jane muttered, pushing at the bin with both hands. 'I think I can—'

'Ouch.'

'Oh. Sorry.'

'That was my foot.'

'How clumsy of me. You can put me down now.'

The long, tough face leered at her. 'You sure you wanna be put down, kid?'

'Yes, please.'

'Oh.' Marlowe glowered at her as if he'd just bitten into an apple and found her there. 'Well, in that case, I guess . . .'

'Anywhere here will do. Thank you ever so much.' As soon as her feet touched the ground, Jane scuttled like a crab running for a train and put the width of the desk between herself and Mr Marlowe. Not that she had anything definite against him as yet; but he hadn't shaved in a while and his breath didn't smell very nice. 'Well, now,' she said.

'Yeah?'

'I expect you'd like to know,' Jane said, 'what I'm doing in your office.'

'I can guess.'

Jane blinked. 'You can?'

'Sure.' Marlowe laughed. 'I'm a detective, remember.' Suddenly his voice became cold and hard, like a leftover fried egg. 'You figured that if Maybury shot Stein, then the pearls must still be here. You double-crossed Pedersen, but it didn't occur to you that Michaels had the stuff hidden in the other sock. When you found the body it was too late, so you put the tablespoon in Gobler's hand to make it look like suicide and called the cops. Then you came here, figuring that if the cops didn't get me, Shaftberg would. Only you figured wrong, sister.' His hand disappeared into his coat pocket again. 'That's the trouble with me, I never do what I'm supposed to. I get letters of complaint about it all the time. Right?'

Jane bit her lip. 'Actually,' she said, 'no.'

Marlowe looked as if someone had just stolen his trousers. 'No?'

'No,' Jane repeated.

'You mean Hellman had the jade all along and really Thelma was Chase's *sister*?'

Jane sighed. Unless she did something about it, this could go on all night. 'I really am awfully sorry, Mr Marlowe, but I actually don't properly belong in your plot. I, er, just dropped in. On my way somewhere.'

Marlowe sneered. 'Sure,' he said. 'Only hundred-thousand-dollar blondes don't just drop in on guys like me. There always has to be a reason. I reckon Pavlinski and Stein—'

'Excuse me,' Jane insisted, feeling a little bit dazed at being described as a hundred-thousand-dollar blonde. She couldn't help glowing a little inside, even though her hair was, of course, a sort of shoe-polish brown. 'I know this sounds a little strange, but I'm not actually from Fiction. I'm real. Really.'

'Sure,' Marlowe snarled, and shot her.

'Who?'

'Hercule Poirot,' Skinner hissed. 'He's a detective.'

'What's a detective?' Titania asked.

Skinner didn't answer. He was beginning to wish he'd stayed in *Painted Saddles*. All right, it was tawdry and cheap and there were always men with guns jumping out and trying to kill him, but at least one day followed another in something like a logical sequence and he knew where all the public lavatories were. If all the future had to offer was diving in and out of other people's books until he finally got stabbed, lynched or squashed by a bookmark, he couldn't see very much point in continuing to run.

The big leather armchairs looked very comfortable. He sat down in one. A thought occurred to him.

'Hey,' he said.

Poirot, who was kneeling beside the body examining something through a magnifying glass, looked round. 'M'sieur?'

'Is there any food in this book?'

'Pardon?'

'Food.' Skinner frowned. '*Quelque chose à manger*,' he said irritably. 'Something to drink'd be good, too. *Le bourbon*. Also, where's the john?'

Poirot's eyebrows furrowed for a moment. 'Ah! *Les*

toilettes.' He stopped, and rubbed the bridge of his nose with thumb and forefinger. 'Now that you mention it, m'sieur, I cannot recall having seen any. In the English detective fiction, *vous entendez*, it is, how you say, taboo . . .'

Skinner shrugged. 'Okay,' he said, 'it's your carpet. What about the food?'

Before Poirot could answer, the door opened and a butler came in. In his hands was a tray, and on the tray—

'Yes!' Titania shouted, vaulting over the chair Skinner was sitting in. 'Hey, I'm beginning to like it here.'

—Cucumber sandwiches, potted meat sandwiches, tea-cakes, muffins, Victoria sponge, shortbread, biscuits. The plate was half empty before the butler was able to put it down.

'Hey,' mumbled Skinner with his mouth full. 'Butler.'

'Sir?'

'If I asked you to bring me a large Scotch, would you?'

'Certainly, sir. Miss?'

Titania shrugged. 'Don't mind if I do,' she said. 'I'll have a Manhattan, thanks. No ice.'

'Whee!' Skinner grinned, displaying a mouthful of half-chewed potted meat sandwich. 'The hell with Reality, let's stay—'

At which point he gagged, choked, writhed like an eel in a blender, turned blue and collapsed to the floor. The crust of the sandwich fell from his twitching fingers.

A moment later, Titania crashed to the ground at his side.

'*Sacré bleu*,' said Poirot.

'The barman stooped. I jumped around behind the counter and jostled him out of the way. A sawed-off shotgun lay under a towel on a shelf under the bar. Beside it was a cigar box. In the cigar box was a .38 automatic. I took both of them.

The barman pressed back against the tier of glasses behind the bar.'

Regalian stopped reading, breathed out, switched off the tape recorder and threw the Raymond Chandler paperback down on top of the pile of Agatha Christies. He felt slightly intoxicated and slightly sick, as if he'd just drunk a teacupful of sweet sherry with a triple whisky chaser. What I do for literature, he muttered to himself.

While the tape was rewinding, he decided to check on the bounty hunter. As far as he knew, basic good/evil theory states that a villain, once tied up, stays tied up, whereas a hero wrapped in string is just an escape in chrysalis, poised and waiting to happen. That was all very well; but this was Reality, not Fiction, and the bodies were flesh and blood, not dreams and verbiage. More to the point, the washing line was Sears Roebuck and about twenty years old. Probably a wise move to stroll down to the cellar and just make sure he's still . . .

Gone.

Shit.

One good thing about being in Reality, Regalian told himself as, armed with the heaviest frying-pan he could find, he embarked on a room-to-room search. In Reality you can swear as much as you like without fear of being edited into confetti to make sure we don't alienate the under-twelve market share. Having developed this happy thought, he spent the next five minutes making the best use of the unaccustomed freedom that his vocabulary allowed.

He had just searched all the upstairs rooms, and was standing on the landing wondering where the loathsome creature had got to, when the airing cupboard door opened and the bounty hunter jumped on his back. In his hands he gripped a leg ripped off a pair of long thermal underpants, presumably intended for use as a makeshift garrotte.

Sigh. Here we go again. Choke choke, gasp gasp, aaargh! Back in the old groove, the well-worn track, the daily grind. A change (Regalian mused as he dropped to one knee and threw the bounty hunter over his shoulder and down the stairs) is supposed to be as good as a rest, but on balance I think I'd rather have the rest. On the other hand (he argued, as a cut-glass vase hurled with extreme force and prejudice hit the wall three inches from his nose and exploded into needle-sharp splinters), it wouldn't do to get rusty. A gentle workout now and again, nothing too strenuous (the bounty hunter, armed with a splintered banister rail, aimed a sickening blow at his head which he was only just able to parry with a hastily snatched chair), keeps you in trim and only takes fifteen minutes or so a day. One owes it to oneself (a brisk kick to the kneecap swept the bounty hunter's feet out from under him, after which Regalian smashed the chair to matchwood over his head) not to vegetate, something which can so easily happen (and followed it up with a swift, sharp kick to the point of the chin, sending the bounty hunter tumbling back down the stairs, rolling across the hall and bumping headlong down the cellar steps) if you get lazy.

'Hello,' he called out. 'Are you all right?'

Silence. Having allowed himself the luxury of catching his breath, he picked up the length of banister rail, trotted downstairs and peered down into the cellar. Now then, he told himself, this is a case in point. I could so easily assume he's out for the count and get on with my work, only to have him jump me again just as I'm priming the bomb. No fear. I'd better just totter down into the cellar and kick the blighter's lights out.

It was dark in the cellar – the light didn't work; how

many villains does it take to remove a light bulb? – and sure enough, there was a conspicuous shortage of unconscious seven-foot-long bodies at the foot of the cellar steps. Not that that was a problem. Any second now (ah, splendid – marvellously punctual chaps, villains; you could set your watch by them) he'll come leaping out of the darkness brandishing a broken bottle and then it'll be steely-fingers-round-my-windpipe time again. Then another judo throw (crash, tinkle; spare a thought for poor Mr Skinner's claret, too late, oh well, no use crying over it), more lashing and dodging (swish! thunk! swish!), groin-kicking (gawd, bet that hurt!) and coup-de-grace administering (hell, I think I've pulled a muscle) and I think we can just about call that done. Now, I don't for one moment suppose there'd be such a thing as ten foot of stout chain anywhere about the place? Well, fancy that.

A moment later, Regalian stood up, brushed himself off and admired his handiwork.

'Get out of that one, Smiler,' he said chirpily, 'and I'll buy you a drink. So long.'

One good thing. All that chasing about had given the tape time to rewind. There's nothing so boring as just standing about waiting.

To business. The tape he'd so painstakingly prepared consisted of ten extracts from cosy English whodunnits, interleaved with ten of the purplest bits of American hard-boiled pulp crime he could find. A little careful editing and mixing, so that the two tracks ran simultaneously. Play back the tape, and if he'd got it right there'd be a reaction similar in nature (and violence) to the meeting of matter and anti-matter. Hey presto, one character bomb, which (with any luck) would tear great big ragged holes in the fabric of crime writing, through which he could sneak. Although it's virtually impossible to guarantee where you'll end up, he had a rough idea of the likeliest place. Once there, of course, he'd be on his own and quite probably facing overwhelming odds and certain death, but so be it. He was used to that. He'd faced certain death so many times in his career that he knew every last pimple on its nose.

Before that, though, he'd be really wickedly irresponsible and selfish, and make himself a sandwich. No point in visiting Reality and going home without having first sampled the local cuisine.

No sandwich, because no bread. After some soul-searching and cupboard-searching he found an old tin of corned beef, a jar of pickled cabbage, a can opener and a bottle of Schlitz beer. Scarcely a heroic banquet; but after a few mouthfuls he'd had enough, and enough is reckoned to be equivalent, all things being equal, to a feast. Anyway, he drank the beer. It was flat, and there were small white bits in it. Then he washed the plate and glass (please leave Reality as you would wish to find it), combed his hair and had a pee—

Always wanted to do that; but in Fiction, you don't, somehow . . .

—And wandered back into the kitchen. Zero hour. Time to set off the bomb.

This time, the bounty hunter hit him between the shoulder blades with a brass candlestick.

CHAPTER ELEVEN

H amlet was bored.
    True, Mr Holmes had plenty of books; but they were all called things like *A Manual Of Forensic Toxicology* and *Wilkinson On Rigor Mortis*, whereas what Hamlet could have done with was a nice, easy-paced whodunnit. Aside from reading, there was nothing much else to do except hammer fruitlessly on the door (locked on the outside), carve his initials on the furniture and make peculiar noises with the violin.

And to think, he reflected bitterly, I chucked in my nice cushy job with Bill Shakespeare because I felt I was getting into a rut and wanted a bit of adventure. More fool me. All right, so it was a bit monotonous saying *exactly* the same words over and over again, but at least there was running about and swordfighting and stabbing people through soft furnishings, followed by a few drinks with the guys after the show. He glanced at the clock on the mantelpiece. Right now, back at the ranch, he'd be getting ready for the big duel scene. His favourite bit.

He stood up, walked round the edge of the Persian

rug three times without stepping on the tassels, pulled a handful of leaves off the aspidistra, found a small screwdriver in a drawer and started taking the handles off the writing desk.

There was a loud bang.

Well yes, you could call it that, just as you could describe the eruption of Krakatoa as a bit of a hiccup, or the San Francisco Earthquake as a traffic hazard. Accept that bang is an understatement, and leave it at that. Blame adjective rationing.

As the windows blew in and the broken glass rained round his head like windblown snow (better? Thank you) Hamlet felt a welcome surge of adrenalin, a pleasing quickening in his pulse rate. Ah, he said to himself, this is a bit more like it.

Like what?

Well, extreme danger, for starters; quite possibly sudden death. He rolled under the desk and put his head between his knees. A bolt of lightning seared across the room and blasted a hole in the far wall.

Me and my big mouth, huh?

The door flew open, and a body flew across the room. Hamlet recognised it as Mr Holmes. As it hit the wall with a horrible thump, he half expected to see a man-shaped hole in the brickwork, cartoon-style. Then the chandelier fell on top of the desk, and he ducked back down again, making *eeeek* noises.

Silence. Very tentatively, he poked his head out, satisfied himself that the fixtures and fittings weren't flying about any more and looked at the spot where Mr Holmes had landed.

'Hamlet?'

Hamlet frowned. 'Skinner?'

'Yeah. Over here.'

'Skinner?'

'Regalian?'

'Jane?'

'Titania?'

'All right, what is this, a ruddy prizegiving? Everybody come out, and let's see what goes on.'

Hamlet extricated himself, scrambling through trashed desk and over chandelier debris like a claustrophobic tortoise, to find that there was quite a crowd scene among the wreckage. There was:

Skinner.

Titania.

Jane.

Regalian—

'Look out!' he yelled, as the bounty hunter rose up from behind a splintered book-case and took a swipe at Regalian's head with the mashed-up residue of a violin. Regalian turned, saw him, clicked his tongue impatiently and threw him out through the open window.

'Christ,' said Skinner, dusting plaster out of his hair. 'How in God's name did we get here?'

'Coincidence,' Regalian answered. 'Time-honoured literary device. Everybody all right? Good. Nice to see you all again.'

'*Coincidence?*' Jane shrieked. 'Come off it, there's got to be more to it than that. Last thing I knew, I was in this Raymond Chandler book, and Philip Marlowe'd just shot me.'

'I was being poisoned to death in an Agatha Christie.'

'Were you really?' Regalian looked at them both. 'How did you come to be there?'

'Well—'

'Because,' said Claudia, entering melodramatically through the lightning hole in the wall, 'I sent you there. Hello, everyone.'

★   ★   ★

For every exit, an entrance.

It was a pool, and he was floating.

Or it was a sky, and he was a hawk with its wings spread, hovering motionless in the warm wind, a still point in an infinity of movement. Or it was the vast firmament itself, and he was a lone star surrounded by infinite blackness. That was nearer the mark, he reflected bitterly. Certainly, there was nobody to share his solitude. He had outlived them all, presumably. He invariably did.

As the focus sharpened, he became aware of the wood and satin around him, the sides of the box pressing his arms on both sides, the lid inches from his face. The confinement irritated him. He sniffed like a dog, but couldn't smell light. It was time to wake up.

Count Dracula, dead and alive, began to move in his coffin. Slowly, to begin with; even after all this time, he still savoured the first pleasure of movement after sleep with the intensity of a gourmet. He allowed his fingers to flex and stretch, like the claws of a cat extending. He tasted the sensation as his fingernails pressed into the satin lining. Touch is the first of the five senses to go, and the last to return. Of the five, it had always been his favourite.

He could feel the blood begin to move again inside his veins. Ah, the wonder of it! The sheer sensual pleasure of life, his great weakness, his addiction. It was at times like this that he almost believed it was all worth it. That was an illusion which rarely lasted for long, but he liked to make the most of it.

Time to leave this little cosy cell. He concentrated his mind, visualised the screws turning unassisted in the wood until the lid was unsecured. He could hear them dropping to the stone floor. He smiled; then he lifted his hands until he could feel the lid, and pushed up.

Funny . . .

Unseen hands grabbed the lid and pulled it out of his grasp. Perplexed, he opened his eyes, and found that he was staring up at a face.

Urgently he tried to sit upright, but the effort was too great and he sank back, snarling noiselessly like a dying fox. The face . . .

There were two of them now; one round, moon-shaped, with a squat snub nose and enormous thick-lensed spectacles, all under an ancient, oil-stained flat cloth cap; the other thin, lined, ancient, a cigarette stub apparently glued to the bottom lip. Their eyes seemed to bore into him, like a wooden stake.

'Igor.'

'Yes, young Norman?'

'Tha knows what's happened.'

'What?'

'Dozy boogers've delivered t'wrong bloody crate, that's what.'

'Tha reckons?'

'Look at it, will tha? Does that look like a bloody flat-pack wardrobe to thee?'

Count Dracula cleared his throat. 'Excuse me,' he said. The faces glowered at him.

'Bloody 'ell,' growled the old one. 'Another flamin' southerner.'

'Excuse me,' Dracula insisted. 'This isn't Transylvania, is it?'

'Tha what?'

'Transylvania,' the Count repeated helplessly. 'You know, down from Hungary and across a bit.'

The younger face scowled at him. 'Nay, lad, this is Dewsbury.'

'Yorkshire.'

'Yorkshire?' Dracula mouthed the unfamiliar syllables as if carefully spitting out a gnat. 'England?'

'We've got a right one 'ere, Norman lad. Tha's right, choom. Yorkshire, England. Where was it tha said tha was from?'

'Trans—' Dracula gave it up. 'Europe,' he said.

'Figures.'

'Look at 'is clothes, for pity's sake.'

For the first time in several centuries, Dracula became suddenly aware of his black, silk-lined cape and shiny black shoes, and wished his working clothes were – well, a trifle less flashy. A nice, comfy old raincoat, perhaps, or a properly broken-in tweed jacket, with leather patches on the elbows. And a flat cap too, of course.

'If tha's coom to t'wrong address, tha can bloody well pay thy own return postage,' said the round face. 'Ah've only got me pension, tha knows.'

Dracula licked his lips, which were as dry as paper. Suddenly he felt horribly thirsty. 'Excuse me.'

'Now what?'

'Could I trouble you gentlemen for, um, something to drink?'

'Huh? Such as?'

'Bl—' Dracula clamped his mouth shut on the word, biting it in two. 'A glass of milk would be fine,' he said meekly.

'There's tea in t'pot,' grunted the old one. ''Tis cold, mind.'

'That'll be fine, really,' Dracula whimpered. 'I'd be ever so grateful.'

He lay back in the coffin and wished he was dead.

A brief note, in passing, about the Scholfield.

Developed in 1875 as Smith & Wesson's answer to Colt's classic Peacemaker series, the Scholfield model was a heavy-calibre, top-break high-quality service-type revolver, featuring double as well as single action lock operation, an improved cylinder latch and simultaneous ejection of the spent cases. Although less powerful than the Colt, it probably deserved a better reception than it in fact received. However, with the military content to perservere with the single-action-only Colt, and the civilian market dominated by the Hartford marketing machine . . .

Yes. Quite. That's a bit like devoting the whole of your guide book entry on Florence to the corporation dump; factually accurate, but somehow missing the point.

Which is, that the Scholfield is the only personal sidearm so far invented whose IQ rating would qualify it for Mensa membership. Forget your smart missiles; compared with the Scholfield, smart missiles are Laurel and Hardy. The only reason Scholfield revolvers don't dominate all the top-league chess championships is that the only way they'd be able to move the pieces around is by shooting them.

Puzzled? Something wrong here? You can't come to terms with the concept of a weapon that's smarter than you are? Think. Weapons are for fighting; but when fighting occurs it's not the *weapons* that get hurt, is it?

Claudia.

So far, we've only taken note of her in her capacity as the universe's foremost, pushicst, most go-getting agent; a significant role, heaven knows, but really only a sideline, ancillary to her principal field of activity.

Claudia has this production company, A. C. Productions. It hasn't actually produced anything yet, but the same goes for 99.997% of all production companies everywhere.

She also has a Property; quite possibly the hottest property in the cosmos. All she's waiting for is the right time and the right people.

The time is now. The people are here.
Roll 'em.

'Hello, everyone,' said Claudia. She was smiling. When agents smile, wise men and women hide under things or charter fast aircraft; but this was a *special* smile. Her face looked like a black hole with a star just disappearing down it.

Regalian looked at her. 'I know you, don't I?' he said. She nodded.

'Everybody knows me,' she replied. 'Oh, excuse me just one moment.'

She stooped down and picked something up off the floor. It was the Scholfield. She thumbed back the hammer and pointed it at Regalian's head.

'Hey . . .'

'Later,' she said. 'I'm on a tight schedule. Now then, everybody, listen carefully. I expect you'd like to know why I've brought you all here.'

Skinner nodded cautiously, his eyes fixed on the revolver. There was something about the gun's manner he didn't like. He knew, of course; you don't spend thirty-six years with a chatty handgun without being able to sense its moods. The Scholfield was . . .

In *love*?

Oh dear. It was probably the masterful way she'd swept it off the ground and jerked the hammer back. At last, he could hear the gun saying to itself, at last I've found a soulmate, a megalomaniac psychotic with a steady eye and sweaty palms. Skinner sucked his teeth thoughtfully.

'Actually,' he said, 'if we could start with *how* you brought us here, that would probably be quite helpful. If you don't mind, that is.'

'Sure.' Skinner's guess was right. Tight schedule or no

tight schedule, Claudia wasn't the sort of girl who'd pass up on a chance to dwell on her own cleverness. 'I bought the rights.'

'What? To Agatha Christie? And Sherlock Holmes?'

'No.' Claudia's smile broadened, until the doomed star went supernova. 'To you.'

'I beg your—'

'You're in Fiction, right? You're all fictional characters. So, I bought the rights. I own you.'

'You can't own us!' Jane snapped. 'We're human.'

'So? I bought the human rights. Sure, I know they're supposed to be inalienable, but everything has a price.' She grinned. 'In this business, anyway. And that means,' she continued, twitching the gun an inch or so until Jane could see straight down the muzzle, 'I can do anything I want with you. Including change the ending. That's a threat.'

Jane, who was on the point of being extremely eloquent, decided not to be.

'Anyhow,' Claudia went on, 'all I had to do then was bring you all together. Wasn't difficult. In fact, Regalian here made it very simple by rigging up that bomb contraption. All I had to do was nudge you two into Agatha Christie and slide you across into Chandler. He was in Sherlock Holmes already. I'd already sent Max to bring Regalian back out of Reality, but I needn't have bothered, since as it turned out he did that for me.'

Regalian quivered slightly. 'Max?'

'The bounty hunter. Sorry if he was a nuisance.'

'*Max?*'

Claudia shrugged. 'It happens to be his name. Where's he got to, by the way? Anybody seen him?'

'I threw him out of that window there,' Regalian said. 'I expect he's all right, though. He seems pretty hard to damage.'

As if on cue, the bounty hunter limped through the door, trailing his left leg.

'Hi, Max.'

'Howdy.'

Claudia frowned. 'Max, dear,' she sighed, 'I know you've been under cover for rather a long time, but I do hope you haven't gone completely native.'

'It's been thirty-six years years, ma'am. A body kinda gets used to it.'

'Max, please try and speak something approximating to English, or if you can't, just keep quiet and kill people when I tell you to. Thirty-six years,' she added with feeling. 'That's ever such a long time, isn't it?'

Hamlet, who had spent the last few minutes trying to work out who was who and what was going on, interrupted. 'Just a minute,' he said. 'Are you trying to say it was *you* . . . ?'

'Ah!' Claudia beamed ironically. 'That faint tinkling sound you just heard, ladies and gentlemen, was the penny finally dropping, proving that gravity always gets its coin in the end. Now then, are we all with it and up to speed? Then I'll begin.'

'Just a minute.' This time it was Titania. 'I still don't follow. Odd, because usually I'm quite fluent in gibberish. Mind you, it helps if it's spoken in a strong sane accent. What do you want us *for*?'

Claudia breathed in. The expression on her face suggested that her patience was overdrawn to the point of demanding the card back. 'If you'd let me get a word in,' she said, 'I'll tell you. I have this project.'

'And?'

'And I need you for it. Actually you weren't my first choices, but Costner was busy, Redford was quite keen but something cropped up and Streisand's people kept making difficulties and Connery was just too expensive . . . You'll do.'

'What *for*?' Titania insisted.

'Cute little property I own the rights to.'

'Which is?'

Claudia stopped smiling and looked grave; messianic, even. She looked like a cross between Jesus Christ and Richard Attenborough receiving an award.

'The end of the world,' she said.

It was some time later.

'Blackcurrant,' mumbled Regalian with his mouth full. He spat out a wad of hemp fibre and returned to his task.

'I still don't get it,' Titania went on. 'I mean, if the ghastly woman wants us for this *project* of hers, why whisk us away to this place—'

'Wherever it is,' Jane interrupted sourly. Her gag had tasted of peppermint, and she loathed peppermint. 'Nobody saw fit to tell us where we are. It's as bad as going by train.'

'—And leave us here? Doesn't make sense. And all that garbage about owning the rights to the end of the world.'

Regalian chewed. The way he saw it, he only had one pair of jaws. He could use them for explaining, or he could use them for gnawing his way through a thick, tough, blackcurrant-impregnated rope. He knew precisely where they were, and he had a pretty shrewd idea of why they were there. In due course, he would have to explain to the others, and put up with their reaction. His chief regret at present was that the rope wasn't thicker.

As for Jane; she spat a couple of times to clear at least some of the foul taste out of her mouth, and found herself looking at Regalian.

Her hero.

Gosh.

In all the excitement of materialising and being threatened with guns and then scooped up by some agency she
hadn't even tried to understand and deposited here, whatever here was – it had, well, slipped past her attention
that here she was, suddenly, face to face with her character. Her hero. The closest thing, she supposed, to her
child; except that in *Bloodblades of Shimmaroon* she'd
pegged his age at thirty-six . . .

Pause for thought. The recurring number thirty-six; if
there was any correlation between real and fictional,
Regalian was born the year Skinner disappeared. Gosh,
she thought. Nuts, she thought.

Her hero. Flesh of her brain, blood of her imagination
– it was little short of a miracle, given her powers of
character-drawing, that he could walk in a straight line
without falling over or bumping into things, and yet there
he was, tall, strong, wise, resourceful, handsome, coura-
geous, tied up with rope . . . I did that, she told herself,
with my little Apple. Or did I?

My dream man? My wish-fulfilment? When I made
you, did I really want you to abseil in through my window
and carry me off to the Castle of Flangorien, far beyond
the twin seas of Ghar? Now then, be honest.

But you aren't *him*. I tried to make you my dream
lover, but that's not how you turned out. I tried to make
you the man I'd want to be if I was a man, but you
wouldn't play ball with that, either. And I don't think I
was being unreasonable; I didn't insist that you stay
home and do your homework, or try and force you into
medical school. When I was a young girl, staring at the
walls and dreaming, I started to write a book, just for
my own amusement, and you were there. Perhaps it was
just that you were young then, too; but when, on a freak

million-to-one shot, the twelfth publisher I sent my outline and sample chapters to wrote back and offered me a contract . . .

Jane looked away. She remembered.

We like the book, they said. We think you've got something there. We like the imaginary world, and the kingdoms and the battles and the dragon and the wizards and the mages and the princesses and the long-lost princes disguised as swineherds and the Talisman of Jarg and the Nine Rings of Being and the Death's Head of Khong, which will look great on the cover and, if we strike lucky, maybe we can have T-shirts too, perhaps even key-rings. But you've got to fix the hero. The hero sucks. Sorry.

No problem. I can fix the hero. You want to see how quickly I can fix the hero? Wait there, I'll be right back.

And so, my hero, I fixed you; I fixed you *good*. I think it was round about then that I lost you as well, stopped hearing you in my head as my fingers peck-peck-pecked at the keyboard. No matter; I could imagine, which is almost the same thing but not quite. And now, ten books later, we meet and I don't recognise you at first. My, haven't you grown. The beard suits you. You've lost weight. And whoever gave you the idea you could wear green with your complexion?

My hero. I don't know what to say.

'God,' Regalian spluttered, 'but I *hate* blackcurrant.'

I must remember that, Jane told herself. And then it struck her that, unless he was doing a very good job of controlling his emotions (improbable), he hadn't shown the slightest interest in her. You'd have thought – Jesus, I'm practically this guy's *god*. I *created* you, buster.

But not in my own image.

Yeah. So what? If on day minus one God had managed against all the odds to get a contract on the basis of a synopsis and ten chapters and they'd told Him, God, we love it but lose all the goody-goody stuff, wouldn't He have done the same? In the beginning was the Word, and the Word was negotiable. It always is.

'Jane,' my mother always used to say, 'Jane, when are you going to grow up and make something of your life?' Hey, Mum, your wish is granted. Admittedly, what I'm making of my life is a pig's ear, but you never properly defined *something*. All your fault.

Maybe he isn't mine. Maybe he belongs to my editor and the publicity department and the marketing boys and the art department and the sales reps and W. H. Smith and maybe, even, the goddamn readers, but not to me. Maybe, my hero, you belong to you. In which case, go write yourself.

Does it matter? You're here and, here, you're *real*; rather more so than I am, I suppose. What does that make us? Pen pals?

'Jane.'

My God, he's talking to me. She pulled herself together, tried not to blush or stare; dammit, I refuse to be sixteen again for anybody. 'Yes?'

'There's something,' Regalian said – he was looking at her – 'I always wanted to ask you. I guess now's as good a time as any.'

'Okay.' Jane nodded, kept her voice steady. 'Fire away.'

'On page 746 of the fourth volume of *Wishblades of Pondara*,' Regalian said, 'there's an earthquake, remember? I come out of the burning temple, okay, I've got sixteen blood-crazed Thargs after me, the tsunami invoked by the Mad Mage is about to take out the whole of downtown T'zpoom with devastating loss of life, the princess is trapped in the ruined castle with revolting Lord Sna'haz and his twelve unspeakable cronies, and what do you make me do? Well?'

'I . . . I can't remember.'

'You can't remember,' Regalian echoed, ominously calm. 'Fine. Let me refresh your memory. You have me stop dead in the middle of the market place, bloody great big chunks of flying masonry and falling roofbeams missing me by inches – see this scar on my nose? That's your fault, that is – you make me sit down on a fallen pillar and spend six pages analysing my relationship with my parents. Why was that?'

Time stood still and nothing happened, except that Jane's face grew steadily more reminiscent of a high quality sunset (or, if you prefer, a beetroot). Eventually she spoke.

'Wasn't me.'

'I beg your pardon?'

'Wasn't me. It was my editor. Said you needed more depth and motivation. So I, er, gave you some.'

'*In the middle of a fucking earthquake?*' Regalian was staring at her, his mouth open. 'You stupid bloody woman. I could have been killed. There were people dying, I could have been saving them. And you had me pratting about down there because some guy told you I needed to be a fully rounded human being? Of all the—'

'I'm sorry,' Jane whimpered. 'But I was three weeks behind and there was nowhere else I could fit it in, and . . .'

Regalian scowled her to silence. 'Not only that,' he said. 'Where did you get off, saying all that about my mother? You never even met my mother. How *dare* you—?'

'But you haven't *got* a mother,' Jane wailed. 'I *created* you. Surely you can see that—'

'What are you gibbering about, woman? What, you think the stork brought me? Hellfire, you're even sadder than I thought.' He looked away, as if considering something. 'Just my luck, eh? All the books by all the authors in all the world, and I have to walk into yours.'

He bit savagely into his rope, and Jane was glad, briefly, that it was blackcurrant. Compared to the ingratitude of characters, she told herself, serpents' teeth are about as sharp as traffic bollards.

Skinner, who had been eavesdropping with a facetious grin on his face, cleared his throat. 'Hey,' he said.

'Yeah? What do *you* want?'

'How much longer are you going to be with those goddamn ropes?' Skinner demanded. 'We gotta get out of here.'

Regalian laughed. There was about as much humour in his laughter as there's meat in an industrial-grade catering sausage. 'I wouldn't worry if I were you. Even when we're free of all this blasted string, we aren't going anywhere. I think all the rope and gags were just in case we felt like a snack.'

'How do you know?'

Regalian smiled wanly. 'Because I've been here before,' he replied. 'And once seen, never forgotten, believe me.'

'Been here *before*?' Jane looked at him, confused. 'How could you have? I've never written anywhere like this.'

'We're not in a book,' Regalian answered. 'Not one specific book, anyway. We're in lots of books. In fact, this is probably the biggest concentration of fiction anywhere in the whole dimension. Trust me, after you've been here any length of time, you'll be *pleased* to be in on the end of the world. Probably that's what she was thinking of,' he added ruefully.

Titania sniffed. 'All right, Mister Clever,' she muttered. 'So where—?'

'I was coming to that. Welcome, ladies and gentlemen, to the Slushpile.'

Abandon hope, all ye who enter here.
Listen.

Listen carefully. You hear it? Good. Listen to it for any length of time, and you'll realise how easily that noise could come to fill the whole universe.

Scribblescribblescritchscritchtippytippytaptap

That, as if you didn't know, is the sound of people writing novels. In every street in every town in every country in every continent on every planet in every solar system in every galaxy in every one of an infinity of alternative universes, there's at least one would-be novelist out word hunting tonight. The brash, the earnest, the very sad, the hopeful, the hopeless, the divinely inspired and the cruelly deceived, those with talent and those with none – is there anybody in all creation who doesn't believe, deep in the secret part of his soul, that he hasn't got at least one blockbusting smash bestseller lurking inside him like an eighty-thousand-word tapeworm bursting to get out? Tales of adventure, tales of true love, thrillers and chillers with chainsaws and gibbets, smut, spit and sawdust, confused lust in Islington and glossy lust in Tinseltown, Martians and monsters, clogs, shawls and cobblestones, a million different versions of the Holy Grail (in the trade they call it Cup and Sorcery), every permutation on every theme and not one of them knowingly undertold. Here's a chartered actuary in Cheltenham dreaming of lost Nazi gold, there's a sentient silicone isotope from the Teacup Nebula carefully plotting out its own weird version of the universal Tolkien derivative. The very chair you sit on probably has the first three hundred pages of its Great Furniture Novel tucked down behind its cushions. So much activity, so much blood, tears, toil and sweat – dear God, so much raw inspiration and uncut ability – and 99.9999999999999999999% of it futile and in vain.

Every publishing house has a cellar, warehouse or disused nuclear bunker where the unsolicited manuscripts go. They call it the Slushpile, and it makes a cemetery look like Mardi Gras. At least the graveyard residents have lived, even if very horribly or very briefly. The Slushpile hasn't. Try to imagine a more dreadful place than this. Can you? You can? You need professional help as a matter of urgency.

And in every novel in the pile, characters; imaginary men and women, pink rabbits and cuddly bears, trolls, treens and sentient silicone isotopes who've all been arbitrarily summoned into existence and left here to rot. And here's a charming thought for you; they outnumber the population of Reality by God knows how many to one. Maybe they brood. Quite possibly, they feel a sense of grievance. For good reason, the walls of the Slushpile are thick.

'Yes,' Regalian went on, 'I was here once. *She* sent me here. I was lucky, I was only in here for eighteen months. The others . . .' His words tailed off, and he sat staring for a minute and a half without speaking. 'Here's one bit of good advice,' he said eventually. 'You two. Whatever you do, *don't* tell any of the inmates that you're – you know.'

'No. What?'

'The W-word,' Regalian hissed. 'Rhymes with lighters, fighters and blighters. People who do the W thing aren't popular down here. You'd last about as long as a side of beef in a piranha tank.'

'Ah,' said Skinner, 'I got you. Thanks for the warning.'

'Whiters?'

'Shut up.' Regalian took a deep breath and set about the remaining strands of rope, pausing occasionally to gag and spit. To judge by his expression, even home-made cakes bought at village flower shows never tasted this bad.

'Right,' Hamlet said. 'Now I think I see. If she's an agent—'

Titania nodded. 'They'd follow her to the ends of the earth; anything, just for the hope of a chance. And there must be—'

'Billions of them,' Regalian confirmed. 'All of them baying for blood. Instant holocaust; just find some way for them to cross over the line into Reality—'

'The way we've been doing . . .'

Regalian spat out hemp, and tugged. The ropes gave way. He fell forwards, picked himself up and began scouring the ground for a sharp-edged stone. 'Personally,' he said. 'I'd be inclined to get out of here, if at all possible. Suggestions, anyone?'

There followed a long, embarrassed silence, during which Regalian sawed rope with his sharp stone. Eventually Skinner cleared his throat. He wasn't quite sure how he'd become the spokesman; he just knew that he was. In the absence of relevant previous experience, vocational training or a copy of *So You Want To Be A Spokesman?*, he took a deep breath and charged in.

'Look,' he said, 'no offence, but . . .' Having signposted, as if with neon lights and a three-month advertising campaign, the fact that he was about to say something offensive, he dried up. Obligingly, Regalian filled in the gap.

'I'm the hero,' he prompted. 'Why don't I get off my butt and do something? Yes?'

'Mphm.' Skinner nodded. 'I mean, that's not to say you haven't done an awful lot already. You have.'

'Thank you for noticing.'

'But . . .' Another deep breath. 'Shit, this is your damn dimension. I've been in it thirty-six years and I haven't a clue how it works. *She's* no use. *He's* no use . . .'

'Excuse me,' said Titania acidly. 'Which she were you referring to?'

'Which leaves you. Also,' Skinner added, feeling the

argument might lend weight, 'there's that crazy broad who's planning to blow up the planet. I mean, if stopping her isn't hero work, what is?'

Regalian nodded. 'Point taken,' he said. 'Trouble is, I've got absolutely nothing in the way of a plan. Usually I have. Not this time.' He sat down and put his head in his hands. 'Pretty strange feeling, actually,' he continued. 'Being a hero, you come to expect it; you know, the flash of inspiration, the perfectly timed brainwave. When suddenly it isn't there, you feel . . .' He waved his hands vaguely. 'Disorientated. It's like happening to glance down and noticing that someone's stolen your trousers while you were wearing them. Anyway, the fact is, I don't know what to do. Hence the request for ideas.'

'I know what to do,' Titania said.

'I mean,' Regalian went on, 'there must be something. There's always *something*. Doesn't matter how harebrained it is. If a lifetime in the heroism business has taught me anything, it's that the dafter the plan, the more likely it is to succeed. But dammit, I can't even think of a *sensible* idea. I'm going to get a complex about it in a minute.'

'I know what to—'

Skinner rubbed his chin. 'Maybe the idea's there and you just can't recognise it,' he said. 'I remember when I was writing the big scene in *North Of The Pecos* . . .'

'I said I know what to—'

'Quiet!' Skinner turned, scowling. 'How can the poor guy concentrate with you chattering away? You have no idea—'

'But I *do*,' Titania snarled, 'that's the *point*. If only you'd listen.'

Regalian looked up. 'Figures,' he said. 'I mean – no disrespect – she must be with us for some reason. I reckoned she was a love interest, but I think I was mistaken there. I'm morally certain she's not the comic relief, and there's no luggage to carry or washing to do, so—'

'Hey!' Titania glowered at him. 'Just listen to yourself, will you?'

'I thought we were meant to be listening to you.'

Skinner shrugged. 'Changed her mind,' he said.

'Woman's prerogative,' Hamlet added.

'*Hey!*'

'Now she's offended.'

'Notoriously thin-skinned, women.'

'That's why they're so unreliable, I guess.'

'Not like us.'

'Exactly.'

'*HEY!*'

'I hate it when they get all shrill,' Hamlet muttered. 'So undignified.'

'Better hear her out. I suppose.'

'Might as well. Otherwise it'll be floods of tears.'

'The tears aren't so bad, it's when they stamp their feet—'

'*WILL YOU THREE CLOWNS JUST SHUT UP!*' Titania suggested. 'And you,' she said, rounding on Skinner, 'you ought to know better. Those two, Captain Machismo and Mister Get-thee-to-a-nunnery-but-first-darn-my-socks, they're heroes, they can't help it. You've got no excuse.'

Skinner smirked. 'Product of my time,' he said. 'Very much a 'fifties thing. Where I come from, women stay home and jump on chairs if they see a mouse.'

'You were right,' Hamlet whispered. 'She isn't a love interest.'

'That's okay, then.'

'You're telling me,' Skinner said. 'I was worried. Sorry, you were saying something?'

'Hang on a minute,' Jane interrupted. 'This isn't right.

All this crass male stuff's a bit sudden, isn't it? Where's it all coming from?'

'It's this rotten place,' Regalian groaned. He was deliberately looking away, not catching anyone's eye. 'All these horrible books we're surrounded by. It's making us revert to type. The longer we stay here, the more cliché-ridden we become. That's why it's so important that we get out of here quick. If we stay here much longer, we'll just be cardboard cut-outs. Sorry,' he said, turning back to Titania. 'Boys' talk. You were about to suggest something.'

Titania, who now understood, nodded. 'It's really quite simple when you think about it. All we've got to do is get a message to the other side. Reality. Find someone who can *write* us out of here.'

Jane raised an eyebrow. 'Come again?' she said.

'That means you,' Titania replied. 'Think about it. You're working on a book right now, yes?'

Jane nodded. 'Hopelessly overdue,' she said sadly. 'Deadline like yesterday. If I ever get out of here, I'm going to be in serious trouble.'

'Great!' Titania clapped her hands together in joy. 'So if you deliver a completed manuscript, it'll get rushed straight off and into production?'

Jane shrugged. 'I suppose so. But how does that help?'

'Easy.' Titania was pacing up and down, excited. 'Get someone else to write the book for you, with us in it as characters. It's as simple as being lifted out of here by transporter beam.'

'Yes, but who . . . ?'

Suddenly, Regalian began to grin. 'Nice idea,' he said. 'For a girl,' he added. To do him justice, he tried to stop the words coming out, but he couldn't. 'Let's just hurry it along, though, shall we, before I say something I'll really regret?'

'Yes,' said Jane, slowly and loudly. 'But who?'

'Easy,' Regalian answered. 'A ghost writer.'

A valid point Regalian has there, because writers never die.

Oh sure, there comes a day when they cease drinking and stop moving altogether, and after a while they start to whiff a bit and go all soft and squidgy, and unless something is done about it the public health people start sending you snotty letters; but the fact remains, writers enjoy a vaguely defined immortality. So long as their books survive, so do they.

Dead and alive, as it were. Or undead, if you prefer.

You can see where this is leading . . .

Cautiously, Dracula lifted the lid and peered out.

God, he muttered to himself, I *hate* Reality. It's cold, the satin in the coffin feels like sandpaper, and horrible people from Yorkshire peer down and stare at you like you were some sort of *freak* . . . Wouldn't be seen dead in a place like this.

Quite.

The *indignity* of it all. Bundled back into his coffin without so much as a quick nibble at a soft white neck, then bumped and jostled about for hours in what he gathered was something called the Postal System, and left somewhere. God knows where. A less even-tempered bloke might get quite angry.

Dracula, however, had always made a practice of not letting the sun go down on his wrath (or, for obvious reasons, on his *anything*); accordingly he'd taken a deep breath, thought a happy thought, sniffed for sunlight (all clear) and thought the screws out of the woodwork. And now here he was; a little bruised, a trifle battered, but all in one piece and ready for a hard day's night. He pushed aside the lid and scrambled out, snagging his cape on a splinter.

Because he'd never been in a sorting office before, he hadn't a clue what the place was. All he knew was that it felt *sinister*. The nearest he'd ever been to something like this was the crypt under the castle chapel back in dear old Transylvania. Crypts he felt at home with; cool, dark places with somewhere to put your feet up and a nice selection of packed lunches. This was different. There was a malevolence here he couldn't begin to understand. Gave him the creeps.

Buck up, he told himself. None of this moping. Let's bustle about and try and find something useful, like a door or a window.

And so he began his misguided tour of the building. He walked past the letter racks, the parcel shelves, the recorded delivery section . . .

The dead letter cupboard . . .

He glanced down.

COUNT VLAD DRACULA
To be held until called for.

He frowned. It wasn't a totally unfamiliar concept. Given his habit of going to sleep for long periods of time, he would often leave himself little notes – the deeds to the castle are in the safe, the back door key is on the hook in the scullery, the bin men call on Wednesdays, that sort of thing – and lodge them with lawyers or bank managers marked *Not to be opened for fifty years*. Presumably, this was one of those letters. Maybe – with any luck – it might tell him what he was doing here, and how he could get home again. He slid a finger under the flap and tore.

Dear Count Dracula,
I was wondering if you could help. My name's Jane

Armitage, and I'm a writer. It's a long story, practically
a trilogy, but here I am, stuck in Fiction, and there you
are stuck in Real Life. So, you help me and maybe I can
do something for you. How does that sound?

'Slow down,' Jane muttered.

Titania frowned. 'Sorry,' she said. 'Where did you get
up to?'

'*Sound.* Before you carry on,' Jane continued, 'I still
don't get it. How do you know Dracula's going to be
there, and how are we going to get this letter to him? It
all seems a bit crazy to me.'

'Basic authorship theory,' Regalian interrupted.

'Ah,' said Jane wearily. 'That old thing. Go on.'

'It's perfectly logical,' Regalian said. 'We use the dead
letter system. Direct line from here to there.'

Jane scratched her neck just behind the ear, thinking.
She could see the similarity between letters that nobody
wanted and books that nobody would ever read; perhaps
that was all the logic it took. She wasn't about to argue,
but . . .

'And Dracula?' she said. 'Bit of a long shot, surely.'

'Ah,' Regalian agreed, 'there perhaps we're pushing our
luck a bit, I'll grant you. What we're counting on is the
system of exits and entrances.'

'Equations,' said Titania helpfully.

'Equations,' Regalian confirmed. 'When you came into
Fiction, that bounty hunter bloke – Max, was it? – got
pushed out, or wanted to leave, one or the other. But he
came back in when I did, which means somebody else
must have been shot out into Real Life.' He paused, as
if suddenly appreciating the flaw in his own argument.
'The key word, I think, is life. Look at it this way. If you
take young Hamlet's big question, to be or not to be,
Dracula's a definite Don't Know.'

'Floating voter,' Titania chimed in. 'Ambivalent.'

Regalian nodded. 'Good word. Ambivalent. So it's a reasonable bet that, in the absence of volunteers to be shot through into Reality, Dracula's a likely victim when the press gang comes round. There's all sorts of clever maths which Titania can show you if you suffer from particularly bad insomnia, but I think that's the bare bones of it. I have,' he added, 'heard sillier arguments in my time, if that's any help. Plus, we do have basic heroism theory, which states that the daffier the plan . . .'

Jane sniffed. 'This is obviously a complete waste of time,' she said. 'Absolutely no way—'

'Hey!' Titania stamped her foot, hating herself as she did so. 'Shut up, you, and take dictation.'

Having read the letter through twice, Dracula put it down on the office table, furrowed his brows and thought for a moment.

It sounded all right. A great many things do, of course. 'Just nip over there and secure those cannons, there's a good lad,' probably sounded reasonable enough to the commander of the Light Brigade. This is the triple-visaged goddess of Life in her aspect as Complete Bastard; you never know whether it's going to be all right until you try it. But still, it sounded all right.

The mission: to go to a specified address (for someone who can fly like a warp-engined bat, no big deal – and it was only a hundred or so miles away, scarcely long enough for the in-flight movie); to obtain access, again a piece of cake to the Count; to sit down in front of a keyboard and type in a few thousand words – and there was the truly amazing coincidence, because although he'd never even so much as mentioned it to anybody in passing, he'd always felt that, one of these days when the time was right and he didn't have much else on, he could sit down and write a really cracking good novel, because it can't be *difficult*, can it?

Then, it seemed, all he had to do was bung the completed typescript in an envelope and post it off to the address given in the letter, and he'd have earned himself the Reward. What the Reward was, the letter didn't exactly say, but it stood to reason, didn't it, that in all probability it was going to be red, liquid and jam-packed full of corpuscles. Unlike relatives by marriage, vampires are exquisitely simple to choose presents for. So, Dracula muttered to himself as he stood in the sorting-office window and spread his cape, here's to it.

Blood for old rope, you might say.

Jane sat back, folded the paper neatly and watched it disappear.

'Think he'll fall for it?' Skinner asked. 'I don't. So maybe he's not too bright—'

'Aristocracy.' Titania sniffed. 'Inbred, the lot of them. Daft as a bottleful of ferrets.'

'Hey,' Hamlet objected. 'I heard that.'

'Case in point,' Titania smirked. 'Even when you're completely sane, what's the summit of your intellectual capacity? Telling the difference between a medium-sized bird of prey and a carpentry tool. Watch out, Einstein, here comes Hamlet.'

Jane frowned. 'Settle down, you two,' she ordered. 'The point is—'

'Can we rely on the caped crusader to fall for the sucker ploy?' Skinner resumed. 'Furthermore, even if he's that dozy, will he be up to doing the job?'

'Good point,' said Jane, nodding sagely. She was thinking of the God-awful hole she'd written herself into; the fight between Regalian and Gordian in the arena of Perimadeia. Maximum security plot cock-up; escape is impossible. If Dracula managed to sort that out, it'd be a miracle. And very, very humiliating.

'Actually,' Skinner remarked, 'I don't see that as a problem. I've always found that people who live by sucking blood are highly efficient.'

Titania sniffed. 'That sounds like laying the groundwork for an Inland Revenue joke,' she said. 'If I were you, I'd leave it in embryo.'

'Get lost.'

It passed through Regalian's mind that, of all his many concerns, Skinner and Titania being a love interest was the least of them. Far from looking like an imminent pink hearts job, they sounded as if they were already married. He decided to call the meeting to order.

'Well,' he said, 'that's all we can do for the time being. If it's going to work, we'll know soon enough.'

'Will we?' Jane's forehead wrinkled. 'He's got a quarter of a book to write, hasn't he? That'll take him, oh . . .'

Regalian shook his head. 'Time's different here,' he replied. 'You've sent manuscripts to publishers, you should know that. My estimate, in fact, is any minute now . . .'

Dracula sat back in Jane's chair and grinned, cutting himself with his fangs as he did so. He didn't seem to notice. He was in a trance.

He'd been right. It wasn't difficult. Even though he'd had to go back virtually to the beginning and write the first three sections again, the words had dripped from his fingers as he typed. It was almost as if the characters had lives of their own.

A quick glance at the window revealed the first telltale smudges of pink. Dawn was on its way, time he was back under the bed. Pity. He was dying to read it through once more from the beginning. Boy, what a book!

As he lay luxuriously back among the fluff, odd slippers, dead beetles and other objects native to the space between bed and floor, he found himself wondering – again – why he hadn't done this before. Strange, the way people made out that there was some sort of mystique to novel writing, when it was easy as falling off a mantelpiece.

He'd even got a title: *Fangs For The Memory*. He liked that. Slick.

A serious problem with first novels, he knew, was the urge to make them thinly disguised autobiography. He'd resolved to avoid this at all costs and his hero, a tall, slim, good-looking young Transylvanian with a liking for fresh draught blood and a seven-foot wingspan, was about as unlike him as it was possible to get. To take only one example; Brad, his hero, impaled his enemies with birch stakes, whereas he'd always used hickory.

The other characters – Regalian, Jane, Skinner, Titania, Hamlet – had just kind of taken off of their own accord, but that was no bad thing. It allowed him to concentrate on Brad, his complex personality, his devastating taste in clothes, his lively wit, his success with women. For two pins, he'd start the sequel right now, while he was in the mood. He'd got a title for that, too; something along the lines of *The Vampire Will See You Now*. Needed fixing, maybe, but definitely along the right lines.

And then, he remembered, he'd be able to collect on the Reward.

Didn't seem fair, somehow; after all, he'd had such fun doing it. On the other hand, that's the writer's life for you. Half your time blissed out of your skull writing the book, the other six months feverishly spending the limitless wealth. It is, after all, a well-known fact that the average writer, on finding a genie issuing forth from a lamp he's been idly polishing and being asked to name his three wishes, would be hard put to it to think of a single one.

Still, now he came to think of it, he was feeling decidedly peckish. A little mild necking would do no harm at all.

Cue the Reward, please . . .

CHAPTER TWELVE

'Basic authorship theory,' Regalian answered.

Jane scowled. 'I'm beginning to get a bit tired of that particular phrase,' she said. 'Exactly which blindingly self-evident slice of dogma had you in mind?'

'Dogma,' Regalian repeated thoughtfully. 'Interesting word, that.'

'How much is that dogma in the window,' Titania chimed in, 'the one with the waggly—?'

'Shut up, you. The main thing to remember,' Regalian said, 'is that this book will be Dracula's first novel, right?'

'Presumably.'

'Oh, undoubtedly. Which is where basic authorship theory comes in. What you have to bear in mind is—'

The ground vanished.

For the first twenty-fifth of a second, nobody noticed. Inside the Slushpile, all surfaces are nondescript to the point of self-effacement. The proper adjective is *bleak*. After all, the place is little more than a rather more than usually desperate Job Centre, but without even the pretence of furniture or, indeed, walls. And in even the most godforsaken Job Centre in, say, Merseyside you'll always find one human touch; a framed photograph of wife and children on someone's desk, a postcard from some colleague's holiday resort pinned up on a notice-board, a grey-leafed, cigarette-burnt avocado plant hiding in a corner. Nothing like that in the Slushpile. So, when the ground suddenly became transparent and faded away, there were no instantaneous cries of *My God! Look!* It was really only when they started to fall through an apparently empty void and the old thirty-two-feet-per-second-per-second routine cut in that anybody paid it any heed.

'What the—?'

'Oh, good, it's worked.'

'Oh Christ, we're all going to—'

'What you have to bear in mind,' Regalian continued blithely, as an endless supply of nothing at all whistled past their ears, 'is that everybody's first novel invariably has the author as its hero. Which means—'

'*Aaaaaaagh!*'

'—That our friend with the pointy teeth will not only be in Reality, he'll now be in Fiction *as well*. And that,' Regalian added with a chuckle, 'is where we'll let him have his reward. Oh yes,' he added, with a certain degree of satisfaction, 'that'll be a positive pleasure. Someone he can really get his teeth into.'

Paul McCartney rarely goes shopping in Marks & Spencer these days. It's been ages since Sean Connery dropped in to a bar for a quiet drink and some peace and quiet. For roughly similar reasons, Claudia sent Max down to the Slushpile to see to the prisoners. Being mobbed by hysterical crowds can be so wearing.

He landed – no doors in the Slushpile, for the same reason that there are no window boxes on a submarine – a little bit off course; not on the deserted outskirts, where the prisoners had been dumped, but rather further in, which was a pity. Almost before he'd scrambled to his feet, a pack of scavenging characters came ambling up, eyes bulging, ribs visible in wasted carcasses, tongues lolling. He recognised them as heroines of attempted clog-and-shawl period romances, all naive innocence and demure cotton halter-neck dresses; but it was all right, he was wearing both his guns now, and after he'd shot five or six of them they went back the way they'd come, carrying their dead with them. They stayed pretty much out of his way after that, although he could hear the soft pad of their feet as they followed at a respectful distance. He did have an uncomfortable moment or two when a small knot of starved and crazy fugitives from the Danielle Steel cloning vats tried to jump him; even a .45 bullet isn't guaranteed to stop a Redditch housewife's idea of Joan Collins who hasn't eaten for three years, and Max was glad he'd remembered his Bowie knife. He gave the science fiction compound a very wide berth, however. You can't carry that much firepower and still walk upright.

Arrived safely. Checked both guns loaded, knife handy down leg of boot. Assumed gunfighter's roll.

'Howdy,' he said; and stopped, bewildered.

Nobody here.

Signs that they'd been there, not long since; chewed-through ropes and more discarded gags than a comedian's dustbin. Just no prisoners, that was all.

Rescued? Surely not. Eaten by characters? More likely, but if so, where were the bones? Even the fluffy kittens from the Children's colony would have left a few scraps of bone, if only for later. Being held hostage? Could be. He clicked his tongue impatiently. The last time they'd used this place as a temporary holding cell, he'd had to go in with a special operations unit to free Superman from a mob of fundamentalist hobbits. With Gatling gun ammunition running at twenty dollars a crate, he wasn't sure his budget would run to a repeat performance.

Gosh-danged pesky characters, he muttered to himself.

Whatever the situation, there was nothing to be gained from hanging about here. She would have to be told. The thought appalled him, but he had no option. It was rather like being Henry VIII's fiancée, looking at the seating plan for the wedding breakfast and seeing that the president of the executioners' co-operative is going to be sitting on the top table.

Just as he was about to give the order to be beamed up, he noticed something skulking in a shadow out of the corner of his eye. Nothing unusual in that; an awful lot of skulking goes on in the Slushpile. It's the nearest thing they have there to a rich cultural heritage. This, however, was skulking with intent to attract attention.

'Howdy,' he said.

The skulker (skulcator? skulksman?) shuffled a few steps forward, hesitated like a hungry alley cat, and then darted back into the shadows. Max sighed. This sort of thing could go on all night if he let it. He had two options, one of which was to establish a bond of trust and confidence between himself and the shy, wild creature a few yards away. He opted for the other.

'You in the shadow,' he said, drawing his gun and thumbing back the hammer. 'Come out before I blow your head off.'

The skulkster quivered a little and then crept towards him on hands and knees. Max recognised it as a Comic Irishman; very much a discontinued line, suggesting it had been here a very long time indeed.

'Top o' the morning to ye, sorr,' the creature hissed. 'An' will you be after bein' Herself's assisthant, faith an' begob?'

Max shuddered a little. A hundred years at least since

anybody's written a character like that. It'd be a kindness to put the poor thing out of its misery.

'Sure am, stranger,' he nevertheless replied.

The creature shuffled nearer, until he could see the poor mad gleam in its eyes. A century living with its own dialogue had long since turned its brains to mush. Pity tightened his finger on the trigger, professionalism restrained it.

'An' if I was to be after tellin' ye where thim newcomers might be after having got to,' the relic wheezed on, 'might ye not be afther considerin' puttin' in a good word with Herself for a pore ole comic relief that's been here since there was afther bein' snakes in dear ole Erin, begob and bejazus?' Then it started coughing and snuffling. Max felt slightly sick.

'Reckon so,' he forced himself to say. 'Figure the agent-lady's always on the scoutaround for—' He closed his eyes. '—promising young talent. Why don't you-all tell me what's on your mind?'

The creature told its tale while Max listened, occasionally nodding while the translator circuits in his brain began to glow white hot. When the narrative had finally spluttered to its barely comprehensible end, he nodded again.

'Thanks, partner,' he said, 'right neighbourly of you.' He glanced down, and just as a fresh wave of revulsion started to course through him, an idea slipped in through the cat-flap of his mind. 'Say,' he enquired, 'can you do Scottish too?'

'Och awa' wi' ye, mon,' drivelled the creature. 'Do ye no ken frae ma accent I was born beside the bonny braes of Strannochmuir? Also Welsh, look you. And Nondescript Rustic, arr—'

'Sure thing,' Max broke in quickly. It was a long time since he'd eaten, but there was still something left inside his digestive tract, and he didn't want it ending up all over his shoes. 'Reckon that Scottish stuff's what we done been looking for. Vacancy aboard the *Enterprise* for a chief engineer. Interested? If you are,' he added rapidly, 'just nod.'

The creature nodded.

'Right,' said Max, as the transporter beam hit him. 'We'll let you know.'

Six coffins . . .

'Hello?' Regalian shouted. 'Anybody there?' He desisted, and tried thinking instead. Logic: if this was, as he suspected, a coffin, then it followed that they were probably in a crypt. If that was the case, chances were there was nobody else in it with them; and if there was, he wasn't sure he *wanted* to be helped out of his nice safe box by one of them.

Think . . . It suddenly occurred to him that he knew how to get out of a coffin. You just apply your mind, and the screws that hold the lid on start to unscrew of their own accord. He tried it; and a moment later, he heard a tiny, distant tinkle, as of small metal objects falling on to a stone floor. He lifted his arms and pushed against the lid, which gave way. He sat up.

God, he thought, that was thirsty work. What I wouldn't give right now for a nice long cool pint of AB negative . . .

What?

Instinctively, his hand flew to his neck. Sure enough, he located a small, tender patch. A bruise, probably, and two tiny puncture marks.

Oh *spiffing.* Just what I need at this particular juncture.

Another lid fell away, and Skinner sat up, massaging his neck and looking as if he'd just received IBM's tax demand by mistake instead of his own.

'You too, huh?' Regalian said. 'It's true what they say about suckers; one born every minute.'

Skinner just swore. Not long after that, Hamlet emerged. His teeth had already started to grow, Regalian noticed gloomily. Those could be a problem, horrible great sharp things, but what could you do? Stick corks on the points?

'Girls?' he queried, 'Come on, we haven't got all day.'

Sure enough, the last two remaining lids fell away, revealing Jane and Titania. Both of them were rubbing their necks and running through a wide repertoire of non-verbal communications. What's the betting that, if you translated the thoughts, each one would prove to begin with the words *If ever I get my hands on the little* . . . Well, quite. They'd have to join the queue, that was all.

He hesitated. He counted. *Six* coffins. He remembered. He rubbed his hands together, and made noises indicative of evil satisfaction.

'I know you're in there,' he said. 'Out you come.'

'Shan't,' said a voice from inside the sixth coffin.

'Sure?'

'Yes.'

'Fine. Skinner, pass me the hammer. Titania, reach me over one of those pointed stakes. Yes, the oak will do fine. Hamlet, look lively and fetch the silver bullets . . .'

There followed the sound, by now familiar, of screws hitting flagstones, followed by the creaking of a coffin lid being raised. A white, ghastly face peeked over the lid.

'You rotten cheats!' it said. 'You haven't got any stakes after all.'

His heroic reflexes made it possible for Regalian to grab the coffin lid and wrench it out of Dracula's hands before he was able to do a snail impression. 'What's this, then?' the hero shouted, pointing to his neck with his free hand. 'And before you make any funny remarks, I may not be able to kill you with my bare hands, but I could have a lot of fun trying my very hardest and eventually failing.'

'All right,' whimpered the vampire. 'Point taken. Look, I can explain.'

'Oh good,' Jane growled. 'He can explain. That's all right, then.'

'It's for your own good,' the vampire said. 'Honest. I'd have thought you'd have worked that one out for yourselves.'

'Our own good?'

'That's right.'

'Being turned into sunlight-shunning, invisible-in-mirrors, make-mine-a-bloody-Mary-hold-the-Mary *vampires* for our own good, huh?'

'Yes.'

Regalian stood for a moment, hand on chin, thinking. 'Do you know something?' he eventually asked.

'What?'

'I think,' he said slowly, 'that the only reason people think you can't kill a vampire by shoving its head up its own arse is because nobody's ever actually tried it. What do you think, guys?'

Skinner nodded vigorously. 'Let's research,' he said. 'I love research. People tell me I should have been a professor or something.'

'Listen!' the vampire shrieked.

'Sorry?'

'Vampires, right? They're undead. Can only be killed with stakes or silver bullets.'

'Reputedly.'

'And now you're vampires, right? Think about it.'

'I'm trying not to, actually.'

'Please,' the vampire urged. 'Talk about helping you guys out. I mean, you lot *are* on the run from Claudia, with her dreaded henchman Max close on your tails. I'd have thought you'd be grateful.'

Regalian frowned. 'How did you know that?' he said quietly.

The vampire grinned feebly. 'Because,' he explained, 'they're standing right behind you.'

'Sure,' Regalian sneered. 'Pull the other one.'

'With pleasure,' said a female voice. Regalian spun round, and found himself peering down the muzzle of the Scholfield, so close that he could see the heads of the bullets in the cylinder. They weren't dull black, like lead, or orange and shiny, like copper-jacketed; more sort of white and shiny. 'Or rather, Max will do it. Max, get the block and tackle.'

Titania made a threatening noise. 'You won't get away with this,' she said. 'We outnumber you three to one.'

Claudia smiled. 'My dear girl,' she said, 'I admit there are half a dozen of you. Have you ever stopped to think where the expression "six-shooter" comes from?'

Titania shrugged. 'He might get one of us,' she said. 'That'd still leave five.'

'Actually.' Skinner edged forward, looking extremely embarrassed. 'Wouldn't try it if I were you. In *Rangers of Texas*, I had him shoot three flies off a cowpat at twenty-five yards in one second. He's good.'

'What harm had the cowpat done him?' asked Titania, interested.

Resignedly, Regalian raised his hands a token few inches, and then let them fall to his sides. 'All right,' he said, 'that'll do. So what happens now? Back to that horrible place again?'

Claudia shook her head. 'You should be so lucky,' she replied cheerfully. 'Time to go to work.'

Jane wrinkled her forehead. 'Excuse me,' she said to Claudia. 'You aren't *seriously* going to destroy the world, are you?'

'I'm not sure,' Claudia replied, picking at a loose thread

on her cuff. 'I may decide to do it seriously. Or I may go for the more frivolous treatment. Slapstick armageddon,' she mused. 'A remake of *Dr Strangelove*, something like that. I don't know, you've given me something to think about there. I do so like dealing with creative people.'

All this while, Dracula had been staring at Claudia's neck with a look of combined awe and hunger such as you might expect from a small boy who's been asked to look after a sweetshop for an afternoon. While Claudia was dealing with Jane's enquiry, Regalian nudged him in the ribs.

'Your oppo Realside,' he said. 'I promised him a reward for helping us out.'

'What? Oh, really. Yes.'

'What I figured was,' Regalian went on, 'if I paid you, it'd be the same as paying him. Agreed?'

'Hm? Oh sure, sure.'

'There you go, then.'

'What?'

'The reward.'

'What reward? Where?'

Half an inch of the side of Regalian's mouth twitched into a smile. 'You're looking at it,' he said. 'Admittedly, it's more sort of Pick Your Own rather than all packaged up in cellophane with a sell-by date, but you won't mind that. I mean, it positively guarantees that peak freshness you never seem to get with the store-bought stuff.'

At that moment, Max slewed round and brought the muzzle of the Scholfield in line with the point where Regalian's eyebrows met. 'Care to share the joke, partner?' he said.

Regalian stared at the gun; and as he did so, he saw something.

Thought he saw something. Surely he'd been mistaken. No, there it was again.

The gun had winked at him.

All right, let's get technical. It had rotated its cylinder one half-station, thus hiding the mouth of one chamber behind the front upright of the frame, before reversing the procedure and returning the cylinder to rest against the bolt and pawl. Same thing.

Accordingly, Regalian dived to the ground, rolled and reached out for Max's feet, with the intention of throwing him to the ground and wrestling the gun away from him. As he did so, he heard Max swear, out of the corner of his eye watched the gun tracking him, watched Max pull the trigger—

Click. Followed by click, click.

At the very edge of his vision, he could just make out Dracula lunging at Claudia, mouth open. By the time he'd connected with Max's ankles, he could faintly hear the sound of Dracula being dealt a horribly savage blow with an organiser bag. Never mind; concentrate on the job in hand, let the other five take care of Claudia.

In retrospect, that was a bit like America declaring that it would see to Martinique, while leaving Monaco and Lichtenstein to deal with China, Russia, Japan and the thousand-battlecruiser task force that'd just arrived that morning from Mars. At the time, however, it seemed reasonable enough; and he was too preoccupied with snatching the Scholfield from Max's hand and clubbing him half to death with the butt to spare too many thoughts for how the rest of the gang was getting on. It was only when he was back on his feet and turning the gun towards where Claudia had last been that he realised that something wasn't quite in accordance with his game plan.

'Where's she gone?' he snapped.

Jane, who was still on her feet, shrugged. Then she too fell over and went peacefully to sleep. Instinctively, Regalian sniffed.

The effect of the tiny free sample he'd taken in was almost enough to sweep him off his feet; but he managed to stagger back a few steps and sit down on an empty coffin in something approaching good order until his head stopped swimming and his eyes cleared. *Stupid!* He should have guessed. That old familiar sweet, fat smell.

Essence of Thomas Hardy, guaranteed to send you to sleep in one second flat. Presumably she had the stuff in an aerosol in her jacket pocket. Mace of the d'Urbervilles, or some such brand name.

He stood up again, swaying slightly (he recognised the symptoms; adjective poisoning) and cursing his own stupidity. As a result, she had made a clean getaway, off to wherever she could call up reinforcements; maybe even the editor's pencil. Nasty thought; back in the Slushpile for good, with no hope of escape.

At his feet, Max groaned and twitched slightly. Dammit, he hadn't even done that properly. His thumb was on the Scholfield's hammer, but he couldn't bring himself to cock and fire . . .

'Why not?'

'Because I'm a hero, you bloodthirsty object,' he sighed.

'I could go off accidentally,' the Scholfield replied helpfully. 'Just think how shaky your hand is after sniffing that loathsome stuff. Tragic accident, poetic justice . . .'

Regalian lowered his hand until the gun was pointing at the floor. 'Nice thought,' he said, 'but no thanks. Besides, you've bent the rules quite enough for one day, surely. Three misfires in a row?'

The Scholfield wriggled its cylinder by way of a shrug. 'Sidearm's discretion,' it replied. 'Did you like the wink, by the way? Took me ages to work out how to do that.'

'Neat,' Regalian answered. 'I owe you one. That doesn't extend, however, to wasting defenceless enemies. Save it for when I catch up with Madam.'

'You won't,' the Scholfield replied wearily. 'Take it from me. Usually I've got nothing against psychopaths, but in her case I'll make an exception. Compared to her, dear old Wild Bill was Gandhi.'

Regalian winced and sat down again, making sure the gun was pointing in a safe direction. 'So,' he said, 'you don't reckon I should go after her. What *should* I do?'

'Don't ask me for strategic advice,' the gun replied, 'I'm exclusively tactical. I'd suggest trussing that pillock up before he comes round, though. That's always assuming you still don't want me to—'

'Correct assumption.'

'Pity. All right. Not that there's much rope in a crypt. You'd better sling him in a coffin and screw down the lid.'

Regalian did so, and then sat on it, just to make sure. He'd had enough of taking chances for one day.

'The others are probably out for the next couple of hours,' the gun continued. 'Look on the bright side, though, it could have been Henry James.'

Regalian nodded. 'Hell of a way to go,' he agreed. 'But if I just hang around here till they wake up—'

'Madam'll have come back with the heavy mob long before then,' the Scholfield anticipated. 'You have a problem, I can see that. And this time, she'll be ready. Wooden stakes, big hammers . . .'

'Quite.' Regalian cupped his chin in his hands. 'Not so long ago, I thought fighting it out with trolls and goblins and crazed wizards was bad enough. Didn't know I was born.'

'Guaranteed to win, too,' the gun sympathised. 'Oh sure, I know you still had to do the actual smiting, but you knew there could only be one result. Bit different now, huh?'

'You could say that. Almost as bad as being in real life, I guess.'

The gun considered. 'Oil's better here,' it said, after a while. 'Better choice of ammunition. You rust less quickly. Otherwise not all that much to choose between them. Actually, I'm disappointed. I'd expected it to be great fun on this side.'

'But now you know better.'

'Sure.'

In the far, shadowy corner of the crypt, something scuttled, but Regalian ignored it. Whatever nameless thing it might be, it wasn't doing him any harm, it had its living to make, same as everybody else. Regalian had spent quite a lot of time in and around crypts during *Thoughtspears of S'nagharz*, and realistically speaking the worst thing that could happen to you in one, provided the doors didn't seize, was extreme boredom.

'I suppose,' he said at last, doing his best to shake off the feeling of lethargy that was doing its best to pick the pockets of his enthusiasm, 'I'd better go through the motions of making a fight of it. How about if I were to try and get these idiots somewhere safe?'

'Could do,' the Scholfield agreed. 'Of course, that might be easier than you think. Like, this is a crypt, they're all now qualified vampires.'

'So?'

'So,' the Scholfield continued, 'the basic life support requirements aren't so desperately stringent for vampires. Put it another way; you can't kill an earthworm by burying it alive.'

Regalian looked up. 'Good point,' he said. 'So if I were to find a way of sealing off this crypt—'

'Go outside and cave in the underground passage that leads down to it,' suggested the gun. 'The basic Edgar Alan Poe gambit. Before you ask, a few well-aimed shots from me into the tunnel roof could easily do the trick.'

'—which would keep them safe from Claudia, and delay whatever her weird doomsday scenario is.'

'For a while, anyway,' the gun replied. 'A few lousy tons of rock isn't going to hold her up for more than a few hours, mind.'

Regalian nodded. 'Unless of course she's preoccupied with trying to chase me. That'd divide her resources a bit, maybe buy a little time.'

Air passed down the Scholfield's barrel, giving the illusion of a sigh. 'It might work,' it said. 'Not as if you're snowed under with viable alternatives. Even so, I always reckon time's only worth buying if you can get a good discount. I mean, it can't be worth much if they were reduced to giving it away free with history.'

'What?'

'Oh forget it,' the Scholfield replied impatiently. 'I dunno. Sam Johnson had Boswell, I have to end up with you. Let's go shoot a roof.'

Dracula – the real-life Dracula, not his fictional clone – stood up, scratched his ear, and sat down again.

God, but this was *fun*. Not just fun fun, but *real* fun. Maybe it was something to do with being Real himself for the first time; whatever. The fact remained that sitting in front of a VDU tapping keys on a keyboard beat flying in through windows and biting women's necks into a cocked hat.

On the other hand, he was thirsty. Oppressively so. What he needed, right now, was a very substantial drink. Hey, he said to himself, now I'm even thinking like a proper writer.

He'd already been through the fridge and the freezer; not a drop of blood anywhere in the whole place. He sighed, and fretted. On the one hand, he already had this marvellous idea for the opening scene of the sequel. On the other hand, he wasn't going to be in any shape to write anything without a good long swig of the old red stuff, quick. The Muse would have to wait, just for a little while.

Reluctantly he stood up again, switched off the screen and opened the window. The cool night air called to him. and suddenly he remembered the thrill of the wind under him, the headlong glory of flight. Raising his arms, he grinned, starlight flashing on his teeth, and jumped.

A very short while later, he landed in a flowerbed.

Shit, he muttered to himself, I've left it a bit late. Can't fly without juice. Pity. Have to walk, instead.

He'd been walking the deserted streets for maybe half an hour when bells started ringing in his head. He could smell young, female blood no more than fifty yards away; good, high-octane stuff, enough to keep him on his feet for a good long time. Idly wondering what sort of young lady would be out walking the streets alone at this ungodly hour, he followed his nose round a corner and froze, like a cat stalking a pigeon. Yo!

A bob of shoulder-length blonde hair, a flash of shapely leg, a supple sway of the hips as she walked; all the signals were positive. In fact, she couldn't be a more obvious mark if she had the words *70 cl – Please dispose of can tidily* tattooed between her shoulder blades. Dracula widened his grin into a snarl, raised his hands above his shoulders and pounced—

'Gotcha!'

—And hit the pavement, chin-first, as at least two extremely heavy bodies crashed down on top of him, informing him as they did so that he was nicked, that he had the right to remain silent . . .

Even depleted and run down as he was, he had enough of his superhuman strength left to be able to toss police-men about like tennis balls. He got rid of the original two by throwing them over his shoulder, then picked up a third and lobbed him through a plate-glass window; and he was just using the fourth as a subject in an experiment to see if policemen's heads unscrew like bottle-tops when the young lady walked up to him, gave him an unfriendly look and kicked him in a part of his anatomy which, although undead and invulnerable to anything except stakes and silver bullets, was nevertheless not exactly improved by sharp impact from a pointed toe. This so demoralised him that instead of leaping on her and draining every last drop of blood from her veins in one long draught, he made do with dropping the copper he was holding and staggering off as fast as he could run while still doubled up with pain.

That was still fast enough. Ten minutes later, having satisfied himself that he'd shaken off his pursuers, he sat down on a low wall, caught his breath and swore quietly for a while. Then, feeling better, he stood up, took a deep breath and crossed the road towards . . .

It was academic where he was going, because he never got there. A car, rounding the corner at excessive speed, hit him a ferocious glancing blow, sending him spinning off like a hard-hit cricket ball, until a wall got in the way and slowed him down to stalling speed.

He groaned. In the distance he could hear car doors slamming, shouts of *Call an ambulance quick* and other picturesque background noises. A torchbeam hit him in the face. Somebody said, 'You all right, mate?' or something similar. He tried to growl, bare his teeth, frighten them away; but all he managed was a feeble moan. He was just about to try again when he fainted.

When he came round, he fancied he was inside some sort of vehicle, moving fast. There was a man in a blue uniform standing over him, and a cute little thing with a white uniform and a really sensational neck off to his left.

Dracula tried to sit up, but encountered technical difficulties.

'He must have lost a hell of a lot of blood,' the man was saying. 'Emergency transfusion?'

'We don't know his group,' the girl replied. 'Oh, hang on, he's coming round.' She bent over him, until her neck was only inches from his face; yet those few inches separated him from his prey as effectively as the plate-glass window of a restaurant separates the people sitting inside and eating from the people outside with their noses pressed up against the glass. 'Hi,' she said. 'What blood group are you?'

'Huh?'

'We're going to give you some blood,' the girl said. 'What group?'

That settles it, Dracula said to himself, this is Heaven, or maybe Valhalla.

'Oh, whatever you've got the most of,' he croaked. 'Litre of the house red'll do fine, really, unless you can recommend something a bit special.'

The girl stared at him, shrugged and turned to her colleague. 'Concussion,' she said. 'I'll bang in a sedative, you do a quick test. Ready?'

There was no point trying to struggle against the needle; he was far too feeble and drained, and besides, lounging on soft pillows while a gorgeous blonde takes your order for blood wasn't something he could convincingly tell himself he wanted to escape *from*. With a contented sigh, Count Dracula lay back, closed his eyes and thought of Transylvania.

'There was no need,' Regalian muttered, 'to get carried away.'

If he'd been addicted to puns, he could have got some mileage out of a performance that had brought the house down without raising the roof; the opposite, in fact. Instead, he coughed out some of the dust he'd inhaled, and scrabbled in the loose spoil for the Scholfield.

'Nice thorough job?' queried the revolver.

'Thorough,' Regalian answered. 'Certainly thorough. You all right?'

'Nothing wrong with me an oily rag won't cure,' the gun said cheerfully. 'Come on, then, work to be done. By the way, I've got two shots left.'

'Bully for you, then. Now, where do you think this tunnel leads?'

'Follow it and see.'

They hadn't gone more than a hundred yards when Regalian stopped dead in his tracks. 'Listen!' he hissed.

'So? You never heard stealthy footsteps before?'

'Coming this way.' Regalian looked back at the way he'd just come. In a long, straight tunnel, hiding space is at something of a premium. 'Shit,' he added. 'Now what?'

'I'd have thought that was pretty obvious,' replied the Scholfield sarcastically. 'In case you haven't had time to read the manual, you fire me by pulling the lever, commonly known as a trigger, which you'll find located just behind the tip of your right index finger.'

Regalian was just about to reply that under no circumstances was he going to start a gunfight against unknown opponents in a pitch dark tunnel when a pale penumbra of light, such as that produced by a torch just around a corner, caught his attention. A split second later, a short, ugly, powerfully built form appeared in front of him and raised a lantern . . .

'Shot!' said the Scholfield with admiration. 'But I thought you said—'

'Changed my mind,' Regalian answered, stepping over the now deceased goblin and picking up the lantern. 'If it's just goblins, I fancy my chances. In *Wishblades* I used

to knock these buggers off by the coachload.' He stuffed
the gun in his belt and picked up the goblin's heavy black
scimitar. 'It'll be good for my self-image to do some proper
swordfighting again.'

'Now's your chance,' the Scholfield murmured, as
another crouched, menacing form lurched round the
corner like a two-legged spider. There was a crash, like a
whole canteen of cutlery falling from a fourth-floor
window, and the goblin fell neatly over the body of its
colleague. 'You want to watch what you're doing with that
thing,' the gun added, as Regalian tried a wristy practice
swing with the scimitar. 'You could put someone's eye
out if you aren't careful.'

'Could have once,' Regalian replied nostalgically.
'Better stick to the orthodox stuff for now, at least till I've
had a bit more practice.'

During the course of the next twenty minutes, he got
all the practice he could reasonably want.

'This,' he grunted, parrying a savage leg glance and
responding with a beautifully timed figure-of-nine cut
to the throat, 'is proper heroing. None of your undignified—' He flicked aside a despairing thrust and made
contact with his counterthrust; five down, two to go.
'—running about and hiding behind things, oh no.
Heroism's all about things going *thunk!* and *splat!* Like,'
he added, whirling round and aiming a double-handed
cut across the cheekpiece of a goblin helmet, 'that. Here,
you rotten little bastard, come back!'

'Quite finished?'

'Apparently. Did you see that? The last one scarpered.
They're not supposed to do that.'

'Shucks. Come on, grab that lantern and let's get out
of here, before you get an overwhelming urge to dress up
in leather.'

'Don't know what you're getting so damned patronising

about,' Regalian grumbled, as he picked his way over goblin corpses. 'Haven't noticed you going a bundle on passive resistance and friendly persuasion. Don't say you're jealous of a goblin scimitar.'

'Get real, you ponce,' the Scholfield growled disdainfully. 'But in case it slipped your mind, the purpose of the exercise isn't actually abolishing goblins. What we're meant to be doing— Oops,' it added. 'Company.'

Regalian grinned. 'Good,' he said. 'I was starting to get a bit lonely.'

'Not that sort of company,' the Scholfield hissed. 'I meant company in the sense of smaller than a brigade but larger than a platoon.'

'Oh. That sort of company.'

'Yes.'

Sure enough, the clatter of iron-soled goblin footwear was starting to get offensively loud. 'Coming this way,' Regalian whispered. 'That's a problem, isn't it?'

'Yup.'

'I mean, being realistic for a moment, I can't fight that many goblins on my own.'

'True.'

'Any suggestions? And don't say run away, because with all these dead bodies lying on the floor I wouldn't get ten yards without ending up flat on my face.'

'Correct.' The gun paused. 'Which leaves?'

'I beg your pardon?'

'Not forward,' said the Scholfield with exaggerated patience. 'Not back. Or up or down. That just leaves—'

'What?'

'Sideways, you idiot.'

'Thanks, but the walls are solid. You had noticed that, hadn't you? I mean it's not as if it's riddled with little doors in the wall every few—'

He stopped. Under his left hand, he could feel wood.

Carefully he lifted the lantern. 'Hey, look at this. A door.'

'Oh, so *that's* what they're called. I knew it began with a D.'

Footsteps nearer, running; very close to the corner. Quickly, Regalian reached out, secured the door handle, turned it and pushed through—

'Hellfire. It's locked.'

The Scholfield made an exasperated noise. 'Doesn't that suggest something to do? A course of action?'

Regalian shrugged. 'Run away? Surrender? Pop next door and see if they've got a spare key?'

'Shoot the lock off, dummy.'

Regalian frowned. 'Easily said, my finely machined chum, but how do you actually—?'

'Oh for pity's sake – mind your stupid feet, there's a good lad.'

BANG!

'All right,' said Claudia into her mobile phone, 'you can have exclusive distribution in Mauritius *and* the Cayman Islands *and* the soft toy rights *and* a ten-year franchise on the Four Horsemen of the Apocalypse™ combination radio alarm clock and sandwich maker. *Now* have we got a deal?'

The telephone assured her that she had, and it had been a pleasure doing business, and one day soon how about lunch, and changing the subject entirely, did she happen to know which of the levers inside the cockpit of a third generation Kawaguchiya Heavy Industries space shuttle closed the doors?

'The blue one third from the left, second row down,' Claudia answered, 'except on the GT1001. Why?'

'Oh,' replied the telephone, 'just curious, that's all. Ciao.'

'See you, Lin.' Claudia shrugged and pushed back the aerial. 'Max?'

'Howdy.'

She peered down the beam of her pocket flashlight until she located him, sitting cross-legged on the floor thumbing cartridges into the gate of his Winchester '74. 'Max,' she said, 'what's going on?'

The bounty hunter clicked his tongue. 'Reckon them no-good skunks all moseyed off into the crypt and caved in the tunnel, ma'am. All of 'em 'cept that danged hero. He's down the tunnel some place beatin' up on mah goblins.'

'I see. And are you planning on doing anything about that?'

Max grinned, and jacked the action of the rifle. 'Reckon so, ma'am,' he said, pulling a cartridge from his belt and holding it up so that the bullet head caught the light. 'Solid silver, ma'am,' he explained.

'Oh right. Well, get a move on, will you? And do try not to damage them,' she added, allowing her drawl to unwind like a rattlesnake at a health farm. 'I'm not too fussed about the hero and Hamlet, but I want Skinner and the Armitage woman in one piece. Understood?'

'Sho' nuff, ma'am.'

He got up, wiped the dust off his trousers, picked up his rifle and stalked off down the tunnel, spurs jingling. Once he'd disappeared from sight, Claudia pulled out the phone again and tapped in a very short number.

'Yes, hello. What? No, it's urgent. Look, I don't care if it is a Sunday, I want to talk to Him *now*, got that? What? Oh, all right then, tell Him to call me as soon as He gets back. Yes. Bye.'

She scowled. That was the trouble with these so-called creative types. Downright unprofessional. She keyed in another number. A clue; it was like the number you would dial for fire, police or ambulance, only upside down.

'Nick? Yes, it's me. Look, the, um, other player in the

game's just horsing around and I've run out of patience so the bottom line is, if you can match His price, the contract's yours. How soon? You can't make it earlier? Oh well then, that'll have to do. Yup, see you around. Cheerio.'

Well, Claudia reflected, at least she now had a definite date, even if it did mean hanging fire for another forty-eight hours. Just enough time, she reflected (for she loved to accentuate the positive) to get all those sweatshirts amended and into the shops. She dialled a third number.

'George? Yes, now listen. The logo. I want you to change it, rush job. Look, just under where it says "The end of the world is", I want you to delete "nigh" and put in "Wednesday". Got that? Fine. Bye.'

She put the phone away, and grinned.

Let's do the show right here.

CHAPTER THIRTEEN

E xcerpt from *Ending The World For Pleasure and Profit,*
p. 176.

*The consequences of conventional Armageddon on the envi-
ronment have in recent years given rise to a considerable
amount of debate in ecological circles. The prospect of littering
space with large quantities of post-holocaust radioactive debris
is not an attractive one for any would-be terricide with even
a vestigial level of ecological awareness; hence the race to
develop an environmentally friendly alternative – the so-called
'responsible apocalypse'.*

*The only viable model so far developed is that proposed in
a recent paper in Catastrophica by Claudia Van Sittaert, the
celebrated dramatic agent. The Van Sittaert option contem-
plates achieving global oblivion by means of breaking down
the spatio-temporal membrane dividing Fiction from Reality.
The underlying logic is quite straightforward; only what is real
can exist, and where reality is so comprehensively diluted with
fictional elements that it becomes impossible to distinguish fact
from fiction, existence itself is likely to be irreversibly compro-
mised. The world, in short, would no longer be sufficiently real
to go on existing, and would quite simply cease.*

The practicalities of the proposal are refreshingly straight-forward. The balance between Fiction and Reality is regulated by one basic law: for every entrance, an exit. If a real person were to be transferred into Fiction and then suddenly sent back again to Reality without a corresponding transfer of another real person back into Fiction, the effect would be to fracture the membrane, thereby creating an interface through which the inhabitants of both sides of the line could pass freely. Once the loophole exists, it will inevitably be used, leading to a collapse of Reality and the desired effect.

Van Sittaert herself attributes the inspiration for this radical new approach to a chance remark of one Hamlet, Prince of Denmark. According to Van Sittaert, the theory sprang fully formed into her mind at precisely the moment when she realised that 'To be or not to be' was not in fact a trick question, as she had always assumed.

'Thought you were going to shoot off the lock.'

'Well?'

'What you have just shot off,' Regalian said slowly, 'was in fact the door handle.'

'Oh.'

Regalian fetched a sigh up from sock-level and sat down, his back to the tunnel wall. Pretty soon, he would be knee-deep in goblins; not a pleasant prospect, if he knew goblins, which he did, rather better than he'd have wished if he'd had any say in the matter, which he hadn't. Say in the matter, now he came to think of it, had been conspicuously absent from his life for as long as he could remember, right up to the moment when Jane had turned him loose to embark on this damnfool adventure. Was it coincidence, he wondered, that ever since he'd been the master of his fate and the captain of his soul, one cock-up had, so to speak, pressed another's heel in a headlong stampede to happen to him? Probably not. The thought that he was worse at arranging his own life than Jane, who was a nice kid but about as bright as the stairwell light in a cheap hotel, didn't cheer him up particularly. The opposite, in fact.

I wish, he caught himself thinking, I was back home in the Hubworld. For one thing, you got a better class of goblin in the Hubworld. More to the point, however many of the little buggers you found charging towards you, it was certain sure that you'd be more than a match for them. True, you did actually have to smite them, and they were perfectly capable of giving you a wicked nip in the ankle if you weren't careful; but at least you knew it was all going to be all right, because you were the hero. Right now, you're still the hero, but there are no guarantees whatsoever.

Thinks . . .

But this is still Fiction, and I'm still me. If I wasn't still the hero, this wouldn't be happening to me; it'd be some other poor bugger hunched in this lousy tunnel waiting for the goblins to show. And if I'm still the hero, then . . .

'Howdy.'

Regalian looked up, puzzled. 'You?'

'Reckon so.'

'I was expecting goblins.'

Max allowed himself a lazy smile. Actually, he was trying to cut down, but the situation seemed to justify the indulgence. 'They'll be along directly. Reckon I got longer legs, is all.' He raised the rifle to hip level. 'Won't be needing them, anyhow,' he added. 'On your feet, part-ner. Little lady wants a word with you.'

Regalian looked at the muzzle of the rifle, remembered the position of the lock on the door behind him, and made a few swift calculations of trajectory. 'Get stuffed,' he said.

'Pardon me?'

'Go play with yourself,' Regalian elucidated. 'Shove off. Go away.'

'Reckon you can't have heard me right, mister. On your feet – that's if you reckon on doin' much more livin' around these parts.'

Thanks to his basic training at character school, Regalian was able to sneer. He did so. 'Nuts to you. Go on, shoot me.'

'You said it, buster.' Max shrugged and pulled the trigger. At the moment when the sear slipped out of the hammer notch, Regalian threw himself forward and rolled. The bullet from Max's rifle cleared the top of his head by eight thousandths of an inch, hit the doorframe and smashed the lock. The door creaked and swung inwards.

'Sheeit,' Max exclaimed, disgusted; but before he could jack another round into the Winchester's chamber, Regalian headbutted him in the stomach and threw him across the tunnel, then dived like an American footballer through the open door, hit the ground, swore, kicked the door shut with his foot and looked round for something to wedge it shut with. Quite by chance there was a section of railway sleeper of precisely the right length leaning against the wall, just handy. He grabbed it, jammed it in place and listened. He hoped very much that Max would try shoulder-charging it. A clatter of footsteps, a bang on the door and a cry of pain followed, and Regalian smiled contentedly.

'You realise,' the Scholfield said, 'that as soon as the goblins show up, they'll have that door down in no time.'

'Oh shut up.'

'Don't you take that tone with me. I'll bet you King Arthur didn't talk like that to Excalibur.'

'Excalibur got chucked in a lake,' Regalian replied. 'Think on.'

'Just for that,' the Scholfield said icily, 'you can get yourself out of this one.'

'Thanks.'

Regalian scrambled to his feet and looked round. This didn't help him much, because it was as dark as a bag and he couldn't see a thing. Nevertheless. To boldly go, and all that crap. He went.

You lose track of time, walking in complete darkness; so it may have been twenty minutes or two hours before he turned a corner and found himself in the light once again. Once his eyes had recovered from the glare, he found himself facing a huge steel door, like a safe or an airlock. There was a tumbler, and one of those things like a miniature ship's wheel. Also a notice, which said:

NO ENTRY
EXCEPT ON OFFICIAL BUSINESS
Please leave fiction as you would expect to find it

A little gust of air tickled his ear. He stood still, listening. There was something or someone scuttling up the tunnel behind him. Three guesses? Only need one, thanks all the same. He reached out and twiddled the ship's wheel until it locked. No joy. Obviously you had to know the combination, and he didn't.

'Gun.'

'Not talking to you.'

'Gun,' he repeated, 'believe me when I tell you that under normal circumstances I'd rather be tied hand and foot and dropped off Niagara into a cauldron of piranha-infested boiling shit than ask you for help. Understood?'

'Still not talking to you.'

'On the other hand,' Regalian went on, 'you're a machine. You have component parts that go round and click and lock in place, and all that jazz. So does this door. If there's a sort of mechanical-twiddly-clicky-things' union to which you and this door belong, do you think you could have a word with your mate here and get this lot open? I'd be ever so grateful.'

Pause. 'You would?'

'Yes.'

'Make a change, that would.'

'Indeed.'

'Oh well, since it's you. Draw me and rest my muzzle against the door.'

Regalian did so. The gun moved in his hand, and knocked on the door three times; whereupon a little hatch slid across and a voice said, 'Yes?'

'Special delivery,' said the gun. 'Gotta be signed for.'

'With you in a jiffy,' replied the voice. The hatch closed, there was a rattling of keys, chains and bolts, and the door swung open.

'Easy when you know how,' muttered the gun under its breath, as Regalian brought it sharply up into line with the doorman's eye. Not long after that, he was inside and the door clanged shut behind him.

'Sorry about that,' Regalian said. 'Only there's these goblins, you see, and—'

''Ere,' said the man. He was a short, round, bald individual in a brown workshop coat with pencils and a Vernier calliper sticking out of the top pocket. 'What you doing in 'ere? You're not allowed.'

'Sorry, but it's an emergency. You see, these goblins . . .'

The man stared at him. 'You're from Fiction, aintcher? Your lot's not allowed in 'ere. Clear off.'

Regalian waggled the gun meaningfully. 'Or?'

'Or,' the man replied, 'put that bloody thing away, come on through and 'ave a cuppa tea. Kettle's just boiled.'

'Ah,' Regalian said. 'Thanks.'

'Got to say all that stuff, you see,' the man explained, leading the way. 'Then if anyone asks, I can say I told you to push off but you frettened me wiv a gun. 'Salright if you fretten me wiv a gun. I could of lent you one if you wanted.'

'I see.' Regalian looked around. 'Where is this exactly?' he asked.

'Non-Fiction,' the man replied. 'Don't spose you've ever been 'ere before. Different department.'

It was a workshop. It reminded Regalian strongly of various wizard's caves he'd visited in the course of the trilogy; the same half-empty teacups on every flat surface, oily rags and cigarette butts on the floor, Pirelli calendar, small elderly transistor radio warbling mindlessly to itself in the shadows. The hardware was different, but not very. For the record, there were CNC lathes, vertical mills, slot mills, universal mills, pillar-drills, planers, bench grinders, cutter grinders, overhead countershafts and lots of other mythical, magical apparatus that only exists in the furthest reaches of the imagination. You could probably create the world in this place, if you had the materials. It would probably only take you five days; four if you took the phone off the hook and left the paperwork to look after itself.

'Sugar?' the man asked.

'Please,' Regalian answered. The man heaped in two tablespoons from a big tin, fished out the teabag and splashed in milk from an oily bottle.

'There you go,' the man said. ''Ave a seat, I'll be wiv you in a tick.'

He pottered over to one of the giant machines, flicked a switch and turned a little wheel. There was a hum and a buzz like steel bees, and a few glittering specks of metal dust flew up into the air. 'Bugger,' the man snarled. 'Taken off two fou too many, gotta do it again.'

'Sorry,' Regalian said. 'I'm distracting you.'

The man shook his head. 'Glad of the company, mate,' he replied without looking up. He twirled a big T-shaped key in the chuck, pulled out whatever it was he'd been working on and chucked it in a bin under the bench. 'Don't get visitors down 'ere as a rule,' he went on. 'You don't, not in Non-Fiction. Shouldn't be 'ere meself, by rights. Should be fully automated, like.' He laughed. 'That'll be the day, right?'

Regalian nodded, on general principles. 'Excuse me asking,' he said, 'but how did I get here?'

'You should know, mate,' the man replied. 'Don't ask me.'

'But I didn't think it was possible,' Regalian went on. 'I mean, the balance of nature, basic authorship theory—'

The man shrugged. 'Books is books, I guess,' he replied. ''Snot as if you'd gone into whatsitcalled, Reality. It's just, up this end, fings in books are sposed to be true.'

'Only supposed to be?'

The man shrugged again. 'Depends,' he replied. 'Like, whatchercall true? All depends on what it says in the specs.'

'Specs?'

'Tolerances,' the man said, winding a new piece of metal into the chuck. 'Like, 'as it got to be true to within one fousandf of an inch? Ten fousandfs? Fickess of a fag paper? Makes a difference, I can tell you. Me, I'm a perfecksionist, gotta be wivin half a fou or it doesn't go out that door. In fact, most of yer Non-Fiction don't need to be anyfing like that precise. Like, yer 'istory, yer politics, that sort of fing, you can get away with murder. Yer sciences, now, that's different. Gotta be careful with the sciences, or the whole planet could get blown up.' He switched on the machine; buzz buzz, crinkle crinkle. 'An' that's why they'll never do wivout the likes of me,' he added. 'Gotta 'ave somebody to make sure it don't go wrong. Right?'

'I can see that,' Regalian replied. 'Vitally important.' He took a swig of his tea and, being a hero, managed to swallow it. 'Um, is there another door?'

''Fraid not,' the man replied. He was measuring something with a micrometer. It was so small that Regalian could barely see it. 'On account of all this is a spatio-temporal anomaly. Dun't exist,' he translated. 'No back door in a spatio-temporal anomaly. No front door either, come to that,' he added, blowing away a grain of dust, 'but it's a bloody pain not 'avin' a front door, so I knocked froo one afternoon when nobody was lookin'. Dozy buggers haven't even noticed yet. That's one of the good fings about not existin'; they leave you alone most of the time.'

'Right. So, if I wanted to leave—'

'Can't leave. On account of, you can't go out of a place you never went in to start wiv.'

'I see,' Regalian said. 'So I'm sort of marooned here, am I?'

'You would be,' the man replied, 'if you existed. But you don't.'

'Don't I?'

'Not since you come in 'ere you don't. On account of nuffin' can exist in 'ere.'

'Because this place doesn't exist?'

'You're catching on, my son. There should be a quarter-be-twenty-Whit tap in that box by yer left foot, if you wouldn't mind.'

Regalian picked up the box and carried it over to where the man was working. 'Excuse me if this is a silly question,' he said, 'but if this place doesn't exist, how come you're here?'

'Some poor bugger's got to be here,' he replied. 'Make sure the machines don't play up. Do all the fiddly jobs. Like this,' he said, pointing. 'That's an equation, that is. For a maffs book. Got to be exactly right, or the whole shooting match'll be up the pictures. You show me a machine'll do that an' I'll show you half a ton of rocking-'orse shit.'

'What he's trying to say—' said the Scholfield.

''Ere, who said that?'

'My gun,' replied Regalian, embarrassed. 'It can talk. I wish it couldn't, but it can.'

'Give it 'ere a minute.'

'Hey, hang on, what d'you think you're—?'

'Stroof,' said the man, 'it can talk. Nice bit of work, too. Nice machining. People knew how to make fings in them days.'

As he took the gun back, Regalian could hardly bring himself to look at it. Revolvers can't smirk, of course, or look revoltingly smug. They can't talk, either.

'As I was saying,' the Scholfield continued, 'none of this exists, because there aren't any imaginary characters in Non-Fiction; but because somebody's got to do it, they bend the rules.'

'Oh,' said Regalian. 'So he does exist.'

'No, of course not. He doesn't exist, this workshop doesn't exist, none of it exists. They just happen to be here, that's all. The universe turns a blind eye.'

'On account,' the man agreed, nodding, 'of if they closed me down, they'd be in shit up to their ears. Which is good,' he added. 'Means I can do what the bloody 'ell I like, and if they try an' stop me I tell 'em to get stuffed. Nuffin' they can do about it.'

'I see.' Regalian leaned back, letting it sink in. 'So it's impossible for me to get out of here.'

'That's right.'

'But since nobody gives a toss—'

'Knew you'd get the 'ang of it eventually,' the man said, grinning. 'Least, they do give a toss, but they can't do nuffin' about it.'

'So,' Regalian went on, 'although it'd be impossible for me to open that door there and find myself ever-so-conveniently exactly where I wanted to be—'

'Do us a favour an' put the kettle on first,' replied the man. 'Any time you're passing, feel free to drop in.'

Regalian had walked to the door and his hand was on the handle when he stopped, thought for a moment and turned back. 'One last thing,' he said.

'Hm?'

'Science. You know all about it, presumably?'

Without looking up, the man pointed to a large tea-chest in a corner. It was full to the top with strange, tiny artefacts, and there was a label on it, which read:

SCIENCE
THIS WAY UP

''Sall in there,' the man said. 'Help yourself.'

Regalian shook his head. 'Actually,' he said, 'it would-n't mean anything to me. I was wondering if you could sort of translate for me.'

'Do me best.'

'Thanks.' Regalian perched on the edge of a huge machine and folded his arms. 'About the end of the world,' he said.

'What about it?'

'How does it work? And how would you go about stop-ping it?'

The man stopped what he was doing, switched off the power and wiped his hands on his trouser legs. There was something – difficult to describe, when you've only got shoddy, post-modernist adjectives to work with – cheerfully reverential in his manner, as if he had just seen the Messiah and remembered that the Messiah owed him twenty quid.

'Ah,' said the man, 'you're one of them, then.'

Basic apocalypse theory.

It is now, for the sake of argument, the End of the World. Earthquakes are shaking the surface of the planet, making life difficult for all the nations of the earth who are trying to exterminate each other in the War To End All Wars – a difficult enough undertaking without the ground suddenly opening up and swallowing the enemy battalion you've spent all day carefully pinning down and enfilading in preparation for the Big Push – while overhead the upper atmosphere is nose-to-tail with executive shuttlecraft trying to make it to Alpha Centauri before the currency in the hold becomes totally worthless. The Four Horsemen™ roam the surface of the planet, trying to find an open blacksmith's forge. The Antichrist paces through the devastated streets, dodging falling bombs and selling lottery tickets.

Seen it. Old hat. Yawn. What's on the other channel?

This is *not* how the world ends.

This is how the world ends . . .

At the top of the hill overlooking Jerusalem, the Antichrist reined in his horse and waited for the Four Horsemen to catch him up.

'It's all right for you,' muttered the First Horseman, who was in fact a Horsewoman. 'All that time you spent schlepping around in Westerns, you obviously learned how to ride one of these wretched animals. I'm still trying to work it out from first principles.'

'Oh for crying out loud,' muttered the Antichrist under his

breath, 'it's not difficult. All you've got to do is sit on the goddamn thing and hold on tight with your knees.'

'That's your idea of not difficult, is it?'

'Well,' replied the Antichrist, 'the other three seem to be managing okay.'

'Sure,' snapped the Horsewoman. 'I can believe it. Hamlet's a prince, so presumably he's been riding to hounds and playing polo since he was in nappies. Regalian's a hero, practically born in the saddle. And Titania, well, from what I gather she's got this thing about equine quadrupeds, so—'

'I heard that.'

'People!' The Antichrist growled, asserting his authority. 'Look, I hate to break up the discussion group, but we do have a schedule to keep to. Right then, where's that bit of paper?'

'What bit of paper?'

'She wrote it all down for me,' the Antichrist replied, scrabbling in the pockets of his jet-black robe. 'Ah, here we go. First, we manifest ourselves.'

'I think we've done that.'

'You reckon? Okay then, one down and nine to go. Next, it says here, we've got to ride through all the nations of the earth spreading death and—'

'All the nations of the earth?'

'That's what it says here.'

'Bugger that,' said the Fourth Horseman. 'According to my pocket atlas, there's seventy-eight of them, seventy-nine if you count the Vatican. Actually, that was before the break-up of the Soviet Union, so—'

'All the nations of the earth,' the Antichrist repeated. 'Otherwise it won't work. Shit, if Michael Palin can do it, so can we. And the sooner we get started—'

'Hang on,' interrupted the First Horsewoman. 'I don't suppose anybody's thought to make any arrangements; you know, hotel reservations, ferry bookings, that sort of thing. You can't just go blithely swanning about the place.'

'Listen to her, will you?' said the Second Horsewoman. 'Where's your spontaneity, your sense of adventure? I vote we just take it all as it comes, and if it turns out that we have to doss down on the beach or under a hedge a few times, then so what, it's not the end of the—'

'Ride through all the nations of the earth,' repeated the Third Horseman. 'All right, what comes after that?'

The Antichrist looked down at the envelope in his skeletal hand. 'Bringing death and desolation, is what it says here. Any idea how we go about that, anybody?'

The Third Horseman sighed. 'She didn't tell you?'

'Well, no.'

'And you didn't think to ask?'

'Well, you were there too. Why didn't you ask?'

'Hey,' broke in the Second Horsewoman, 'you two, break it up. I expect we'll find out what we've got to do when we get there. It'll just come naturally, I expect. I mean, we're the heralds of global destruction, they're probably expecting us.'

'What, you mean brass bands, banners stretched across the street, that sort of thing? I wouldn't set your heart on it, because—'

'I reckon,' said the Third Horseman, 'we don't actually have to do anything. Just being there'll be enough. The violation of physics. The breach in the integrity of the fiction/reality continuum. Wherever we go'll stop being real and start becoming a story. And,' he went on, his voice becoming just a shade brittle, 'when everything's in a story and nothing's real, that'll be it. Nobody left to read the story, so the story can't exist any more.'

'Like in the Slushpile,' agreed the Second Horsewoman thoughtfully. 'Not a pleasant concept, really.'

The Antichrist shrugged. 'Oh well,' he said.

'Oh,' said Regalian.

The man nodded. 'Won't affect me, of course,' he said, 'on account of me not existing anyway. There'll just be me an' all this Non-Fiction, all the science and maffs an' stuff, like in Plato.'

Regalian frowned. 'That's out the other side of Neptune, isn't it? They always told me it was uninhabited.'

'That's Pluto, you pillock. Plato's in Filosofy. It's where all that's material and corruptible is purged away, leavin' only the eternal verities in their true spiritchual essence. That's here,' he added, making a wide gesture towards the machines, the workbenches, the teachests and the carefully labelled plastic dustbins full of shiny metal bits. 'All this lot. Goin' to be borin' as fuck, you mark my words.'

Regalian nodded. 'That,' he said, 'is why I'd like some help making sure it doesn't happen.'

'Wot, you mean stop the end of the world?'

'Mhm.'

The man grinned. 'That's impossible,' he said.

Regalian grinned too. 'God, I'm relieved to hear you say that.'

With a crash, the crypt door fell inwards. Dust settled.

'Right,' said the goblin captain, turning his back on the vault. 'That's that, then. Don't suppose you'll be needing me and my lads for the rest of it, so we'll be on our way . . .'

'No,' said Claudia. 'You stay there.'

'Ah *shit*,' whined the goblin. 'Don't make us go in there, please.'

Claudia looked at him, amused and bemused. 'Why ever not?' she asked.

'Well.' The goblin shuffled his feet. 'It's just – well, don't like crypts. Spooky.'

'Oh get a grip, you silly little man. Whatever can there be in there that can possibly hurt you?'

– Whereupon five coffins simultaneously opened, their lids hitting the ground in unison, and five hideous spectral figures loomed up out of the darkness –

'Eeek!' the goblin explained, pointing. 'Ghugug . . .'

'Not ghosts,' Claudia sighed, 'just vampires. Honestly!'

'Eeek! Vuvuv . . .'

'Oh go away, then, see if I care,' Claudia snapped. 'And I don't expect to receive a bill, either.'

Much pattering of iron-shod feet; then silence, broken only by the *shunk-shunk* of Max chambering a silver-headed bullet into the chamber of his rifle.

'Well, here we all are,' Claudia said briskly. 'Or at least, almost all.' She frowned, then shrugged. 'Can't waste any more time, we'll just have to make do with three horsepersons. Jane, you can double up as Famine and Death. On second thoughts,' she added, looking Jane over, 'not Famine, you wouldn't fool anybody. You'd better be Pestilence and Death. Ready?'

'No.'

Claudia allowed herself a moment to soliloquise about bloody prima donna starlets who hold everything up, and then said, 'Max.'

'Howdy.'

'Shoot them for me, there's a love.'

'Sure thing, ma'am,' he replied, and did so.

As the smoke cleared and the echoes of the shots died away, Jane found herself thinking, *Odd. Death's obviously not so very fatal in these parts*. She sat up and, instinctively, felt the side of her mouth. The big, pointed teeth had gone.

'All done,' said Claudia cheerfully. 'In case you're wondering, by the way, that was all it took. Look around. Better still, breathe in.'

The ex-vampires did so, and gagged. It smelt *horrible*. Claudia nodded.

'Welcome to Reality,' she said.

The consultant bent down to glance at the chart at the foot of the bed, then straightened up and put a big, professional smile on his face.

'Now then, Mr . . . Oh dear, we don't seem to know your name.'

'Smith,' Dracula replied. 'Vlad Smith.'

'Ah, right.' The consultant scribbled something in a notebook, and sat down beside the Count's bed. 'Now then, Mr Smith, I've been looking at your case notes and I have to admit, I'm puzzled.'

'You are. I mean, you are? Why's that?'

The consultant's forehead furrowed over for a moment, as if a stray thought had crept up behind him and hit him with a brick. 'I have to tell you,' he said, 'your case is – well, I'll admit, it's a new one on me. You see, we keep on pumping blood into you, and we can't seem to see where it goes to.'

'Really.'

The consultant nodded. 'Twenty-six gallons of the stuff we've put in over the last ten days, and according to our scans it's just vanished. Hollow legs, as it were. Very curious.' He paused. 'Er, how do you feel? In yourself, as it were?'

'Oh, fine.'

'Do you indeed? That's very—'

'Apart from the pain, of course,' Dracula added quickly. 'Really terrible, the pain is. Ouch. Ouch ouch.'

The consultant looked at him over the rims of his spectacles. 'Whereabouts is this pain, exactly?'

'Oh, all over. Everywhere. It's agony, Doctor, really it is.'

The intravenous drip on the rail over his head burped and ran dry. The consultant waved to a nurse, who installed a fresh bottle. 'Well,' said the consultant, 'I'm afraid we're going to have to keep you in, just for the time being. Until the condition stabilises, I mean.'

'I see,' replied the Count. 'And what does that mean, exactly?'

The consultant smiled wanly. 'Until we manage to pour some blood into you and keep it there, I suppose,' he said. 'This pain, you're sure it's everywhere?'

'Positive,' Dracula replied. 'Ooh. Ouch. Ooh.'

'Well, in that case . . .'

Suddenly, Dracula sat bolt upright, tearing the drip tube from his arm. A look of sheer fury crossed his face, and he covered his heart with his hand. A sticky red patch began to grow under his fingers.

'Fuck,' he said, and fell back on to the pillows.

The consultant bent over him and moved the hand aside, saw the bullet-hole, glanced up at the skylight and ducked. 'Nurse!' he yelled.

'Doctor?'

'There's someone shooting the patients.'

'Yes, Doctor.'

'Seems to have cured this one.'

'Yes, Doctor.'

'Well, sort of. He's dead.'

Claudia glanced round.

'Your friend,' she said, 'the chap with the cape and the teeth. Where'd he get to?'

Skinner looked down at the pile of empty clothes, and shuddered. 'I think,' he said, 'he actually was a vampire, if you follow me. Name of Dracula.' The penny dropped and Skinner looked up, astonished. 'This *is* Reality,' he said. 'That's why he *really* died. Jesus!'

'Told you,' Claudia said. 'Why do people never seem to believe what I tell them?'

'Jesus,' Skinner repeated softly. 'I'm home.'

'Indeed you are, Mr Skinner. And you too, Ms Armitage. All part of the service.' Claudia glanced down at her watch. 'And now, if you don't mind. If I may put it this way, if you think we've got all the time in the world, think again. Places, please.'

Something hot and wet blew in Skinner's ear. He whirled round. It was a horse.

'Do we have to?' he groaned. 'Only I get this rash, right up the side of my legs. Wouldn't a Buick do just as well, really?'

'No.'

There were, indeed, four horses; one pale, the others jet black. Jane felt in her pockets for a lump of sugar and wondered whether, if she asked nicely, she could have hers fitted with training wheels.

'Ready?' Claudia asked.

And then the wall caved in.

'Mind how yer go,' the man said, and then he closed the door behind him. Regalian nodded, and then found himself falling forward—

Into the damn crypt, the one he'd been at such pains to leave. Buggery!

—Except that now it seemed to be full of horses. And Claudia. And Max, pointing that blasted rifle at him. He ducked down behind a horse, and the bullet sang off the rock behind him, which was now of course an archway.

'How in hell's name—?' Claudia was shouting, and that at least sounded promising. He heard Max's rifle cycling, and glanced over his shoulder, the way he'd just come—

Out of, apparently, the desert.

To be precise, Arizona.

He was only guessing; but the rock formations, the huge tree-like cacti, the sand, the burning sun. Arizona, New Mexico, one of those places. Maybe Nevada. The geography of Reality wasn't his strong suit.

Reality . . .

'Oh bloody marvellous,' he muttered, and ran.

'Don't just stand there,' Claudia yelled. 'Get after him.'

'Sure thing, ma'am.'

'And before you go,' she added, 'tie up these idiots.'

'Right away, ma'am.'

'No, on second thoughts, don't do that.' Claudia scowled horribly through the hole in the crypt wall, temporarily dazed. It had been a long, long time since she'd felt like this, not knowing what to do next. Take the ground out from under her feet and she'd find a way to cope. But suddenly to have the initiative snatched away from her; it was intolerable.

Then she smiled. No need to worry.

'Let him go,' she said. 'He'll keep. Max, you just make sure this lot behave themselves and don't try running away.'

'But the other one, ma'am,' Max objected, pointing at the archway with his rifle. 'You ain't jes' gonna let him—'

Claudia shrugged. 'Why ever not? Fictional character loose in Reality, just what the doctor ordered. Let him run as far as he likes.'

Max thought about it for a moment, and grinned. 'I surely see your meaning, ma'am,' he replied. 'Kinda, let him do the job for us.'

'Quite. Can we have a couple more horses, please? One for you and one for Ms Armitage. I think she'll have to make do with just being Pestilence.'

'Sho' nuff, ma'am. But I thought . . .'

Claudia took the reins of the pale horse and vaulted lightly into the saddle. 'The hell with it,' she said. 'It's my show. Why shouldn't I get to act in it too?'

Having checked that he was alive and no worse damaged than the average first-class parcel, Regalian picked himself up and looked around.

'How.'

He groaned. Around him in a circle he could see feathers, buckskins and the shiny heads of newly polished arrows. The painful bruise on the back of his head probably had something to do with the lump of rock which had rolled down the side of the narrow gorge just as he was passing through it.

'I refuse,' he announced wearily, 'to be party to crude racial stereotyping. No pre-Columbian Native American ever said "How" except for the tourists, and I'm not a tourist, I'm here on business. Now . . .'

The seven-foot flowerpot-coloured giant who towered over him had no discernible facial expression. He could have been a statue, until he started to talk.

'How,' he repeated. 'Me Take Forty-Two. Cigar Store nation. You fight with me or go in anthill.'

'Just a minute,' Regalian snarled. 'This is supposed to be Reality, dammit.' An unpleasant thought occurred to him. 'Or are you—?'

'We come from hole in rock,' said the Indian, pointing in the direction Regalian had just come from. 'We from Fiction, where damn sight better than this. In Fiction, we goblins, knocks being crude racial stereotype into cocked hat, on account of which we well pissed off. Now, you fight or you want go in anthill? All same to us.'

'Please yourselves,' Regalian said, and his hand swooped down on the grips of the Scholfield. The ring of warriors parted, something about their manner suggesting that while they were unquestionably braves, they drew the line at being bloody stupids. He drew the gun.

'Psst!'

'What?'

'Keep your voice down,' the Scholfield hissed. 'I hate to have to tell you this, but I'm empty. No cartridges left. You used the last one shooting off the door handle, remember?'

Regalian closed his eyes. 'Thank you,' he said. 'Thank you ever so much. I'll be sure to remember this as long as I – well, teabag memory or not, I should be able to manage that. Thanks a *lot*.'

Take Forty-Two was frowning at him. 'What paleface saying to obviously empty handgun?' he demanded. 'Let's get show on road. We fight with knives.'

'Knives?'

'Sure. You got better idea?'

'Plenty.'

'Very probably you do. We fight with knives anyway.' A coffin-handled Bowie knife whizzed through the air and buried itself in the sand at Regalian's feet. With obvious distaste he leaned forward and picked it up.

The crowd was silent. Nobody was buying popcorn. Nobody was selling popcorn. The sky was blue instead of green, but otherwise; business as usual. Except that, in real life, when you get killed you die.

He glanced down at the knife he'd been issued with and compared it with the trainee meat cleaver in the other guy's hand. Maybe it was all subjective, but as far as he could see, the one he'd got was smaller, flimsier and really only suited to opening letters; air-mail letters, for choice. He got the impression that if these characters had ever heard of sportsmanship, they'd have assumed it referred to some sort of purpose-built racing canoe.

'Excuse me,' he said. 'Before we start, can I just have a quick word with the umpire?'

'Me umpire.' The voice came from something Regalian had taken to be a totem pole. In fact, it was a very large man. 'Me Five Tupperware Dishes, Coldfoot nation. What you want now?'

Regalian looked at Five Tupperware Dishes until the crick in his neck became painful, and decided not to bother. Having this guy for an umpire, he reckoned, was a bit like having a kleptomaniac for a store detective. What do I do now? he asked himself. Well, you could try fighting. What an inspired suggestion. Yes, I think I'll give that a try.

The thought was still being processed in his mind when Take Forty-Two's knife whistled past his jaw, proving that, no matter what claims they make for modern hi-tech electric razors, the cleanest, smoothest shave you can get is still a Bowie knife in the hands of a seven-foot-tall psychotic warrior. Regalian swayed clear, stepped back and folded his arms.

'Excuse me,' he said.

A fraction of a second later he had to move again, thereby cheating himself by the thickness of a lightweight Rizla of eligibility for a Vincent Van Gogh Look-Alike contest. He could see, however, as the maniac facing him recovered his balance for the next blow, that the first seed of doubt had been sown. He concentrated . . .

'Excuse me,' he said, 'but do you mind waiting till the umpire gives the signal?'

'Huh?'

'For the fight to start,' he explained, moving smartly to his left to avoid a blow that would have decapitated an elephant. 'Although actually . . .'

Take Forty-Two stood still, his knife hand hanging limp at his side. 'What you mean, actually?' he grunted.

Regalian slowly dropped the knife. 'You've lost,' he said. 'Sorry.'

'What you say, I lost?' demanded the warrior angrily. 'I not lost. I still alive. You hold still, I prove it.'

'I hate to be pernickety,' Regalian said, shaking his head, 'but you forfeit the match. Rule Seventeen, striking a blow before the umpire gives the signal.' He pulled a book from his pocket (it was, in fact, his concise English/Elvish dictionary, but he guessed he'd be safe) and tossed it at the warrior's feet. 'Look it up for yourself if you don't believe me.'

For a moment. Take Forty-Two looked as if he was going to explode. Then he turned slowly round and stared hard at the umpire.

'Hey, you,' he thundered, 'what big idea? Me undefeated champion. Now I lose match. I pull out lungs and make you eat.'

A moment later there was a really good fight going. Nobody gave the signal, but (Regalian reasoned to himself as he ran, unnoticed, towards the rail the horses were tied to) it probably didn't matter, because it wasn't a championship bout, only – chunk, chunk, *scream!* – a friendly.

CHAPTER FOURTEEN

M ain Street.
You've seen it over and over again. You could
draw a map of it blindfold.

Here we have the Lucky Strike saloon; swinging doors,
pianola tinnily tinkling *Dixie*, raucous voices implying that
the cowpokes are cutting the dust after six weeks on the
Lone Star trail. Next door, the general store, presided
over by a nervous Swede who knows for a fact that before
long some bastard in a poncho is going to come in, load
up a buckboard with his entire stock of dynamite and
leave without paying. Sharing a party wall with the general
store, the barbershop-cum-funeral-parlour, presided over
by a long, thin, elderly loon who wears wire-framed John
Lennon spectacles and giggles a lot. Due south lie the
livery stable, the blacksmith, the dentist (J. Holliday prop^r;
painless extractions guaranteed; CLOSED) and the bank,
miraculously open between robberies. On the other side
of the street, we have the sheriff's office (W^{tt} Earp, prop^r;
CLOSED), the Silver Dollar saloon (see above under
Lucky Strike), the Wells Fargo office, the dry goods store
(for dry, read inflammable, as some clown with an oil

lamp will inevitably demonstrate before the titles roll) and one or two other establishments not essential to the plot and accordingly left anonymous. Main Street. All human life is here; although, quite often, not for very long.

In a cloud of dust, six horsepersons thunder into town, draw up in front of the Lucky Strike and tether their horses to the rail. Quite soon, they have the front stoop to themselves. Trouble has come to Main Street, punctual as ever. You can set your watch by Trouble in this town.

'Where . . . ?' Skinner began to say; then Max tapped him on the shoulder and pointed to the sign over the doorway of the Bank.

BANK OF CHICOPEE FALLS

Skinner's mouth fell open, as if some joker had cut the tendons in his jaw. He stared, unable to speak.

'Welcome home,' Claudia said. 'Of course, you're a bit early. In thirty-odd years or so—'

'Thirty-six, ma'am,' Max amended.

'Thirty-six years, you'll be born. Yes, I know,' she said, before Skinner could interrupt. 'Last time around you were born in Chicago. Well, this time you're going to be born here. Or rather, you won't, because the world's about to end, but don't worry about it. You're home, that's the main thing.'

Skinner nodded. 'That's my place over there,' he said. 'Look, where it says W^{tt} Earp Prop^r CLOSED. Hey, I never knew it used to be the sheriff's office.'

'You learn something new every day,' Claudia replied cheerfully. 'Pretty futile under the circumstances, but it's the right attitude. Congratulations, Mr Skinner, Ms Armitage, on a job well done.'

Jane stared. 'Excuse me?'

'Your quest,' Claudia replied. 'Your mission, to rescue our tubby friend here and bring him back into Reality. I had every confidence in you, of course.'

'I . . .' Skinner tried to think of something to say, but couldn't. He was *home*, dammit; the question which still nagged away at him was, which home? Yes, it was Chicopee Falls, the armpit of Iowa, his Real home, but it looked uncommonly like the ghastly places he'd spent the last thirty-six years dodging about in, through and round. And the trouble was, he couldn't tell them apart any longer. And yes, he *was* home; it was no more and no less of a homecoming than that of the man returning unscathed from the War to find his street flattened by a land-mine, or pulled down to make way for Progress, or simply painted another colour and sold to the upwardly mobile. Turn your back for more than a minute and Home changes. 'Gee,' he said. 'Good to be back.'

'Excuse me,' said Hamlet.

'Sorry, we're neglecting you,' Claudia said, smirking.

'I couldn't help noticing,' Hamlet said, 'that we're standing in front of a saloon.'

'Quite right.'

Hamlet nodded. 'I'm going to have a drink,' he said.

'What a perfectly splendid idea,' Claudia said. 'You won't mind if I don't join you, I've got a few things more to see to. Come along, Max.'

They were halfway down the steps before Titania called out, 'Excuse me.'

'Yes?'

'Does this mean we're not prisoners any more?'

Claudia shrugged. 'Up to you entirely. I've finished with you, you see. If I were you, I'd enjoy the rest of your life. Ciao.'

Alone on the stoop, Titania watched them ride away.

Inside the saloon, she could hear Hamlet's voice asking everyone what they were having, the pianola still playing *Dixie*, Jane asking where the Ladies' was. No reason, she told herself, why I shouldn't go through and join them. No reason why I should, either.

No reason . . .

Ever since she'd found herself involved in this strange sequence of events, she'd been waiting for the reason; the oh-so-that-was-it reason, the answer to the question *Why me?* And now the world was about to end – was ending, in fact – and she still couldn't see the answer. A very good reason for not seeing something is because it isn't there.

A wagon rolled by, piled high with logwood and chased by three small children and a dog. She waited for it to become relevant to the story. It didn't. It just kept rollin'.

Welcome to Reality.

In Reality, there is no plot. In real-life newsreel footage of the bomb going off, the fatal shooting, the tanks rumbling through the rubble-strewn street, there's always one little man, quietly dressed and respectable, standing peacefully at the edge of the picture and *looking the other way*. In Fiction, he couldn't exist. Everybody is involved. They have their exits and their entrances.

This is Reality, and I have no part in it. Oh, she wasn't naive, she'd heard stories; innocent ingénues fresh from the country, young and easily led, get roped in as last-minute love interests because the editor has pointed out to the author that he's got an all-male cast, and then get quietly forgotten about and abandoned at the end of Chapter Twelve. That's Fiction. Fiction's a bitch and then you're cut. Reality . . .

Characters in Fiction aren't much given to introspection, except in the line of duty. No character ever slumped across a bar at three in the morning and moaned, 'How come I've made such a fuck-up of my life?', for the simple reason that no character in the universe of poetry and prose ever fucked up his own life. That's what authors are for.

Why, Titania mused nonetheless, me? Let's think about this.

All right then, who is Titania? Well, she's this ravishingly gorgeous upper-class bint who falls for a funny, fat, middle-aged, working-class guy with artificially big ears. The term *stooge* tends to spring irrepressibly to mind. Great. This Is Your Life, and so on.

So far, so comprehensible; because Skinner's (a) funny, fat, middle-aged and American (equivalent to working-class as far as suitability is concerned) and (b) the unwilling plaything of a malicious destiny, translated willy-nilly into an alien dimension in circumstances connected with a work of dramatic fiction. A nasty trick to play on a girl, but logical. It would explain why me rather than, say, Modesty Blaise or Anna Karenina. But . . .

But it hadn't *happened*. There hadn't been any suggestion that she should fall for the poor sucker. All she'd done was tag along. The Jane creature had been the heroine, and she'd just been Spare Girl.

Plausible enough in Reality; in Fiction, impossible.

So?

She looked up. A face was grinning at her from behind the stoop rail.

'Ill met by moonlight, proud Titania,' it said, and its voice sounded funny. It sounded like an actor.

Golly, she remembered, that's my cue. Even before she found the place in her mind, even before her tongue started to move . . .

'What, jealous Oberon? Fairies, skip hence. I have forsworn his bed and company. Hey, what the . . . ?'

The face came back with the next line ('Tarry, rash wanton'; a line she'd particularly hated ever since she'd found out that wantons are also little suet dumplings you get in Chinese soup) but there was something about it not quite, not altogether, not entirely . . .

It wasn't Oberon. That was, of course, a pretty sweeping statement, because Oberon rarely looked the same two days running; for the simple reason that he looked like whoever happened to be playing him at the time. Anybody can be Oberon – the postman, the milkman, the snotty clerk in the building society – provided he belongs to an amateur dramatic society and waits his turn. To be Oberon, all you have to do is say Oberon's lines, like that man was doing.

But that man, nevertheless, wasn't Oberon. That was somebody else.

She had an idea he answered to the name Max.

Seven glasses of whisky later, Skinner suddenly found himself feeling strangely weary.

'I think,' he yawned, 'I'll just go lie down. That's if you don't need me for ten minutes.'

Jane, who hadn't spoken to him, or anyone, since they'd walked into the saloon, nodded her approval. Hamlet, who was playing poker with five savage-looking men in enormous hats, didn't look up. Titania had wandered off somewhere. This is the way the world ends, apparently.

He wandered out on to the stoop, which was empty, and sat down in a rocking chair. Somebody had left a bottle of whisky and a glass handy, and there was a fine view down Main Street which, Skinner felt, was probably quite conducive to sleep. After a while, his head began to nod—

—And to reverberate with strange words, words wanting to be said aloud. Alarmed, Skinner woke himself up. All alone. Main Street. Whisky. Probably needled whisky, accounting for hallucination of offstage voices. Nasty whisky. Sleep it off, wake up healthy and happy and sane.

The words drifted back, lurked just out of his field of vision, crept up on him. Just before he drifted into sleep, they pounced.

Just before, mind; not after.

'I see their knavery,' Skinner mumbled (and a tiny part of his brain clung, as it were, to the door handle and screamed, *Look out, you fool, they're coming to get you!*). 'This is to make an ass of me, to fright me if they could. But I will not stir from this place, do what they can. I will *Skinner you crazy bastard, get outa there, now before you drown in wet shit* up and down here and I will sing . . .'

He raised his head and noticed, for the first time, that there was a girl asleep in the other rocking chair, the one opposite. At once his mind was full of voices. There was a rough, crude voice, hoarsely muttering the Elizabethan equivalent of *Cor yeah, thassa bit of all right, innit?* There was a high-pitched American voice saying, *Nooo, you fucking idiot, it's Titania, you know her, get the hell outa there, something terrible's about to* . . . And there was a wordless braying sort of voice suggesting that what he really wanted, most in all the world, was a nice warm stall, fresh straw and a carrot.

The girl sat up. Their eyes met. For a fraction of a second they shared the single telepathic concept, *Oh shit!*

'What angel,' mumbled the girl, 'wakes me from my flowery bed?'

The ninety-five per cent of Skinner's mind that was no longer his own yelled *Cue!* at him. He ignored it. Slowly he reached up and felt his ears.

In a cloud of dust, a horseman thunders into town, draws up in front of the livery stable, and glances up at the clock.

Five minutes to twelve. High noon.

'Hell,' Regalian muttered under his breath. He reined in the horse and looked round, then caught sight of two familiar faces.

'Howdy.'

'Hello there.'

For a moment he contemplated riding away, or steering the horse straight at them to ride them down. Pointless. Instead, he jumped down from the horse and tied it to the rail. Let them come.

'You're late,' said Claudia. 'But we managed without you.'

'You managed . . . ?' Regalian caught his breath. 'But this is . . .'

'Reality.' Claudia did her Cheshire cat impression. 'And Fiction too.' She looked up at the clock and smiled. 'You're just in time,' she said.

'For the fight?'

'For the wedding.'

Something banged on the door of Regalian's brain demanding to be let in, but he ignored it. 'But the showdown,' he said. 'Surely . . .' He hesitated. 'Claudia,' he went on, 'what *are* you playing at, you evil bitch?'

Claudia tried to look offended but her smirk got in the way. 'Nothing at all,' she replied. 'Your friends are free to go. Any time they want to.'

'But . . .' He scowled. 'What wedding?'

Claudia shook her head. Regalian noticed that Max had somehow disappeared. *Kill Claudia! Now might I do it, pat . . .*

'Do you know,' she said, 'what day it is?'

'What?'

'The date. In real-time.'

'No. Why?'

Claudia's grin widened, threatening to unzip her entire face. 'June the Twenty-first,' she said. 'Midsummer's day.

Ah well, things to do. No hard feelings?'
'You *bitch*!'

Jane's head nodded on to her folded arms. Despite the smoke and the noise and the piano still tinnily tinkling *Dixie*, she was tired. She slept.

Hamlet leaned back in his chair while the poker game clattered around him, the players moving and grunting like robots, mechanical toys. He'd folded in this particular hand long since. His eyelids felt heavy. His eyes closed. The other players quietly got up and left. The saloon was empty.

Except for a vague, almost translucent figure, like a huge mayfly, hovering in the cigar smoke. From a fold of his shimmering robe he took a small purple flower, which he proceeded to squeeze, like lemon over scampi, directly above the eyelids of the sleeping female. A moment later, he repeated the procedure with the male sleeper.

He snickered; *hna-hna-hna!* You can't hope to do that convincingly unless you've spent at least three terms at Baddie School. It's all a matter of breath control and, of course, hours and hours and hours of practice.

You could just about call this fleeting, ephemeral figure a fairy, just as you could theoretically describe Hitler as a statesman; after all, he was a man, and at various stages of his career he had quite a lot of states. This fairy, however, is different. He's the sort of fairy who, when assigned to tooth duty, would have with him at all times a pair of big, rusty pliers.

His name is probably Max.

The clock ticked on. One minute to twelve.
Twelve noon, or twelve midnight.

Jane woke up.

She couldn't remember having fallen asleep; but so what, she felt better for it. She remembered. And hey! the world was still here. She opened her eyes.

Yow!

She closed them quickly and started to rub. Soap!

When it was safe to open them again, she discovered that she was looking directly into the eyes of . . .

'Hello,' she said.

'Hello,' Hamlet replied.

There was still one small, hidden part of Jane's mind that wasn't knee-deep in violet-scented pink goo, courtesy of the love-philtre. It was the part she used for being a writer.

This is how it goes with writers, even piss-awful ones like Jane. There's this tiny hidden cell bunker-deep inside their heads which operates on totally different rules and sees things from entirely different perspectives. It's a bit like an embassy; regardless of its location, it's a wee sliver of somewhere else – sovereign territory, operating under its own jurisdiction. And, like an embassy, it's the last safe place to run to when things on the outside start to get hairy.

Having barricaded herself in and jammed the mental equivalent of a chair under the door handle, the real Jane took a deep breath and called a staff meeting.

Oh dear. In love again. Shit.

Brain, she commanded, access memory for previous outbreaks of love and analyse.

Computing.

Well?

You really want to hear this?

Yes.

You're the boss. You want them in chronological order, or by magnitude of fool made of self, or alphabetical, or what?

Chronological will do just fine.

Computing. Well, if we forget about teddy bears and music teachers for the time being, we start with Kevin. Remember Kevin?

Jane shuddered. Let's skip Kevin, shall we?

Good idea. That brings us on to Damian. Tall. Skinny. Unfortunate skin condition. Wrote poetry about derelict machinery and how dismal life is. Further analysis?

Next, please.

Fast-forwarding Damian, we come to Malcolm. World-weary, cynical, devil-may-care, affected a Franz Kafka dying-of-consumption cough, in reality brought on by smoking French cigarettes; worked in the pie factory at the bottom of Gough Whitlam Boulevard. Curious and really rather disgusting half-moon-shaped birthmark on his . . .

Next, please.

Is this really achieving anything? I mean, wouldn't you be more usefully occupied knotting sheets together and climbing out through your left ear?

Next, please.

If you insist. Ye gods, Stuart. Could we bypass Stuart, because if you throw up in here, I'm the one who's going to have to live with the smell.

Further detail, please.

Computing. Stuart, five foot four, fourteen stone, his deter-mination to sample every new experience at least once finally led to his having a bath in, let's see, nineteen seventy-nine, March, to be precise. Owned a scruffy Toyota about seven years older than he was, on the back seat of which you could always be certain of finding the remains of the previous day's hamburger, usually at incredibly inappropriate moments. Arguably the nadir of your romantic career to date, although these things are necessarily subjective. Had enough? You realise we haven't even got through your teens yet.

She hadn't; and so the catalogue continued . . .

(And outside that small, safe place the rest of her gazed

into Hamlet's soft, slugbelly-coloured eyes and sighed; and in the orchestra pit, the phantom violinists pulled on their asbestos gloves to protect their fingers from the glowing heat of tortured catgut . . .)

That's the lot?

Thank God. Unless you want Him included as well. You know, Mister Something-is-rotten-in-the-state-of-Denmark-or-maybe-it's-just-time-I-changed-my-socks . . .'

Not just now, thanks. Session ends.

Logout sequence completed. Ciao and good luck.

As she'd suspected; and the record confirmed it. Hopeless and feckless she may have been in her choice of kindred souls, but always consistent. There was a definite pattern to it (for a very general idea, imagine the brain of a Dalek linked up to a computer dating program) and Hamlet quite simply didn't correlate.

Put-up job. Somebody's doing this to me.

Guess who.

And, the real Jane realised, as she gazed into Hamlet's eyes, sod all I can do about it.

Help! Rescue!

My hero . . .

Not just sheer vindictiveness. Not just an evil mind having fun moving the counters around.

Fictional boy meets real girl; real boy meets fictional girl. They fall in love.

Fiction mixed with Reality, Reality with Fiction.

This is the way the world ends.

Stands the town clock at one to noon? And will the shootout happen soon?

But the clock also reads one minute to twelve at the end of *Midsummer Night's Dream*, just before Theseus's iron-hand-of-midnight speech; that poetic and, in context, highly sinister version of *Last orders at the bar, please.* Then the play finishes, the happy-ever-after begins.

Happy ending; highly subjective term. Happy for who? Ending of what?

Even now, in the fifty-ninth minute of the eleventh hour, there was a tiny nodule in the most obscure box-room of Skinner's mind that said *No, this isn't. And Titania doesn't, she goes back to Oberon and lives happily . . . And above all, I'm not. Not what? Can't remember. Just not, is all.*

The sky is a stained-glass window, all different shades of light and dark blue. The air is that heavy, sweet, fresh smell unique to midsummer midnight. The little white light in Skinner's brain flickers for the last time and goes out. A big stupid grin splurges across his face, like a custard pie from the hand of God.

Cue Theseus, whose name is probably Max. He opens his mouth . . .

'You bitch!' Regalian shouted, and ran.

Where to, he wasn't sure, Fiction or Reality, all one big happy . . . He stopped running, his breath coming hard. No point running. Main Street.

What had the man said?

All you gotta do, son, is fight and lose. You know that. Fight and lose.

He looked up; and he was facing Max. The clock started to strike twelve.

Max, in black, two guns on his belt, looking more like Jack Palance than Mr Palance could ever hope to do even if he took lessons.

The tumbleweed wobbled and fell over. Far away, the swinging door of the saloon banged in the wind. A bell rang. In the background, the wedding party stopped to watch; otherwise, the street was deserted, the way Main Street always is.

All you gotta do is fight and lose.

Yes! Restore Reality, have the hero die at the hands of the villain. Fat chance.

'Okay, stranger,' Max drawled. 'This town ain't big enough for the both of us.'

Basic authorship theory.

The hero always wins. He has no choice.

There are times when this can be a confounded nuisance.

'Oh, I don't know,' Regalian replied. 'Tell you what, you can have the whole of the top bit, from the bank down as far as the general store and the watering trough, and I'll even throw in the big open space behind the smithy. You could build a whole factory estate on that if you wanted to.'

Max didn't reply. On his right hand he wore a skintight black leather glove. It was hovering about an inch and a half above the pearl grips of his Peacemaker. He grinned.

And the realisation hit Regalian like an express train hitting a cow on the line; he'll draw and I'll be faster, and I'll kill him. And that'll mean Fiction has won, and there'll be no more Reality, ever. Even if he manages to shoot me, I'm still a sodding vampire, I can't die. Not that it'll come to that, of course, because I'm the hero. And the hero's always faster on the draw. Always.

From the direction of the upper saloon balcony, he heard the grinding click of a Winchester rifle being cocked. Of course, he realised, the sniper; the one who always gets shot and falls through the balsawood railings. Only he's not here to kill me, he's here to make sure, in case I miss . . .

But I can't.

I *can't*, dammit. If I turn through a hundred and eighty

degrees and shoot straight up in the air, the bullet will fall on his head and kill him. If I somehow manage not to shoot at all, he'll miss, his bullet will ricochet off a wagon wheel and come back and hit him straight between the eyes.

This is the way the world ends; not with a whimper, but a bloody loud bang.

And . . .

Max went for his gun. And before he'd cocked the hammer, before the Peacemaker was even clear of the holster, the Scholfield was out and cocked and levelled at his heart and—

There was absolutely nothing Regalian could do. He felt his finger tighten on the trigger, and the sear broke and (Max's gun was out now, and his thumb was on the hammer; too late, too late, too late) the hammer fell.

The Scholfield cleared its throat.

It had only one line, but it was a honey. When the film was over, it would be the line everybody would remember.

'Click,' it said.

The bullet from Max's gun – sterling silver, ninety-nine-point-nine per cent fine – hit Regalian smack in the heart. He jerked, hit the ground like a sack of potatoes and lay still.

Max screamed, turned, raised the gun to put it to his head and fire it into his own ear. He pulled the trigger, missed; and the bullet went past him and hit Skinner on the saloon balcony. *Crash!* went those balsawood railings. *Thump!* went that heavy body.

Horrified, Max tried to back away but there was nowhere for him to go. He threw the gun from him. It hit the ground, the impact jarred the hammer, a shot rang out; the bullet ricocheted off a wagon wheel, missed Hamlet's head by a fraction of an inch, sang off the tin-plate sign over Barker's Store, smashed through the window of the saloon and hit the pianola, which immediately began to play *Buffalo Girl*.

With a sickening *crunch!*, the bomb in Hamlet's chest exploded.

Max whimpered and stared at his right hand. The black glove had gone. He glanced up. The rim of his hat was now white.

'No!' he screeched. 'No, please!'

He sank to his knees; and Jane, making her way sedately towards the train that sat puffing quietly like a contented pipe-smoker at the end of the street, stepped over him without looking down.

Hamlet woke up.

He was sitting at a table. On either side of him was a child; to his right, a boy of about twelve, and to his left a six-year-old girl, with pigtails and freckles like a foxed mirror. In front of him was an empty plate. Everyone else's plate was heaped with slices of grey, sad-looking meat and vegetables boiled into semi-deliquescence.

'Why isn't Hamlet having any?' demanded the girl.

On the other side of the table, a harassed-looking woman who was obviously Mummy made a little Give-me-strength sighing noise.

'Hamlet isn't hungry, dear,' she said.

'I think Hamlet's very hungry,' replied the girl. 'I think Hamlet should have some too.'

'Actually,' Hamlet said, and then stopped. It suddenly occurred to him that he was invisible.

Except possibly to the girl, who turned and gave him a long, serious stare. 'Don't you?' she said.

'Actually,' Hamlet replied, 'I'm not all that hungry,

thanks all the same. Look, can you actually see me?'

'Of course I can,' replied the girl.

'Sarah,' said Mummy, 'I think we've had enough of Hamlet for today, so just eat up your nice tea and then you can watch television.'

'Can they see me?'

'Of course not,' said the girl. 'They're *silly*.'

The sour-looking bald man who was palpably Daddy clicked his tongue and scowled at Mummy. 'I told you,' he said. 'I said to you, Don't encourage the child, it'll get out of hand.'

'I think Hamlet's gone to bed now,' said Mummy loudly. 'You can say goodnight to him later if you like.'

The girl shook her head. 'Hamlet hasn't gone to bed, have you, Hamlet? He says he'd like some food now, and ice cream for afters.'

'No, really, it's very kind of—'

'Another peep out of you, my girl,' growled Daddy, 'and it's straight up to your room for you. Understood?'

'She's crazy,' said the boy to nobody in particular. 'My teacher says people who talk to people who aren't there are crazy and ought to be locked up, otherwise they turn into serial killers and go around stabbing people.'

'Mummy, Kieron's being horrible again, tell him to stop.'

'Kieron . . .'

'Central Casting? Hello? Is anybody there? Look, what the bloody hell . . . ?'

'Mummy, Kieron's upset Hamlet and made him cry. Make Kieron go to his room, Mummy.'

Yes, hello? Now what?

'What the devil is this?' Hamlet growled. 'And how do I get out?'

Some people are never satisfied.

'I think Sarah ought to go to her room,' said Kieron,

pouring gravy into the ravine between the mashed potato mountain and the cabbage swamp. 'She's the one who's gone crazy and started talking to people who aren't there.'

'What exactly do you mean by that?'

I mean, we find you a perfectly good job . . .

'Perfectly good job? You call being some brat's imaginary friend a perfectly good job? In your dreams, chum.'

It's all we've got going at the moment. Either that or a bit part in a Mister Blobby cartoon. Take your pick.

'Kieron, leave Sarah *alone*. Oh God, now look what you've done. Go and fetch a cloth.'

'Mummy, Kieron's spilt gravy all over Hamlet's sleeve. That's not *fair*, Mummy.'

'Did you say a Mister Blobby cartoon?'

Yes.

'On reflection,' said Hamlet slowly, 'and looking at it, you know, holistically, I can see where the character has potential. Okay, a limited audience, but certainly potential. I'll take it.'

That's all right, then. Ciao.

'Kieron? *Kieron!*'

'Mummy, Hamlet's gone ever such a funny colour. Do you think he's going to be sick?'

Titania woke up.

What angel wakes me from my flowery bed? It was, she realised, her voice. And the man standing over her, smelling of vinegar, sweat and something extremely pungent which might well have been jute, had a long, hairy snout and enormous ears. Hey ho, back to work again.

Now what, she asked herself, the hell was all that about?

(And, in the back office at Central Casting, Julie turned to Christine and asked exactly the same question.

Christine hesitated. She could explain how, in order to

revitalise the imagery and counterpoint the structural device
of the Bottom/Titania sequence, which was just beginning to
lose a teeny bit of its bite after three quarters of a million
performances, it had been decided that it'd be fun to do to
Titania something quite like what they'd been doing to Bottom
all these years, only more so; that it would undoubtedly have
a tremendously positive effect on her future interpretation of
the role knowing exactly what a pillock one feels when one
gets caught up in a divine comedy and put through Aristotle's
mangle; how it was a combination holiday, training course
and potential-unlocking role-playing scenario all rolled into
one. Or she could basically ignore the question.

'Dunno,' she said accordingly. 'Bit of fluff on the terminals
somewhere, I suppose.'

'Poxy thing.'

'Yeah.')

The Scholfield woke up.

The ceiling had turned, it noticed, to glass; and the
floor was green baize. And someone had tied a ticket to
its trigger guard reading *$10 garanteid one carful oner.*

'Where am I?' it murmured.

'Hogan's Ironmongery and Provisions,' replied a
battered-looking Remington. 'Main Street. Dodge City.
Second hand, sorry, I beg your pardon, pre-owned
section, main display case. Where'd you come from, then?
Last time I looked, you were a ratty ole Webley with a
knackered cylinder axis pin.'

'I heard that.'

'Oh, he's still here, then. Don't mind him, he's British,
they're all a bit snotty.'

'I just got here,' murmured the Scholfield thoughtfully.
'Are we for sale, then, or what?'

The Remington snickered quietly. 'Could say that,' it
replied. 'More like Special Offer, actually. Ole man

Hogan, he'll be giving us away free with them colourfast cotton-rich shirts next.'

'No demand,' added a nickel-plated Colt Navy in the corner of the case. 'Quiet town, this.'

'*Dodge City!*'

'Armpit of the goddamn galaxy,' sighed the Remington. 'When they're not in church they're sitting at home embroidering samplers. No injuns. A body could rust right through and nobody'd care a blind cuss.'

With a terrific effort, the Scholfield moved its barrel thirty thousandths of an inch to the left, until it was able to see the date on the copy of the *Dodge City Tribune* which someone had left lying on top of the case. June 15th, 1883.

Marvellous, muttered the Scholfield to itself, absolutely marvellous. Thanks to my quick thinking, ingenuity and imaginatively flexible approach to the rules of heroic fiction, there's a happy ending. All the rest of the gang are probably on some amazingly wonderful new assignment somewhere as a reward, and what do I get? I end up in a dusty case in a junk shop in a, open quote, quiet town, close quote. Comes of being a gun, I suppose. They never stop and think a gun's maybe got feelings too. Drop us; do we not break? Take us apart; do our springs not fly across the room and disappear forever behind the sofa? Has not a gun screws, pins, cylinder latch bolts . . . ?

Just then the bell over the shop door rang, and a tall, dark man with long black hair and a bushy moustache strode across the threshold. The storekeeper looked up from his ledgers and switched on a retailer's special smile.

'Good day,' he simpered. 'Mr Hickock, ain't it? How're you settling in down at the Old Parsonage?'

'Swell,' replied the stranger. 'Say, I'm interested in buying a pistol. You got any?'

The Scholfield held its breath . . .

⋆   ⋆   ⋆

Skinner woke up.

The first thing that he noticed was that his coffee had gone stone cold. The second was the broken window.

'Goddamn kids,' he muttered.

Among the things he didn't notice was the lack of a Scholfield revolver in his desk drawer, largely because (as things now stood) he didn't expect there to be one. He'd never owned a Scholfield. Firearms in general made him nervous, which was one of the reasons why he'd given up writing cowboy stories years ago and now confined himself to wholesome tales for kiddies with a high fluffy-bunny-to-page ratio and no sex and violence whatsoever.

More money in it, too.

Under his elbows was the keyboard of his trusty Remington typewriter, and he observed with a scowl that, by falling asleep on it, he had caused it to type *oghurqwoieh*, which wasn't the sort of word his readership could relate to. Most of his readers had difficulty with *horse* and *cow*, let alone *oghurqwoieh*. He reached for the typewriter rubber.

And then he remembered his dream. Weird, he told himself as the mental review ended, wasn't the word for it. One hell of a dream; and a tiny part of him that hadn't quite got used to the idea that any book by A. Skinner had to have at least five furry animals in the first two paragraphs made the tentative suggestion that he might care to write it down while it was still fresh and use it for something. Lord only knew what, but something.

Well, quite. A dream in which he'd travelled to a strange and terrifying place where the characters in books had all come to life; in which he had a short but extremely instructive liaison with the Queen of Elfland before being chased about by mad gunmen, and . . . Hell, there was more, but it was leaking out like ink from a broken fountain pen. It was gone. Pity.

He was hungry. He could murder a big plate of stinging nettles . . .

Stinging nettles?

Hay?

Carrots?

He shook his head, finished rubbing out *oghurqwoieh*
and phoned the glazier.

Jane woke up.

Third time this week she'd fallen asleep in front of the
screen; and this time, her forehead had hit the keyboard,
producing a three-inch row of asterisks. She deleted them,
and glanced up to see where she'd got to.

Ah yes. The bit where Regalian gets killed.

She hesitated, and frowned. Hang on a minute, she
thought, he's the damn hero. What do you think you're
. . . ?

Her fingers started to move across the keys. This was
an unusual occurrence in itself, since Jane was a lifelong
member of the two-fingers-and-keep-looking-down school
of typing, and whenever she tried to touch-type her words
ended up more full of buckshee consonants than a water-
melon is full of pips. Without slowing down production in
any way, she glanced up at the screen to have a look at
whatever the devil it was she was churning out.

*'But why?' Jane demanded. 'Why does it have to end this
way, just when we've finally found each other?'*

*A faint smile drifted across the hero's pain-scoured face.
'Even love,' he said, 'cannot bridge the gap between dimen-
sions . . .'*

'Oh for crying out loud,' Jane said, and pressed the
delete key. Nothing happened. Her left hand was still
typing. She couldn't make it stop.

*'When I shot Max,' Regalian continued, his breath coming
in short, painful gasps . . .*

Just a cotton-picking minute. He didn't shoot Max, it was the other way round. I think. And who the hell is this Max guy anyhow?

'I put everything back the way it should have been. Not the way it would have been if Skinner hadn't shot him in the mirror the first time, because that couldn't have happened in the first place if something wasn't badly wrong. I don't . . .' He broke off as a horrible spasm of coughing racked his tortured frame . . .

'No, please,' Jane said. 'You can't make me say tortured frame, whoever you are, it's just not fair.'

'Maybe,' said Jane, 'Skinner was never meant to write that book. Wouldn't that account for it?'

Regalian shook his head. 'I don't suppose anyone will ever know the real reason,' he said. 'All I know is, we've got back to Reality but it's changed. Things aren't the way they were, but somehow I know they're as they should be. And that includes my death, and the two of us never . . .'

'Hush,' said Jane softly, 'don't say any more, just lie still. I'll . . .'

'Hey,' Jane objected aloud, 'knock it off, sister. I want to know what's been going on.'

She caught her breath as Regalian shuddered and closed his eyes, his face white with pain. 'No,' she said, 'you can't die, not now, not like this.'

'This is how it has to be,' Regalian answered faintly. 'Not for us, but for everyone else. Without sacrifice there can be no Jane, is that you, why are you making me say all this bloody pompous bullshit, I wouldn't be seen dead making a deathbed speech anyway . . .'

'Regalian!' Frantically, she clasped his head to her bosom, but too late, too late. He was gone.

'Regalian!' she murmured softly through her tears. 'My hero!'

Jane leaned back in her chair and sat on her hands. For

a fraction of a second there, she'd almost believed . . .

No, the hell with that. Too many late nights, too much strong coffee. She pressed BLOCK, then DELETE. Nothing happened.

The bloody thing was just out of warranty, too.

With a sigh, she reached forward, pulled the disk out of the machine and switched off. The screen went blank . . .

For a moment, and then letters began to appear. They were persistent buggers, because she could still see them with her eyes closed.

DON'T WORRY ABOUT IT, YOU'LL HAVE FORGOTTEN ALL ABOUT IT IN TEN MINUTES OR SO. LOOK, SORRY ABOUT ALL THIS, YOU'LL NEED TO FIND YOURSELF A NEW HERO. PROBABLY JUST AS WELL. I WAS STARTING TO GET A BIT BLOODY PREDICTABLE.

SKINNER GOT BACK SAFELY, IN CASE YOU WERE WONDERING. UNDER THE NEW REGIME HE WRITES SOPPY STUFF ABOUT BETSY BUNNY AND SARAH SQUIRREL. HE'S BETTER AT THAT THAN COWBOYS, BUT EVEN SO I DON'T THINK HE NEEDS TO START MAKING ROOM ON HIS MANTELPIECE FOR THE PULITZER PRIZE JUST YET.

WHAT ELSE? OH YES, HAMLET'S COME TO A BAD END. THAT IS, HE'S SORT OF PERMANENTLY STUCK IN REALITY, EXCEPT THAT HE'S BECOME SOME KIND OF DISEMBODIED THINGY. ACTUALLY IT'S GOOD STEADY WORK, THERE'S ALWAYS A CALL FOR SPOOKS AND STUFF WITH A SPECIES AS DEPRESSINGLY SUPERSTITIOUS AS YOURS. MICKEY MOUSE IS HAMLET NOW. IN FACT THEY'RE RECASTING THE WHOLE BLOODY THING. I HEAR TOM AND JERRY HAVE GOT ROSENCRANTZ AND GUILDENSTERN AND

THE GHOST IS NOW MR MAGOO. PROBABLY BE
AN IMPROVEMENT.

HEY JANE, IT WAS GREAT FUN BUT LET'S NOT
DO IT AGAIN, OKAY?

CHEERIO FOR NOW.

The screen went blank.

Jane began to snore.

Regalian woke up.

It was cold, and dark. The only light was the afterglow
of the green sky. He was alone.

'I see,' he said aloud. 'Right, fair enough. I didn't expect
gratitude anyway, so I'm not disappointed. A souvenir
would have been nice, a printed T-shirt or something, but
what the hell.'

His voice sounded strangely hollow, almost artificial,
or at least a long way off. There was sand under his feet.
He checked to make sure he was wearing suitable shoes.
He was. Good.

He tried to remember, but the last thing that he could
bring to mind was Claudia's face, a Ralph Steadman cari-
cature of rage and hatred, yelling, 'You bastard, you'll
never work in this business again!' Well, fine. Nobody
loves a smartarse, and you're only as good as your last
job. Who needs a hero who forgets to reload his gun before
the final shoot-out?

And there are no happy endings for characters; because
at the end of all things, after the shoot-out, after the hero
folds the heroine in his arms and the background music
swells to a crescendo, the lights go off and then come up,
everyone takes off their make-up and puts their costume
back on the rack and goes home to wait for the phone
to ring with a new job. And quite frequently it doesn't.
And then you're here. Stuck. For ever.

'Excuse me.'

He looked down. Just under his left foot, which he'd been on the point of putting down on the ground, was a small brown scorpion. He wobbled frantically and staggered sideways.

'Excuse me, but are you Regalian?'

He blinked. ''Fraid so,' he replied. 'Or I was, anyway. It's a bit complicated.'

The scorpion waggled its tail. 'I just wanted to say,' it continued, 'how much I liked your last book. Well, not the last one, actually, I didn't think that was all that special, it's the one before that I was thinking of. I really liked that one.'

'Gosh. Um. Thanks.'

'Particularly,' the scorpion went on, 'that bit where you're fighting the six spectral warriors who jump up out of the ground where the wicked grand vizier has just emptied his teapot. I thought that was really great, how you ducked down behind the stone and then jumped out and bashed them over the head.'

'Did I? Oh yes, rather. Well, er, yes. Thanks very much. Glad you liked it.'

'And another bit I liked,' went on the scorpion, 'was that bit a few chapters later where you're trapped in the burning temple and you swing out through the stained-glass window on the bell-rope just in time to save the girl from the merciless desert nomads. I thought that bit was dead good, too.'

'That wasn't me, actually,' Regalian said. 'In fact, that was the, er, baddie, and he wasn't so much rescuing her as kidnapping—'

'Oh.' The scorpion twitched slightly. 'Anyway, it was dead good.'

'Great.'

'One other thing I wanted to ask,' the scorpion said. 'You don't mind me asking, do you?'

'No, no, you go right ahead.'

'Thanks.' The scorpion waggled its front legs. 'What I want to know is, where exactly do you get your ideas from? I mean, do you just sit down and think them up, or do they just come to you? Because—'

'In actual fact,' said Regalian gently, 'that's not me, that's the writer. She thinks of all the things to do and then I just do them.'

'Really?'

'Yes.'

'Oh. Who's she, then?'

Regalian stifled a sigh. 'Her name's Jane Armitage,' he said. 'She's terribly nice, actually. I've met her and—'

'And so all that stuff was really her idea?'

'Yes.'

'Oh. Well, it was nice meeting you anyway. Um, would you just sign my shell for me, please? To Jonathan.'

'Sure.' Regalian groped in his pocket, found a pen and stooped down. As soon as he'd finished signing his name, the scorpion stung him.

'Thanks a lot,' it said. 'Well, must rush. Bye.'

Regalian tried to wave at the small, scuttling form as it disappeared among the dunes; however, since he was lying on his face, paralysed from the neck down, he couldn't quite manage it.

He died.

It wasn't nearly so bad this time; because when he woke up he wasn't in the desert any more. He was sitting on a horse, wearing a buckskin shirt and cowboy boots, riding across a green landscape at a pleasant ambling pace.

'Hi,' said a voice at his side.

'Don't tell me,' he said, without looking down. 'You're a Smith and Wesson Scholfield model, and you used to belong to . . .'

'Don't insult me, please,' replied the voice; and Regalian

noticed that it was female, quite soft and pleasant. 'I'm a Colt. A *proper* cowboy gun, none of your gimmicky rubbish. My name's Cindy.'

'That's an unusual name for a gun, isn't it?'

'I'm only for show. Come on, it *is* a musical. And by the way, why aren't you singing?'

'Should I be?'

'Yes. *Oh, what a beautiful mornin'*. Forgotten it already? I'll hum it for you.'

Regalian nearly fell off his horse. '*Oklahoma!*' he exclaimed.

'No,' said the gun, 'that comes later, right now it's *Oh, what a beautiful mornin'*.' It paused. 'Hang about,' it said. 'You're not the usual guy, are you?'

Regalian grinned. Well, why not? A hero is a hero, after all.

'Depends,' he said.